J

CREW OF ELMWOOD PUBLIC

J

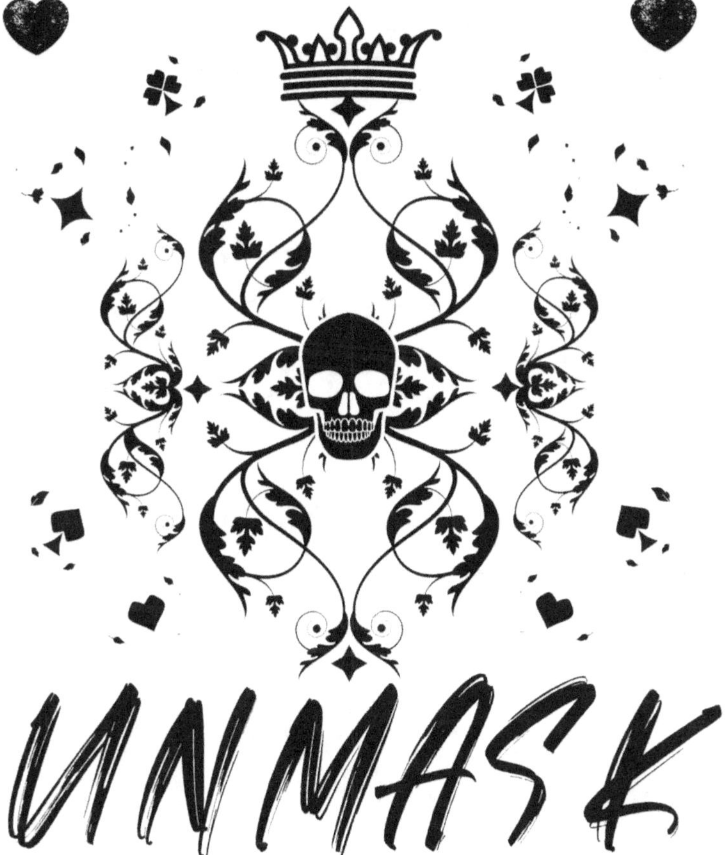

UNMASK

USA TODAY BESTSELLING AUTHOR

BLURB

Some hearts are too dangerous to heal. Some boys are too beautiful to trust. And some revenge is worth dying for.

KAYLOR

Fool me once, shame on you. Fool me twice, shame on me.

They broke me once. I won't let them break me twice.

Raine. Kreed. Maddox. Mason.

They weren't just the kings of Elmwood Public. They were the devils who taught me that love and destruction wear the same beautiful face. I thought escaping their gilded cage meant freedom. I thought the nightmares would end, that the scars would fade, that I could forget the taste of their betrayal on my lips.

I was wrong.

Because the monsters hunting me now make the Corvo boys look like saints. And the only way to survive the darkness closing in? I have to let the four devils who destroyed me back into my life again. Not that they gave me much of a choice.

But I'm not that broken girl anymore, and I'm done playing nice.

KREED

I let her walk away. I told myself she was safer without me, that she belonged with the Vipers. That was my first mistake. My second? Thinking I could forget her.

I wasn't supposed to fall for her.

But when Kaylor looked at me with those sad eyes, she made me believe I could be more than the monster everyone expected; she became my obsession. My salvation. My destruction.

I'd battled monsters before, on the field, in the ring, in the streets that bled Elmwood dry. The kind that came with brass knuckles and back-alley deals. The kind that didn't flinch at the sight of blood, especially not mine, but Kaylor Steele wasn't a battlefield I could blitz through with fists or threats. She was all sharp edges and deep scars. And the fight for her? It wasn't about power or pride.

It was about survival, and I had no intention of losing. Not her.

Never again.

Sign up for an exclusive first look at new releases and exclusives from bestselling author J.L. Weil and receive a bonus scene from the Raven series from Zane's POV, as well as *two free* eBooks, Losing Emma and Breaking Emma, bonus stories from my Divisa Series as a thank you!

Want to discuss what you've just read? Get exclusive teasers or connect with other readers and authors?
Join my reader group on Facebook!

Published by Dark Magick Publishing, LLC
PO BOX 633
Crystal Lake, IL 60039-0633
jenniferlweil@gmail.com
ISBN (Paperback) 978-1-954915-38-1
ISBN (Hardback) 978-1-954915-39-8

Printed and Bound by IngramSpark

ALSO BY J.L. WEIL

ELITE OF ELMWOOD ACADEMY
(New Adult Dark High School Romance)
Turmoil
Disorder
Revenge
Rival
Unchained
Broken

CREW OF ELMWOOD PUBLIC
(New Adult Dark High School Romance)
Liars
Unmask
Endgame

MOONSTRUCK MATES
(New Adult Paranormal Romance)
Kelsey
Liam

DIVISA HUNTRESS
(New Adult Paranormal Romance)
Crown of Darkness
Inferno of Darkness
Eternity of Darkness

DRAGON DESCENDANTS SERIES
(Upper Teen Reverse Harem Fantasy)
Stealing Tranquility
Absorbing Poison
Taming Fire
Thawing Frost

THE DIVISA SERIES
(Full series completed – Teen Paranormal Romance)
Losing Emma: A Divisa novella
Saving Angel
Hunting Angel
Breaking Emma: A Divisa novella
Chasing Angel
Loving Angel
Redeeming Angel

LUMINESCENCE TRILOGY
(Full series completed – Teen Paranormal Romance)
Luminescence
Amethyst Tears
Moondust
Darkmist – A Luminescence novella

RAVEN SERIES
(Full series completed – Teen Paranormal Romance)
White Raven
Black Crow

Soul Symmetry

BEAUTY NEVER DIES CHRONICLES
(Teen Dystopian Romance)
Slumber
Entangled
Forsaken

NINE TAILS SERIES
(Teen Paranormal Romance)
First Shift
Storm Shift
Flame Shift
Time Shift
Void Shift
Spirit Shift
Tide Shift
Wind Shift
Celestial Shift

HAVENWOOD FALLS HIGH
(Teen Paranormal Romance)
Falling Deep
Ascending Darkness

SINGLE NOVELS
Stolen Summer
(New Adult College Romance)
Corrupt Me
(New Adult College Romance)
Starbound
(Teen Paranormal Romance)
Casting Dreams
(New Adult Paranormal Romance)

Ancient Tides
(New Adult Paranormal Romance)

For an updated list of my books, please visit my website:
www.jlweil.com

Join my VIP email list and I'll personally send you an email reminder
as soon as my next book is out! Click here to sign up: www.jlweil.com

To my readers: buckle up. To my characters: behave (just kidding, please don't).

KAYLOR

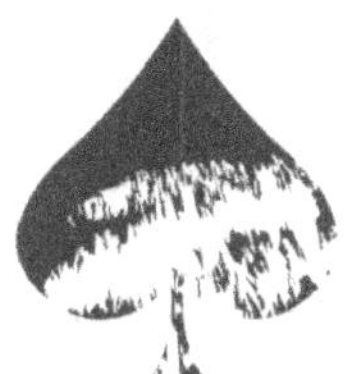

How could a hand have so much meaning?

It was just a hand. Five fingers. Five sexy fingers, each with a playing card suit tattooed below the knuckle. Heart. Spade. Diamond. Club. A hand I'd seen inflict pain, and a hand with knuckles that had been bruised and broken. The hand of a quarterback, who could throw a perfect spiral down the field with such control and precision. But also...a hand that had once, however briefly, made me feel beautiful, treasured, wanted, and even loved.

I never paid much attention to hands before, especially on guys. But Kreed's? His fingers could be, *had been*, a lot of things.

Seductive. The way his thumb had brushed across my bottom lip and he smirked when I sucked in a breath like he knew exactly what he was doing to me.

Dangerous. The way they fought, such power in a strike, such anger in his fists.

Gentle. The way they had once, just once, caught a tear on my cheek before I could pretend it wasn't there.

Now, that hand hung between us, waiting.

The warehouse's docking door was open, the night air biting

against my skin as I stood at the edge of everything I'd ever known. My heart pounded so hard I could hear it in my ears, a steady, deafening rhythm of doubt.

The Vipers Nest loomed behind me, cold, dark, and full of ghosts, but it wasn't the warehouse I was running from.

It was Kreed.

My heart pounded against my ribs, a frantic, confused rhythm. I didn't understand how something as simple as a hand could unravel me, how it could make this choice feel suddenly impossible.

I squeezed my fists to keep from shaking. I knew what I had to do, but it didn't make the decision easier. I took a step back, my eyes ensnared by the silver depths of his. I was so damn angry, so hurt that it made me feel stupid because I'd actually started to fall for him. How had I thought for even a second that he wasn't the asshole everyone claimed him to be? That under the cold exterior, a heart beat in his chest? That I'd been thawing the ice erected so tightly around the organ?

The step away from him wasn't dramatic, wasn't even far, but it might as well have been miles because Kreed felt it. I saw the moment it hit him, the fraction of a second before his face fell, before the storm in his gray eyes dimmed into something almost...hurtful.

Almost.

But it was quickly gone, his famous mask slamming into place, the one that said he didn't give a damn, that this was nothing but another game. That I was a fool to think he cared. He dropped his hand like it had never meant anything at all and scoffed under his breath. "You're making a mistake, little raven."

The words lashed through me. I almost asked him if the roles were reversed if he wouldn't have done the same. I almost asked him which mistake he referred to. Leaving him? Or falling for him in the first place?

My lips remained pressed together because it didn't matter. I already knew the answer.

I shook my head.

"Kaylor," he growled through gritted teeth.

The use of my name pierced my bleeding heart. It was as if each of the Corvos had jabbed me with a dagger, their betrayal a lash, but Kreed... He sliced my heart more than once. My chin lifted as I stared into his gorgeous face that not even his betrayal could dull. "What you did... I-I can't forgive you," I stammered.

His jaw tensed as he continued to hold my eyes. "I'm not asking you to forgive me, little raven. You're not safe here."

My laugh was hollow. "And you think I'm safer with *you*?"

He didn't answer.

So I gave him one. "You killed my parents." I hurled the accusation, desperate for him to deny it.

His expression didn't change. "You know that's not true."

Something inside me snapped, hot like a rubber band smacking against skin. "Why? Because it wasn't your fingers that pulled the trigger?" I spat, stepping toward him, wanting, needing him to feel a fraction of the pain burning within me. "That doesn't absolve you of your part in their death. *Or* what you did to me after. You uprooted me from my entire life. Your father pretended to be my godfather. Why? What sane person does that?"

Kreed didn't flinch.

Didn't blink.

Didn't do a goddamn thing but watch me as if I was delicate and breakable when we both knew I wasn't.

Maddox's voice cut through the tension. "We had our reasons."

I whirled on him, on Nash, on Mason, on all of them. "Don't." My voice shook. "I don't want to hear your excuses. They mean nothing to me." I'd heard what happened to their mother, but the last thing I wanted to feel was sympathy toward them. Not yet. I needed more time to process my problems before I thought about anyone else's, particularly theirs.

Rusty shifted beside me, his presence steady. "You heard her," he directed at the Raven Crew.

Kreed's eyes zeroed on him, dark and unreadable. "Fuck you," he hissed at him, and the entire warehouse tensed. "If you think I'm going to let her go... This isn't over. Far from it." His threat lingered in the air, an invisible weapon pointed at Rusty's head.

I had to get Kreed out of here before shit hit the fan. I wanted them gone, not dead or hurt. For reasons beyond my understanding, I cared what happened to him; even after he ripped out my heart and betrayed me, I still fucking cared, and that was on me. I'd have to learn how to deal with my feelings, but I couldn't do that with him here. I needed space to think without Kreed and the Crew clogging my thoughts.

"Walk away while I'm still inclined to let you keep the use of your legs," Rusty replied, his coal-dark eyes never leaving Kreed's as the two continued to stand off. I'd never seen Rusty like this. He'd always been like a giant teddy bear to me.

Kreed exhaled through his nose, jaw clenched so tight I swore his teeth ground. "This isn't over. It's personal for me, and I'm not my fucking father. Perhaps I'm worse."

Too many thoughts ran wild in my head. My parents. Kreed's mother. The Vipers. The Ravens. My life would never be the same. "It's never simple with us," I replied sadly. "It never has been."

Would he let me go?

If I chose to stay with Rusty, would Kreed walk out alive? Would he fight? Would he get hurt? Would any of them? Would Maddox, Mason, and Nash step in and force Kreed to leave?

Why do I fucking care?

After everything they'd done to me, why did I give a shit what happened to them?

Kreed stood in front of me, the two scars under his right eye glowing by the dim overhead lights. His veins pulsed under his skin with barely restrained fury. "You're really doing it. You're really going to stay with *him*," he spat venomously.

I swallowed hard. "And the alternative is to go home with the people who kidnapped me. In what world does that make sense?"

He raked a hand through his already disheveled hair. "Things might have started out like that, but it's different now."

"Maybe to you." Doubt lingered in my voice, but I steeled myself against it.

And yet...I hesitated.

Not because I trusted Kreed, or because I believed things would ever be okay between us. But because of something in his eyes, a glint deeper than hurt that made my stomach twist.

"You don't understand. Shit is so much more complicated," Kreed said, stepping closer. "This isn't black and white. I'm trying to protect you. Believe it or not, it's all I've done. If you leave with him, we're done. I won't be here to save you, little raven."

A knife. That's what his ultimatum was. A blade to my ribs, a final twist that had been bleeding out for a long, long time, because he meant those words.

I forced myself to meet his stare. "Then don't. The only person I need to be saved from is you."

Lies.

We both knew it. No matter how much I might want to deny it, there was this pull between us, twisted and toxic and inescapable. It wouldn't die just because I wanted it to, but I had to do this.

Couldn't he see that he left me no choice?

What his father had done to me...to my parents...it was unforgivable.

Kreed's jaw ticked. "Fine." He took another step, the heat of him suffocating. "But before you go, tell me the truth."

I swallowed. "About what?"

His voice dropped lower. "About why you're really running."

My throat cinched. "I'm not running."

"You are." His eyes flicked to mine as he held my chin between his thumb and finger. "Not from Rusty. Not from me. From whatever the fuck is inside you that you don't want to face."

I stiffened. "That's not—"

"You're scared."

I shook my head.

"You think he's going to protect you?" Kreed glanced at Rusty, lips curling as his hand fell from my face. "He's not. Someone still wants you dead. You better hope he's up for the challenge. You had four of us protecting you before. Five if you add in Nash. That was real, little raven."

"That's enough," Rusty boomed. "You need to leave before I kick your ass out."

Kreed's smirk was a thing of cruelty, but his gaze stayed locked on me, daring me to say something...anything that wasn't a lie.

But I couldn't.

The truth was...I didn't know if I was making the right choice. So, I did the only thing I could.

I turned before he could see the war raging inside me, before he could catch the single, stupid tear threatening to fall.

Each step deeper into the warehouse was heavier than the last, but I kept going. Rusty's hand rested on my lower back, and I swore I heard Kreed inhale like I just knocked the wind out of him.

Still, I refused to look back. If I did, I might break, and I couldn't afford to lose my shit again.

"You're going to regret this!" Maddox yelled at me, and I stumbled.

I reached out to steady myself on the wall. Something skidded across the floor, landing at my feet. My phone. The one Rusty's guys had taken from me.

"When you come crawling back for his help, I'll be the first to remind you of this moment," Maddox promised.

I glanced over my shoulder to see Maddox's broad back heading into the night. Kreed and Nash were already gone. Only Mason lingered behind.

I didn't think it would be easy, but I also hadn't anticipated it being as hard as it was to watch Kreed walk out of the warehouse, leaving me alone. Had I expected him to fight harder for me? Was I disappointed?

The only thing I was sure of was what a fucking mess I was.

Mason shook his head at me, a well of sadness and remorse pooling in his light-green eyes, not a wink of his usual boyish humor. "I don't want to leave you like this. It feels...wrong."

"That's because everything about what happened is wrong," I murmured.

Mason shoved his hands into his pockets. "I thought we were friends."

How could he make me feel like shit when I hadn't done anything wrong? "So did I. I guess we were both wrong. There's too much shit between us for a friendship to be possible."

His gaze shifted to the four beefy guys standing in the warehouse corners, waiting and watching, before finding mine again. "Our parents' shit isn't our shit."

There might be some truth to his statement. I wasn't my father. Perhaps they weren't their father either, but they'd still been compliant. "It doesn't feel like that."

"Maybe you're right, but staying won't bring them back. This isn't the answer, and you know it, kitten."

Not my little kitten but just kitten. I never thought I would want to hear their possessive nicknames ever again. Maybe I didn't.

I hated the expression on Mason's features and that we had an audience for what should be a private conversation. A vulnerable Mason wasn't something I was used to. "Kreed doesn't let people in. Ever. But he let *you* in. *You.* Think about that while you're alone tonight. Whose bed will you sneak into? His?" Mason's eyes shifted to Rusty's as he snorted in disgust. Giving me one last suffering glance, Mason walked out.

Go after him!

Go after them!

I couldn't figure out where the voice stemmed from. My wounded heart? Or my head?

Bending down, I picked up my phone, and this time, I didn't look back despite the conflict pressing inside me.

I LOCKED the office door behind me, pressing my spine against it, sucking in a breath that did absolutely nothing to steady the riot inside me. The walls were closing in. The world spiraled around me.

"What the fuck have I done?" I muttered under my breath. My knees buckled, and I hit the floor hard, curling into myself, trying to hold everything in, trying to contain the hurricane of emotions threatening to rip me apart from the inside out.

But I couldn't.

A sob tore from my throat, raw and violent, my forehead dropping to my knees. Then another. And another. Until I was screaming. Silent at first, then louder, the sound clawing its way up, choking me, shaking me apart. I wailed into the empty room and let out one long, tortured scream brimming with anger, agony, loss, loneliness, heartache, and betrayal.

I didn't know how to process it. Any of it.

My father. My parents' death. Kreed. His brothers. His father. The lies. The truth.

If I thought I had come close to dealing with a fraction of my grief, I was so wrong. My body trembled; my breath came too fast, too shallow. A high-pitched buzzing filled my ears, spreading to my fingers, making my hands feel both weightless and unbearably heavy at the same time.

Breathe. Just breathe.

I pressed my hands to my chest, trying to force air into my lungs, but it wasn't working. My vision blurred, darkening at the edges.

I needed—God, I didn't even know what I needed.

My phone.

I turned it over with shaking fingers, barely able to see the screen through my tears. Kenny. Carson. My best friends. The ones who had always been my go-to when my world was falling apart, but my thumb didn't tap their names.

Instead, it hovered over one contact.

Kreed.

What the hell is wrong with me?

My stomach twisted. When had that changed? When had *he* become the person I wanted to call when I couldn't breathe?

No. No, I can't do this. Won't.

I hated how my traitorous heart wanted him even as my mind screamed he was poison. Trauma did that; it scrambled the compass until north looked like south, until danger felt like home. Kreed was just as much a part of this mess as the rest of them. I had to separate myself from the chaos so I could see clearly. Right now, everything was muddled.

With my jaw clamped, I swiped away from his name, pulling up Carson's number instead. Before I pressed call, a knock echoed through the room.

My heart stopped.

For a second, I thought it might be Kreed. Had he come back? My throat worked as I swallowed. I started to shove away from the door.

"Kaylor?"

Shit. Rusty.

Disappointment dropped like a severed wrecking ball in my gut. I'd nearly forgotten him, forgotten where I was. Relief ribboned through me, but it didn't last. Why was my first thought always Kreed? He was gone, and I should be happy. I should be feeling anything but sad and broken. Anger, hell yes.

"You okay?" Rusty asked through the office door.

A bitter laugh bubbled up. "No."

The shifting of his feet sounded from the other side of the door. "Come on, kiddo. Let's get you out of here. It's been a long day. You'll feel better after you've rested."

I swiped at my face, the black makeup I'd been wearing for the football game smeared over my still shaky fingers. The football game. It seemed like years ago I'd been sitting in the stands with Poppy. *Oh*

God. Poppy. Was she okay? "Go where?" I squeaked, wiping at the snot dripping from my nose.

"Somewhere you can cool off for a bit. No one will bother you there." His voice, that deep, gruff timbre, easily carried through the door.

That wasn't exactly reassuring.

Unease twisted low in my stomach, but this was Rusty. Not a stranger. Not like when I had been thrown into the Corvos' world, forced to navigate a house full of people who saw me as nothing more than a pawn in their twisted game.

That had been hell, but I had survived. I had to keep reminding myself. I was alive. I was lucky. I needed to keep living.

Forcing myself to my feet, I wiped my palms against my jeans before unlocking the door. Rusty stood there waiting in his oil-stained pants tucked into his dusty, untied, black combat boots. Behind his bushy beard, it was difficult to read what was going on, but that had always been Rusty.

"Can't I just stay at my place?" I asked, my voice hoarse.

Rusty's lips thinned behind his mustache, sympathy crossing his features. He was a bigger and bulkier guy than my father had been, but he'd always been this gentle giant to me. "It's not yours anymore, kiddo. Donovan sold it." Contempt weighed heavily in his admission. He didn't like having to tell me any more than I liked hearing the hard truth.

My stomach bottomed out. "What?"

Rusty leaned a shoulder against the door, filling the entire entrance. "Some other family bought it and moved in about a week ago."

The words barely registered. My house. The only thing I had left of my parents. Gone. Sold.

I swayed on my feet, my mind racing. How could Donovan do that?

And more importantly, why the hell hadn't Kenny or Carson told me?

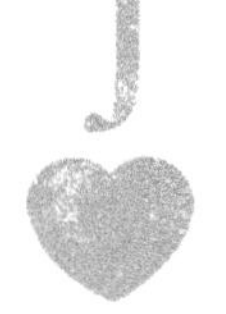

2

KREED

The cold night air did nothing to cool the fire burning through me. Nash, Maddox, and Mason followed as I left the warehouse, but I barely registered them as I pulled my keys from my pocket. Wordlessly, I tossed them to Nash and got into the passenger seat of *my* car, not even checking to see if he caught them. I didn't give a shit, but when he didn't climb in right away, I glanced over to see what the damn problem was.

Nash opened the driver's door and hovered just outside, his chestnut brow lifting at me, my keys dangling from his middle finger. "You sure?"

No.

The last time I'd ridden shotgun in my SUV had been when I'd been too drunk to drive. That was nearly two years ago. No one drove my wheels. Not even my brothers. To hand over the control now only spoke volumes about the state of my mental health.

Not good wouldn't even begin to cut it.

If I got behind the wheel, I'd kill us all. The surge of rage and pain brawling within me went beyond dangerous. It was fucking deadly.

That was how I felt. Like a weapon on the verge of slicing the throats of everyone in my path.

"Drive," I muttered, shoving a hand through my hair as I slammed the door shut. The others climbed in, knowing it was best to keep their mouths shut when I was like this.

The ride was quiet, the tension thick, stifling. They were waiting for me to break the silence, watching me from the corners of their eyes, expecting me to snap at any second.

They weren't wrong.

As we crossed back into the southern part of Elmwood, I took a deep breath. "Drop me at the club." The last fucking place I wanted to be was the house. I didn't care what my father had to say, not about us running out on the game or failing to bring Kaylor back.

Nash's brown eyes flicked to me as his fingers adjusted on the wheel. "That's a bad idea."

I laughed, the sound empty. "No offense, but fuck off."

In the back seat, Maddox swore under his breath, rubbing a hand over his jaw. "We should go home."

"Can't." The word slipped out before I could stop it. My fingers curled against my thighs as I shook my head. It wasn't just my father I was avoiding.

I couldn't go home.

Not to the room across the hall. Not to the empty space where Kaylor had slept. Not tonight. Perhaps not tomorrow either, but all I could think about was now.

Maddox sighed, tipping his head back against the seat. "Fine. Then we're all getting drunk."

I ground my teeth. "I don't want company."

Mason smirked, flipping a joker card between his fingers, a habit he used to channel his excess energy into. He'd been doing it since he was a kid. "Tough shit. You're not drinking alone."

I didn't argue. Not because I agreed, but because I didn't care. They could do whatever the hell they wanted. I was getting into a fight tonight. It was the only way I knew how to work out the shit churning me inside out. My fists needed to pummel something, particularly flesh and bone. "Have it your way."

The moment I stepped into the club, the bass thumped through my chest, drowning out the flashing lights, the press of bodies, the thick scent of alcohol, the ringing of the casino room, and the topless girl on the catwalk. The club should have been a distraction.

It wasn't.

I went straight to the bar, ordered a whiskey, and downed it in one go. Nash smirked at the bartender as he turned on his charm. Flirting was the last fucking thing on my mind, but at least she would keep Nash occupied and out of my way. Maddox and Mason were another story. The twins eyed me as they flanked me on either side, knowing it would take both of them to try to keep me out of trouble. *Good luck.* I snorted and ordered a second round.

My fingers curled around the glass Lacy set in front of me, and I frowned at her overly friendly smile, not that I didn't consider for a hot second taking her up on what her eyes suggested, but I didn't want sex. I wanted pain, and in this place, it wouldn't take long for trouble to find me. It rarely did. I just had to wait for someone to look at me wrong or say the wrong fucking thing.

A group of guys near the poker tables caught my attention. Hell, I think half of the club had noticed them. They were hard to miss with the amount of ruckus they were causing, getting a little too aggressive with the dealer. Drunk, cocky, stupid. They were less about losing their money and more about seeing if they could get her to take off her clothes. The club had strict rules. If you wanted to see tits and ass, you went to the lounge. The girls working at the casino were there to encourage the guests to empty their wallets. Flirt a little, but hands off. Each section of the club had a job, and the workers knew the part they were to play.

I kept my eye on them, just begging one of them to look at me or to cross a line. I got my opening as one of the idiots stumbled toward the bar, and I might have *accidentally* gotten in his way, my elbow sliding into his path, so when he bumped into me, it looked like it was his fault. He was drunk after all.

I turned slowly, setting my empty glass down hard on the bar top, slightly surprised it didn't shatter. "You got a problem?" I asked not so nicely, lifting a brow.

Mason and Maddox knew my tricks. "Shit," they muttered in unison, turning on their stools.

The guy scoffed, barely glancing at me. "Nah, man. It was an accident. I'm just here to have fun. Let me buy you a drink."

This douchebag was about to have the worst night of his life. I almost felt sorry for him. Almost, until I remembered how he had been pawing the dealer, patting her ass, and looking down her shirt. "Lucky for you, I'm in the mood for a little fun too. *And* I can buy my own drinks."

I grabbed him by the collar and slammed him into the bar. Despite being drunk, his reaction time surprised me. The first punch landed before I even registered it, a sharp crack against my jaw, splitting my lip. I barely felt the sting before my instincts kicked in, sending a vicious grin curling across my face.

Finally.

I didn't hesitate.

I drove my fist into his ribs—once, twice—each hit sending a satisfying jolt up my arm. He grunted, stumbling back against the bar, his face twisting in pain. His friends lunged, cursing, and the club erupted into chaos.

Someone grabbed me from behind, locking an arm around my throat. I slammed my elbow into his gut and twisted free, spinning to drive a brutal right hook into his temple. He crumpled, knocking over a table on his way down. It crashed, glasses and booze spilling over the floor, a hazard if there ever was one.

Another came at me, swinging wild and sloppily, so damn predictable. I ducked his punch, caught his wrist, and yanked him forward, straight into my knee. His nose shattered with a sickening crunch, blood splattering across my shirt, followed by more fists and more shouting.

I hardly flinched when a glass bottle shattered against the bar next to me, missing my head by inches. Some dumbass tried to use the distraction to tackle me, but I pivoted, grabbed his arm, and threw him face-first into the counter. The bartender cursed, backing away, but I barely heard her over the pounding in my ears. Everything was a blur of movement, adrenaline, rage, and fists connecting with flesh.

The next guy to rush me was bigger, bulkier, but I didn't give a damn. I let him charge, let him think he had the upper hand, until I sidestepped at the last second, grabbing the back of his head and slamming him down onto my knee. His skull bounced off my leg, his body going limp as he crumpled to the floor. My knuckles burned and bled, but damn, if it didn't feel good.

"Fucking hell, Kreed!" Nash hollered, glancing at me as he pinned some random dude to the wall.

My eyes located the twins in the thick of it, fists flying, bodies crashing into tables and into walls. Maddox took down two guys at once, dodging a punch and delivering a brutal uppercut that sent one sprawling. Mason was grinning like a psychopath as he drove a chair into someone's back, the wood splintering on impact. And Nash handled business, keeping his strikes efficient. He didn't fight for the thrill like the rest of us. He fought to end it.

Me?

I was just getting started.

A hand yanked on my shoulder, trying to pull me back. I spun, already throwing a punch, only to be caught by a bouncer. "Enough!" Alexus growled, gripping my wrist midair.

I wrenched free, chest heaving, blood dripping from my knuckles. Around me, the fight had dissolved into a mess of groaning bodies and overturned furniture. Security swarmed in, grabbing Maddox, Mason, and Nash, dragging us toward the back, not in the mood for our shit.

They hauled us into one of the rooms, shoving us onto a worn leather couch. Alexus, the security guard in charge, crossed his arms and glared. He had dealt with us for most of our lives and was the only person in this club with balls big enough to put his hands on us. "Sleep it off," he ordered. "You're cut off. All of you."

I wiped the blood from my nose, my pulse still thrumming, my knuckles still tingling with the rush. "Whatever. You don't have anything here I want."

Maddox grinned, his teeth stained red. "Good talk, Alex."

Alexus's stare hardened as he pointed at me, putting his finger in my face, not the place to be unless you wanted it broken, regardless of how big you were or if you were a friend. "And if you start any more shit, I'm calling your father."

My body locked up. The rage burning so violently inside me shaped into something cold. I leaned forward slowly, resting my forearms on my knees. The room had gone quiet, the twins watching carefully.

Then, I laughed. Low, rough, humorless, reclining deeper into the couch. "Do it," I retorted. "See what happens."

Alexius hesitated. I was still the boss's son.

Smart man.

My head fell back against the couch, my ribs throbbing, blood staining my shirt. My restraint was tested to the end of its rope, and I just sat there, my knuckles stinging and whiskey burning in my veins.

None of it felt like enough.

None of it touched the real fight sweltering inside me.

I'd never in my life crashed out over a girl. I was angry at her. At my father. At my life. But mostly myself.

I never should have left her at the warehouse, or perhaps I never should have touched her to begin with, but it was too late. She'd already gotten to me, and I couldn't shake her out of my system, but fuck me if I wouldn't try.

I WOKE up with my skull feeling like it had been split in two and my mouth tasting like I'd swallowed a damn ashtray. My fingers touched my temples, which did the exact opposite of offering relief.

"Christ." I winced. This had to be the mother of all hangovers. My head lolled to the side, pressing against the cool leather of—

Wait.

Why am I not in my bed? And why am I sleeping at such an awkward angle?

I cracked one eye open, the dim morning light stabbing through my brain, to see the back seat of one of my father's sedans. The one Roman, his driver, used to shuttle him around like a fucking king.

What the hell?

Where's my car?

Better question, where the hell am I?

I had no memory of crawling into the back seat, let alone someone bringing... I glanced at the window. Home. I was sitting outside my house. Had my father sent the car? Had someone called him? What I didn't need this morning was him harping on my ass. The last thing I remembered was walking out of the club with a bottle of liquor in my hand, stumbling under flickering streetlights.

Yet, here I was.

I groaned, forcing my aching body to move. My muscles protested as I pushed the car door open and stepped onto the pavement, swaying slightly. The cold air slapped me in the face, but it did nothing to clear the pounding in my head.

I staggered up the steps to the house, my limbs heavy and movements sluggish as every inch of me screamed in protest, urging me to get off my feet and find the quickest bed. *Fuck,* the driveway was looking pretty comfortable right now. My knuckles throbbed, and I didn't have to question why. Those assholes deserved what they got, and the bruises and stiff ribs were worth it. In fact, I had a feeling there were many nights like last night to come.

But first, I needed painkillers. Now.

Inside, the house was quiet. Too quiet.

Where the hell is everyone?

I assumed Maddox and Mason had come home with me, but perhaps the assumption was wrong. They could have very well shoved me in the back seat and asked Roman to drive me home. This place was rarely empty. If Maddox and Mason weren't bickering in some room, their voices traveling through the house, then security was usually underfoot.

I stumbled into the kitchen, yanking open a cabinet and grabbing the bottle of ibuprofen. The pills rattled in my shaking hand as I dumped a few into my palm, my eyes darting to the half-empty whiskey bottle sitting on the counter.

How damn convenient.

Fuck it.

I reached for a glass, pouring the liquor with shaky fingers. One swallow to take the edge off. One drink to dull the pain.

The booze and the pills went down smoothly, and I refilled the glass before dragging my ass into the family room, seeking the couch. I had to get off my feet. Walking hurt. Hell, any movement at all was torturous.

The couch more or less caught me as I plopped down, somehow not spilling a drop of whiskey, but before I brought the glass to my lips, a hand snatched it away.

"That's enough." The voice was firm, steady. Unyielding.

Annoyance joined the other aches and pains in my body. I lifted my gaze, and there he was. My fucking father.

He stood above me, the picture of cold authority, his piercing light green eyes taking me in with barely concealed disapproval. He held my glass between his fingers, the expensive whiskey swirling in the tumbler. "You smell like you showered in Jack Daniels," he said, nose wrinkling in distaste.

I barely swallowed the urge to tell him to go to hell. I didn't have the energy for one of his lectures, but being the good son I was, I rubbed the back of my neck instead, my temples pulsating as I leaned against the couch, exhaling through my nose.

"Where's Kaylor?" he asked, his tone clipped as he crossed his arms over his wide chest. Back in the day, Daddy Dearest had been a linebacker like Maddox. Years of dedication and treating his body like some damn temple kept him looking fit.

I tensed. Just the sound of her name made my stomach twist. I focused on the glass tumbler in his hand, wishing I'd brought the bottle instead. "I don't know," I muttered.

Dad took a step closer, dressed in a crisp, pressed striped suit, and sat down on the coffee table so we were eye level. "What happened last night?"

I wasn't in the mood for this shit. Not now. Not with my head splitting open and his voice scraping against my last nerve. "Ask Maddox or Mason," I said flatly. "They were there."

He exhaled, losing patience. "Get your shit together, Kreed. Go take a shower. Scrub the stench off you, and when you're done cleaning up, we're going to figure out a way to bring her back."

I let out a bitter laugh, finally lifting my gaze to his. "She doesn't want to come back." My voice was hoarse, raw from all the yelling and all the drinking. "She knows everything. She knows what you did. How you basically kidnapped her."

My father's face didn't so much as twitch. "That doesn't matter."

Something inside me went cold.

He threw back the tumbler of whiskey before setting the empty glass on the coffee table in front of me like a taunt. "I'm not done with her yet."

The way he said it. So fucking casual. So damn final.

My temper flared bright, fast, and dangerous, curling up my spine. Leaning forward, I snatched the tumbler off the table.

"Get her back." Dad straightened, turning his back to me, already moving toward the door, already dismissing me as if I were nothing but another chess piece in his carefully constructed game.

My teeth ground together.

I wanted to hit something. If I were being honest, I wanted to sink my fist into him. However, I did the next best thing. As soon as he was out of sight, I reared back and hurled the forgotten glass into the fireplace. The shattering crystal echoed through the empty room, the flames swallowing the pieces whole. Yet no matter how much I wanted to, no matter how much I burned inside, the one thing I couldn't destroy was the part of me that still wanted her.

The fire crackled, swallowing the shattered remains of the glass, but it did nothing to silence the chaos in my head. I turned away, running a hand down my face, and then I saw it.

Her hoodie. Well, my hoodie, to be precise, the one she borrowed and kept wearing.

It was draped over the back of the armchair; the same hoodie she always wore when she curled up in the corner after sneaking out to the porch for air. The same one she'd shrugged off absentmindedly last week when she was arguing with Mason over some bullshit movie trivia.

A lump formed in my throat, thick and suffocating.

The pain I'd spent the whole night trying to drown, trying to fight, came back with a vengeance, heaving into my chest with the force of a freight train.

I wanted another drink.

Needed one.

But the whiskey was gone, the roaring flame consuming it just like every last piece of her that had been left in this house, and I was too damn tired to get up and raid the liquor cabinet.

I had no one to blame but myself. Why the fuck did I care what Kaylor Steele did? Why the fuck indeed?

Get her back. It was just like my father to issue an order and expect it to be obeyed. Especially by his sons, but I was no longer playing by his rules. *If* I decided to get her back, it would be on my terms and for my reasons, not so he could continue using her to further his corrupt agenda.

I used to love being part of a crew, but lately...the things we did... didn't sit right with me. I had to make a choice.

3

KAYLOR

The road stretched before us, nothing but thick trees and darkness pressing in from both sides. The only sound in the cab was the low hum of the truck's engine and the occasional thump of loose gravel kicking up beneath the tires. Rusty's large hands dwarfed the wheel, his expression somber as he kept his eyes on the winding road.

I stared out the window, my breath fogging the glass as my mind reeled over everything that had led to this moment. Leaving. Running. Kreed's face when I stepped back. The way his hand had lingered in the air between us before he'd clenched it into a fist and let it drop.

It was for the best.

So why did it feel as if I'd ripped something open inside myself?

Rusty cleared his throat, pulling me away from my turbulent thoughts. "You'll be safe at the cabin. No one knows about it but your dad and me. Not even Jesse." Jesse was Rusty's son, who was a few years older than I was. Rusty and Jesse's mom never had a relationship, and he hadn't found out he had a son until Jess was seven.

"There's no Internet or TV, but we do get spotty cell service, depending on the weather."

If he was trying to sell me on this cabin, it wasn't working. No Internet or TV sounded like a prison sentence, not a retreat. Swiping at my eyes, I stared straight ahead, refusing to shed another tear over a traitor. "Where is it?"

He glanced over his shoulder before changing lanes, the snake tattoo coiling around his entire arm drawing my eyes. "Outside city limits, deep in the woods. It used to belong to an old friend of mine before he moved out of state. He left the place to me," he said. "Figured it might come in handy one day. Or at the very least, a place to escape and relax. Your dad and I used to come out here to get away when things got hot."

I studied him in the dim glow of the dashboard lights. Rusty had always been solid. Dependable. He hadn't given up on me after my parents died and had fought to get me out of the Corvos' control, to make sure I knew the truth. And yet, the way he and the Vipers had gone about getting me back unsettled me. Maybe it was just my paranoia. Maybe it was the exhaustion gnawing at the outskirts of my mind. Maybe it was having my heart yanked out of my chest a second time, but I had so many more questions.

I started with something simple. We'd get to the nitty-gritty details eventually. "Why are you doing this?"

His jaw tensed slightly, causing his beard to twitch. "I had to get you away from them. You don't belong with the Corvos, and it's what your father would want. They might be gone, but you still have family. The crew will take care of you."

I swallowed hard. "You don't know what I've been through."

"I know it's a lot to take in with everything you've learned about your father. But the Corvos only see you as something to use, but you're not a damn tool. You're not theirs. You belong with us. I'm sorry that we couldn't protect you sooner. I had no idea what Donovan had planned. If I had...well, things would have gone differently."

My stomach twisted at his words. Perhaps because a part of me knew he wasn't wrong. Or maybe because I didn't know who I belonged to anymore. Or that I wanted to belong to myself. Why did I have to choose? I wanted nothing to do with either side or the hatred they'd built between them. I had my own anger to work through. Adding to it would only make it difficult. It would harden me, make me bitter and jaded, and I'd already changed so much.

"If you wanted to protect me, what was the purpose of the masks?" I asked. They had the opposite effect of safety. I had thought they were the killers or associated with them. My mind couldn't reason why the Vipers would wear them if not to frighten me, which they had.

The truck hit a bump, jostling us in our seats. "To throw the Corvos off. We were trying to avoid them knowing it was us, not just for your safety, but for the crew and their families. We hadn't meant to scare you, but it had to look real for the Ravens to believe it."

"Oh, it looked and felt very real," I mumbled, toying with the ends of my sleeve that was starting to tatter from my constant stress.

"Yeah, well, it didn't go exactly according to plan."

"No shit." But that was the story of my life.

"I know it was a mistake, kiddo. But Donovan watches everything, and we couldn't risk him linking it back to the Vipers too soon."

I turned back toward the window, watching as the trees grew denser, the night even darker. "How much longer?" Turned out I was too fucking tired to grill Rusty.

The unmistakable scent of grease and oil filled the cabin of the truck, mostly from Rusty's clothes but some from the seats. "Almost there."

A few minutes later, the truck slowed as we turned onto an overgrown driveway, branches scraping the sides of the vehicle. Up ahead, the outline of a small house emerged through the trees. The tires crunched over unplowed snow as Rusty pulled the truck to a stop in front of a small, weathered cabin, nestled deep in the woods. The place was dark, silent, and unnervingly isolated except for the single porch light flickering and barely cutting through the night.

Cabin was a generous word for what sat in the middle of the clearing. The structure was small, almost forgotten, with a slanted roof and a front porch that sagged. The paint on the exterior was peeling, and the wooden shutters hung loose.

Rusty cut the engine, leaving just the howling winds blowing through the trees as he glanced at me. "It's not much, but it's remote and safe. No one will come looking for you here. Not unless you want to be found."

Safe.

I wasn't sure I even knew what that word meant anymore.

"What about Donovan?" I asked. If he had gone through so much effort to get my guardianship, it seemed unlikely he would just let me go and cut his losses.

"I don't want you to worry. I'll handle Donovan and his Ravens. The only thing you need to be doing is thinking about your future."

Those Ravens included Kreed, Mason, Maddox, and Raine.

Not that I gave a shit. Fuck them. Fuck them all.

My arms wrapped around myself as I huddled into the seat. I should have felt relief. I should have been grateful, instead of the unease coiling unrelentingly in my stomach, but exhaustion weighed heavier. My body ached, my head was a mess, and right now, I didn't have the energy to question anything.

After I slid out of the truck, my boots sank into a layer of snow as I took in the rest of the place. The air was thick with the scent of damp wood and earth, and the wind whispered through the trees, rattling the bare branches like bones clacking together.

Rusty unlocked the door and pushed it open, flicking on the light inside. A dull yellow glow flooded the cabin, revealing a space that hadn't been touched in months, maybe longer. Dust clung to the sparse furniture, including a worn-out couch with a crocheted throw draped over the back. A wooden coffee table littered with old magazines sat beside the couch, and just over the threshold to the right was a small kitchenette with a single-burner stove and an outdated fridge.

I stepped inside cautiously, cedar lingering thick in the air as my fingers brushed against the edge of a counter. A fine layer of dust coated the surface, confirming my suspicion. "No one's been here in a while?"

Rusty shrugged, setting his keys on the counter and moving to put a kettle of water on the only burner. "Haven't had a reason to use it lately, especially during the winter. The roads can be treacherous and slick during a storm."

I nodded slowly, my gaze drifting to the one hallway leading to what I assumed was a bedroom and bathroom. The whole place felt...abandoned.

Rusty pulled a mug from the cabinet and filled it with hot water from a kettle. He dropped a tea bag in before handing it to me. "Drink this. It'll help you sleep."

I accepted it, the warmth seeping into my fingers. "How long can I stay here?"

His frame seemed to occupy the entire kitchen as he leaned against the counter. "For as long as you need."

The promise should have been comforting, but something about this place, about being so far removed from everything, made me feel...trapped. Ironic because I'd just escaped one cell only to feel boxed in another smaller, grossly dirtier one.

Maybe I was just tired.

Maybe I was overthinking things.

Maybe I was missing that plush, oversized bed across the hall from Kreed's room.

I sat on the couch, cradling the tea, exhaustion pulling at me. "Thanks, Rusty." I took a sip, the warmth spreading through me.

His lips lifted in a small, tired smile. "There's a bedroom down the hall. I'll take the couch. Get some sleep, kiddo. We'll figure out what happens next after you've rested."

A yawn pulled at the corners of my mouth, and I nearly told

Rusty to take the bedroom. Getting up again sounded like a chore when it would be so much easier to curl up right here on the couch, but I took my tea and ordered my body to move. I barely made it to the bedroom before the burden of everything crashed down on me. The tea was still warm in my hands as I tucked myself beneath the thin blanket fully dressed, my body finally surrendering.

For the first time in days, sleep claimed me fast and hard. And for the first time in weeks, I didn't dream.

I WOKE UP GROGGY, my head fogged with sleep, and my eyes blurry with tears. Blinking them away, I stared at the unfamiliar wooden ceiling, trying to shake off the heaviness pressing down on me. Crying in my sleep wasn't a new concept, and I doubted it would stop anytime soon. Especially now.

How long had I been out?

Crash.

A clatter of what sounded like glass breaking from somewhere in the small cabin jolted me upright in bed. Strands of my silvery hair fell into my face as my head whirled toward the door, and a moment later, Rusty mumbled a curse in his gruff voice.

Shoving my hair out of the way, I scooted to the edge of the lumpy bed, stretching the kinks out of my back and neck. Definitely not the best sleep of my life, that was for freaking sure.

I made quick use of the bathroom, mostly because I didn't have anything to do my normal hygiene routine. No toothbrush. No tooth-paste. No hairbrush. No face wash. Nada.

Rusty was crouched on the floor, sweeping up broken glass into a makeshift dustpan when I emerged from the hallway. He glanced up, sensing my presence. "Everything okay?" I asked, hovering awkwardly in the doorway.

"Just being my normal, clumsy oaf," he retorted, scooping up the last few bits of glass before standing up. "Did you sleep okay?" he asked, keeping his voice light as if it would make this situation any less weird.

I tried to recall how many times I'd ever been alone with him. Other than a few times when I was little and he used to watch me at the shop, I couldn't think of anything in recent years. I shrugged. "I haven't been sleeping well since..."

"You don't have to say. It's been rough. Probably really hard for you." He let out a heavy sigh, dumping the glass into the trash before facing me again. "I'm sorry about what happened, for not being able to save your parents. If I had known..."

"How could you have?"

"It's a guilt I'll carry with me forever."

My lips turned down. "My dad wouldn't want that."

Setting the broom aside, he leaned against the counter. "He also wouldn't have wanted his little girl in the clutches of his enemy. I should have done a better job finding you sooner."

"You found me. That's enough. You lost him too." It felt so good to talk about my parents with someone who knew them, with someone who loved them. I hadn't realized how much I needed this, not to forget about them.

Rusty swallowed before pushing off the counter. "Sit. I made some coffee. You're probably starved."

I sat curled up in the oversized chair, a knit blanket pulled around my legs as Rusty set a steaming mug of coffee on the side table beside me.

"Sorry, it's not Starbucks," he said, placing a box of doughnuts down next. "Best I could do on short notice. I'm not exactly Gordon Ramsay."

I offered a small, flat smile. "It's fine. Thank you."

He hovered for a second longer, hands in his pockets like he wanted to say more but couldn't find the words. Finally, he gave a nod and stepped back toward the kitchen.

The coffee smelled like burnt hazelnut, and the doughnuts were slightly stale, but none of that mattered. Nothing did because everything I thought I knew was a lie.

My fingers trembled as I wrapped them around the warm mug, trying to ground myself, find my bearings, but it didn't work. I was still floating, untethered and raw.

Donovan hadn't just altered my parents' will; he'd orchestrated their deaths. For revenge. A long, meticulous plan that ended with them dead and him sitting like a king on a throne built from the ashes of my life, and I had nothing. No clothes. No room to call mine.

The blanket suddenly felt suffocating. I kicked it off and stood up too fast, the room tilting slightly as the pressure of it all bore down again.

Rusty turned from the sink. "Kaylor?"

"I don't have a home." My voice cracked. "I don't have anything, Rusty. Not even a goddamn pair of socks to my name."

He moved but kept a careful distance. "You have people who care about you. We'll figure it out. You're not alone."

"But I am." I choked out a tart laugh. "I don't even know what to do next. My whole future just...collapsed. It's hard to think about tomorrow when today is already unbearable."

He nodded slowly, rubbing the back of his neck. "I know it's bleak right now. I know it's not what you need, but the cabin's safe. It's yours for as long as you want it. I'll stock the kitchen later. And I'll make some calls. Try to find someone, anyone who might help."

I blinked back the tears forming again. I was so tired of crying. "You don't have to fix this," I murmured. "I'm not you're burden."

"You could never be a burden." Rusty gave me a sad smile.

The coffee had gone cold, the doughnuts untouched.

THERE WASN'T much to do in the cabin. I contemplated going for a walk to clear my head, but I didn't know anything about the area, and it would be just my luck I'd end up lost. Not to mention, the temps had dropped overnight to a bitter cold that took my breath away. It was an easy decision to stay cozied up in the chair, especially after Rusty started a fire.

I must have dozed off, because when I woke, the cabin seemed dimmer than before. Pushing the blanket off my legs, I listened, wondering where Rusty was. Silence greeted me. No footsteps. No low murmurs from another room. Even the fire had fizzled out, leaving nothing but ash in the burner. I swung my legs to the floor, rubbing at my arms as a chill settled over me. Stepping cautiously into the kitchen, my stomach twisted when I looked out the window, seeing at least another inch of snow blanketing the ground, but more importantly, Rusty's truck was gone.

No note. No explanation.

Okay, where the hell did he go? Nothing like dropping me off in the middle of nowhere and then dipping.

My stomach growled, reminding me I hadn't eaten yet today.

Abandoning my seat at the table, I went on the hunt for fuel. At least Rusty hadn't just dumped me here to fend for myself. I tried to imagine myself foraging in the woods for berries. It was laughable. I lacked actual survival skills. Unless there was a Black Friday sale at Prada, the only survival instincts I had were emotional trauma shit.

Since I didn't have it in me to make anything complicated, I opted for the quickest option. I obviously could handle toast. Right? How hard could it be?

It took me longer than I was willing to admit to finagle the toaster, but I could reheat coffee like a pro *if* this place had a microwave, which, of course, it didn't. I'd been here for less than twenty-four hours, and I already missed my life and all the things I took for granted, like having a fully stocked fridge and pantry at my disposal any time of the day.

I wasn't going to last a day here. Something about being alone and isolated in a strange place set me on edge, and cold coffee alone wasn't going to be enough to calm me.

Opening the freezer, I improvised, pulling out a tray of ice and popping a handful of cubes into my coffee. While I waited for my toast, I sat at the kitchen table, staring out into the endless stretch of trees.

What the hell am I supposed to do now?

Process what happened and what I learned?

Yeah, I sure as hell didn't want to do that.

I could hardly believe last night was real, and shoving all the feelings inside a nice little compartmentalized box somewhere in the dark crevice of my brain seemed so much healthier than dealing with it. I was fucking tired of crying. My eyes couldn't handle any more, puffy and bloodshot as they were.

Sipping on the iced coffee, I winced at the bitterness. What I wouldn't do for some sugar and cream.

The harshness of my situation settled deep in my bones, whether I wanted it there or not. Controlling my brain wasn't as easy as snapping my fingers.

The betrayal. The fucking stupidity of it all. How could I have been so foolish?

My chest ached, a slow burn of anger and something else. Something I wasn't ready to name. I had started to trust Kreed. Not just tolerate him but trust him. And Mason and Maddox, too, at least a little. But not like Kreed. No, he was different. I thought I saw another side to him. Was that all part of his persona? Was any of it real? God, I'd fucking slept with him!

He didn't just make me trust him. He made me want him, and that was the most dangerous part because I had started to believe the lies wrapped in skilled hands and stolen glances, in the quiet moments when he wasn't a Corvo and I wasn't the girl his father stole. I had started to think that maybe, just maybe, he wasn't as bad as I thought. That *he* was on my side. How fucking foolish. Kreed *was* the bad guy. Well, relatively speaking, considering my father had apparently been one, too. That realization cracked deep and jagged inside me. If I couldn't trust Kreed and I couldn't trust my father's memory, then who the hell could I trust? The answer curdled in my gut. No one. Not anymore.

The toaster popped.

I jumped, the sound yanking me out of my rabbit hole. "Screw this," I murmured. I couldn't stay here. The cabin felt too small, too cut off, like I'd been stranded in the middle of nowhere with nothing but my thoughts. *And* my thoughts were the last thing I wanted company with.

Grabbing my phone, I dialed the only person I still trusted.

Brock answered on the third ring. "Kay?"

"Hey." My voice came out hoarse, but I tried to steady it.

"What happened? Are you okay?" Brock rattled off. I could picture his pinched, dark brows. "I've been trying to reach you since last night."

My fingers dug into the side of my head as my elbow braced against the table. "No."

"Are you hurt?"

My lip trembled. I shook my head even though he couldn't see me. "No."

"Did Kreed do something?" he demanded, nothing friendly in his tone.

I let out a hollow laugh. "Depends on your definition of something."

"I'll kill him."

"I don't want him dead. There's been enough death."

A pause. Then, softer, he asked, "What do you need?"

"Can you come get me?"

"Where are you? At the house?" he replied without any hesitation.

He meant Kreed's house, an obvious assumption since he didn't know what happened last night. "A cabin. I don't—" I exhaled. "I don't know where I am," I admitted, hating how weak I sounded. "Somewhere in the woods."

"Stay put. I'll get Fynn to track this number. Keep your phone on." The shit my cousin and his friends could do still baffled me. I could barely make toast and coffee. At my age, they had reputations that stretched beyond high school. "I'm on my way," he assured, and through the phone, I could hear him moving, already in motion.

"Brock?" I hesitated. "Does your offer still stand?"

A series of dings came through the line that sounded like a car door opening. "To stay at my house?"

"Yeah."

"Always."

I swallowed the lump in my throat. "Okay. See you soon."

As I hung up, I let out a breath I hadn't realized I was holding. I didn't know what the next move was, but at least I would be somewhere familiar *and* with civilization and within reach of DoorDash. Brock's house, however, wasn't a very inconspicuous location. It was a risk. Kreed or Donovan could easily find me, but I was banking on my cousin having something up his sleeve to keep me hidden.

He was good for shit like that.

Now I just had to wait and figure out what I planned to tell Rusty. He'd gone out of his way to drive me here last night, give me a safe haven, and I ran the first chance I got.

Some habits died hard.

Each minute that ticked by felt like an hour. I couldn't decide if the anxiety in my stomach was because I didn't want Rusty to come back or if I did. Regardless, I sucked at waiting. It gave my brain too much free range.

With nothing else to do, I scrolled through my phone, searching but telling myself I wasn't looking for *his* name. I should block his number and delete him from my phone, but as I stared at Kreed's contact, I couldn't bring myself to do it. Not yet.

4

KAYLOR

The low crunch of tires against gravel and snow sent a spike of adrenaline through my veins. I moved toward the window, peering out through the dusty glass just as a sleek black Land Rover rolled to a stop outside the cabin. Brock. And he hadn't come alone.

Grayson stepped out of the passenger seat, scanning the area like he had too much experience in shady situations. He was bundled in a puffer coat and had a beanie pulled over his head. The Elite in general were extraordinarily good-looking, but I'd always thought Grayson the sexiest, and becoming a dad hadn't changed his appeal. If anything, it made him weirdly hotter. His gaze assessed the cabin before he turned toward the front door.

Brock, on the other hand, took a less cautious approach, stalking right for the cabin, finding me the only thing on his mind, knowing Grayson had his back. Classic Brock, scowling, unfazed, as if nothing rattled him, but I knew better.

I'd always envied the friendship my cousin had with Grayson, Micah, and Fynn. The Elite. It was more than a name. It meant something. To each other. To everyone in this town. To the girls lucky enough to call them theirs. Some bonds went deeper than just friendship. The four of them were tied together in ways I would never know.

Probably for the best.

I'd learned that sometimes ignorance could be bliss.

The image of my father had been forever altered by the truth.

Not wasting another second, I flung open the door and rushed toward the car. Grayson's gaze locked on to me immediately, his head tilting slightly. "Anyone inside we need to worry about?"

I shook my head as I opened the back seat door, eager to get out of here. "Rusty left. I don't know where he is. Probably at the shop."

"Let's go. I don't want to be here if he comes back," Brock said, still frowning at me. His gaze was too intense, and I felt him studying me as he and Grayson climbed back into the car.

Neither of them spoke right away, but as soon as I slammed the door shut, Brock shifted the SUV into drive and pulled back onto the path. The tires kicked up snow as we wound through the dense trees, bumping over uneven ground. The farther we got from the cabin, the more I realized just how deep in the woods Rusty had taken me. The path was barely visible, the snow-draped trees pressing in on either side, thick and unyielding. I hadn't noticed last night. I'd been too damn exhausted, too numb, but now? It made my stomach twist. If Rusty had wanted to keep me hidden, he could have.

Kreed wouldn't have found me. No one would have, and yet, here I was, willingly walking right back into the Ravens' lair.

I turned my head to stare out the window, my throat thick. Maybe I was making a mistake. Maybe I should've stayed in that cabin, gone off-grid until I turned eighteen, but the thought of being alone, of hiding, made my chest squeeze with panic. And Brock... My cousin was safe. He always had been.

When we finally reached the massive iron gates leading to Taylor's mansion, I rubbed the heel of my hand over my heart. The estate loomed ahead, glistening under the late February sun, with its Greek and Roman influences, sitting on more land than any normal person would know what to do with. It wasn't my home, but it was familiar, and that was enough.

Brock pulled into the driveway, killing the engine before twisting in his seat to look at me. His aqua eyes gave nothing away, but the flicker in his jaw betrayed him, a sure sign he was holding something back. "My parents are out of the country for the next few months," he said, nodding toward the house. "You won't have to worry about them showing up unexpectedly."

His parents' absence was nothing new. Brock spent most of his life alone, being raised by a nanny or the staff. My aunt and uncle weren't bad people; they just weren't hands-on and were very focused on their careers. I had so many memories of coming here when we were younger, popping in when Uncle Sutton and Aunt Char were back in town. They'd always brought me little trinkets from wherever they'd been overseas.

I tried to give Brock a smile of gratitude, but it fell short. "Thanks. Seriously. I mean it. I don't know what I would do without you."

"You're family. Now let's go inside so you can tell me what kind of trouble we're dealing with," he said, reaching for the door. I climbed out, clutching my phone as Grayson followed behind. As soon as I stepped through the front door, Brock shut it with a quiet click before turning to face me. His eyes were brimming with concern. "Have you eaten?"

"I had a piece of toast," I admitted to my pathetic food intake. I hadn't had a decent meal in what felt like days.

He nodded toward the hallway leading to the kitchen. "Grayson will fix us something to eat."

Brock's best friend snorted. "Since when did I become your chef?"

My cousin hooked an arm around my neck, giving me a quick squeeze before he answered Grayson. "Since you're the only one of the three of us who can make something edible. Dad life has taught you a few things."

Grayson rolled his eyes. "Do you even have any food here?" he asked, raising a brow.

My cousin's lips thinned as he went to the fridge, me tailing behind. "Definitely not."

"I'll order us something," Grayson grumbled, digging out his phone as he went to sit at the table.

Brock grabbed three drinks, handing me one as he passed by, and sat across from Grayson. He slid the can down the table, and Grayson snagged it before it went sailing off the edge. "Tell me what happened yesterday," Brock said, popping the top on his can, the carbonation hissing.

Sitting in an empty seat, I gave Brock and Grayson the rundown of events while we waited for our food to arrive. When I finished, the kitchen was quiet, except for the soft hum of the refrigerator and the occasional scrape of Brock's fingers against the wooden table. As Brock and Grayson digested everything, my fingers gripped the edge of my chair. I thought unburdening the secret would take away some of the pressure pressing on my chest, but my pulse still hadn't settled after spilling everything, the lies, the manipulation, the fucking betrayal.

I expected Brock to be pissed, but the storm brewing in his eyes was something else entirely. "So let me get this straight." Each syllable dropped like a threat, fury braided into every breath. "Donovan Corvo didn't just manipulate his way into getting guardianship of you. He rigged your father's will to make sure it happened?"

I nodded, my throat tight. "Yeah. And his sons were in on it. *Kreed* was in on it."

Brock muttered a curse under his breath, pushing back from the table so abruptly that his chair scraped against the tile. He got up, pacing, shaking his head like he was trying to make sense of it. "I knew it was weird when your father gave *him,* of all people, guardianship. It didn't make any sense to me. They're gonna fucking pay for this," he growled. His hands curled into fists at his sides. "They messed with the wrong family. I gave him one shot. He won't get a second. Not from us."

My chest squeezed at the possessiveness in his voice. Brock had always been protective. "I just want to forget they exist," I admitted.

"Do you think Kreed or Donovan will let you walk away?" Grayson asked, voice deceptively calm, giving Brock a moment to collect himself. He didn't need to press the question. It already clawed at the back of my mind.

"I don't know why they'd want me to begin with." I wrapped my arms around myself, the chill in the room suddenly more noticeable. "My parents are gone. They got their revenge. What importance could I have now?"

Grayson didn't blink. "Control."

The word hit harder than I expected. "I don't understand."

"You know about the Vipers Nest now," he said slowly, watching me like he wasn't sure how much I could handle. "You know your father was the head of the crew."

I let out a dry laugh. "Yeah, don't remind me. I still haven't come to terms with that side of my dad yet."

Brock and Grayson exchanged a brief glance, but it was enough to set uneasiness squirming in my chest.

"With you under their thumb, they can use you as leverage. A bargaining chip. They can force the Vipers' hand and make them surrender what your father spent his life building." Grayson's gaze sharpened, voice dropping low. "Your dad didn't just build the Nest, Kay. He hid things in it, things bigger than drugs, bigger than money."

I swallowed hard. "What do you mean?"

"Ledgers. Records. Names," Brock cut in. "Politicians, cops, businessmen—all the assholes who kept the city in his pocket. He wrote it all down. Insurance. Blackmail. Enough dirt to bury half of Elmwood alive if it ever saw the light of day. Where do you think we get half of our intel?" Brock's brows lifted. "That's what Donovan's after. Not just you. Not just revenge for his wife. If he controls you, he controls that legacy. He can use you to unlock everything your dad left behind."

I shook my head, my stomach twisting. "I don't have any of that. I don't know where it is."

Grayson leaned forward, his elbows braced on his knees, his eyes never leaving mine. "You don't have to know. You are the key. The bloodline. The heir. As long as you're breathing, you're leverage to be used to give up this information, and every crew in this city knows it."

Cold sank into my bones, heavier than the snow still clinging to my boots. My father's sins were chained to me, inked into my skin like some invisible mark I couldn't scrub away.

Brock sighed, rubbing a hand down the stubble peeking from his chin. "It's a fight you never should have been brought into. I'm telling you what your father would want me to say. You don't want to get mixed up in that world. He didn't want that for you."

A shiver crawled down my spine, but I refused to look away. "So what the hell am I supposed to do?"

He braced a hand on the counter, casual in a way that felt anything but, a glint gleaming behind his eyes. "I should tell you to leave, to get the hell out of Elmwood."

"Is that what you would do?"

"I think you know the answer to that. If it were me, I'd go back to school."

I blinked. "What? Isn't that the opposite of what I should do?"

"Probably," he agreed, but the calculation in his expression didn't change. "Lying low is an option. Or...you walk into Public with your head high, and you show them that they didn't break you. That you're stronger than their lies. That you won't fucking run and hide. That they don't own you. You take your life back."

The words hit deep inside me. "Rusty won't like that. He thinks I *should* stay hidden, tucked away somewhere in the middle of nowhere."

"And then what?" The question dangled for a moment between us. "The decision is yours, but it's going to take more than a house in the woods to stop the Ravens from finding you. Take my word for it. If it were me, I wouldn't stop."

He was right. If I disappeared, if I let them win, then I was exactly what they wanted me to be, weak and afraid.

"I'm not saying be reckless," Brock added. "You're not alone. You have us now. And you know the truth; that's power right there."

Before I responded, the doorbell rang.

Grayson pushed out of his chair and made his way to the door, grabbing the takeout bag from the delivery guy without a word.

My cousin sat back down, his expression turning serious. "Take a few days. Think about it," he said, sliding a container toward me. "But the Corvos only win if you let them. You have more fire in your veins. The Kaylor I know wouldn't hide. She'd fight back."

I swallowed hard. He was right. Life had beaten me down lately, but I was still the girl who didn't take shit from anyone. Certainly not some moody bad boy from the other side of town.

"The cycle of retaliation ends with you, Kaylor," Brock continued. "Or we hit back. Revenge is my specialty. Either way, I'll back you. And I'll do whatever it takes, starting with seeing if I can get our lawyers to discredit your father's altered will. There might be an original copy out there. And if there is, Fynn can find it."

I should be a little afraid of what means of revenge he was willing to take, but I wasn't. Brock and the Elite were damn good at what they did.

BROCK AND GRAYSON left hours ago, giving me space, but now that I had it, I didn't know what to do with myself. They couldn't stay but would have if I had asked. And he asked. Repeatedly, but the truth was, I needed a moment to myself; although at the same time, I feared being alone.

Being in Brock's house was so different than being in an isolated cabin in the middle of bumfuck nowhere. There was a strange comfort here, a pulse of normalcy the cabin had lacked. Out there, it had felt like the world had ended. Here, it just kept spinning.

Before leaving, Brock had ordered groceries, fully stocking the kitchen and leaving me with one of his credit cards. He assured me that Fynn would monitor the house and grounds through the security system and gave me a quick rundown of how it worked. If I were ever in trouble, a button was all it took to alert the police.

Now I had to deal with Rusty. That was a call I wasn't looking forward to. Hopefully, he was still at the shop and hadn't returned to the cabin and found me missing. He would assume the worst, that the Ravens were involved. I should have left a note. The last thing I wanted was to add to the strife between the crews.

Unlocking my phone, I wavered between my phone app and the text app, my finger hovering midair. *Fuck it.* I sent Rusty a quick text, letting him know I appreciated everything he'd done, but I needed a few days to myself. I told him not to worry, I was safe, and I'd be in touch soon, leaving it at that. I had a feeling he wouldn't be happy about my choice, which made a text easier.

I could only handle so much shit in a day, and my brain was currently clogged with all things Corvo. What I needed was a shower to clear my mind. I did my best decision-making in the shower, scrubbing all the gunk off me physically and metaphorically.

I took one of the guest rooms upstairs but stopped at Brock's bedroom to grab some sweats. I didn't think he would mind if I borrowed some. Eventually, I would have to figure out what to do about clothes...and my life. Thanks to Donovan and his illegal alteration of my parents' will, I didn't have access to a single penny. Even if I managed to prove his fraud, by then, he could have taken or spent every cent my parents worked for.

Nothing seemed clear to me. It was all still so confusing and impossible to believe. This couldn't be real. It was easier to believe I'd wake up from this nightmare than it was to accept how messed up my life was.

I was so fucking mad at myself for being so trusting, for letting Kreed in, for thinking for a second that Donovan might have had my best interest in mind. I'd wanted so bad to be out of that house, but now that I was on the other side, it wasn't better. I wasn't happier.

Just the opposite.

I never felt more alone or lost.

Dragging myself toward the attached bathroom, I turned the water on as hot as I could stand it and stripped off my clothes. Steam filled the room, thick and suffocating, but I welcomed it. Stepping under the spray, I let the scalding water pound against my back, tilting my head down as droplets streamed over my face.

I scrubbed my skin harder than necessary as if I could erase the last few days, the confusion, the betrayal, and the way my body still reacted when I thought about him.

Kreed.

Fuck him.

He made his choice. He played with my life, helped manipulate me, and let me believe I could trust him. That I could want him.

And yet...

I slammed my palm against the tile, letting out a breath.

I didn't want to miss him. Didn't want my heart to squeeze every time I thought about the way he looked at me, touched me, and made me feel like I was his. I should hate him. I *did* hate him. "I hate him," I murmured, thinking saying it out loud would make it true, but at the same time, I hated myself more for still caring. For still feeling anything at all.

As I braced my hands against the shower wall, drops of water rolled down my skin as I squeezed my eyes shut.

Screw them.

Screw Kreed. Screw Donovan. Screw the Corvos.

Brock was right. I couldn't hide. Or more like I didn't want to.

They had fucked with the wrong girl. I would finish my senior year at Public, graduate, and make the Raven Crew wish they had never set eyes on me.

I wasn't normally a vindictive person, but circumstances had changed me, and the fire kindling in my blood crackled for revenge.

Even if it killed me to see *him*...to see *them*.

The second I stepped into Elmwood Public Monday morning, I scanned the halls, searching for Poppy. I didn't give a damn about the whispers that followed me as I moved through the crowd. People always stared. Envied me. Feared me. That wasn't new, but today, I wasn't in the mood for their bullshit.

I needed to find her.

I caught sight of Poppy near the lockers, rummaging through her bag. She wasn't hard to spot—bright red hair, black combat boots, distressed stockings, and an oversized hoodie that swallowed her frame. The moment I strode up, her head snapped to me, and her expression twisted into a scowl. "What the hell do you—"

"Have you heard from Kaylor?" I cut her off.

Her scowl morphed into confusion as she slipped her bag strap over her shoulder. "You mean you don't know where she is?"

No. And that fact alone was enough to make me fucking unhinged. "She's gone," I gritted out.

Poppy's brow furrowed, concern flashing across her face. "What do you mean *gone*? Like...dead."

"God, no. She's fine… I think."

Her gold eyes widened. "What the fuck happened, Kreed? Where is she?"

I clenched my jaw, inhaling deeply through my nose. "I mean, she's not at the Corvo estate, and she sure as hell isn't answering my calls."

Poppy hesitated, then shook her head. "I was about to ask you the same thing. I haven't been able to get a hold of her since Friday night…since the game." She swallowed hard. "Since we snuck out and those guys took her."

My stomach twisted. I already knew what happened that night, knew Kaylor walked away from me, chose the Vipers, but hearing it out loud sent a fresh wave of fury through me.

I ran a hand over my face. *Think, Kreed. Focus.*

I needed to find her.

I needed to talk to her.

Poppy was my best shot at making that happen. "Listen," I said, deciding to be as straightforward as I could. "I need your help."

Poppy slammed her locker door shut with a metallic clang that vibrated down the hallway. She turned slowly, arms folding across her chest like a barrier she had no intention of lowering. "Why the hell would I help you?"

I didn't flinch. Just leaned against the wall, one boot scuffing the floor as I held her stare. "Because you're worried about her. And so am I."

Her brow furrowed, eyes narrowing as if searching for the lie between my words. "Is she avoiding you or something?"

"Or something," I conceded, the corner of my mouth twitching though there wasn't a trace of amusement behind it. "Will you help me, Poppy?"

She tilted her head, studying me like I was a strange specimen under glass. "Never thought I'd hear those words from Kreed Corvo's mouth."

"I'm asking nicely," I replied.

"And if I refuse?"

I straightened, just a little, letting the quiet stretch, letting her feel what I wasn't saying. "Then we move to me not asking nicely. Either way, I'll find out where she is. Don't give me a reason to unleash what I'm barely restraining."

Hesitation fluttered across her face, perhaps. A sliver of fear she quickly masked. "Why is this so important to you? It's not like you haven't been a complete dick to her."

"A complete dick, huh? I'll own that, but I don't have time to explain everything," I said. "But the people she's with? They're dangerous."

She arched a brow, lips parting slightly. "More dangerous than you?"

My gaze held hers. "Yeah."

Her arms dropped an inch, and the sarcasm drained from her face. "Holy shit. You're not kidding."

"I wish I were."

Poppy shook her head slowly, almost like she couldn't believe she was about to say what she did. "It's hard to imagine someone worse than you and your brothers."

I huffed a breath. "Cute."

She hesitated. "Fine. What do you want me to do?"

"Will you text her or call her?" I asked. "Set up a meeting. Tell her you want to see her. *But* don't tell her I'll be there."

Poppy's expression darkened. "That's a horrible idea."

I sighed, my patience wearing thin. "Poppy—"

"No, seriously," she cut me off, glaring. "If Kaylor wanted to talk to you, she would. You wouldn't need me to play fucking messenger. Not to mention, I've tried calling her. It seems she doesn't want to talk to either of us."

The words stung, but I pushed through them. "I don't care. *I need* to see her. Reach out to her friends from the Academy. They might know where she is."

Poppy let out a breath. She'd never seen me like this before. No one had, and maybe that's why, after a long moment, she muttered, "Shit," under her breath. "Fine. I'll try again. *But* only because I need to know she's okay."

Relief cut through me.

"Don't get too excited, Corvo," Poppy added, pointing a finger at my chest, "if she hates me for this, I'm blaming you. *And* after I do this, you'll tell me why she's in so much danger that it has you on edge."

I'd agree to anything, but it didn't mean I would deliver. I just needed Poppy to say yes.

MASON LEANED AGAINST MY DESK, his arms crossed, watching as I sent Poppy the phone numbers he'd dug up for Kaylor's friends from Elmwood Academy. It was scary the personal data you could pay to acquire online. "You sure about this?" he asked, his fingers messing up his hair.

"No," I muttered, tossing my phone onto the bed. "But I'm doing it anyway."

The card flipping between Mason's fingers halted. "She's not gonna be happy to see you."

"No shit."

"She might actually try to kill you."

I gave him a flat look. "If she wanted me dead, she wouldn't have run."

Mason smirked, but there was something behind it, something thoughtful. "Maybe she's plotting her revenge. I still think you should let me go instead."

I already knew where this was headed. "Not happening."

"Come on, man. She hates you right now. Me? She hates less than you."

I didn't say anything.

Mason shrugged. "Might be easier for her to talk to someone she doesn't associate with breaking her heart."

My fists clasped at the word. "Yeah? And what exactly would you say to her?"

"I don't know. Probably something like 'Hey, sorry we kidnapped you and manipulated you into trusting us, but in our defense, we kind of like you now.'"

I shot him a glare.

Mason smirked again, but his expression sobered. "Look, I get it. You need to talk to her. Just... don't make it worse."

My jaw locked.

Mason sighed, pushing off the desk, dropping the joker card on top of the table. "I can't believe you're going rogue. Do whatever the fuck you want, but if you come back looking like she took a baseball bat to your ribs, don't say I didn't warn you."

I didn't bother responding because I already knew the risk, and I was taking it anyway. I couldn't keep living with this feeling inside me.

Needing an outlet for the turmoil buzzing and the nagging impatience within me, I headed downstairs to our home gym, letting loose on the punching bag. It was either the hundred-fifty-pound bag or someone's face. The urge to drown myself in booze was just another reason to wear myself out in the gym. It was too easy to get drunk and forget her name. The only problem was I had yet to find out how much booze it would take. She never seemed to stray from my mind.

It was easy to convince myself I was tracking Kaylor for my father, but it was an excuse. I wanted to find her for purely selfish reasons, and it was time I acknowledged that I didn't just want her back; I wanted *her*.

There was also the fact that there was a mole in her father's crew, and no matter how many pieces I tried to force into the puzzle, I couldn't figure out who it was, and my father sure as hell wasn't volunteering the information. He had an arrangement. One that my father benefited from and would continue to profit from.

Someone had been feeding him information. Detailed shit. Timelines. Movements. Conversations that should've never left private circles. That betrayal was how her parents died. Not because of a business deal gone sideways, but because someone close to them, a friend, a fucking traitor, sold them out, and now my father was still pulling strings, still manipulating everyone like the greedy bastard he was.

For Donovan Corvo, it was never enough. No one knew the impossible expectations of him better than his sons.

I didn't want to be concerned with Kaylor, but the fact that I couldn't seem to stop thinking about her drove me nuts. If the only way to make this insanity stop was to bring her back, then the choice seemed obvious.

Someone in her crew had blood on their hands. Her blood. If she got too close, if she trusted the wrong person again…

I pumped my fist into the bag over and over, my already raw knuckles protesting at the repeated pain.

I shouldn't care.

I shouldn't be concerned with what happened to her.

I was raised not to give a damn about anyone outside the family and the crew. Taught to shut down emotions, ignore feelings, focus on loyalty, strength, and power, but somewhere along the way, she cracked my shield.

Kaylor fucking Steele.

Whack. Whack. Whack.

The girl with sadness in her eyes and stubbornness in her soul. The girl I was supposed to isolate. Keep close until my father was done using her, but I lost control the second she looked at me like I was more than my name. The second she trusted me. The second she chose me.

And I broke that.

I broke her.

All I could think about was how to fix something I never deserved to have in the first place. I didn't get to have people. Not like that. But I couldn't let her go.

Not when the same people who betrayed her family could be circling again.

Not when there was still a target on her back.

I didn't understand why her safety mattered more than anything else, but it did. It did in a way that scared the shit out of me. I thought maybe...that was what love was.

Or maybe it was just guilt dressed up in softer colors.

Either way, I was in too deep.

I SAT in Poppy's car, my fingers raking through my already messy hair. Slumping against the passenger seat, I squinted against the morning light stabbing through the windshield. My head throbbed, drums slamming against the inside of my skull, and the bitterness of last night's booze still coated the back of my tongue.

The engine idled, and the windows were cracked just enough to let in the piercing brink of winter air. Two days had passed before Kaylor finally responded to Poppy, and in those forty-eight hours, I'd been wasted for most of them. I'd stopped long enough to sober up once I got the text from Poppy, and when she pulled up to the house, I almost didn't smell like a brewery. Maybe. It could also be that I'd become immune to my own stank.

Poppy crinkled her nose as she steered the car down my driveway. "Jesus, Corvo. You look like shit. And you smell like you spent the night passed out on a bar floor."

I grunted, rubbing a hand over my face. "You're not far off."

"I was joking, but...wow." She shook her head and adjusted the volume on the radio, low enough not to aggravate my hangover but loud enough to kill the silence. "You seriously got wasted?"

"I needed to think," I muttered even though thinking was the last thing I managed to do with a bottle in my hand. "I didn't exactly sleep."

"Things are worse than I feared." She shot me a side glance, brows arching like she wanted to see if I'd flinch. "I kept my end of the deal. I know where she's staying. Now you owe me answers, Corvo. I'm betraying my best friend right now *for you.* So don't insult me by pretending this is no big deal."

I didn't respond right away. The truth was heavier than my hangover. She wasn't wrong. She deserved to know what she was walking into. I adjusted the sunglasses shielding my bloodshot eyes from the morning light. "Kaylor's dad..." I started hoarsely. "He was the head of the Vipers Nest."

Poppy's gaze widened, her head whipping toward me, taking her eyes off the road for a few seconds. "The crew? Like—crew, crew?"

I nodded.

"Holy shit," she whispered, then blinked at me, the many bangle bracelets on her arms chiming together as she turned the wheel. "Wait, so, why was she even living with you? Aren't the Vipers and Ravens like rivals?"

"My father blackmailed a judge to alter her parents' will and get guardianship. It was all part of his plan." I stared out the window. "She didn't know. None of us told her the truth. She found out Friday night. That's why she ran."

Poppy's nose scrunched. "Well, no wonder she hates you."

I deserved that. "There's more," I added, stretching my legs out as far as I could in the compact car. "There's a traitor in the Vipers. Someone gave my father inside information that led to her parents being killed. I don't know who it is, but it means she's not safe under their protection."

Poppy gave a laugh, more disbelief than humor. "And you think she's safer with you?"

Her words punched a hole in my chest. "I can keep her alive."

"Who will protect her from *you?* I should kick your ass out of my car." When I didn't say anything, Poppy glanced over again. Her expression softened, just a fraction. "You fell for her, didn't you? That's what's got you so twisted up inside."

I didn't answer. I didn't have to.

"Goddamn," she whispered, frowning. "Kreed Corvo, the untouchable king of Public, caught feelings."

"I never said I had feelings for her," I grumbled as I stared out the passenger window at the blur of suburban houses passing by.

"You don't have to. Have you ever been in love before?"

I leveled her a look.

"I'm going to take that as a no." She turned back to the road, a small smile playing at the corners of her mouth. "You were falling for her. Why is that so wrong?"

My chest tightened, and emotion clawed its way up my throat. "It's not supposed to be like this," I said, the words grinding out like broken glass. I stared ahead through the windshield. The leather of the seat creaked as I shifted, trying to escape the snare of her scrutiny. "You're right, though. She will be safer as far from Elmwood as she can get and far from me."

"Could you let her go?"

I sighed and rubbed my hand down my face, wishing I could scrape the guilt off with it. "If it was the only way, yes."

The car slowed as we approached a familiar intersection, and Poppy drummed her fingers against the steering wheel, a nervous habit I'd noticed she had when she was thinking too hard. "What are we going to do if she refuses to come back with us?"

"It's not an option."

Poppy rolled her eyes. "Wonderful. You could have told me before we left that there was a chance we'd be committing a felony. I'd never kidnapped anyone before."

My lips twitched. "Then you're in for the biggest rush of your life, Pops."

Poppy pulled up to a guardhouse and rolled down her window to give her name to the man screening the cars coming in. I shouldn't have been surprised to see Kaylor was tucked behind a gated community with security. This part of Elmwood was her comfort zone, where she would feel secure, but if I could get inside, it would only show just how vulnerable she was.

The guard let us through without pause once Poppy gave her name. She chewed on her lower lip, her nerves growing as we approached the house, and what a fucking house. I lived in a pretty elaborate home, but this...

The house was too perfect, pristine, screaming old money and power. This wasn't some temporary safe house. This was a home, and it sure as hell wasn't the one we had forced her to leave behind.

I swallowed hard, forcing down the raw edge that curled beneath my ribs. She was here. Breathing. That had to be enough. Even if I shattered whatever fragile thing still existed between us, it would be worth it, because this was the only way I knew how to keep her alive.

"We're really doing this?" Poppy muttered as she stared up at the house like it might bite.

I didn't look at her. Just kept my gaze fixed ahead. "All you need to do is go up to the door and ring the bell. I'll take care of the rest."

She didn't move. Didn't breathe either. "She's never going to forgive me." Her voice cracked just slightly. "I don't know if I can forgive myself."

I turned in the seat. "Poppy, get your shit together." The words weren't gentle. They weren't meant to be.

Her jaw dropped, eyes narrowing in a flash of wounded disbelief. "You're an ass," she snapped, but her voice wobbled.

Scanning the house, I took mental notes of the numerous cameras. They were well hidden, and there were probably a few more I didn't see. This place wouldn't have been easy to get to without Poppy being on the approved guest list.

Just who the fuck lives here? And how does she know them?

This definitely wasn't Rusty's. Someone else from the crew?

"That's been established," I replied.

"Don't be surprised when she slams the door in our faces," Poppy said, getting out of the car and closing the door hard.

My eyes tracked her angry steps as she walked up to the house, my lips twitching. It made sense that the two of them gravitated to each other and became friends. I waited a beat, giving Kaylor a moment to come to the door before I got out of the car. I didn't want her to catch a glimpse of me on the camera. The only way this worked was if I caught her unawares.

From ahead, I heard their voices. Poppy's was soft and careful, but Kaylor's voice hit me like a fist to the ribs, knocking the breath from my lungs. I hadn't realized how much I needed to hear it until now.

My sneakers scuffed over the concrete. The place was too quiet, too fucking elegant, and it made me itch. The Corvo estate was a fucking fortress, but this? This was different. It wasn't a prison.

It was a sanctuary.

A sanctuary that didn't include me.

As I rounded the corner to the front door, Poppy was stepping over the threshold, giving me a slightly obscure view of Kaylor. Damp strands of platinum hair waterfalled down her as if she'd just gotten out of the shower, and she was wearing sweatpants and an oversized sweatshirt, one that wasn't mine.

Whose damn hoodie is it?

I gritted my teeth, shoving the possessive thought away.

Not mine. Not anymore.

Before Kaylor could see me and slam the door in my face, I moved, coming up behind Poppy. Poppy must have sensed me, her body instantly tensing. She shifted uncomfortably as if suddenly regretting everything about this plan.

My palm flattened on the door as it started to close. Kaylor's gaze pulled away from her friend, speckles of fear widening those light-blue eyes before they landed on me. I didn't stop moving, knowing I had to fully commit and push my way inside. It was the only way I could get her to listen without influence or interruption.

Confusion flashed across her face.

And then?

Fucking ice.

Her entire body went rigid, her face locking down so fast it made my stomach drop.

And what a freaking face. I knew I had very little time, so my eyes drank up the unobstructed view of her, greedier than I wanted to admit. Where there had once been heat and something dangerously close to love, there was now only frost in her eyes. No trace of warmth.

Her full pink lips turned down, and I wanted to kiss them like a starving man, like I dreamed about every goddamn night since. Regret burned through me like acid—regret, need, something deeper I didn't want to name yet. It all surged up so fast I froze. Forgot what I was doing there. Forgot the plan, the lies, the betrayal. All I saw was her, and all she saw was the one person she never wanted to see again.

It had been days since she walked away from me, but it felt like months, like someone had toyed with the hands on the clock, stretching time just to fuck with me. Standing here and seeing her again... It hit me like a sucker punch to the chest.

Get a fucking grip, man.

I closed the door behind me, bolting the lock. "Hey, little raven."

6

KAYLOR

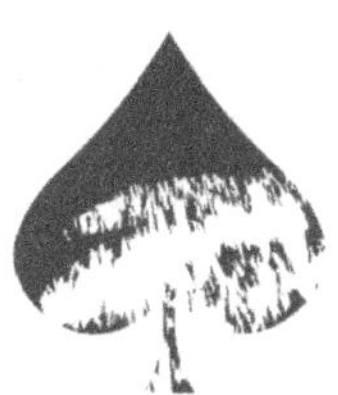

And to think I thought I might never hear that nickname again. *Little raven.* The way his voice curled around the two words did ungodly things to my insides. How annoying and surprising was the fact that he stood in front of me. "What is this? Why the fuck are you here?" I meant for it to come out cold, biting, but it didn't hit as hard as I wanted. Not when I looked at him and the ground beneath me was suddenly unsteady.

Kreed didn't say anything at first. He just stood there, staring at me like he was trying to memorize every inch of my face as if he wasn't sure I was real.

I understood the feeling. My eyes, despite my brain telling them not to devour him, did just that. From his head to his toes and back up, I took in the state of his appearance, the black hoodie and jeans, the two tiny scars under his eye, the tattoos on his hand and fingers, and the stud twinkling on the side of his nose, as well as some added features like the dark circles under those silver eyes. Only Kreed could make being tired and haggard hot.

"Did they touch you?" he asked, voice low.

I blinked, wondering what the hell he was talking about. My

brain could only come up with one conclusion, but it made no sense to me. "Who? Do you mean Rusty?"

His jaw clenched so tight I could practically hear the pressure crack in his teeth.

Ew. What the hell? "Why would you think Rusty would touch me?" I asked, wondering what was going on in his head.

"Did he?" he demanded again, danger shimmering behind his eyes.

Jesus. "No. What the fuck is this, Kreed?"

The way his eyes fluttered closed at the sound of his name made my heart flutter in spite of myself. Like hearing me say it hurt and healed him at the same time. "Say it again," he said, opening his eyes, locking on to mine.

I still hadn't figured out why the sound of his name affected him, but it only seemed to be when I said it, giving me an edge over him. However, Kreed showing up put a wrench in my revenge plot, which consisted of just the thought of revenge with no details. I wasn't prepared to see him. Somehow, his face destroyed all my damn walls. It wasn't fair. A face alone shouldn't have that kind of power. "Not going to happen." I folded my arms across my chest, trying to contain the whirlwind in my gut. *Get a hold of yourself, Kay.* "And not that it's any of your fucking business, but I'm not staying with Rusty. I left."

His whole body seemed to exhale as if I'd released something inside him just by saying those words. "Good." Relief descended into his features.

Had he believed I'd been hurt? Emotions twisted in me that I didn't want to examine. It didn't explain why he would give a shit. I wasn't his problem anymore. Perhaps that was the relief I was seeing.

"What's going on?" I asked warily, then immediately shook my head. "Wait. No. I don't want to know." I stepped around him toward the front door, but of course, he blocked me, his frame planted between me and escape.

Kreed didn't move. Didn't flinch. Just watched me with that

maddening calm, one hand braced against the door frame. "Not gonna happen, little raven. You didn't think you'd get rid of me that easily, did you?"

My heart skipped, but I refused to acknowledge that he made me feel anything but rage. "I thought I made it clear I never wanted to see you again."

He took a step closer, slow and deliberate, like every inch of ground he reclaimed was his by right. "Too bad. You wouldn't listen to me that night, so you'll hear me out now."

My gaze cut to Poppy. She stood frozen by the wall, guilt written all over her face. "What the hell is this?" I breathed, betrayal wrapping around my heart.

Poppy's expression fell. "I'm sorry. After Friday night—"

"You set me up," I lashed out at Poppy, and although I was hurt that she'd brought the damn enemy to where I was hiding, it was Kreed I was truly pissed off with. I understood how she'd be worried, and I'd been ignoring my phone in fear that every message or call might be a Corvo. Especially one in particular. Look where that got me. He was here in the flesh, which was so much worse than a call or a text.

Poppy flinched. "I was worried, and Kreed was the only way I could make sure you were alive."

The jerk in question moved toward me, and I took a step back without meaning to. Not that I had far to go in the foyer. "It's not her fault. I didn't give her a choice. And besides"—he motioned around us, at the locked door—"it proves my point."

Was he defending her? There had to be something off with the universe, a retrograde moon. "Which is what?"

He stared at me like the answer was obvious. "You're not out of danger. Not yet. If I can find you...so can anyone else."

I laughed once, but there was no humor in it. "Who could hurt me more than you?"

His signature scowl deepened. "There's more you don't know," he said, the admission raw as it scraped out of him.

I shook my head. "There's nothing left you can say."

I wanted to be mad at Poppy, especially for bringing the one person I wasn't ready to see, but if the roles had been reversed, I couldn't say that I wouldn't have done the same in her position. I was partially to blame. Of course, she would worry. It was what a good friend did, and Poppy had been nothing but a good friend to me, my only friend. I was the one who left her hanging. I should have texted to let her know I was okay, but I'd lumped her into a part of my life I hadn't been ready to deal with. That wasn't fair to her.

Ignoring Kreed for a moment, which was difficult to do because I always seemed so damn hyperaware of him, I hugged Poppy, whispering an apology. "I'm sorry I made you worry."

Kreed, on the other hand, wasn't going to get any grace from me, let alone a freaking hug. Not today. "Poppy can stay, but you can't," I told him.

He remained rooted in place, motionless like the stubborn ass he was or like someone who was used to getting what he wanted. "I'm not leaving. Hate me all you want, but it doesn't change that I'm not going anywhere without you."

My hands balled into fists. Oh, I wanted to hit him, to subject him to half the amount of pain I carried at his betrayal. "I do hate you."

The sting in his expression almost made me flinch. Almost. "Good. I warned you. I told you I wasn't a nice guy. I'm not someone you should be involved with."

Poppy shifted awkwardly. "I'll, uh...give you guys a minute," she muttered before slipping behind Kreed and out the front door. Of course, he didn't try to stop her when she left, and just like that, it was just him and me.

Again.

"Why is it so important that I live in your house?" I didn't know why I bothered to ask. Curiosity mostly.

"Because we're the only ones who can protect you. My father has no intention of letting you slip through his fingers when he's so close to getting what he wants. Rusty can't stop him, not when there's a traitor amongst his midst."

My brows furrowed. "A traitor? What are you talking about?"

"Look," he said, dragging a hand through his black hair. "Someone in the Vipers betrayed your father. They fed us information."

"It's done. Why does it matter who the traitor is? It won't change the past. My parents will still be dead. And you'll still be the asshole who kidnapped me."

His face remained expressionless, but his eyes were troubled. "You're not wrong. What we did... It was fucked up."

He had no idea how much he hurt me. "That's an understatement."

And for a second, just a second, emotion flitted behind his eyes. Regret. Pain. Maybe even something akin to genuine worry, but I shoved the thought deep where it couldn't reach me. "It will be easier if you come with me instead of my father finding you. I'm trying to help you, but you know this ends with you back at the house."

My chin lifted. "Until I'm eighteen. That's only four months."

The features in his face tightened. "So much shit can happen in four months. Let me help you."

"You hurt me, Kreed," I said, the anger finally bubbling to the surface. "All of you did. You used me. Lied to me. You let me think I was safe with you."

He backed me into a corner. "I didn't lie about everything."

Don't touch me. God, please don't touch me. I wasn't strong enough to resist him. Not yet, but I'd get there. "Doesn't fucking matter."

"Yes, it does," he said, firmer now. "Because I need you to understand that I—" He cut himself off. Whatever he was going to say stayed locked behind his teeth.

Good. Because I wasn't sure I could survive hearing it.

My throat burned, and I hated how tired I must have looked. I hated that part of me still missed him even as every inch of me screamed to push him away, but I forced my walls back up. "You never stop, do you?"

He leaned in, and I had nowhere to go, our bodies nearly touching, the flutters in my belly warning me to retreat.

I caught a whiff of alcohol. "Are you drunk?"

"Not in the last hour."

At a closer look, Kreed looked like he was suffering. Bloodshot eyes. Dark circles. His fingers slid to my hips, and my breath caught with it. I loathed how easily my body responded to him, how the heat of his palms lit something deep under my skin, something I'd tried so hard to smother. A buzz in the air vibrated between us, this magnetic pull that made every nerve stand at attention, vibrating with want and warning. I was supposed to hate him. I wanted to hate him, but with his body so close, his strength practically wrapping around me like a promise, all I could think about was how badly I wanted to lean into him, just for a second. To let my guard drop. To pretend I wasn't so fucking tired of carrying everything alone. Kreed was chaos, but right then, he felt like the only thing holding me together. And worse, he was offering to carry the weight I was still dragging.

I didn't want to make a rash decision, especially with him clouding my common sense. His presence messed me up. I needed a moment to think. Without him.

"What could they want with me?" I asked, wishing this nightmare would end.

"It's what my father wants, and you're the key."

"I don't need you. I have my cousin and his friends. I trust them a hell of a lot more than I do you. Speaking of Brock, you've probably got about five minutes before the police show up, courtesy of my cousin." I was banking on Fynn having seen Kreed on the security cameras.

He didn't even blink. "We'll be gone by then."

My head screamed at me to push him away. My heart longed to fist my fingers into his shirt and tug him against me. What was a conflicted girl to do? Be reasonable? Or reckless? I shook my head. "Not we. *You.* I'm not going with you. Nothing's changed."

"I'm not playing."

"Don't be a jackass."

"Yes, I'm a jackass," he said, his fingers tangling into my hair. "But I'm a jackass with your best interest at heart. Can you say the same about Rusty? Or any of the Vipers?"

I couldn't. Not when I didn't really know any of them except for Rusty. He'd been my father's best friend and like an uncle to me.

Sirens blared in the distance. Our time was up. If he didn't go soon, he would be talking to the cops. For reasons I couldn't process, I didn't want Kreed detained by the police. Despite everything, a part of me wanted to protect him. Why the fuck was I having such a hard time staying mad at him? "I want you to leave."

He didn't move. "Little raven..."

"Get out." I shoved at his chest, but he barely budged. I loathed how much that part of me hoped he'd stay, that he'd fight for me.

His silver eyes maintained uncontrollable contact with mine as his fingers drifted through my damp hair. "You can keep running all you want, but I'll always find you. That's a promise."

A promise? He was joking, right? But then I whispered, "Please, Kreed."

Those two words worked.

He stepped back slowly, as if the movement cost him something. Like each inch between us tore him open as he turned and left. No parting words. No final look. Just silence. It cracked something deep in my chest. Something I hadn't realized was his to break.

Revenge wouldn't be as easy as I figured.

My heart wouldn't stop racing. I stood in the middle of the hallway, staring at the door like he might walk back through it as if maybe he'd left something behind besides the storm still spinning in my chest. It blew my mind how he had the power to rattle me.

With a breath, I waited for the cops to show. When they arrived, I assured them everything was fine and it was a false alarm. With a forced smile and apology, they were on their way. I turned and wandered back into the living room, reaching for the remote to flick on the TV, hoping the noise would drown out the whirlwind in my head. Anything to keep me from thinking too hard about the way my body had responded to him or the way my heart had tried to crawl out of my chest when he looked at me.

As I started searching through Netflix, my phone buzzed. Viper's Auto Pro popped up on the screen. My dad's shop. Rusty.

For fuck's sake. How much more could I deal with in a single day?

I'd been avoiding him, and despite wanting to keep putting off this conversation, I knew I was on borrowed time. The last thing I wanted was *Rusty* showing up on my doorstep.

I stared at the number glowing on the screen, thumb hovering over the green icon. I owed Rusty more than a return call. I owed him an explanation. Without him, I'd still be locked inside that house, a puppet in Donovan's twisted theater.

My chest rose and fell with a steadying breath before I hit accept and put the phone on speaker. "Hello."

"Kiddo, thank God." He exhaled loudly. "I've been trying to get a hold of you. Are you okay?"

I glanced at the TV. "I'm fine. Safe," I added quickly, settling deeper into the couch. "Sorry I left. I couldn't stay there."

"After everything you've been through, it makes sense you would want to be somewhere that makes you comfortable. I just want to make sure you stay that way." The strain was evident in his tone.

I rubbed a hand down my arm, already knowing where this was going. "You're worried the Corvos might try something." If he only knew who I just kicked out of the house. Perhaps Rusty had a reason to worry. Perhaps *I* did.

"Aren't you?"

I chewed on my lip, thinking about my surprise visit from Kreed. Did I think he would try something wild? "I don't know," I replied honestly. I didn't know who to believe, who to trust. If what Kreed said about the Vipers having a traitor was true, then I had a reason to be suspicious of everyone.

"At least let me send a few guys," Rusty said, already sounding like he was reaching for keys. "Where are you staying?"

The TV caught my eye as a picture of a girl flashed on the screen. "Rusty, I've got to go."

"I don't think this is a good idea," he rushed out. "They'll look for you there."

"Uh-huh," I replied, my eyes glued to the news. "I'll think about it." I hit the end call button as the screen lit up with a breaking news banner.

Sixteen-year-old girl reported missing late last night...

My stomach dropped.

It was the fourth one this year. Four girls. Same age range, near mine, which was why it hit so close to home to me, *and* they'd all been taken from my town. Same nothing-to-go-on circumstances. Just vanished without a trace.

Elmwood might have looked polished on the outside, but it was rotting beneath the surface. People liked to pretend it was just rumors, and the missing girls had run away, but no one really believed that anymore. How could they? This was a fucking pattern, and I didn't need to be a criminologist to figure out we had a big problem.

My fingers tightened around the remote. The image on the screen showed the girl's school photo, a bright smile and innocent eyes. A name and age flashed beneath it, but all I could focus on was the pit forming in my gut. I was alone in Brock's giant house. Alone in a neighborhood that was probably safe by most standards, but still...I was *alone*, an easy target, and the thought didn't sit right with me anymore.

A shiver ghosted over my spine, and I reached for the blanket on the back of the couch, wrapping it around myself even though I wasn't cold. Maybe I was being paranoid. Or maybe I was finally realizing just how dangerous Elmwood was. Kreed had said I wasn't safe.

I'd assumed he meant because of his family or my father's crew. But this? These girls?

This was a different brand of danger.

As much as I hated the thought of going back to the Corvos, especially after everything, I couldn't deny the part of me that thought their house might be the only place in Elmwood no one dared to cross.

Unless, of course, you were me.

Was I even entertaining the thought of going back to their house, under Donovan's care? The person who murdered my parents?

I couldn't.

Let him force me.

The pit of uneasiness grew. The streets weren't safe. Things seemed to have gotten worse, or maybe I was more aware of the shady shit happening outside my perfect bubble now that it had been popped.

The clock on the wall ticked too loudly.

I was curled up on the couch with the blanket wrapped around me like a cocoon, but no matter how tightly I tucked it around me, I couldn't get warm. Brock's house was massive, an overbuilt mansion with too many rooms. I used to think it was cool... Now it just felt like I was being watched by shadows I couldn't see.

A creak came from upstairs, and my heart knocked into my ribs. I held my breath, eyes locked on the ceiling, waiting for another sound—footsteps, a door, anything—but silence followed, thick and heavy.

I tried to convince myself it was nothing. Old pipes, maybe. Or just the wind. Until a thud came from down the hall.

"Okay, nope," I muttered, grabbing my phone and unlocking it.

My fingers were drawn to Kreed's name, and I stopped myself from hitting his number a second before I made a huge mistake. Annoyed that he was always the first person I thought of, I had the urge to throw my phone across the room.

I didn't want to think about him right now. I didn't want to be scared in this house. Or alone. I tapped into my group chat with Kenny and Carson.

Me: **SOS. Come over? Please.**

It took less than a minute for both of them to reply.

Kenny: **On my way. Wine or ice cream?**

Carson: **I'll grab snacks.**

An hour later, the three of us were sprawled across the couch in a fortress of blankets and throw pillows. The TV was on, playing some random rom-com none of us were really watching. I was sandwiched between them, safe in the warm bubble of friendship, even if the air was laced with all the things we didn't say.

"Okay," Kenny said, eyeing me over her bowl of popcorn. Strands of honey hair spilled out of her messy bun. "I know *he* is a touchy subject, but we've got to just get the elephant out of the room. Rip it off like a Band-Aid. Let's talk about Kreed."

I groaned and buried my face in the blanket. "No."

"Yes." She nudged me with her foot. "You've been so MIA since transferring to Public, and now you're texting us in the middle of the night like a horror movie finale girl. It's so obvious you're not okay. Spill."

I peeked at Carson, who looked suddenly interested in the popcorn bowl in his lap. His jaw was tight, his shoulders even tighter. I missed it at first, but Kenny didn't as my gaze slid to her.

She saw it. She always noticed Carson's mood because Kenny was in love with him. And Carson... Well, I didn't know who he was interested in. He never had a serious relationship or dated. Sometimes I wondered if Kenny and I were the problem. We were always around, which could be intimidating to potential partners.

"I don't even know where to start," I said, scooping a handful of popcorn.

"Try," Kenny said softly, her bravado slipping. "It's me. Us. We've always talked about everything. There's nothing you can't tell us. This is and has always been a judgment-free zone. We love you."

So I did.

I told them everything. The lies. The setup. The betrayal. The way Kreed looked at me like I was his beginning and end, and how that look infuriated me. What I didn't say was how it felt when his hands found my hips again, firm and certain. Or how part of me wanted to fall into him, to forget everything just for the heat of his skin against mine. Even when I hated him most, my body betrayed me.

Kenny sat cross-legged at the edge of the couch, her fingers tapping a restless rhythm against her thigh. Shock and disbelief glinted in her big brown eyes.

Carson leaned forward, forearms braced on his knees, his gaze unfocused—haunted. He hadn't spoken since I'd started. He didn't need to. His silence said enough.

When I finally finished, the room held its breath. Just the low hum of the TV playing some sitcom neither of us cared about filled the dead space.

Kenny blinked. "What the fuck, Kay. That is some seriously messed-up shit. It doesn't seem real."

"Tell me about it," I mumbled.

"He hurt you," Carson muttered.

I looked over.

His gaze was fixed on the screen. "You don't need someone like him."

"I know," I whispered.

Kenny's fingers brushed mine. "But you still want him."

My heart ached. "I don't want to. I'm working on it. The anger helps. As long as I stay mad at him, it's easier."

Carson finally looked at me. "I should never have let you leave the hospital with him."

The guilt on his face broke my heart. "This isn't your fault. We can't begin to understand the mind of a madman."

"But you're willing to go back to that school."

I understood Carson's hesitancy. "I have little choice if I want to graduate." I sank deeper into the cushions, exhaustion lacing my words. "It's only a few months. Despite knowing the truth, on paper, Donovan is my godfather. I don't have the energy or resources to fight him on this."

Kenny shifted beside me. "You know Brock and his family would fight it for you."

"They would, but by the time the courts got involved and overturned the guardianship, I'll be an adult. I'm not giving up, not on my inheritance. I'm just conceding to the guardianship until my birthday."

Carson rose from the couch and crossed to the window, his arms folding across his chest. "I don't like this."

"When do you ever like any of our plans?" Kenny pointed out.

Carson glanced over his shoulder, the flickering of the TV hitting the side of his handsome face. "They generally suck, as does this one. Several things could go wrong."

I gave a ghost of a smile. "That's why I have you guys."

"We can't be there with you at school," Carson said, the helplessness in his voice a slow punch to the gut.

"No," I admitted. "But Poppy will be."

Kenny raised a brow. "You trust her?"

Before today, I would have answered without hesitation, but her blindsiding me with Kreed gave me pause. Her intentions were good, but I just wish she hadn't brought him here. Now I had to worry about Kreed showing up whenever he damn well felt like it, which I feared would be more than I liked. He wasn't someone who was easily deterred when he wanted something, and somewhere along the way, Kreed decided that what he wanted was me.

The idea shouldn't make my stomach feel funny. I shouldn't feel anything but disdain.

If only I could control the way I reacted when it came to Kreed Corvo.

"ARE you sure you're okay with this?" I asked, crossing and uncrossing my legs for like the tenth time.

Carson drummed his fingers against the steering wheel, his eyes flicking between the road and me like he wanted to say something but kept swallowing it back. "It's more than okay. I'll swing by after school and pick you up. It will hopefully give you enough time to get all your missing assignments together."

I took my cousin's advice and decided to go back to school. I couldn't hide out in his house forever. Carson and Kenny weren't keen on the idea when I brought it up a few nights ago, justifiably worried about me, but seeing Kreed made me realize I wanted to get on with my life. He tortured me, and I planned to return the favor every day at school until I graduated, and then I'd never have to see his damn face again.

Except in my dreams.

Which happened far too often. Last night had been the worst, filled with restless sleep, twisted blankets, and dreams that started with Kreed's hands on me and ended with the sound of a girl screaming in the distance.

I cursed him for showing up and reminding my body of shit I wanted to forget. Dreaming of him was preferable to living the nightmare of my parents' death, but only marginally, as it reminded me of what we could have had.

"I don't mind waiting. Seriously," I assured Carson, not wanting him or Kenny to worry more than they did. "I wouldn't be able to do this without you."

"Are you nervous about seeing him?" Carson asked, his left eye twitching as if the thought of Kreed made him agitated.

"Yeah, but not as much as I thought. Seeing you guys really helped." I felt stronger. They reminded me of the girl I'd been before my life got blown up.

"I don't like this, you going back to Public with *them*," Carson said finally as we pulled into the lot behind Elmwood Public. The vein in his neck pulsed.

My stomach turned at the unspoken names—Kreed, Mason, and Maddox. "I'll be fine," I said unconvincedly, but I was committed, so I continued the facade. "I swear. Plus, Poppy will be there to keep me from doing anything stupid."

He shifted into park and turned toward me, his jaw working like he was trying to bite back another dozen words. "I'll be here after school. Right here. Don't wait around. Just come straight to the car, okay?"

I nodded, clutching the strap of my bag tighter. "Thanks for the ride." I moved to get out of the car, but Carson's fingers wrapped around my wrist.

"Kay, I..."

With my hand on the door, I glanced back at Carson, waiting for him to finish.

"Just be careful."

I leaned over the center console and hugged my best friend before stepping out of the car. He might have held on a few seconds longer than necessary, but he was worried. So was I.

Here fucking goes nothing.

7

KAYLOR

The cold hit me first, followed by the low thrum of student chatter as I stepped onto campus. It was like walking into a spotlight, too many eyes, too many whispers, too much crap pressing down on my shoulders.

I was back.

It was so strange, like a ghost haunting my own life. Everything was the same, the chipped bricks, the faded mascot banner flapping weakly in the wind, and the sound of sneakers shuffling over gravel, but I wasn't the same. Not even close. The world had shifted under my feet, cracked wide-open by secrets and betrayals, and yet somehow it just kept turning. Students laughed, gossiped, and scrolled through their phones as if nothing had happened. As if girls weren't going missing. As if my parents hadn't been murdered. As if I hadn't been played. I stood there, feeling the strangeness of it all sink deep into my bones, this sense of being awake in a dream everyone else refused to see. Oblivious. Untouched. Free in a way I couldn't even remember how to feel.

I refused to let them break me.

I wouldn't hide.

I won't run.

Nothing like a little internal affirmation to get me through the day. Now I just had to walk through the front doors of Public with my chin high. Fuck them all.

I could do this.

I had Poppy.

I wasn't alone.

If there was a traitor, and I was still in danger as Kreed believed, this might be a really bad decision, but I didn't know if his claim had any weight. It could be another lie, another tactic to manipulate me. It wasn't like I was some gang heiress. It wasn't like Rusty expected me to take up my father's position in the crew.

That would be absurd and something I had no interest in. I'd leave the criminal activity to Rusty and the Corvos. Turned out, I didn't have the stomach for it despite it being in my blood.

And then I saw them.

Mason and Maddox stood by the lockers near the main entrance, their dark hair and clothing a sharp contrast against the pale gray walls. Mason noticed me first, his expression unreadable. Maddox's gaze followed a beat later.

But no Kreed.

My heart twisted in my chest before I could stop it. I hated that I noticed his absence more than anything else. Before I fully spiraled or crashed into someone from sheer distraction, an arm looped through mine, grounding me. "God, you really were about to freeze like a baby deer in headlights, weren't you?" Poppy said, her voice a low whisper laced with amusement. "Come on, babe. You're not walking these halls alone."

Relief washed over me as I leaned into her, grateful and already a little steadier with her by my side. The hallway pressed in around us, but Poppy's presence carved out a little bubble I could breathe in.

I didn't look back at Mason and Maddox again.

And I didn't let myself think about Kreed.

Not yet.

"He's not here, by the way," Poppy informed me as she ushered me into the crowd like she didn't give a single fuck, her black platform boots stomping against the tile like thunder. A pleated plaid skirt swished around her thighs, paired with ripped fishnets and an oversized hoodie featuring a moody anime girl with bleeding-heart eyes. "If you're looking for him."

"I'm not. And I didn't ask."

Two space buns perched high on her red hair like little gothic crowns. Silver piercings glittered along her ears, and a black choker hugged her throat. She could have stepped out of a Tim Burton dream and into a Tokyo street scene. She somehow made it work. "You didn't have to. Your eyes haven't been able to stop looking for him."

"Sorry. I just don't want him to blindside me again," I reasoned.

"Hmm. Is that all? I'd be more concerned with that duo if I were you."

I followed her gaze to see Mason and Maddox still watching me. "Shit," I mumbled.

"He hasn't been at school for the last few days in case you were wondering. Not since we went to see you."

"Why not?" The question tumbled out of my mouth before I could stop myself.

She shrugged. "Probably too drunk in some corner, but he's going to be pissed he missed you."

I hugged my bag against my chest. "Good."

I HAD SO much work to catch up on that when the final bell finished ringing through the halls I could hardly believe the day was gone. I grabbed my stack of missing assignments and shoved them into my bag; the weight was heavier than it should be. Perhaps because everything was now. I just wanted to get to my locker, collect the rest of my stuff, and disappear before I had to navigate any more awkward stares or whispers.

I was halfway there when it happened.

A hand clamped around my upper arm and yanked hard. My feet slipped, nearly sending me sprawling as my bag fell off my shoulder. Another body sidled up beside me, too close, reeking of sweat and arrogance.

"I was wondering when I'd get you alone again," someone whispered, breath hot against the shell of my ear.

The dread in my stomach solidified into ice. I recognized them; all three played for the football team. Bodie. Keenan. And Dawson. Big. Cocky. Too confident in how much they could get away with. I remembered seeing Bodie smirk at me earlier in the hallway, but I hadn't thought much of it. Now, that same smirk twisted darker. Bodie was in my chem class. I didn't know Dawson and Keenan well, but they'd all been in the cellar on Raven Night.

"What the—let go!" I snapped, jerking my arm, but another one flanked me. My spine stiffened, every nerve screaming danger, but my feet still moved. I was being funneled. Herded. It was like being pulled into a nightmare.

They shoved me through a door, and I instantly knew something was wrong. The stench of urinals and disinfectant slapped into me. The boys' bathroom.

I twisted to bolt, but one of them blocked the exit, and another pushed me back against the wall so hard my head hit the tile. "Hey—get off me!" I tried to twist again, but Dawson shoved me so hard the breath flew out of me. My bag hit the ground with a loud smack.

"No more Raven boys to protect you, huh?" Keenan sneered, his breath a mix of mint gum and ego. "Did Kreed get tired of playing house?"

Bodie grabbed my wrists. "Word around school is he got bored and tossed you aside, just like he does with all the girls."

Heat surged up my throat, thick and choking.

Dawson leaned a shoulder on the wall beside me. "Don't worry, baby. We'll make you feel wanted."

"Kreed doesn't fight for anyone," Bodie said, grabbing my chin and tilting my face up. His grip was bruising, fingers digging into bone. "But you...I don't see the appeal."

I didn't move. Couldn't. My muscles were locked, a thousand alarms blaring behind my eyes. What was the angle here? What could they possibly want with me besides the disgusting obvious? Did this have something to do with Kreed?

"He's never protected a girl before," Keenan added, his eyes raking over me like I was a meal, not a person. "Only ever bled for his crew. But you? You're not a Raven."

"Do you want to bet your life on that?" My voice was hoarse, but I latched on to it like a lifeline. "What do you think he'll do if he finds out you've got me trapped in here?"

It was a bluff. It had to be. But maybe, just maybe, that sliver of doubt would buy me time.

"He's not here today. That's the best part. How fucking convenient for us," Bodie muttered, dragging a finger down my cheek, not soft enough to be a caress. "We don't mind Corvo's leftovers."

Shit.

Terror lanced through me. I tried to scream, but a palm clamped over my mouth, rough and unrelenting, silencing the sound before it left my throat. My body writhed in instinctive panic, but it was useless. I was trapped, and nobody was coming. Evan wasn't here to burst in like a guardian angel. Brock was miles away. And Kreed... was probably at the fucking club drunk. Useless to me in this situation.

Bodie grabbed my chin roughly. "Because of you, my nose will be permanently crooked."

I tried to jerk my head out of his grasp, but his fingers only pressed deeper.

Dawson licked the side of my cheek, and revulsion rolled through me. "I spent a week in bed. It hurt so much to just breathe."

They were pissed they got their asses beat and thought it would be a good idea to take it out on me? I'd thought my association with the Ravens granted me a certain amount of protection. My first day back at Public, I was learning the hard way that might not be the case, particularly since it seemed everyone at school knew the Corvo boys and I had a falling out.

I fought. I did. I kicked, scratched, and shoved, but it wasn't enough.

I was outnumbered. Outmuscled. Out of options.

Basically fucked.

My skin crawled with disgust, and my vision blurred as a coldness seeped into my veins. Every cell in my body screamed for oxygen, for space, for help. I tried again, kicking, biting, clawing, but they were too strong.

Tears pricked my eyes, and just when I didn't think I had any more fight left in me, the door burst open with a crash. Bodie gripping me was suddenly gone, yanked back so fast he let out a startled yelp before his head cracked against the stall door. I stumbled forward, only to see Keenan get slammed into the sink with a force that cracked porcelain.

Mason.

He stood like a shadow peeled from the corners of a nightmare, jaw locked, his light-green eyes darker than I'd ever seen them with rage. Maddox was beside him, even quieter, even deadlier.

"What the fuck—" Dawson began, but Maddox cut him off with a punch, crumpling him to the ground like a rag doll.

Mason was a blur of motion, his fists flying, slamming into Keenan's stomach and then his jaw. Blood spattered the mirror. The boy dropped like dead weight, gasping and cursing as he crumpled onto the floor.

But Maddox was the storm.

He didn't say a word. His expression was purely dangerous as he tackled Bodie with enough force to send them both into the far wall. His football teammate fought back, but he was no match. Maddox drove his fist into his face again and again, knuckles slick with blood, eyes glazed feral.

I couldn't look away.

"Mad—Mad, stop!" Mason yelled, grabbing his brother's shoulder, trying to haul him off. "He's down, man, it's over!"

But Maddox didn't stop.

If these assholes thought Kreed gave them a beating before, they were about to die.

It took both of Mason's arms to wrench his twin back, and even then, Maddox was snarling, trying to shake him off, eyes locked on the broken mess of the guy on the floor.

Mason, still hanging on to Maddox, glowered at his teammates. "Now you'll think twice about touching what's ours. The next person who thinks about putting their hands on her will leave in a fucking body bag. Spread that shit around."

I didn't even realize I was shaking until Mason turned to me, tempting fate by releasing Maddox to place his hands on my shoulders. "Are you okay?" he asked, his voice brimming with concern.

Maddox clenched his fists like he wasn't quite finished.

Blinking, I forced my eyes to focus on Mason's face, my breath heaving and heart racing. The bathroom looked like a war zone now, groans escaping from the guys who'd dared to corner me.

Mason's gaze scanned over me for damage. "Kitten, hey, look at me. Are you okay?" he asked again.

I nodded, but the truth was, I didn't know. I was shaking too hard to feel anything, and my knees nearly gave out, but Mason was there to keep me from falling, his arms firm as he pulled me against him.

Maddox finally stilled, his chest heaving, eyes still wild. Mason was breathing hard too, one hand resting on his brother's chest to keep him back. Maddox stepped closer, eyes still sharp, voice calm and low. "No one fucks with you. Not while we're breathing."

Somehow, even though I knew this whole thing was so messed up and terrifying and shouldn't have happened at all...I believed him, believed them both, and despite being ridiculously mad at them, I never wanted Mason to let me go.

He must have sensed it, the way my body locked up, the tremble that stole into my limbs. Maybe he even said my name, but the ringing in my ears drowned everything out, a white noise hollowing me out from the inside.

Then arms were beneath me.

Mason dipped low, one strong sweep lifting me clean off the ground as if I weighed nothing at all. He carried me from the bathroom without a backward glance, leaving Maddox behind with the bloodied assholes and the shattered remains of my composure.

Somewhere passing through the halls, I remembered that Carson was to pick me up. I glanced at the wall clock as we passed by, noticing he would be about ten minutes away from the academy, which gave me ten minutes to get Mason to put me down. I didn't need Carson to see Mason carrying me outside on my first day back at Public.

"You can put me down now," I said despite my arms remaining curled around his neck. He smelled so good. Not as good as Kreed, no one did, but still, Mason's scent brought a wave of familiarity I wasn't sure was a good thing.

"Not yet," he murmured, smirking just enough to be insufferable. "I'm enjoying this too much. And let's be honest, if Kreed were here, I wouldn't get the chance."

My lungs started to cooperate again. "Where is he?"

Mason gave me a cocky-as-fuck grin, pieces of his dark hair falling over his eyes. "So, you noticed."

I didn't dignify that with a response.

Footsteps thudded behind us. Maddox emerged at Mason's side, his eyes sweeping over me. His jaw ticked. "We need to bounce. Now."

Mason adjusted his hold, carrying me easily through the halls. "Why do you care where Kreed is?" he asked me.

"I don't," I replied coolly.

His lips smirked. "Liar. You were hoping he'd storm in like your dark knight. He's got that antihero complex, doesn't he?"

I loosened my death grip from around his neck. "What do you want?"

Mason's chest vibrated under me as he chuckled softly. "We missed you."

"Bullshit."

"Don't be like that," Maddox said with a cocky smirk. "You know damn well you missed us. I've been keeping your bed warm."

"There's only one bed I'd ever consider climbing in again in that house, and you're definitely not sleeping in it." Nothing in that statement was remotely true, but Maddox didn't need to know that. I wanted to rile him, to hurt him, to piss him off. It only seemed fair after all the shit he put me through.

"You think Kreed would touch you after the way you rejected him twice?" Maddox countered, challenge written in every inch of his expression.

I tilted my head, a slow, dangerous smile curling on my lips. "You wanna put money on it?"

Maddox veered toward an empty classroom and pushed the door open. Mason followed without hesitation. I was too caught up in the moment to question it. His eyes flared with interest. "A bet? I like the way your twisted little mind works, menace."

What the hell am I doing?

Why am I baiting him like this?

Have I officially lost my last working brain cell?

Maddox side-eyed Mason. "You sure you don't want me to take her, bro? You look like you're struggling."

Mason's arms tightened around me like a reflex. "Get the fuck out of here. Touch her and I'll break your fingers one by one."

I squirmed. "Okay, caveman. Seriously. Put me down. I'm fine." The playful bickering had grounded me, brought me back to myself, and I could breathe again.

"And deny Kreed the pleasure of seeing your pretty face on his phone?" Mason said, far too casually.

My feet hit the floor, and I spun on him. "What the hell does that mean?"

He just smirked, pulling out his phone and sliding an arm around me. "Smile, my little kitten."

Click.

He snapped a photo of me on his phone.

I lunged for the device, but he danced back, grinning like a devil as my hand swiped air. "Delete it."

His finger tapped on the screen, no doubt shooting a text off to his older brother. Mischief danced in his eyes. "I don't think so. That was gold. Think I can get one of you shirtless? For my personal stash."

I deadpanned, "Sure. Let me strip. Actually, why stop at the top? Full nude sound good?"

Mason winked. "Tempting. But risking Kreed's wrath? I'm pretty, not suicidal."

"Delete. The. Photo," I growled, my arms winging on either side of my hips.

"Sorry, menace," Maddox cut in with a smirk, walking backward toward the door and tossing my bag across the room so it stopped near my feet. "No can do."

"Wait—what are you doing?" I asked, still breathless, still trying to process the fact that I was nearly assaulted and then rescued in the span of two minutes.

Maddox turned to me with that same ruthless calm he'd worn during the fight. "Just to make sure we don't have any repeat instances. Stay put, menace."

Disbelief had my mouth dropping open. "What the fuck are you doing?"

Mason gave a half-hearted shrug. "Keeping you out of trouble... Just until Kreed gets here."

They were already halfway out the door.

My eyes volleyed between them. "You're kidding." And as soon as I realized they weren't screwing with me, I darted toward them, but I wasn't quick enough. The heavy door swung shut with a loud clang, and then it clicked. The fuckers locked me in. *No way.*

I blinked at the door, completely stunned, thinking this had to be another one of their games. "Are you serious right now?" I hissed at the solid door.

Silence.

The disbelief melted into irritation as I yanked at the handle. It didn't budge.

They wouldn't. Nuh-uh. No way they would lock me inside a classroom and actually leave.

I pounded on the door hard. "Let me out! I'm not some fragile little damsel. What the hell is wrong with you?!"

No answer. Just the faint echo of footsteps fading down the hall.

Fuck no, I'm not staying put.

I groaned, turning in a slow circle as if a secret door might appear behind the whiteboard. Of all the dramatic, overbearing, Corvo-boy nonsense, this was peak. I'd almost been assaulted, sure, but I didn't need to be locked in a room like some porcelain doll waiting for a knight in bloodstained armor.

God, it's just like them to lock me up.

And they wanted me to believe they'd changed. *Jackasses.*

First order of business, I needed to find a way out of here. I had no intention of sticking around waiting for Kreed.

Reaching for my phone, I debated calling Poppy or Carson. Carson was on his way to pick me up, probably only a few minutes out. Poppy might still be on the grounds and would absolutely lose her mind hearing about this, but before I hit send, something else caught my attention.

The windows.

We were on the first floor, and the south side of the wall was lined with small square windows. And thank God, they weren't bolted shut.

I shoved the phone in my pocket and crossed the grimy floor, grabbing the metal frame. It gave with only a little resistance, squeaking open an inch, then two, then wide enough for me to get my arms through. I tugged at the screen, and with a little force and a lot of cursing, it popped out. I let the screen clatter to the ground outside.

Climbing onto the ledge wasn't exactly graceful. I slipped once, swore again, and finally got both knees up without busting my head open. Hoisting myself up, I wiggled halfway through before I remembered my backpack. I tossed it down onto the snow below and squeezed the rest of the way out, dropping unceremoniously into a crouch on the other side.

The air outside felt like freedom.

I brushed myself off, glancing back at the window. It was crooked now, and the screen lay beside the building like a discarded clue in some juvenile escape plan.

A smirk tugged at the corner of my mouth. Let Maddox and Mason have their stupid "wait for Kreed" plan. I almost wished I could stick around, invisible in the corner, just to see the looks on their faces when they came back and found the classroom empty.

Too bad I'd already made my exit.

I lingered in the shadow of the school building, heart still hammering from my less than glamorous escape through the window. My palms were scraped, my knee ached from the landing, and my pride had taken a serious hit, but at least I wasn't locked in school anymore.

I shifted from foot to foot, eyes locked on the front lot like a hawk, willing Carson's BMW to appear. The next time I saw Mason and Maddox, they were going to get a swift knee to the junk. *Assholes*.

How dare they leave me locked in a classroom.

As I plotted several ways to exact my revenge, I spotted Carson's sleek black car pulling in with its usual purr of power. The Elmwood Public parking lot didn't have many expensive cars, unlike Elmwood Academy, where every kid drove something flashier and pricier than the next person. Only a handful of kids who attended Public had parents who could afford such luxuries; the Corvos were one of them.

Relief hit me so fast. I didn't wait. I bolted across the snowy grass like a girl being chased by a serial killer or the Corvos, practically the same thing, darting between students and skidding to a stop just as Carson stepped out of the driver's seat.

He lounged against the side of his car, his eyes scanning the parking lot for me, but his expression shifted the second he saw me. "Kay?" he asked, pushing off the car. "What's wrong? What happened?"

"I don't want to talk about it," I said quickly, breathless. "Can we just—please—can we get out of here?"

His brow furrowed, and for a moment, he didn't say anything. "That fucking bad?"

"You have no idea."

Then he opened his arms, and I didn't hesitate. I folded into his chest, letting myself have that one second of comfort. That one breath of feeling grounded.

Of course, it couldn't last.

Carson was suddenly ripped away from me, so fast I floundered from the loss of his support. A loud crack thundered as a fist connected with the side of his mouth, and I barely had time to react before Carson stumbled back with a groan.

"What the fuck!" I shrieked, staring into Kreed's dark, silver eyes.

8

KAYLOR

Kreed had Carson by the front of his hoodie, fists clenched so tight the fabric puckered between his knuckles. They were chest to chest, Carson tense but unyielding, his jaw locked and dark-blue eyes hard.

"Kreed!" I shouted, heart slamming against my ribs. "Let. Him. Go."

He didn't flinch. His glare never left Carson, fury simmering just beneath his skin, like a fuse that had already been lit.

I stormed forward, boots scuffing the cold concrete. "I swear to God, if you don't take your hands off my best friend right now, I'll never forgive you."

His head angled toward me slowly, silver eyes burning like coals. "It's not your forgiveness I want."

My breath caught. Something fragile inside me cracked, and I forced the words out anyway. "Then why, Kreed?" My voice broke around the edges. "Why the hell did you hit him?"

His nostrils flared, the muscle in his jaw ticking as he finally released Carson with a shove that sent my best friend stumbling back. "He had his hands on you," he growled, chest heaving, his eyes wild

and unreadable. He looked like hell. His hair was a mess, his lips were in a frightening scowl, and his eyes were bloodshot and unfocused. He smelled like liquor and smoke, like sweat and rage, and all the things I hadn't missed about him. He was a violent storm barely holding itself together.

"What is wrong with you?!" I screamed, rushing to Carson's side.

Blood trickled from the corner of his lip, and Carson wiped at it with the back of his thumb, eyeing Kreed with disdain that could rival mine.

Kreed didn't answer.

He just glared at Carson like he wanted to hit him again, the two of them in an epic showdown. There was only one way to get their attention before things escalated.

"We're not doing this," I said, stepping between them, pressing a hand to Kreed's chest, not to soothe him but to stop him. "Not here. Not like this."

His chest rose against my palm, breath ragged and uneven, but he didn't move. Didn't argue. Just stood there with too much emotion in his eyes and blood on his knuckles.

I didn't know whether to scream or fall apart.

Kreed's eyes flicked down to me, emotion fractured in them. Regret. Fury. Hurt. It was all there, tangled and twisted and too much to take in at once. "I'll hurt him and anyone else who gets in my way."

My spine locked, pulse thrumming in my throat. "You're psycho," I said, but it came out quieter than I meant.

He stepped closer, the space between us crackling. "Only when it comes to you."

I shook my head. "If I didn't already hate you, I'd hate you so much right now."

A ghost of a grin tugged at the corner of his mouth, dark and cruel and so heartbreakingly familiar. "We both know that's a lie," he murmured, brushing a knuckle along my jaw, slow enough to make me shiver. "And I'd be more than happy to prove what a liar you are... in front of your little *boy* friend."

I slapped his hand away like it burned, but he didn't flinch. Didn't move. Just stared at me with that feral gleam, as if he'd already claimed me and would raze the earth to keep me. The worst freaking part? My body remembered the feel of his touch before my mind could catch up.

"Let's go," I said as I grabbed Carson's hand without thinking, threading my fingers through his and tugging him toward the passenger side of his BMW. A piece of me wasn't sure Kreed would let me go. If he tried to stop me from leaving with Carson, what would I do?

Carson didn't say anything, didn't look at me, just followed, his jaw locked. The second the door shut behind me, he slammed his closed and gunned it out of the school parking lot, tires screeching across the blacktop. His hard eyes glanced one last time in the rearview mirror at Kreed.

I refused to look back. My concern was Carson, and as much as I wanted to make sure he was okay, I'd known Carson long enough to recognize his mood.

The silence in the car was heavy. I didn't dare break it. I sat there, letting him breathe, letting him cool off, letting the hum of the engine fill the space between us.

Eventually, he pulled up in front of Bean & Barley, the little coffee shop off Main we tended to go to after finals or on weekends to gossip when we didn't have a fucking care in the world. So very different from today. I spotted Kenny through the window instantly, her honey waves bouncing as she fiddled with her drink and her phone.

"I'm sorry," I whispered, finally speaking.

Carson didn't respond, just shook his head and got out of the car. I followed silently.

The bell above the shop door chimed as we stepped inside. Kenny's head snapped up, and the second her gaze landed on

Carson's face, she gasped. "Holy. Shit, Car. What the hell happened to your face?"

Carson strode straight over to the booth and dropped into the seat across from her. "I met the infamous Kreed Corvo," he said flatly. "It didn't go well."

Kenny blinked, wide-eyed. "I can see that." Her warm brown gaze softened as she leaned forward. "Does it hurt?"

Carson shrugged like it was nothing. "I'm fine." But his body was coiled, and I knew better. He wasn't fine.

Kenny glanced between us, eyebrows drawn, sensing the obvious tension. "Okay, so...I'm guessing the two of you aren't talking?"

I winced, sliding into the booth next to her. "I didn't know he would react like that."

Kenny's stare sharpened. "Why did he punch you?" she asked Carson. "What did you say?"

Carson looked at me once before answering. "Nothing, but I'm assuming it was because I hugged her."

Something Carson and I had done a million times before. I hugged my friends. It wasn't a reason for Kreed to lose his shit.

Kenny let out a slow breath, sitting back in her seat. "Seriously?"

I looked down at the table, cheeks burning, heart heavy. Nothing about this was fair. Not to Carson. Not to Kenny. I never should have involved them in my mess because everything felt broken, and I didn't know how to fix any of it.

"It's a good thing you're not still living there," Carson grumbled, reaching across the table for Kenny's drink and taking a sip.

"She didn't just live with him. She slept with him," Kenny muttered, adding salt to the wound.

I pinned her with a what-the-fuck glare.

"You didn't." Carson nearly spit out Kenny's drink before touching the corner of his lip, blood smearing on his fingers. "You fucked that guy." Hurt and disappointment flashed through his dark-blue eyes. "Fuck, Kay." Shaking his head, he stood from the booth. "I need to clean this up."

My heart ached as Carson walked to the back of the café toward the bathrooms.

Kenny gave me an apologetic glance, scooting her coffee cup toward me.

"How mad is he, do you think?" I asked, my knee bouncing under the table as I sipped Kenny's latte.

"Pretty pissed, but can you blame him? He got punched for the first time."

I winced, the guilt curling in low and bitter. Carson wasn't a fighter. He was soft edges and quiet loyalty. "I never meant to involve either of you. I definitely never meant for Carson to get hurt."

Kenny reached up to tuck a curl behind her ear. "He'll get over it. Just give him space... And maybe an ice pack." Her lips cracked into a partial smile.

I could count on Kenny to find the humor in any situation. I snorted, but the lightness didn't last long. "God, he is so confusing," I complained, taking another sip of the latte before passing it back to Kenny. I was too flustered to go to the counter and order one for myself.

"Who, Carson?"

I shook my head. "No, Kreed."

Kenny's lips twitched with a knowing sort of amusement, her expression too understanding for my comfort.

"Sorry," I said quickly. "I know I shouldn't be thinking about him. Not after what he just did, but I can't seem to help myself. It's maddening. *He's* maddening."

Kenny's gaze drifted toward the window, unfocused and distant. "I get it. You can't always help who you fall for."

My heart twinged. I reached across the table and laced my fingers through hers, squeezing her hand. "No. You can't." We were a wreck, the both of us. She was quietly breaking over a boy who didn't see her, and I was unraveling for one who saw too much.

"Neither can Carson," she said quietly.

My hand stilled. "What does that mean?"

She raised an eyebrow. "You *have* to know. There's no way you don't know that Carson's been in love with you since, like, seventh grade."

Had I known? Had I just not wanted to see, fearing that our friendship would change? I couldn't be sure. "What? But I thought—"

"That *I* was in love with him?" Her laugh was dry. Sad. "I am. Doesn't change how he feels about you."

Sagging back in my seat, I closed my eyes briefly. "What a fucking mess."

Kenny's elbows pressed on the table as she leaned her chin on her hands. "So that guy, Mason... Does he have a girlfriend?"

I shook my head. "No. Nuh-uh. Not happening."

She cocked her head. "So, he has a girlfriend or he doesn't?"

My eyes rolled. "Kenny, you just saw what Kreed is capable of. Mason might have a charming smile and dimples that make your lady bits tingle, but you do not want to get tangled up with a Corvo. Take it from someone who made that mistake."

She gave a small shrug, playing with the edge of her sleeve. "I don't know. I thought it sounded kind of hot—Kreed getting all possessive and alpha male."

Heat prickled at the back of my neck. She wasn't the only one. "Don't mention that to Carson. I doubt he'll agree." Even if in some dark, twisted way, I did too.

THE DRIVE back from the coffee shop was quiet, but this time, it wasn't angry silence. It was heavier and aching. Carson shifted the car into second gear, his bottom lip split and crusted with a thin line of blood. Every time I looked at it, guilt twisted deeper into my chest.

When we pulled up to Brock's house, I didn't even think before saying, "Come inside. Let me disinfect that cut." Whatever he'd done in a public bathroom wasn't enough. It was the least I could do.

He hesitated but nodded, and I took that as a good sign. Things weren't hopeless between us, not that I thought Carson would hold it against me forever, but it sucked having tension between us.

Shadows darkened the corners of the house as the late afternoon light waned. I led him to the kitchen, searching for the first-aid kit in the drawers. He sat on a stool at the counter, eyes following me as I pulled out the supplies. Standing in front of him, I dabbed a cotton pad against his lip gently, trying not to wince every time he did.

"I just don't get it," Carson said quietly, his breath warm on the side of my cheek.

I hadn't realized how close we were or how I was positioned between his legs until then. Stepping back, I opened the ointment and peeled a bandage from its wrapper. "Don't get what?" I retorted, although I had a pretty good idea what he was referring to. I just didn't want to talk about Kreed, not right now, not with him.

Carson looked up at me, his eyes shadowed with emotion too raw. "I don't understand what you see in him." His gaze locked on mine, full of that thing I didn't want to name, didn't want to be real. "Why would you hook up with someone like that?"

Kenny's voice went through my head. *He's been in love with you since the seventh grade.* How could I have been so blind? How had I had no idea? He'd been my best friend for years. We'd grown up together. When had it all changed?

Did I want it to change?

I never considered Carson as anything but a friend, but I couldn't help but wonder if perhaps I'd overlooked what could be between us. Wasn't the foundation of any good relationship friendship? Kreed's name flashed in my head like a warning sign. With him, everything fell fast and uncontrollably, all teeth and fire. We didn't build anything slowly. We devoured. We destroyed. We could barely stand to be in the same room together. Things only went two ways when Kreed and I were alone. Explosive or...explosive. One more passionate, the other more volatile.

Carson reached across the space between us with trembling

certainty, his fingers brushing my hair behind my ear, lingering. "You should be with someone who treats you good," he murmured. "Who'll make you happy. Give you the life you deserve."

My heart skittered. I could hear it, feel it, everywhere, in my chest, my throat, my fingertips. "Do you have someone in mind?" I asked even though I already knew.

He didn't speak. Just looked at me like he wanted me to see him, for real this time. The boy who had always been there. The man trying so hard not to beg. His thumb brushed over the side of my cheek gently, and this time, *I* pulled away.

"Carson..." My voice cracked. "You're amazing. You are. But if I say yes to this, whatever this is, I ruin us. I ruin you. And I can't do that."

His brow furrowed. "Why? Because of him?"

"No." I shook my head slowly. "Because of our best friend."

Confusion flashed across his face.

"Kenny," I said. "She has feelings for you."

His face twisted in confusion. "What are you talking about? Kenny doesn't—"

I shook my head slowly. "She does. I'd know. She's told me."

The heaviness of it landed between us, a fault line cracking open. Carson leaned back, as if the truth had shoved him there, his hand raking through his hair as if he needed something to hold on to, but everything was slipping.

I stood frozen in the silence that followed, watching my best friend splinter in real time because no matter what path I chose... someone was always going to end up hurt.

9

———

KREED

The burn of whiskey hit the back of my throat, but it didn't do shit to quiet the war in my chest. I sat hunched at the end of the bar, elbows on the scratched wood, half-empty glass in one hand as if it were the only thing keeping me sane. I'd started my day here. Seemed only right I ended it here, too. Full circle in the worst way possible.

I could still see Kaylor in Carson's arms, her fingers tangled in his shirt like she needed him. Like he was her safe place.

I didn't think. I didn't breathe. I saw red, and the next thing I knew, my fist was in motion and Carson's mouth was split open.

I'd hit him. Her best friend, and I hated myself for how right it had felt. It was second nature to rely on my fists.

"Word is you had a little altercation with the best friend," Raine drawled, sliding onto the stool beside mine. His leather jacket creaked as he leaned forward, elbows on the counter to signal the bartender. That lazy grin tugged at his lips, the one that always made me want to land a punch just to wipe it clean off his face.

Running a finger over the rim of my glass, I stared at the amber

105

liquid. "If the twins sent you here to come get me, you can see yourself out."

He let out a low whistle, reaching over the bar for a half-melted ice cube and popping it in his mouth. "Well, someone needs to babysit your sorry ass. Honestly, though, I'm surprised it's you. Not sitting in the corner like some exiled prince, but jealousy? That's usually Maddox's lane."

I downed the last of my whiskey in one drag, the burn barely registering. "I'm having a moment," I muttered, glaring at the empty glass.

Raine raised a brow. "Getting wasted every day won't win her back."

I stiffened. "Why the fuck would I want her back?" I hissed.

He didn't back down, just tilted his head and smiled wider. "Then you won't mind if I shoot my shot?"

I was out of the stool before his last word hit the air. My fist flew, landing with a sick crack against his jaw. Raine stumbled back a step, hand flying to his face, blinking like he hadn't quite expected me to move that fast. "You done?" he growled.

Every nerve still hummed inside me from the hit.

Raine straightened, working his jaw with a wince. "That's what I thought. If just hearing me say her name sets you off, maybe stop pretending you don't have feelings for her. You do. We both know it."

"Fuck. Off."

"Still got a hell of a right hook," he muttered, rubbing his chin. "Though you might want to work on your impulse control, Romeo."

I sat back on the stool, my blood still rushing through my veins. "Keep pushing me and you'll lose more than your pride, old man."

"Old man?" Raine laughed under his breath. "Ha. I can still take you. Besides, you're the one unhinged. So dramatic."

I ran a hand down my face, the stress pressing into my skull. The anger was already burning out, leaving only the ache. "I need to see her."

"You're not driving," he said immediately, already anticipating the next fight.

"Then get out of my way." I shot him a look. "I'll walk."

He sighed, grabbing his keys and tossing them in the air. "You're lucky I'm in a charitable mood. But you owe me. Gas, emotional trauma, dental work..."

"Yeah," I muttered, heading for the door. "Add it to the list."

The night air hit like a slap, but it didn't clear my head. Nothing would, not until I saw her again. Even if she hated me, even if she slammed the door in my face, I just needed to explain. One more chance to see her eyes before she looked through me like I didn't matter because she still fucking did to me, and I didn't know how to stop giving a shit about her.

RAINE HAD that annoying charm about him that made people soften before they even realized it. Gender didn't matter. Age didn't matter. He walked into a room, and people instinctively leaned in, drawn to whatever calm confidence he bled without even trying.

It made getting through the gated community too damn easy. The same rent-a-cop from last time sat at the booth. His eyes flicked to Raine, then me, and he grinned like we were old buddies. "I'm good with faces," he said, lifting the gate.

Thank fucking God.

I wasn't in the mood for obstacles today.

Clearly.

"Apparently not good with judgment," I muttered under my breath as Raine rolled his car past the gatehouse.

My older brother smirked. "Be grateful. You've got all the charm of a mugshot right now. You wouldn't have made it inside without me."

I didn't answer. My pulse had started to spike the moment we turned onto her street. "Fuck" breezed through my lips at the sight of a familiar BMW as Raine pulled into the driveway.

He followed my gaze. "A friend of yours?" he asked, nodding to the car.

I shoved the passenger door open, barely waiting for the engine to cut. "Hardly. That asshole's climbing the charts on my enemies list."

"Ah. The best friend," Raine concluded, dragging the words out like a sigh as he leaned on the steering wheel. "Try not to kill him. These are new shoes, and blood doesn't wash out of suede."

But I wasn't listening anymore. Not really.

The minute my boots hit the pavement, the buzz that had clung to me like a second skin started to evaporate. What was left was fire—hot, reckless, coiling under my skin as I spotted Carson.

The douche was already halfway down the steps, tension pouring off him in waves, shoulders locked, fists flexing at his sides, and jaw tense enough to snap. His eyes met mine, fury radiating in them with no attempt to mask it, no veil of civility. "You've got to be kidding me," he bit out, a scornful breath of disdain slipping from his throat. "You just can't take no for an answer, can you?"

I stepped forward, my shadow swallowing the sidewalk between us. "Would you?" My voice dropped, rough around the edges. "If you had a shot with her, are you telling me you wouldn't burn down the whole goddamn world to get her back?"

Carson stopped at the end of the porch, his expression dark. "You never had her."

I smiled, but it was all teeth and bad intentions. "I've had more of her than you have."

His hands curled into fists at his sides. "She deserves better. You'll never be good enough for her."

My breath burned in my chest. "The only thing we can agree on. But I'm a selfish bastard, and I want her. Don't think I haven't noticed how you look at her. She might not be aware that you've been harboring a hard-on for her, but you couldn't be more obvious where I stand."

Carson took a slow step toward me, his voice a low warning. "If you hurt her again..."

Behind us, Raine let out a long sigh and muttered something about testosterone and therapy.

I cocked my head. "You'll what?" I baited, and neither Carson nor I looked away because this wasn't just about a girl. This was a declaration of claim, and I had no plans of losing. Not this time.

An arrogance I hadn't anticipated descended into his pretty-boy preppy features. "You're not the only one with resources available to them."

The corner of my mouth twitched. "Stay out of my way, and I'll stay out of yours. We don't need to be friends. Hell, we don't even need to like each other."

He scowled, but he stepped aside, brushing past me and then Raine. I didn't miss the way he hesitated, glancing back at the house as if he didn't want to leave her alone with me.

Smart man.

The front door creaked open, and Kaylor stood framed in the threshold like a guardian angel with fire in her eyes. One hand was braced against the door frame, knuckles white with tension, and her brows were drawn together in a line of barely contained fury. Her gaze volleyed between Carson and me. "What the hell was that?" The words cracked through the air as she stepped out onto the porch, her bare feet silent against the tile. She crossed her arms over her chest, creating a barrier between us and the vulnerability flickering beneath her anger. The afternoon light caught the silver highlights in her hair, haloing her in flame.

I forced a breath through my nose, slow and measured, trying to keep the jagged edge out of my voice before it could betray just how much seeing her again was unraveling me. "Nothing. Just clearing the air."

Her icy blue eyes narrowed, storm clouds gathering behind them. "What are you doing here, Kreed?" My name on her lips was both a caress and a condemnation, and I felt it in places I'd tried to forget existed.

"He's having a bad day," Raine cut in smoothly, appearing at my side as if he'd materialized from thin air. His hands were shoved deep in the pockets of his worn leather jacket, shoulders loose with that practiced nonchalance he wore like armor, his tone breezy as if we weren't all standing in the middle of an emotional land mine. "Thought we'd drop in. You know, for mental health."

Kaylor didn't move, didn't even blink, but I caught the subtle shift in her posture, the way her weight transferred from one foot to the other like she was calculating distances, measuring her chances of getting back inside before either of us could stop her. Her fingers twitched against her arms, a nervous flutter betraying her composure. Then she bit down on her bottom lip, teeth catching the soft pink flesh in an unconscious gesture that had always been my undoing.

God, that habit. The sight of it hit me like a sucker punch to the solar plexus, stealing the air from my lungs and making me forget how to fucking breathe, especially now, when she was looking at me like I was the biggest asshole.

I probably was.

"I'm not sure that's a good idea," she said, studying my face with the intensity of someone trying to solve a particularly complex puzzle.

I stepped forward, my boots heavy against the porch. Not too close, I knew better than to crowd her when she was already spooked, but just enough for her to catch the desperation I couldn't quite hide when I dropped my voice low and rough. "Little raven...please."

Her lashes fluttered in response. The word, *please*, I never said it. Ever. Not to anyone, Kaylor being the only exception. "Fine," she agreed. "But only if you promise never to lay a hand on one of my friends again."

The muscle in my cheek jumped as I ground my molars together, fighting the urge to tell her exactly what I thought about her precious friend and his wandering hands. I wasn't the type to make empty promises, particularly to her. She deserved better than pretty lies and hollow words. "As long as he keeps his hands off you."

"Kreed." Her spine straightened as she fixed me with a glare. "I'm not kidding."

"Neither am I, little raven." The endearment rolled off my tongue like a confession, completely at odds with the hard line of my shoulders.

She stared at me, her internal debate playing out across her features as she weighed her options, whether to scream, slam the door, or both. Finally, with a soft breath, she stepped back, pulling the door open just wide enough to let Raine and me squeeze past. "Don't make me regret this."

Small victories. I'd learned to take them where I could find them.

The warmth inside wrapped around my skin and seeped into my bones after too many nights sleeping rough. As I passed her in the narrow doorway, our bodies nearly brushing, I caught the barest hint of lavender, that soft, clean scent that had haunted my dreams and followed me through countless sleepless nights.

She wrinkled her nose at me. "You need a shower."

I arched a brow, letting a hint of my old cocky smile ghost across my lips. "Are you offering yours?"

Her glare could have cracked granite, could have stopped a charging bull in its tracks. The temperature in the room seemed to drop several degrees as she leveled me with a look that promised swift and painful retribution. "Don't flirt with me."

Still, despite the ice in her voice, she turned and headed toward the kitchen, her bare feet silent against the hardwood floors. Her voice floated back over her shoulder as she added, "Oh, and you're switching to coffee. It's time to fucking sober up."

Raine chuckled behind me. "Yep. We're definitely staying."

Kaylor disappeared down the hallway, leaving only the lingering scent of lavender and the soft whir of the coffee pot kicking to life. Raine and I drifted into the family room, and I sank onto the couch, head tipping back, eyes falling shut. For the first time in days, maybe longer, the stiffness in my shoulders loosened. I hovered somewhere between awareness and sleep, clinging to the stillness. Every distant clink from the kitchen, the soft percussion of ceramic against granite, the whisper of cabinet doors opening and closing, settled something in my chest. Every rustle of movement, every sign that she was there, real and safe and within reach, soothed the beast that had been clawing at my insides.

Footsteps padded back toward the room. I didn't open my eyes, unready to shatter the moment. Across from me, Raine cleared his throat. "He looks like shit," he muttered.

The corner of my mouth twitched.

"He's looked better," Kaylor replied dryly, her voice carrying that particular brand of understated sarcasm. Even with my eyes closed, I could picture her perfectly, arms crossed over her chest in that defensive posture she'd perfected, chin tilted just enough to project that air of unimpressed authority. The coffee maker gurgled and hissed in the background, punctuating her words with mechanical indifference.

"He needs to sober up," Raine said, his voice dropping to that conspiratorial whisper. "And he can't do that at home."

"Why not?" She'd always been direct, cutting straight through bullshit to get to the heart of things. It was one of the things that drew me to her in the first place, the refusal to dance around the truth.

Raine chuckled sourly. "Our father isn't thrilled with him. Between skipping practices, showing up wasted, and nearly decking a teacher last week, Kreed's not exactly a poster boy right now."

"Because of me?" she asked.

"Partly." Raine's honesty was brutally efficient. No sugarcoating, no gentle lies to soften the blow. "But mostly because he's spiraling. You know how Corvos are. We don't unravel. Not publicly, anyway." He paused, and the leather groaned softly under his weight. "But he's unraveling anyway."

I heard the hitch in her breath, and the sound pierced through the fog of my pretended sleep, and I forced myself to keep my breathing even, my body loose and relaxed against the cushions.

"And you think I can fix that?" Her voice had gone smaller now, rearing those primitive and protective instincts in my chest. She shouldn't sound lost and fragile.

"Can't you?" Raine challenged.

"I don't see how."

"You can start by forgiving him," Raine said, and the simplicity of it was devastating.

"You don't beat around the bush, do you?" I sighed. "I'm not there, Raine. Not with any of you, but definitely not with Kreed."

My heart cracked down the middle, the pain of it immediate, visceral, radiating through my chest and settling in my bones.

"But he can sleep it off," she conceded after a beat. "A few hours. Then you *both* leave."

Relief flooded through me so fast it left me dizzy, a rush of gratitude so intense I nearly forgot to keep breathing. Not forgiveness, we were nowhere close to that, but not complete rejection either. Somewhere in between, which was more than I deserved and less than I needed.

Despite the fact that this entire conversation was centered around me, around my failures and my spiral into self-destruction, I didn't want it to end. Didn't want to break whatever fragile spell had settled over this house, this moment of almost peace. I didn't want her to kick me out, to send me back to the crushing gravity of my father's disappointment and the empty bottles that had become my only reliable companions.

Was it a cheap move to pretend to fall asleep so I could stay as long as possible? Maybe stretch it into the night if I played my cards right? Absolutely. But I didn't give a shit about playing fair anymore. Desperation had a way of stripping away pride, leaving only the raw need to be close to the one person who could quiet the chaos in my head.

The only thing that would make this night better was if Raine made himself scarce, disappeared into the darkness, and left me alone with her. I wanted him gone with a fierce, selfish intensity that surprised me. But I also knew she felt safer with him there, a buffer between us, a familiar presence that kept her from being alone with the person who'd shattered her trust.

I'd allow it for now, swallow the jealousy and the need for privacy, but eventually, when she'd relaxed enough to let her guard down, Raine would have to go.

"I know he'll appreciate it," Raine said. "How are you holding up?"

"Seriously?" Kaylor laughed disbelievingly. "You're asking me how I'm doing?"

"Is that a crime?"

"Coming from you? Yeah, it kind of is." The bitterness in her tone was fresh, recent, like a wound that hadn't quite scabbed over yet.

Raine chuckled a little grimly. "Would it help if I said you're nothing like I expected?"

"Not really." Her response was immediate.

"Fair enough." His tone shifted, softer now. "But if I could go back, I would've done things differently. It took me too long to realize that you're as much of an instrument as we are. More so if I'm being honest."

"That sounds like a manipulation tactic."

"It's not. Though I've definitely used worse."

"Was that your version of an apology?" she asked curiously.

"I'm sorry you got dragged into this," Raine said. "Sorry that we didn't protect you when it mattered."

Those were my words, my apology, yet it sounded so much more sincere and believable from Raine's lips, and I half envied, half cursed him for it.

"That's not good enough," she said eventually. "But I'm tired, Raine. Hating you all takes effort. And I'm running low."

"Don't let it fester," my brother murmured. "Trust me. It'll eat you alive and turn you into something you won't recognize. Kreed... he's fucked up about how things unfolded."

"Good."

"You're ruthless." Admiration laced in Raine's voice now, the type of respect he reserved for people who could match his own capacity for calculated cruelty. "It's that spirit that makes you more Raven than Viper."

"I'm not part of any crew." The denial was immediate, fierce, but I caught the slight tremor underneath it, uncertainty perhaps.

"Remember that, killer Kay," Raine said, and I could hear the smile in his voice, quiet amusement threading through his words like silk. The nickname rolled off his tongue with easy familiarity, and a stab of possessiveness twisted in my gut.

I kept my eyes shut, body still, feigning sleep while the last traces of alcohol fogged my head. Kaylor's soft voice mixed with Raine's deeper one in the background, the kind of low conversation that should have lulled me. It didn't. Not when I heard the slight shift in Raine's tone, the way it warmed like honey when he said her name. My jaw tightened. Then I heard him move, the couch springs groaning slightly, and her breath hitched just barely. I cracked my eyes open a sliver, enough to see his damn hand brushing a strand of her hair behind her ear.

"What did I tell you about touching her?" The words tore from my throat in a growl, rough and jagged from sleep and the bitter after-taste of whiskey still clinging to my tongue. My voice cracked, the muscles in my neck straining as I pushed the words through gritted teeth.

Raine's chuckle rolled through the room. "Just being friendly."

Fire shot through my veins, hot and immediate. I jackknifed upright, the couch cushions groaning under the sudden shift of my weight. My vision swam for a split second, too much movement too fast, but I pushed through it, scowling as I swung my legs over the side and planted my feet on the hardwood floor as I reached for the ceramic mug Kaylor had left on the glass coffee table. "Go be friendly somewhere else." The coffee was cold, but I sipped it anyway. My eyes caught on the grease-stained pizza box sitting next to my mug, cardboard edges soft with moisture, and something twisted in my gut.

I couldn't decide if I was grateful she'd thought to feed me or pissed that she felt the need to take care of someone who'd destroyed her so completely. Probably both.

Raine draped one arm along the back of the couch, his posture screaming casual indifference even as his light-green eyes tracked my every movement. "If only I could trust you not to do something reckless or say something incredibly stupid."

I cursed. Having brothers was the damn worst when it was inconvenient and the absolute best when it was convenient. The duality of it all made my head throb as I shot him a dull glare. "Then you clearly don't know me."

He snorted, but it held no real surprise, just the weary acceptance of someone who'd watched me self-destruct in spectacular fashion more times than either of us could count.

My gaze drifted to Kaylor like a compass finding true north, and I swallowed hard. "Thanks for the coffee."

"This is a one-time thing." Her spine straightened, shoulders squared in a defensive posture that meant business. "And you need to go back to school."

My entire body went still. "Will you be there?"

She blinked once, lashes casting shadows on her cheekbones. "It doesn't matter where I'll be. It's not your concern."

I leaned forward until my elbows rested on my knees. "Everything you do is my concern."

"Kreed." My name came out threaded with exasperation, and the sound of it on her tongue was both salvation and torture, familiar as breathing and foreign as a dead language all at once.

My fist pressed hard against my sternum, knuckles grinding into the bone as if I could physically hold my heart together through sheer force of will. "You can't do that to me. Not after everything."

Her eyes rolled skyward, but I caught the slight tremor in her hands before she crossed her arms, tucking them safely away from view.

Raine raised one hand like he was about to deliver testimony at a congressional hearing, his expression caught somewhere between amusement and genuine discomfort. "The tension in this room is making me uncomfortable. You two either need to kiss and make up or have really loud, angry sex. Preferably when I'm not in the house."

Kaylor shot him a flat look. "I'm not the one who fucked it all up."

I absorbed the blow, letting it settle into the collection of guilt and regret that had taken up permanent residence in my chest. "How long are you going to punish me?"

She didn't hesitate. "You want to earn my trust back? Start by not disappearing into the club and actually showing up to class."

I lifted one eyebrow, the gesture automatic despite the way my pulse hammered against my throat. "For how long?"

Beside me, I caught the subtle twitch of Raine's lips, the barely suppressed smile of someone who already knew exactly what was coming and found it endlessly entertaining.

"Until we graduate." The word dropped between us like a gauntlet thrown down

A slow smirk tugged at my mouth. "What do I get?"

"The privilege of still breathing."

And just like that, the knot of tension that had been strangling me for weeks loosened a fraction. Not gone, not even close, but enough that I could draw a full breath without feeling like my ribs were caving in.

Damn. I'd missed her fire, missed the way she could cut me to ribbons with nothing but words and still somehow make me feel more alive than anyone else ever had. I would do just about anything to keep that flame from burning out even if it meant getting scorched in the process.

Raine's phone buzzed. He glanced down at the screen, cursed under his breath, and stood. "I've got to take this. Don't set anything on fire while I'm gone." He strutted out of the room as he answered the call, and it was just me and her again.

Fucking finally.

This was what I wanted, what I'd been waiting for. A chance.

Kaylor sat curled into the corner of the couch, arms around her knees. I crossed the room slowly and dropped onto the cushion beside her, leaving just enough space for her to move away if she wanted to, but she didn't. That was all the permission I needed.

"You want me to go to school? Fine," I said quietly. "I'll go, but you have to agree to let Evan detail you."

Her light blue eyes narrowed. "For how long?"

Before I could answer, the television behind us flickered with static, the screen's blue glow washing over the room like cold moonlight. A polished news anchor materialized through the interference, her red suit crisp against the sterile backdrop of the studio. The headline crawled across the bottom of the screen in bold white letters: **Teen Girl Still Missing—Authorities Search for Leads.**

A photo of the girl flashed across the screen, and Kaylor's entire body went rigid beside me, every muscle locking up.

"You know her?" I asked, my attention shifting from the screen to study the profile of her face.

She shook her head. "No." But her eyes remained glued to the television screen, pupils dilated with emotion dangerously similar to panic. Not until the segment ended and cut to a commercial for car insurance did she finally blink, finally breathe.

When she turned back toward me, she found me closer than I'd been before, close enough that I could count the flecks of silver in her blue eyes, close enough to catch the faint tremor in her exhale. Our knees brushed, denim against bare skin, and the contact sent electricity shooting up my spine. I couldn't stop staring at her, couldn't tear my gaze away from the way her pulse fluttered at the base of her throat.

"What are you doing?" Her cheeks flushed, wariness darkening her eyes.

A slow release of air breezed through my nose as my fingers flexed against my thigh, as I fought the overwhelming urge to reach out and touch her. "I don't know." The confession scraped my throat raw, honest in a way that made me feel exposed. "I can't stop fucking thinking about you. You're in my mind twenty-four-seven, and I never get jealous, but now it feels as if I'm in a constant state of jealousy. I want to kill everyone who touches you."

Her lips parted in shock, a small sound escaping that might have been my name.

I shifted my weight, draping one arm behind her along the back of the couch with deliberate casualness. The leather was warm under my forearm as I angled my body toward her, creating a cage of muscle and bone that blocked out the rest of the world. "You might not be ready to accept it, but I'm not relinquishing my claim on you. You're mine, little raven. No one else will touch you."

"You can't just claim me." Fire blazed in her eyes. "I'm not a possession."

I smirked. "It's already done. Unless you find someone brave and stupid enough to go against the Crew."

"Does it matter at all that I don't want you?" Her mouth said one thing, but her eyes kept darting to my lips.

I leaned in, closing the distance between us until our faces were separated by nothing but heated air and stubborn pride. Her breath fluttered against my skin, and I caught the faint scent of lavender clinging to her hair. "Liar," I whispered, dropping my voice to that low, rough register that I knew got under her skin. Whether she wanted to acknowledge it or not, I knew exactly how to get to her, knew which buttons to push and which walls to tear down. "Prove that you feel nothing for me."

The challenge hung in the space between us, loaded with implications that made her pupils dilate. Indecision played out across her features, desire battling with anger, need wrestling with pride.

I hadn't come here to seduce her, hadn't planned on using desire as a weapon in whatever twisted game we were playing. But the way her body responded to my proximity, despite her words, and seeing her resolve crack under the strain of our shared history, I realized that seduction might be the only way to break through the walls she'd built around her heart.

Sex was a great way to stir up all those emotions she was so determined not to feel about me. Physical desire had a way of overriding rational thought, of making people forget why they were angry in the first place. I had to keep reminding her that she wanted me, had to chip away at her defenses until there was nothing left but the truth of what existed between us.

I'd take her anger, her pain, her desperate attempts to push me away. I'd take it all and transform it into something else entirely. Something that looked like forgiveness, tasted like redemption, felt like coming home after years of wandering in the dark.

I was coming to realize there wasn't much I wouldn't do for her and no line I wouldn't cross to keep her in my life.

Except walk away.

Never again.

That wasn't an option anymore, not when she was sitting close enough to touch, not when I could see the pulse hammering at her throat and feel the heat radiating from her skin. She could hate me, could fight me, could make my life a living hell, but I would never, ever let her go again.

She snorted. "That sounds like a ploy tactic." She angled her head to the side, her eyes falling to my lips. "You want to play games, *Kreed*?" She intentionally purred my name.

Having her flirt back with me took me by surprise. I expected a snarky quip. "Are you toying with me?"

"How does it feel?" Her lips parted as her tongue darted out to touch her top lip.

If her plan was to torture me, it was working, but she should know better than to taunt me. I was used to taking what I wanted, and her eyes were daring me to try. What was the worst that could happen? She rejected me? I could deal with that. Maybe not gracefully, but what I couldn't deal with was losing her without trying to earn her forgiveness.

Did I deserve a second chance?

Probably not, but it wouldn't stop me from getting what I wanted, and I started to accept it was her I damn well wanted.

I didn't wait for her to pull away and put space between us. I swooped in and kissed her. She didn't shove me away, but she also didn't kiss me back at first, and I fought to go slow, to give her a moment to accept what I offered. I was about to lean back when a soft moan escaped her, and then her mouth shifted under mine. That was it... I was fucking gone.

Her lips parted, and any thoughts on taking my time vanished. Our tongues met, tangling together, and the tension snapped like a pulled wire. My hand slid behind her neck, the other gripping her waist. When she climbed into my lap, straddling me, it was like a match striking dry tinder. Her fingers tunneled into my hair as she settled on top of me, consciously or unconsciously rubbing against the swollen bulge straining in my pants, and I groaned against her mouth, everything inside me coming unstitched.

Oh fuck.

She felt so good against me, my cock throbbing for me to move. She felt like fire and home and chaos and mine.

Mine.

She was mine.

My little raven.

Having her on top of me wasn't enough. Desperation to be closer to her clawed within me like a caged beast, frantic to be set free. I wanted her free of clothes, naked underneath me, and begging me to take her. I wanted to circle my tongue around her budding nipples, to graze them with my teeth and hear the quick inhale of her gasp.

Her mouth ripped from mine, a palm pushing at my chest. The separation happened so quickly I wasn't prepared, and I reached for her, but she shook her head. "I can't do this." She breathed in hot, quick pants.

I tucked a strand of hair behind her ear, needing to keep touching her as my lip curved upward. "I'm not forcing you to kiss me, little raven. You're free to climb off me anytime you want," I murmured, brushing my mouth against hers. I didn't want her to move unless it was closer.

Her breathing quickened, and despite being desperate to have my lips moving over hers, I forced myself to wait, to let her make the choice instead of me being the aggressor, but that didn't mean I couldn't entice. I caressed the side of her cheek, letting my fingers trail down the column of her neck to toy with the gold chain hanging between the slope of her breasts.

Those light-blue eyes darkened, causing my blood to heat.

"I hate you," she murmured before sealing our lips into another kiss.

She tasted like fire and every memory I'd been trying to drink away. I was lost in her, my hands in her hair, her legs still warm on either side of mine, and the world narrowing to nothing but the feel of her against me. I ached with needing her this badly.

My fingers moved to her thighs, squeezing as I went higher. She rolled her hips, grinding against me, and I groaned, my hands unable to decide where to touch her next. Everywhere. I wanted to feel every part of her. The button on her jeans seemed like a good place to start.

"Ahem." A throat cleared loudly.

We both froze. There was only one other person in the house, and the prick chose now of all times to interrupt this fucking moment.

I'm going to murder him.

Kaylor jumped in my arms as if she'd been caught red-handed, scrambling off my lap so fast I almost yanked her back again just to keep her there.

Frowning, I pinned Raine with a death glare that promised pain. He stood in the doorway, one brow arched, amusement stamped across his smug face. "Why is it every time I walk into a room you have your tongue down her throat?"

I flipped him off without hesitation as my head hit the back of the couch.

Kaylor reattached the button I'd just freed.

My brother had the nerve to chuckle. "Anyway, now that things seem to be going in the right direction here, I've got to head out. Something came up."

I caught the glance he threw me, brief, but a look that meant something was happening. Something bad enough that he didn't want her alone or involved. He would fill in the details for me later. I crossed my arms over my chest, already settling back into the couch. Too bad my dick wouldn't calm down.

"You"—Raine pointed at me—"are staying."

Kaylor's head snapped up. "No. No, definitely no," she said, shaking her head. "That's not what we agreed on. He needs to go with you. He's not staying in this house."

Raine shrugged like he didn't hear her. "Kick him outside for all I care, but it's best if someone stays. Besides, he needs to sober up and stay clear of our father until then."

"Fine by me," I said smugly. "I'll stay."

"No," she barked, eyes wide now, panic edging her tone. "Absolutely not. You can't stay here."

"It's just one night. After what I just interrupted, I'd say the two of you have some unfinished business." Raine was already halfway down the hall. "I'll send a driver in the morning," he tossed over his shoulder.

Kaylor jumped up from the couch, her voice echoing after him. "You can't just leave him here!" She rushed after my brother, and I wouldn't be surprised if she tackled his ass to get him to stay. I considered watching from the hallway, but I leaned back, smirking at the ceiling, the taste of her still on my lips and the warmth of her lingering on my thighs, and I swear to God, for once, I wanted to hug my damn brother for being such a genius.

Manipulative, yes, but most people didn't realize how manipulative Raine could be. He did it so flawlessly.

10

KAYLOR

Dashing down the hall after Raine, I kept his broad back in my sights, contemplating tackling the lying asshole. I shouldn't have expected anything less from a Corvo.

Prick.

Screw it. What do I have to lose?

I picked my pace up to a jog, closing the space between Raine and me, and right before he reached the front door, I launched onto his back, wrapping my arms around his neck. I never had a chance. It was as if Raine expected me to try something, anticipating my last-ditch effort, and before I could secure my hold, I was being flipped through the air like a damn amateur gymnast over Raine's shoulders. He did the entire maneuver gracefully. The next thing I knew, I was blinking up at him, my head slightly disoriented from the jarring flip.

Kreed laughed from the other room, but despite the curl in my belly at the sound, I ignored him, spinning and facing the eldest Corvo. "If he stays, then take me with you," I bartered.

Raine's fingers trailed down the side of my arm, his light-green eyes sparkling. "Do me a favor, killer, use this time to work your shit out. Forgive Kreed and put the rest of us out of our misery. He doesn't know how to handle what he's feeling for you because he's never had feelings for anyone before. Have mercy on him. Yes, he isn't absolved of all guilt, but Kreed isn't responsible for what happened."

"He still lied," I pointed out. "You all did."

"That was before you stole his heart. He doesn't fully understand why he can't stop protecting you, but you and I both know the reason. Kreed isn't as cold as he likes to portray. Be careful with him. He's been through more than the rest of us have. Life hasn't been easy on him. You, of all people, can understand his pain." The front door shut with a click. I stood in the hallway, frozen in disbelief, staring at the empty space where Raine had just been.

What the hell did he mean? Understand Kreed's pain?

What have I gotten myself into?

Forgive Kreed?

Raine had lost his ever-loving mind.

"You can't just leave him here!" I shrieked at the now silent door.

No answer. Of course not.

I spun on my heels, anger rising so fast it made my vision go white at the edges. My heart was racing, still trying to calm down from that kiss or maybe from the way Kreed looked at me before it happened. Like I was oxygen and he'd been drowning.

Raine wasn't the only one who had lost his mind. I'd kissed Kreed! After telling him I hated him. Talk about confusing. What was crazier, I hadn't even minded the taste of him, booze mixed with coffee.

I needed to get my head on straight and figure out what the fuck I was doing because, if toying with Kreed for revenge was going to backfire on me every time, I was the one who would end up getting hurt. Again.

Fuck. My. Life.

I stormed back into the living room, my eyes immediately searching out Kreed who was lounging on the couch like he owned the damn place. One arm was slung across the backrest, his head tipped back, that infuriating smirk tugging at the corner of his mouth.

My throat was dry, and I couldn't swallow. "You can't stay here."

"I'm not leaving," the stubborn ass replied.

"I hate you," I hissed, feeling my cheeks burn.

A single brow arched, the stud in his nose twinkling under the dim lighting. "That so?"

"Yes. That's so." I stood my ground, glaring at him, doing everything to look at only his face. If I let my eyes wander over him, I was fucking cooked. "Wipe that smug look off your face. This isn't some win for you."

"You sure about that?" he asked, flexing his fingers and drawing my eyes to the suit of tattoos inked into his skin. "Because from where I'm sitting, it feels like a win. If this is how it feels to have you hate me, I can't wait to see how it feels when you fall for me."

"That's never going to happen." I shook my head, my shoulders slumping. "You're unbelievable."

"And yet, here I am. Believably on your couch. Alone. With you." He grinned, and I wanted to throw the throw pillow at his stupid face.

"This is temporary," I growled. "One night. That's it. Don't get comfortable."

His gaze swept over me with deliberate slowness, and those silver eyes missed nothing, not the way my chest rose and fell too quickly, not the slight tremor in my hands, not the flush creeping up my neck despite my best efforts to remain unaffected. He looked completely unbothered by my declaration, as if he could see straight through every desperate defense I tried to erect between us. "I've never been comfortable a day in my life, little raven. Except for the nights you were in my bed."

The nickname stole the air from my lungs, making my knees go weak. My hand flew to my chest instinctively, fingers pressing against my sternum as if I could somehow hold my heart together through sheer force of will. I hated that he remembered those stolen moments.

Hated even more that I did too, that my treacherous memory could conjure the exact cadence of his voice when he used to say it like a prayer. "And that kiss on the couch can't happen again." My tongue darted out to wet my lips, a nervous habit I couldn't suppress, and I caught the way his eyes tracked the movement with laser focus. "You keep your lips, your hands, and your dick to yourself."

A slow smile spread across his face, making my stomach flip with unwanted heat. "I love it when you get bossy."

"Stop it." The command cracked, but even I heard the tremor underneath it. My body was already turning toward the hallway, muscles coiling with the desperate need to run before I did something irreversibly stupid. "I'm sleeping in my room."

"I'd hope so." His voice followed me, warm with amusement that made my skin prickle with awareness. "Unless you wanna share the couch."

My spine went rigid at the suggestion, every nerve ending sparking to life despite my brain's frantic protests. I didn't look back, couldn't risk it, couldn't trust myself to see whatever expression was painted across his face, because if I turned around, if I caught even a glimpse of that look he used to give me, the one that made me feel like the only person in his universe, I'd crumble.

My feet carried me down the hallway on autopilot, the walls seemed to close in around me, familiar family photos blurring together as I forced myself to keep moving forward instead of running back to where he waited.

And that was the problem, wasn't it? The ugly truth I couldn't admit out loud, couldn't even fully acknowledge in the privacy of my own mind.

Despite everything, despite the lies and the betrayal, despite the way he'd shattered my trust so completely, some traitorous part of me still wanted him.

My bedroom door loomed ahead like salvation, but even as my hand closed around the cool metal of the doorknob, the feel of his presence burned at my back. I could imagine him sprawled across the couch, waiting for me with such arrogant cockiness.

I twisted the handle and stepped inside, closing the door behind me with a soft click.

HOW THE HELL was I supposed to get any sleep with Kreed downstairs? Somehow, not having eyes on him was worse. I had so much homework to catch up on, but studying or working on a paper was the last thing I wanted to do. I had zero concentration unless it was on the asshole sleeping on the couch.

Still, I flopped onto the bed, grabbed the borrowed laptop from Brock, and attempted to get shit done. I must have fallen asleep, exhaustion finally claiming me. My nights for weeks had been restless and long, anything but peaceful, except for the nights I'd been with Kreed.

I didn't know what time it was when the nightmare started, only that I was drowning in it. Screams. Blood. My mother's voice cut off too fast. My father's hand, reaching, covered in crimson. The stench of smoke. A creaking floorboard, too close. And me, too late.

I gasped awake, my throat raw from crying, chest heaving like I'd run miles. My sheets were tangled around my legs, drenched in sweat, and the laptop had slid off my lap, the screen blank. The darkness of the room was familiar, but it didn't feel safe. Not yet. Not with my pulse still in my ears and my hands shaking.

"Kaylor."

Kreed.

My eyes found him sitting on the edge of my bed, half shadowed by the glow of the hallway light leaking in behind him, so close to me his warmth seeped into me. His brows were drawn together, eyes scanning my face as if he was trying to fix me with just a look. His fingers were tangled in the side of my hair, his palm cupping my cheek. "You were crying," he said softly. "The nightmares still keeping you up, little raven?"

I swallowed hard, shame and pain catching in my throat. Papers were scattered on top of the bed, alongside the open laptop. "I—I didn't mean to wake you."

"You didn't." He untangled his fingers as the pad of his thumb brushed along the outline of my jaw. "I couldn't sleep. You're not the only one haunted by things they would love to forget."

You, of all people, can understand his pain. Raine's voice popped into my head.

Had he been referring to their mother's death? Was that the pain Kreed and I shared? If that were true, wouldn't it have been trauma we all shared? Raine, Mason, Maddox, and Kreed? The loss of a parent?

I should tell him I was fine, to stop touching me, and demand he leave. Having Kreed in my room late at night was never a good idea, but I didn't want him to go. *And* I definitely didn't want him to stop touching me, not when every cell in my body came alive, despite that voice of reason inside me screaming *bad idea*, but none of them were louder than the silence lingering after a nightmare. None of them drowned out the shaking in my chest or the way my skin still crawled with old ghosts as Kreed did. He banished the nightmares. Perhaps it was that his darkness overtook mine, blanketing me in his chaos, fierce, consuming, and strangely safe.

He sat on the bed, barefoot, hoodie rumpled, hair a wild mess as if he'd run his hands through it a hundred times tonight. He looked at me, waiting to see if I would tell him to get out, but it took one glance into his silver eyes to know I wouldn't.

I didn't want to be alone even if it meant having the company of the enemy. "What's keeping you up at night?" I asked, breaking the silence before it could swallow us whole.

His shoulders lifted in a faint shrug, but his gaze stayed locked on mine as his hand fell from my face. "You. My mom. My dad. Crew shit."

I sat up slowly, pulling my knees to my chest and wrapping my arms around them, refusing to admit how much I missed his touch. "Tell me about her." Talking was far safer than silence. I didn't know much about the woman who gave birth to Donovan's children, and I wanted to know more about his mom and why they rarely spoke of her.

He hesitated, and for a moment I thought he'd shut down like he always did when things got too real, but his voice broke through the quiet. "What do you want to know?"

"Whatever you're comfortable sharing." I couldn't help but be curious about her. I hadn't noticed a single photo of her in the house, only what I'd seen online. She'd been beautiful, passing most of her stunning looks to Kreed, the eyes, the onyx hair, and the strong chin.

"She was everything. Light, warmth...soft in all the places this world is hard. She loved music, used to sing around the house when she thought no one was listening. And she had this laugh. God, you would've liked her laugh. It filled up a room. She would have adored you."

I didn't say anything. Just let him talk, the charge of his words filling in the space between us, like they carried more than memories.

"My dad...he didn't deserve her," he continued. "He broke her down piece by piece. She was an accomplishment, having a beautiful woman on his arm as his wife. I was the one who found her." His voice cracked then, just barely. "Laid out on the floor like she didn't matter. She did. She mattered more than anything."

My throat burned. "I know that feeling," I whispered. "Seeing them go. Wanting to stop it and not being able to do a damn thing." Was this what Raine had alluded to? We'd both been there when people we loved passed on? I sensed there was more to the story, but I didn't push. I could see what it cost him to open up this much.

He looked at me then, really looked, as if he saw every broken piece of me and wasn't scared of the mess. "We never talk about her. It hurts too much. And the more time that passed without speaking her name, the easier it got, but doing so feels like we're forgetting her, and I don't want that. It's a loneliness that never leaves," he said softly. "It carves a hole inside you."

"Yeah," I said. "It does."

We sat like that for a while, two kids shaped by grief, haunted by memories we couldn't undo, and for once, it didn't feel unbearable.

It just felt...understood.

Beep. Beep. Beep. Beep.

The shrill scream of the security alarm shattered the quiet. My body jolted upright, heart in my throat, every hair on my body rising as fear sank its claws in. The sound was so sudden, so violent, that it took me a second to process what it even was, but it was the why that caused ribbons of fear.

Someone had triggered the alarm.

Someone was outside.

Someone was trying to break in.

My eyes widened, immediately flying to Kreed, who was already moving. One second, he was beside me, and the next, he was on his feet, every muscle in his body coiled, his expression unreadable except for the flash of something deadly in his eyes.

Danger.

"What the fuck—" he growled, then turned to me. "Are you expecting anyone?"

"No," I whispered, shaking my head as I scooted to the edge of the bed. "No one." Hell, I wasn't even expecting him, but it hadn't stopped Kreed from getting inside.

His gaze darkened. "Stay here."

"Like hell." I scrambled out of bed, not even trying to hide the panic in my voice. "You're not leaving me alone to get hacked to pieces. I'm coming with you."

His hesitation was brief, but it was there, yet he reached for my hand, interlocking our fingers. "You've seen too many horror movies."

"Maybe, but I've also seen real-life horrors," I whispered, staying close as he turned toward the door.

We crept down the stairs, not bothering with the lights, my

fingers in his. The house was pitch-black except for the faint red glow of the alarm panel blinking at the end of the hallway. Every creak in the floorboard felt deafening. I was practically glued to Kreed's back, breathing shallow, trying to listen for any sound, footsteps, a window sliding open, or a breath that wasn't mine.

Kreed stood still for a beat, shoulders tense, head tilted slightly like he was listening to something only he could hear. He reached for the butcher block with precision, fingers closing around the biggest knife my cousin had. The blade caught the pale moonlight bleeding in through the window, glinting silver as he turned it over once in his hand.

Without breaking stride, he moved toward the back door, his steps quiet and stealthy. His hand curled around the knob, but he paused, looking at me, eyes growing dark and stormy as they found mine. "Lock the door behind me," he ordered.

My stomach clenched as I clung to his hand, refusing to let go. "What? No fucking way. Don't go out there. It's dark. You don't know who's out there. This is a bad idea." Was I actually worried about him? The thought of Kreed hurt made me sick.

His jaw flexed, but his tone didn't waver. "I need to make sure whoever set off the alarm is gone. If I don't check, neither of us is sleeping, and as much as I like the idea of keeping you up all night, this wasn't what I had in mind."

I wanted to argue. I wanted to scream, but I could see in his eyes that he was going, no matter what I said. I hated how calm he was. Like walking into danger was just another Tuesday for him. Maybe it was. "I swear to God, Kreed Corvo," I muttered, chest throbbing with dread as I unraveled my fingers from his, "if you get yourself murdered, I'll never forgive you."

He turned to face me fully, one corner of his mouth lifting just slightly. "It's good to know that no matter how much you hate me, you still care."

"It's me I'm concerned about. If you die, what chance do I have?"

"If I'm not back in five minutes," he said, holding my gaze, "call

Raine." He didn't wait for my response. He just turned, yanked the door open, and disappeared into the night.

My fingers fumbled with the deadbolt, locking it with a hard click that felt final. I pressed my forehead to the cool glass pane, eyes straining into the darkness beyond the porch light. My breath fogged the glass, shallow and fast. Somewhere out there, he was alone with only a knife and whatever anger he was running on.

Seconds dragged.

I counted my heartbeats just to fill the silence.

A shadow shifted along the fence line, and my pulse spiked. "Kreed?" I whispered even though he couldn't hear me.

The figure stepped into the light, and a breath whooshed out of me. Kreed emerged from the side of the house, knife still in hand, his expression masked. He stepped up to the door, knocked once, and I unlocked it as fast as I could, pulling him inside.

"Well, you didn't die," I said, using sarcasm to cover up what was really happening inside of me.

He shook his head slowly. "No one out there to kill me, but I wish they had tried."

I didn't miss the tension still in his shoulders. "That's messed up. Do you think it was a false alarm?"

"Could've been," he said, but we both knew better. His eyes swept the hallway behind me, then met mine again. "Or someone wanted us to think that."

Goose bumps raced up my arms. Whatever had just happened, one thing was clear. I was glad he was here, *and* I wasn't letting him sleep on the couch tonight.

Gnawing on my lip, I led the way back through the house. The hall was dark, the only light coming from the sliver of moon filtering through the window at the end. Shadows stretched along the walls like quiet ghosts.

We reached my bedroom, and I hesitated in the doorway, hand hovering near the frame. "Leave the door open," I said softly, stepping inside. The room smelled faintly like lavender and old pages, comforting. I climbed into bed, the sheets cool against my skin, pulling the blanket up, but it did little to soothe the chill in my chest. I swallowed hard, hesitating again as I stared up at him.

Kreed lingered near the door, one hand braced against the frame like he was giving me a chance to change my mind.

"Will you stay?" I whispered. "Just for tonight?"

His eyes locked on to mine, and for a beat, he didn't move. Didn't speak. Just watched me, reading between the cracks I couldn't seal up fast enough.

"I might have regrets in the morning," I admitted, my voice barely audible over the wind outside, "but tonight...I just want sleep. Uninterrupted. Without the nightmares. And you..." I swallowed the rest, but the meaning lingered in the air.

He stepped inside without a word, closing the distance in a few careful strides. He didn't say anything. He didn't need to. The way he moved, slow and deliberate, told me enough. He slid onto the mattress beside me, careful not to touch, but he was there, a steady presence.

Somehow, the cure for our disturbed sleep was each other.

"When I say sleep. I mean *sleep*," I clarified. "No funny business. You stay on your side. There's an invisible line, and if you cross it, I swear I'll kill you in your sleep."

The corner of his mouth twitched. "Wouldn't dream of it, but if we're being honest, it might be worth dying to touch you again."

"Keed, you can't say shit like that to me."

"And you know what happens every time you say my name."

"Just get in before I change my mind."

"Gladly, little raven." He took off his hoodie and jeans, letting them fall to the floor as I gathered the papers and laptop, placing them on the nightstand. Then he moved slowly, almost cautiously, around to the other side of the bed as if he were afraid to spook me or I might change my mind. He'd brought the knife with him and set it down on the bedside table. "I've been waiting all week to get into your bed."

Rolling my eyes, I turned onto my side and faced the wall, thinking it would be safer than seeing him. The mattress dipped slightly as he mirrored me, his breath soft at my back. Close, perhaps too damn close, yet comforting all at the same time.

"When did they start coming back? The nightmares?" he asked, his fingers toying with my hair.

I knew what he was doing, attempting to divert my mind from the possibility that someone might still be out there, watching, waiting. I was grateful. My brain needed a distraction, and Kreed was the epitome of diversions for me. Rolling over, I faced him. Just looking at him scrambled my thought process. "I thought I said no touching."

He held his hand up with a smirk, making my stomach cartwheel before resting it on the pillow.

Sighing, I answered his question. "Most nights since the warehouse."

The soft rustle of the wind outside and the occasional creak of the house settled around us. "You shouldn't have to go through that alone." He shifted, his body angling toward me even though we weren't touching.

I didn't have the words because in what felt like forever...I didn't feel alone. Even with an invisible line dividing the space between us, the warmth of his presence was known, as was the depth of his gaze and the quiet understanding we hadn't had before. Somehow, for tonight, that was enough.

"I still hate you," I murmured into the dark, voice muffled by the pillow, barely carrying past the quiet.

From the threshold of my vision, I caught the corner of his mouth twitching. Not quite a smile but close. The moonlight spilling through the curtains cut soft shadows across his face, drawing lines over his perfect cheekbones and stubbled jaw. "Let me cross this invisible line," he said in a husky drawl, "and I promise in thirty seconds you'll be feeling the opposite of hate."

A breath of laughter slipped out before I could catch it, and damn him and the way his eyes warmed, just a little, the smallest crack splitting through all the frost I'd been holding on to. "Kreed."

"Now that's just unfair, little raven." The way he said it, as if he could taste every syllable, sent a small shiver down my spine. Not from fear. From something else entirely.

I should have looked away and reminded myself why I hated him, why I needed to keep the walls up.

I didn't.

I stared at him even as the shadows blurred and my eyelids grew heavy. He just stayed. A steady shape in the dark, anchoring me without chains, and when my body finally sagged into the mattress, breath slowing, heart easing into something that didn't feel like a constant war...I felt it.

His fingers brushed mine.

With a careful patience I hadn't expected, he laced our fingers together one by one until his hand was wrapped in mine.

The logical part of my brain warned me to pull away, telling me this was too intimate. I should have shoved him out of the bed, out of the room, out of my life. Instead...I curled my fingers around his, and in the dark, I let myself believe for just a moment that he wasn't the enemy, that he could be someone I loved, and that maybe I didn't have to carry it all alone.

Maybe I didn't want to let go. Not yet.

I WOKE SLOWLY, the slow that only comes when, for once, your nightmares don't find you. Warmth blanketed me, steady, solid, and familiar.

Kreed.

My hand was resting on his chest, rising and falling with each breath he took. His arm was curled beneath me, holding me as if I belonged there. At some point in the middle of the night, our bodies had betrayed us, nature taking over. We hadn't crossed any lines intentionally, but I'd ended up here anyway, tangled with him.

God help me, it feels good.

His scent surrounded me, a mix of woods, hints of the sea, uniquely his that I was drawn to. I lifted my gaze, careful not to stir him, and found myself staring at his face, so peaceful in sleep, like the demons haunting him had given him a rare reprieve.

He was so fucking gorgeous.

That infuriating jawline, the way his lashes brushed the tops of his cheeks, the slight part to his lips as if he was on the verge of whispering something. My heart squeezed painfully in my chest.

My heart...yearned for him.

My body craved him.

And my soul...it reached for his in a way I didn't know how to stop. Or if I even wanted to.

A slash of sunlight cut across his face, painting a line down the hollow of his cheekbone and catching on the two faint scars beneath his right eye. I'd never asked how he got them. I wasn't sure I wanted to know. Some part of me feared the answer, but I remembered the first time I saw them, wondering who put them there, what kind of pain he'd endured. They weren't the type of marks that faded. They stayed etched into skin, into memory.

My fingers itched to trace them, to feel the raised skin with the pads of my fingers. To press a kiss to the old wounds like I could somehow erase them, but I just lay there, watching him breathe, because moments like this, unguarded and fragile, were rare, and deep down, a part of me was terrified it might be the last.

His breathing changed. Subtle. The pause between inhales stretched a fraction longer. His fingers twitched beneath mine, just slightly, barely enough to register unless you were watching like I was. He was waking up.

I should have looked away or shut my eyes and pretended to be asleep, but I didn't. I couldn't. My gaze stayed fixed on his face, on the slow blink of his lashes as he fought against sleep's retreat, and when those familiar silver irises opened and locked on mine, I forgot all about propriety.

He looked at me with heavy-lidded eyes and an expression carved in stone, but his eyes... God, his eyes burned.

My heart kicked hard.

Rolling away would be smart. Distance, that was what I needed, but instead, my traitorous fingers drifted down the center of his chest, stopping at the flat press of his abs. The worn cotton of his shirt annoyed me. *Why the hell was he still wearing it?*

These were the intrusive thoughts I shouldn't be having. It was too hard to remember I hated him when he was this close.

He continued to watch me, waiting to see what I would do next. I didn't even know. A blaze of heat began to burn hotly inside me. The air between us thickened, heat rolling off him in quiet, pulsing waves.

His lips brushed mine, softly at first, tentatively in a way that lit my blood on fire, giving me the chance to stop this before we went too far.

I didn't.

I leaned in, tilting my chin and catching his mouth with mine, and it was over. The change was immediate. His hand slid behind my neck, fingers threading through my hair and tugging my head back. His lips were soft but possessive, and he dragged my bottom lip out with his teeth. *Sweet baby Jesus. I'm in so much trouble.*

My palm pressed to his chest but lacked any substance. "Wait. I can't think."

"Good. Open up for me, little raven," he murmured, desire thick in his eyes.

As if I had a choice. I was starting to think my need for Kreed would never end. It wouldn't matter what he did or how horrible he was. I was powerless to the way he made me feel.

My lips parted, and the tip of his tongue touched mine as I let him in, but it was hardly enough. I ached everywhere. I glided my tongue against his, feeling him tremble, and a heady sensation danced within me. Power. I had power over this tough, dangerous, broody guy, and it was nearly as addicting as he was.

His mouth moved over mine with desperation, his teeth scraping my bottom lip, and I gasped into the kiss. He growled low in his throat and rolled, pinning me beneath him, the weight of him both terrifying and grounding. Every inch of him was hard, and our bodies aligned too perfectly, remembering each other. My legs wrapped instinctively around his hips, his thigh pressing between mine.

This could be bad, leading to all kinds of complications I didn't need, but my feelings had taken over, and I was lost. Kreed had that effect on me, making me forget who he was, who I was, and our thorny pasts.

His mouth left mine to find my neck, trailing hot kisses up to my ear. "God, I want you," he whispered, the tickle of his breath hot on my skin. "You have no idea how much."

My fingers fisted in his shirt, my heart thundering. We were fire and gasoline, and a spark ignited with every second that passed. "I think I have a pretty good idea," I whispered, my hips grinding against that very evidently hard part of him.

"I swear I've been hard every day since I first saw you."

My hand slipped under his shirt, gliding up over rippled muscle that shifted under my touch. God, he was so beautiful. It wasn't fair. How could I possibly stay away? "That must be"—I traced the edge of his boxer's waistband—"uncomfortable."

"Jesus," he hissed between his teeth. "Are you trying to kill me?"

"Yes." I wasn't sure when or how, but he'd inched up my shirt, and I gasped as the pad of his thumb brushed over my nipple.

"I'd die happily between your legs knowing you want me."

Wanting him would be my downfall. I couldn't seem to stop kissing him at every chance I got. "Against better judgment." I ached for him. Wrapping my legs around his, I lifted my hips, rubbing against him.

His lips curled against mine before he kissed me again, sliding his tongue between my parted lips. My fingers wove into his hair. I freaking loved this, loved kissing him and feeling his weight on top of me. "Tell me yes. Tell me you want me. You want this."

My fingers wrapped around him through his boxers. "I want you inside me." It was the best he was going to get. Wanting him and wanting sex with him were two things I was trying to separate. It wasn't working, but Kreed didn't need to know that. Let him think this was just sex and nothing more.

He hooked a finger into the corner of my underwear, and I held my breath as he grazed my lower belly, moving lower and lower and—

Knock. Knock.

We both froze.

A breath locked between us.

Knock. Knock. This time louder and more urgent.

What the—

The door creaked open wider, and Kreed cursed under his breath. Standing there, arms crossed and glowering, was my cousin. Brock's gaze took in the entire scene in one sweep: the bed and me flushed and wild-eyed, and when they landed on Kreed, his posture went still.

I scrambled off him like I'd been electrocuted, suddenly very aware of his state of undress in my bed, hair a mess, and eyes dark as they glared across the room, the heat in them shifting to shadowy darkness. His gaze followed the sound, silver eyes darkening, no trace of softness remaining. Whatever glint of vulnerability had existed a moment ago was gone, replaced with something hard.

"Shit," I whispered.

No one moved.

KAYLOR

Brock's eyes locked on me first before glaring at Kreed still in my bed, smirking smugly with his hands resting suspiciously near my thighs. Kreed had the nerve to look unapologetic, his chin lifting as he met Brock's glare head-on, testosterone flooding the room.

I smacked Kreed's hand off me. "Brock—" I started, sitting up straighter, yanking the blanket up with me. Thank God, I still had my clothes on and we hadn't been... I didn't want to even think about Brock walking in my room in the middle of Kreed and me having sex.

"Get your hands off my cousin," Brock thundered at Kreed, low and loaded with enough steel to make even Kreed flinch.

Oh hell. I hadn't even had coffee, and already we were diving headfirst into a brawl. I shot Kreed a look that screamed don't. Don't get cocky. Don't provoke him. Do. Not. Start.

But Kreed's smirk deepened like the damn devil's son he was.

Before either of them could say something they'd regret or throw punches, I swung my legs over the side of the bed and stood up between them, holding up both hands like a human peace treaty. "Okay," I said, voice firm, grateful that the oversized tee I wore hung

mid-thigh and Kreed hadn't gotten the chance to remove it. "Everybody, calm down. No one's dying this morning. Not before breakfast."

Neither of them looked away from each other, like two lions circling the same damn territory. The air between them practically vibrated with tension as they waited for the other to make the first strike.

"Brock, nothing happened," I lied. Or maybe it was half true. "I swear I was about to tell him to stop."

"Liar," Kreed muttered under his breath but not so quietly that Brock hadn't heard.

Brock's eyes flicked to mine. "Why is he here?"

I hated disappointing him. "It's a long story, but he was just leaving," I gritted, throwing a glare over my shoulder at Kreed.

The bastard didn't budge.

"Bullshit," Brock hissed, glaring harder.

"He's right," Kreed muttered behind me. "I was definitely not—"

I turned and shot him a look sharp enough to draw blood.

"—leaving," he finished anyway, unfazed. "I told you. I'm not leaving you alone. Not in this house. Not at school. Nowhere."

I groaned, dragging a hand through my hair. "Oh, for fuck's sake. Can we not do this right now?"

Brock took a threatening step forward. "Get dressed." His glower shifted to Kreed. "*And* you, get out of her bed."

"Brock," I said louder this time, planting a hand against his chest to stop him from charging. "I'm okay. There's no reason to make this into something bigger than it is. We just slept. That's it."

He finally looked at me. Really looked. Some of the tension bled out of his shoulders but not enough. "That's not what it looked like," he said roughly. "And trust me, I know what he was thinking."

Fuck. Why me?

Now was definitely not the time to admit I'd kissed Kreed first. I sighed, tugging at the hem of my shirt, feeling the heat crawl up my neck. "It doesn't matter. He didn't force me into anything."

Kreed let out a dry chuckle behind me, the twinkle of his nose ring mocking me. "Don't defend me. It's cute but unnecessary."

"I'm not defending you. I'm trying to stop you from getting a punctured lung or a cracked rib," I hissed out the side of my mouth.

Kreed moved to the edge of the bed, dragging his gaze up and down Brock's frame. "You don't think I could take him?"

"I don't want to find out," I retorted.

"I've always wondered if I could," Kreed said, eyes gleaming now with the glint of a challenge.

"I'm game." Brock cracked his knuckles, shoulders rolling like he was warming up. "Trust me, I've been dreaming of getting my hands on you."

Kreed tipped his head. "Usually, it's the girls who say shit like that to me, but hey—I'm flattered."

"Kreed," I snapped, whirling on him, "I swear to God. Shut. Up." I turned back to my cousin, my expression pleading. "Give me five minutes. Please."

Brock's eyes narrowed like he was calculating how many bones he could break in exactly five minutes. "Make it two. I don't trust you alone with him for longer than that."

Kreed laughed, low and smug. "Smart man."

Brock didn't find it funny. He glowered at Kreed one last time, eyes full of warning, before stepping back into the hallway. He muttered something under his breath, probably about how many different ways he could bury a body, and stalked off.

I turned toward Kreed, who was now lounging against the side of the bed like he hadn't nearly ignited World War III. His black T-shirt clung to his chest, rumpled and slightly twisted from sleep, and his boxer briefs rode low on his hips.

Ugh, I despised how good he looked in the aftermath of chaos.

"I really hate you," I muttered, grabbing the nearest pillow and smacking him across the face with it. The sound was muffled but satisfying.

Kreed caught the pillow one-handed, unbothered, that devil-may-care grin already tugging at his mouth. Before I could retreat, his other hand snaked out, fingers wrapping around my wrist with practiced ease, tugging me off balance until I stumbled forward, right between his legs.

My breath hitched as my knees brushed the inside of his thighs.

"No, you don't," he murmured.

Unfortunately for both of us, he was probably right, but that didn't mean I had to like it. Or him. Or the way his touch turned my spine into liquid steel. "Last night changes nothing between us," I muttered, placing my hands on his shoulders, trying to create space I didn't actually move into. Now I had to go downstairs and deal with my cousin.

The pad of his thumb caressed the inside of my wrist. "And this morning?"

"Never should've happened," I whispered even though the lie sat like glass in my throat.

His smile slipped, just barely, and I hated the speck of disappointment I caught before he looked down. His hands fell to his sides, fingers twitching like he wanted to grab me again and couldn't justify it now.

I stepped back, the space between us stretching with every inch.

He let me go.

Brock wasn't joking about his threat, which gave me a single minute to throw on a sweatshirt and hoodie and use the bathroom. Kreed was waiting for me when I emerged, looking far too calm for what we were about to face.

I'd deal with him later.

I could only handle one freaking problem at a time, and currently, Brock was a more pressing matter.

Following behind me, Kreed and I headed downstairs. Voices carried from the kitchen, and I realized Brock hadn't come alone. Kreed's elbow brushed mine as he came to walk beside me through the hallway, and I snuck a glance at him, seeing the amused expression morph into an unpleasant frown.

He was outnumbered.

I took a deep breath before we rounded the corner, my eyes sweeping through the packed kitchen, and I blinked. The whole damn crew was here. My cousin's crew—the Elite.

Brock stood by the counter, coffee in hand, arms crossed in a brooding statue form. Josie was perched on a stool beside him, legs crossed, her hair in a sleek high ponytail, and judgment in her eyes the second she saw me enter the room with Kreed in tow.

Fynn leaned against the fridge, Kenna curled into his side like they were made of the same damn soul. Micah sat on the edge of the kitchen island, lazily flipping a butter knife between his fingers, Mads shaking her head at him. Ainsley was frowning at Micah. Kenna and Josie exchanged some silent, sister-telepathy look, and Grayson... I scanned the room again to make sure I hadn't missed him. He wasn't here, which meant he was probably home with his daughter, Kensie.

Shit.

Kreed stiffened beside me. Not such a tough guy after all, but fuck me, if I didn't want to hold his hand.

You do not need to offer him support, I reminded myself.

"You brought the crew," I said to my cousin.

Brock grinned, sipping a cup of coffee that literally made my senses buzz. My cousin's aqua eyes brimmed with a mix of concern and suspicion. "You've been quite busy the last few days."

Ugh. The cameras. Of course, Brock had seen Kreed and Raine. "Not on purpose. Trust me. People have a way of just showing up."

Josie stepped forward, softening the air with her presence. She rounded the island and pulled me into a hug that pressed something hot against my chest. "Hey," she said quietly. "Don't worry. We're not here to bust you."

Ainsley and Mads flanked her, both offering comforting squeezes that were too gentle for the guilt in my gut. I hadn't seen them in months. I swallowed hard, blinking fast. *Don't get emotional now.*

Behind them, Micah's gaze zeroed in on Kreed. "Like this one?" he said, lips pressing around the words.

The Kreed who was in my bed was gone, and in his place was all hardness, his expression masked. "You all throw intervention brunches often?"

No one laughed.

Except Micah. His smile was razor-edged, armed with dimples. "Only when a Corvo is somewhere he isn't wanted."

Even Mads looked ready to launch her latte at Kreed.

I winced. "Is there something going on?" I asked quickly, trying to cut through the tension before it exploded.

Josie took another sip of her coffee, nodding. "We wanted to make sure you were okay."

"All of you?" I arched a brow. "Not that I don't appreciate seeing you, because I do. Trust me. Living alone isn't all that glamorous."

Josie tilted her head, chocolate eyes gleaming. "Sure. That's why you let someone you hate sleep in your bed."

My throat dried as Kreed turned to look at me. "Don't start," I warned him.

"So that's why you let him stay?" Fynn leaned on the counter, his voice cool. "You didn't want to be alone?"

"Not exactly," I admitted, my shoulder hitting the doorway as I unleashed some of my weight onto the wood.

"*I* didn't want her to be alone," Kreed piped up, his voice low but unwavering.

Brock glowered at the Corvo in question. "Since when do you make decisions about my cousin's well-being?"

"Or anything to do with her life?" Fynn added, pinning Kreed with his unrelenting green eyes.

"You never had that privilege to begin with," Micah said.

They were ganging up on him, and I wasn't supposed to care, but the way Kreed stood, unmoved and enduring it like he thought he deserved it, itched under my skin.

Kreed's tone didn't change. "If I don't, who will? None of you was here. I know what my father did was fucked up, but I'm not him."

Brock gave a slow nod of understanding despite his eyes narrowing. If anyone got the I-want-to-be-different-from-the-people-who-raised-me thing, it was my cousin. "Still, you have your own reputation. Your own crew. And that comes with risk."

Kreed glanced around the room, gaze hard as stone. "They'll do whatever it takes to make sure she doesn't get hurt."

My cousin angled his head. "Believe it or not, I think you mean that. Physically, I think you'd protect her, but what I worry about is what happens after. The emotional shrapnel you leave behind."

"Brock," I hissed under my breath. "Could you not act like I'm invisible?"

Kreed leaned against the doorway. "If I have to choose between hurting her feelings and protecting her life, I'll hurt her feelings every damn time."

Josie broke the silence. "Does that mean you still think she's in danger?"

Kreed nodded. "Yeah. I do."

That single sentence changed the air. Tension dropped into something heavier, more grounded. "Care to tell me what happened last night? I got a notification from the security system," Brock said.

Kreed's jaw ticked. "Someone tripped the alarm, but by the time I got outside, they were gone."

Fynn frowned. "How do we know you didn't plan it? That it wasn't one of your crew or your brothers who set it off?"

I'd seen Kreed's face when the security system sounded. He'd been genuinely alarmed, his protective instincts kicking in in a way that was ingrained. He hadn't faked it. I was certain, but I understood why my cousin had doubts. Kreed had already proved to be a skilled liar.

"Check your cameras," Kreed countered. His arms stayed loose at his sides, posture casual, almost bored.

"We did," Brock replied evenly, tapping his mug against the granite. "They wore a mask."

Kreed and I shared a glance as a creeping dread curled down my spine like smoke. "They weren't behind it," I said before I could stop myself, again defending Kreed for reasons that escaped me. I'd clearly lost my fucking mind. This was my opportunity to get him out of the house...out of my life, and yet...I couldn't make myself take that step.

"He could be trying to scare you into moving back in with him," Micah theorized, and it was possible, a reasonable doubt. I wouldn't put anything past the Corvos. Donovan especially.

"Believe it or not," Kreed said almost thoughtfully, "I've been weighing the pros and cons. There's no perfect fix. We could send her out of state, make her disappear, but if they want her badly enough...they'll find her. For now, I think it would be better if she stayed here."

I blinked. Unable to believe what I was hearing. "You do?"

Mads's brows lifted. "What changed your mind?"

Kreed's eyes darkened, haunted. "Last night. Whoever tripped that alarm wasn't just testing the perimeter. They were sending a message. The traitor in her father's crew, the one responsible for his murder, knows she's a threat. She's the only link left, a loose string. They won't stop until she's eliminated."

The room stilled.

Josie leaned forward on the stool, her hand touching Brock's shoulder. "And you've been trying to uncover who it is?" she asked Kreed.

He nodded once. "There are some parts of my father's business we don't even have access to. But I'm digging."

Brock's expression shifted, something brewing behind his eyes. "I might be able to help with that." His focus turned to me. "But until we identify the bastard stupid enough to cross your father's legacy, you don't stay anywhere alone. Understood?"

"I'm staying," Kreed said firmly, shifting his weight so he leaned close to me, a hand propped on the door frame above my head, claiming his spot beside me.

Brock laughed once, humorless. "In my house? Not a fucking chance, mini boss."

A smile curved on Kreed's lips. "I'll be wherever Kaylor is."

Micah ran his thumb over the top of the butter knife. "You really don't give up, do you?"

My cousin leaned back slowly in his chair, studying the middle Corvo. "I don't know whether to be impressed or annoyed."

Fynn dragged a chair out, dropped into it with a heavy sigh. "Something tells me that even if we beat the shit out of you that you still wouldn't leave."

"Brock," I protested, not in the mood to clean blood off the floors this damn early.

My cousin didn't spare me a glance, his focus solely on Kreed. "You'd welcome the pain, wouldn't you? Because you think you deserve it. I understand that too well."

A beat passed.

Brock just nodded once, like something unspoken had passed between them. A mutual understanding of the kind of damage men like them carried. He turned back to his coffee.

The tension didn't exactly vanish... It just redistributed. The rest of the room loosened slightly, the crew giving in to the fact that Kreed wasn't going anywhere. Not today.

And me? I stood in the eye of the storm, pulse pounding, mind spinning.

What the actual fuck just happened?

THE POP-IN VISIT from the Elite threw me off. When the front gate called about a car coming to pick me up, I'd completely forgotten Raine had sent it *and* that we were most likely going to be very late for school.

Josie, Ainsley, Mads, and Kenna had quietly gathered a few outfits they thought would fit me, laying them out like it wasn't a big deal, but it was. They had thought about me. Gone out of their way when I hadn't asked. When I hadn't even known I needed it.

The thought of wearing Brock's oversized sweats for another day hadn't exactly been torture, but the fabric swallowed me whole, reminding me with every step that nothing I had actually belonged to me. Slipping into something that didn't hang off my frame would be nice. Necessary, even. Kreed offered to have Mason and Maddox get what clothes they could from the house and drop them off after school.

Look at us working together. A sight I hadn't thought possible this morning.

Given that we only had a few minutes, I dashed upstairs to change and brush my teeth and hair before rushing out the door with Kreed still in his clothes from yesterday. Evan waited beside the black town car parked outside. He opened the door for us as we approached, Kreed nodding at him. "I brought a change of clothes for you," he said to Kreed before shutting the door like this wasn't the first time he'd picked him up early in the morning after being gone all night.

The soft hum of the car was the only sound between us as Evan drove, the morning light cutting angles through the tinted windows. I kept my gaze fixed on the blurred landscape, refusing to look as Kreed peeled off his shirt beside me. The quiet rustle of cotton sliding over skin was an all-too-vivid reminder of this morning. I didn't need to see his abs to recall the way they rippled under my fingers. Didn't need a visual when the memory was scorched into my brain.

God help me.

I pressed my cheek to the cool glass, trying to drown the rising warmth in my chest. Why was it suddenly so awkward to be alone with him?

When I finally glanced back, he was tugging a clean black tee over his head, muscles flexing beneath the fabric. The bastard was smirking at me.

I rolled my eyes hard enough to see stars. "You could at least pretend you're not proud of yourself."

"You could've snuck a peek, little raven. I wouldn't have minded. And it's not like we haven't seen each other naked."

"Let's get one thing straight," I snapped, sitting up straighter, pretending my pulse wasn't a damn drumline. "This morning shouldn't have happened. You caught me with my defenses down. That won't happen again."

His smirk deepened as if I'd issued a challenge instead of a boundary. "So no more sleepovers?"

I shot him a glare.

His grin faltered for a fraction of a second. "What happens when you have another nightmare?"

"I'll deal with it." I paused, eyes narrowing. "Just keep your lips and hands to yourself."

He leaned in slightly, not enough for Evan to notice but just enough to rattle me. "But I do my best work with these lips and hands."

Did he ever.

I turned away, biting the inside of my cheek until I tasted copper, trying not to give him the satisfaction of a blush.

Outside, the school gates loomed closer.

Inside, I was already unraveling.

You hate him. You hate him. You hate him.

It was getting harder and harder to hold on to that feeling.

Wait. Wasn't I supposed to be seeking revenge, going for the jugular? This was the perfect opportunity to crush Kreed, to rip his heart out, but sneaking a peek at him, I didn't know if I had it in me to be so coldhearted, not when my own feelings were a knotted mess.

I had to get it together, straighten out my head, or I'd end up another of Kreed's victims.

The town car rolled to a smooth stop at the edge of the student lot, the low purr of the engine fading as Evan stepped out and opened our door. Kreed climbed out first, already tugging on his backpack, and I followed, tucking a stray piece of hair behind my ear as I slid into step beside him.

We moved in unspoken sync across the lot, the steady crunch of gravel under our shoes oddly grounding, but the second we crossed into the courtyard, peace evaporated.

"Look who finally decided to grace us with his presence." Mason's smug voice rang out.

I didn't even get a chance to brace before an arm looped around my shoulder and yanked me into a very Mason-style chokehold. I stumbled with a surprised grunt as he leaned in and planted a kiss on the top of my head like I wasn't two seconds from stabbing him with a pen. "Morning, my little kitten," he said, grinning.

I shoved at his chest, but the bastard barely budged.

Kreed was on him a heartbeat later. "Keep your lips off her."

Mason just beamed wider as if poking the bear was his favorite pastime. "The gang is back together again."

Maddox sidled up beside us, shooting Kreed a narrowed look. "Where were you last night?"

Before Kreed could answer, Mason threw his hands out. "Seems obvious, doesn't it? They showed up together. Smells like sin and regret."

Kreed didn't take the bait. He slid his hand into his pocket calmly. "I'm staying with her."

That silenced them for all of two seconds.

"We're protecting her now?" Maddox asked as we strode up onto the sidewalk leading into school.

"It's not her fault what happened," Kreed replied.

Maddox's gaze narrowed. "Just because she sucks your dick doesn't make her one of us."

"Hey!" I protested, not that anyone gave a shit what I had to say. They just railed right over me like they had forgotten I was there.

A muscle feathered along Kreed's jawline. "Don't be bitter because she chose my dick over yours."

Mason's brows shot up. "Can we stop talking about your junk?"

"I'm being serious," Kreed bit out. "I don't want another death on my hands."

Maddox opened the school doors, the warmth beckoning me inside. "Is that the only reason you're staying with her?" he pried.

"Why does it matter?" Kreed countered. "I'm not asking you to get involved."

"But we *are* involved," Maddox said, stepping in behind us. "We're crew. Always have been. We don't let each other fall, and I'm not about to let you break up the crew over a girl."

"That wouldn't happen," Kreed muttered, his lips turning into that brooding frown.

Mason flicked my nose. "We seem to be breaking all kinds of rules for you, kitten."

"Dad won't like this," Maddox added, glancing down the hallway like Donovan might step out of the shadows.

"I'm done following his rules," Kreed said simply.

I became too aware of the number of eyes on us as the Corvo boys ushered me through school, and despite my attempts to break ranks and sneak off into the crowd, they seemed to always know, blocking me off.

Maddox clapped a hand to Kreed's shoulder. "Then you're not doing it alone. That's not how we work."

"For once," Mason said, sobering slightly, "he's right. Crew is crew. We do this together. Even when it's a disaster. With or without Dad."

Maddox risked death and slung an arm around my shoulders. "So that means we're staying too."

I'm sorry, what? I held up both hands like I could halt a freight train and stopped dead in my tracks. It took only a second for me to have three brooding Ravens glaring at me. "Absolutely not. I can't have all of you squatting at my cousin's house. This isn't some kind of crew stakeout."

Kreed removed Maddox's arm from around me.

"Why should it only be Kreed?" Maddox asked, tilting his head in that careful, observant way of his.

"We should take turns," Mason added, the glint in his light-green eyes pure chaos. "Fair is fair. Equal opportunity and all that."

Kreed's expression was flat and lethal. "As if I'd trust either of you alone with her."

Let Raven mayhem rain.

The boys started bickering with snarky remarks, growled threats, and shoulders squaring as if the school was suddenly a battleground. I groaned and shoved myself between them. "Does anyone care what I want?" I snapped.

Maddox snorted.

Mason huffed. "How much do you know about keeping someone alive? It's not as easy as it seems. Trust me. We know."

I narrowed my eyes. "Are you implying I'm a difficult case?"

"Yes," the three of them replied in unison.

I snapped my mouth shut as the bell rang. I was supposed to be in class.

Kreed rubbed a hand along his jaw, glancing over at Maddox and Mason. "I need at least one of you at the house. I want ears on the ground. Dad's been quiet...too quiet. He's holding something back about who the Viper informant is. I can feel it. He's got something on the bastard. We need to find out what and, more importantly, who."

Maddox tilted his head, smirking. "Still think we should rotate. Keep it fresh. What do you say, menace? You and me? A proper sleepover?"

We stopped at my locker, and I turned the dial. "Drop dead, Maddox."

Maddox's lips twitched. "That's my girl."

Kreed pressed his back into the locker beside mine, shooting his brother a cold scowl. "She's not yours."

Maddox shrugged one shoulder, completely unfazed. "Yeah, so you've said, but you're not the only one who gets to claim her."

I was starting to think agreeing to this was a bad freaking idea.

"No one is claiming me. Is that clear?" I shoved shit in my bag, uncertain it was the right stuff. I turned to look at each of them one by one. Mason with his lazy charm, Maddox with his calculated grin, and Kreed with his unreadable storm cloud gaze. "I'm not property. I'm not a prize. I don't belong to anyone."

The words hung between us, brittle and daring someone to challenge them, but none of them did. Instead, they all smirked, amused, like I was theirs anyway and they didn't need to say it out loud to make it true, and damn it, part of me hated how that didn't make me want to run.

It made me feel...anchored even if they drove me crazy. Even if they made me want to scream and punch walls and possibly commit actual crimes. I had them, and in a world like this, where loyalty was rare and betrayal was a currency, that meant everything.

The bigger question was, what the fuck was I going to do about them?

12

KREED

Practice hadn't even officially started, and already I was on edge. I sat on the bench beside Maddox, Mason, and Nash, watching the team warm up on the field. I didn't want to be here. Football no longer held the importance it once did or the release. I couldn't stop playing last night over in my head. The idea that someone had been lurking outside, someone who probably expected Kaylor to be alone, nagged at me the entire day. If I'd had a clearer head, if I hadn't indulged in so much alcohol, perhaps I would have been able to catch them before they were able to run off or hide.

"She needs security at school," Maddox said, his helmet dangling from his fingers, sweat glistening on his forehead.

Coach yelled across the field at Dylan, one of our defensive ends, as he landed flat on his back. "What the hell are you talking about?" I asked, my mind only partly listening to Maddox.

"You weren't here yesterday."

My spine stiffened, and I slid my eyes to him, getting this bad feeling that I was about to get pissed off. "So?"

"Well," Maddox continued with a shrug that was far too casual, "there was an incident. With Kaylor and a few guys from the team."

My jaw clenched hard, muscles ticking as a slow burn crept beneath my skin. I didn't like where this was going. "Define incident."

"We handled it," Mason assured, leaning forward on the bench, elbows resting on his knees as he let his helmet hit the ground.

Something was definitely up. I scanned the field, and that's when I saw them, Bodie, Dawson, and Keenan leaning against the bleachers with bruises blooming across their jaws. The sight flipped a switch. "Is that why their faces look like roadkill?"

"They're lucky it wasn't worse," Nash muttered. "If it had been you who found her—"

My hand curled into a fist. Blood pounded in my ears. "What the fuck did they do?"

Mason toyed with the strap of his helmet. "Don't freak out."

Too late. "You're telling me not to is only going to make things worse."

"Shit," Nash mumbled under his breath, and I sensed not a single one of them wanted to tell me what happened. If it was that bad, why hadn't Kaylor mentioned it?

Maddox sighed. "They cornered her in the guys' bathroom," he said, straight to the point. "We got there before it went too far, but it scared her."

I was up in an instant, a buzzing vibrating in my ears. "What the fuck. Why am I just now hearing about this?"

"Because," Mason gritted out, "we handled it. The last thing she needed was you going full-blown psycho and ending up suspended. Or worse."

"Don't dodge. I asked for details, not damage control," I growled, the familiar heat of anger coursing through my veins.

Mason got to his feet, leaving his helmet on the ground. "And I'm telling you—we were keeping you from going nuclear and getting suspended."

I let out a humorless laugh. "Guess that plan failed because now I'm exactly there. I'm about to make sure none of them can walk again unless one of you starts spilling details. Or I can just ask Kaylor."

"I'm surprised she hasn't already told you," Maddox said.

My fingers curled. "We haven't had a lot of time to talk."

Mason smirked. "Oh, I just bet. Who has time to talk when your lips are otherwise engaged?"

I didn't even dignify that with a response. "Give me their names. All of them. Or I'll just start picking the team off one at a time."

Nash looked at me. "I thought we were done killing people."

Tugging off my pads, I tossed them to the ground. "They should have considered that before laying a hand on her."

No one said anything, and I'd run out of patience. Fine. If they weren't going to volunteer the information, I'd take matters into my own hands. Someone was going to start talking, and I wasn't going to wait for permission.

I shoved off the bench and stormed across the field, vision tunneled. Dawson didn't even see me coming. Perfect. I launched at him with everything I had, tackling him like a battering ram straight into the turf. His helmet tumbled off his head as he hit the ground hard, a startled gasp tearing from his throat.

The entire field stopped. My knee pinned his chest, and I grabbed the front of his jersey with one hand, the other locking around his throat. "You ever lay a hand on her again," I snarled, my voice low, "and I'll fucking kill you."

"What the hell, Kreed? What is your problem?" he wheezed, fighting for air.

"You know damn well," I seethed into his face.

He tried to speak, but I squeezed just enough for the message to land. "I figured you didn't give a shit anymore," he struggled, hands trying to push me off him. "You never cared in the past."

Everyone else on the field knew better than to interfere unless they wanted to end up on their asses. I didn't have to think twice about watching my back because my crew would. "My personal business is mine. *And* even if I had lost interest, *she's* off-limits."

His eyes widened as I squeezed, just enough for him to understand I meant it.

"That goes for all of you," I added, projecting the threat loud and clear over the field. "One hand. One word. One fucking breath in her direction, and I'll bury every one of you."

A shrill whistle tore through the tension. "Break it up!" Coach roared from the sideline, storming toward us.

I released Dawson and stood slowly, breathing hard but steady. My gaze flicked to the rest of the team, who looked like they had just seen death walk across the field.

I didn't say another word.

I didn't need to.

I turned and stomped off the field, fire in my blood and one singular vow in my head: They would never touch her again.

PRACTICE HAD JUST WRAPPED UP, and a light dusting of snow began to fall, frosting the field in a thin white sheet. My breath fogged in the cold air as I headed toward the bleachers, slinging my gym bag over my shoulder.

That was when I saw her.

Kaylor sat in one of the middle rows, scowling down at her phone as if it had personally offended her. She was breathtaking, fat flakes of snow drifting slowly around her, giving her this frozen princess aura.

My lips curved downward, and I slowed my steps, drawn to her like gravity. "What's got you frowning so deeply?" I asked, dropping down onto the bench beside her, her nearness and scent expelling some of the fury churning within me.

She startled, her shoulders jerking. It took her a second to orient herself, blinking up at me like she forgot where she was for a second. Cute. She shook her head. "What?" She finally glanced up, her eyes landing on me. "Oh, it's you."

I wavered between amused and annoyed. "Who were you expecting?"

"Anyone but *you*," she replied, glancing out over the field at the snow.

"Liar." Little white flakes stuck to her long lashes, and I stared at them, my lips twitching. "You never answered the question. Who's making you frown, little raven?"

She sighed heavily. "It's Rusty."

My entire body bristled at the name. I didn't even try to hide the way my eyes narrowed. "What does he want?"

She shrugged, peering back down at the screen. "Just checking up. Making sure I'm okay. Telling me again what a mistake this is. Same shit. Different day."

I bit back a curse, my fists curling against my thighs. I didn't trust Rusty. Never had. Something about the guy rubbed me the wrong way, something slick beneath the surface he tried to hide, and it was more than him being the rival. "How very parental of him," I grumbled, settling my bag on the bench at my feet.

She rolled her eyes. "It's no secret he didn't agree with me coming back here," she added, a trace of guilt in her voice. "He'd rather have me tucked away in some cabin in the middle of nowhere, and he is doing his damn hardest to convince me."

I grunted. "That's not concern. That's control. Creepy as fuck, little raven."

Before she could answer, a noise snapped through the stillness, a crunch of boots on fresh snow. My head whipped toward the sound instinctively, my senses flaring to life. Without thinking, I reached for her hand and pulled her up from the bench. "We need to go." Those texts from Rusty were more than just checking in. I couldn't shake the feeling that he was confirming where she was. She might believe his concern was friendly, but my instincts pointed to somewhere else. He'd gone to such lengths to take her from us. He'd do so again.

She noticed the tension in my body, but smart girl that she was, she didn't question it. She followed my lead as I quickly walked, but not suspiciously, toward the school building. As we neared the side entrance, I leaned down, my mouth brushing her ear. "Someone's watching us. Don't react. Just keep moving."

Her body tightened against mine, but she didn't so much as flinch. Fucking proud of her for that.

We approached the maintenance building, and I spotted our opportunity, yanking her behind it and pressing her back against the freezing brick wall. Her eyes widened, about to complain, no doubt, but I shook my head and put a finger to her lips. *Silent. Stay still.* I tried to convey both with my eyes.

Two shadows appeared at the perimeter of the field, moving purposefully. I recognized the tattoos on the side of their necks immediately. Vipers. Fucking Rusty.

My heart hammered, instincts screaming to act. I could fight. I could take them, but it wasn't just me. I had Kaylor to think about, and if one of them even touched her, even for a second, I'd never forgive myself. It's what I would do if I were them... Use a distraction to grab the prize.

I needed a different play.

Voices echoed from the side of the building as a group of students spilled out, laughing and shoving each other, heading toward the parking lot.

Perfect.

I pulled Kaylor into the stream of kids, moving fast, keeping her tucked to my side, but not before one of the Vipers started to look our way.

Think fast.

Without hesitation, I grabbed Kaylor's face and kissed her. Hard.

She stiffened for a fraction before melting against me. I cupped the back of her head, angling her so her face was shielded from view. I didn't care who was watching. I didn't care if it was the whole damn world. All I cared about was keeping her safe, and maybe I let myself enjoy it for a beat longer than I should have.

Her hands fisted in the front of my hoodie, clinging to me like she didn't know where I ended and she began.

God help me, I don't want to stop.

But I forced myself to pull away, keeping my body angled between her and the Vipers as I slid my hand down her arm, lacing my fingers through hers. "Walk," I murmured against her temple. "Now."

She nodded, her face flushed, but she stayed glued to my side as we merged deeper into the crowd of students. I kept my senses honed, tracking the Vipers out of the corner of my eye. They lingered by the edge of the field.

Too late.

We slipped into the building, the door swinging shut behind us. I didn't stop until we rounded a corner and ducked into an empty stairwell, finally out of sight. Only then did I let myself breathe.

Kaylor shoved at my chest lightly, her brows furrowed. "What the hell was that?" she whispered harshly.

I dropped my forehead to hers, needing the contact, needing her to understand. "Until we find who the traitor is, I don't trust anyone. Whether you want to believe me or not, I'm trying to protect you," I said roughly. "They were looking for *you*."

Recognition sparkled in her eyes. Fear. Anger. The edges of both. "Vipers," she said quietly. "Why would Rusty..." Her voice trailed off. "I'm sure they were here to *persuade* me to come back to the shop. Rusty did say he wanted to send a couple of guys to watch the house. That protection probably extends to school."

"To keep you away from us." I tightened my grip on her hand.

Her throat bobbed as she swallowed hard.

For a second, I just stood there, forehead to hers, listening to the thunder of my heart trying to crack through my ribs. "Is that what you really want, little raven? To never see me again? To never have me touch you?" I swept the pad of my thumb along the inside of her wrist.

"You don't play fair, *Kreed*."

The use of my name was deliberate, knowing how it churned me up inside. I still couldn't figure out what it was about my name on her lips that made me so damn hard. Even now, under a stairwell probably covered in cobwebs, hiding, I wanted her. "It's the only way I know," I murmured, dragging my eyes from her lips.

"I'm not saying being cautious isn't wise, but I've known Rusty my whole life. He was my dad's best friend. He wouldn't hurt me. It's *you* who hurt me... Who I can't trust." Her voice was a soft tremor.

It wrecked me.

I moved fast, backing her into the wall, my hands slamming down on either side of her head, boxing her in. "You can trust me because of this," I growled, right before I covered her lips with mine. The kiss in the parking lot had been nothing compared to this. That had been a taste. A tease. This was a goddamn claim.

Her lips parted under mine, soft and eager, and the second her fingers curled into the front of my hoodie, yanking me forward like she needed me just as badly, I surrendered.

My hands found her waist as I pressed into her, chest to chest, thigh between hers, every inch of my body demanding contact. One hand slid down her side, fingers fisting at the hem of her shirt, and I was on the verge of losing myself entirely.

She gasped into my mouth, and I took it, swallowing it.

The kiss turned messier, hungrier. Desperate.

Our teeth clashed. Tongues tangled. Breath shattered between us like glass underfoot. She clawed her hands up into my hair and yanked, just hard enough to punch a groan from my throat. I pushed harder, needing her to feel everything I couldn't say. That I hadn't stopped wanting her. That the emptiness inside me had only gotten worse without her.

I was starved for her.

Every press of her mouth against mine burned into me, branded itself into memory. Her fingers trembled against my skin, clutching at me as if she was afraid I'd vanish the second she let go. I wouldn't. Not now. Not ever.

She tasted like guilt and want. Like salt and sweetness. Like a secret whispered in the dark.

I kissed her harder, deeper, tasting the sadness she tried to hide and wanting to consume every broken piece of it. Every broken piece of her. I wanted to rip it all from her and take it as mine. Break it apart. Shatter it into nothing.

She changed me. She wrecked me, and I'd let her do it again, a thousand times over, just to feel this. To feel her.

Her fingers dragged down my back, knuckles catching against the fabric, and her body tremored as I slid my hand up to cup her face, thumb brushing her cheek like I could erase the grief still hiding in her eyes.

Did I completely forget where we were when I shoved up her sweater and unclasped her bra? Yes. Did I care? Not in the moment, but these cursed straps needed to go, along with everything she was wearing. My lips craved to take the rosebud of her nipple. I settled for a quick brush of my thumb, reveling in the gasp that escaped her.

The problem was, it only spawned a stronger desire within me, and just sneaking a feel or two wasn't going to cut it for either of us. I had to feel her. I needed to hear her soft, breathy gasps.

I fumbled with the button on her jeans, moving my hand inside and under her panties. She gave me no resistance when I slipped two fingers inside her. She bit her lower lip, her head falling back. My fingers began to move as I pressed my lips to the sensitive spot below her ear. "Let go for me, little raven."

She shook her head, teeth still sinking into her lip even as her hips lifted to take my fingers deeper. My thumb flicked over her, drawing out a moan as she arched, moving with me as I stroked in and out of her.

"That's it, little raven," I coaxed, nipping at the column of her neck, my dick hardening as I watched her skin flush. I didn't think it could get harder. Boy, was I fucking wrong.

I was intoxicated by her.

My rhythm increased with the change in her breathing. Her nails dug into my back, her eyes squeezing shut. She was so wet, already on the brink of release. "Oh, God," she whimpered seconds before her muscles tightened around my fingers, pulsing as she climaxed.

The sight of pleasure on her face was so fucking beautiful, and knowing that I was the one who brought her such elation felt fucking good. I drew out her orgasm for as long as I could before slipping my fingers out, her body going limp.

"That's how school should end every day," I whispered along her jaw before leaning back.

"Shit" breezed through her lips, a hand forking through her messy hair. "Why did you—"

"Because I'm not always a selfish asshole." I made sure to flash her a dazzling smile, but it didn't have the desired effect. She still had this haunted glint in her light-blue eyes, the look that made me feel things I never let myself feel.

"Until you get tired of me," she whispered, sadness threading through her words like a needle through cloth, stitching wounds I wanted to tear open so I could heal them myself.

Those words nearly dropped me to my knees.

I gripped her chin gently, forcing her to look at me, making sure she saw the truth bleeding out of me. "I've tried to get you out of my head, little raven. I can't. I'm not built that way. You're not just a complication. And you're most definitely not just some girl. You're the only thing that makes this fucked-up life make sense." I cupped her face, my thumb dragging across her bottom lip with a reverence I didn't know I was capable of. "I never wanted a commitment. Never wanted the complication. But you—" I dragged my thumb slowly down the side of her throat, feeling the frantic beat of her pulse. "You're the only risk I'm willing to take."

She swallowed hard, her hands sliding from my neck to my chest, playing with the frayed strings of my hoodie like she didn't know what else to do with them...or herself. "I can't think when you're this close," she said breathily, her eyes glazed and dazed in a way that made my chest feel too tight, so goddamn sweet it nearly undid me.

"Good," I murmured against her mouth, stealing another kiss, slower this time, a deep pull that made her body melt against mine. "I don't want you thinking. I want you feeling everything."

"Kreed." She sighed my name, her fingers curling deeper into my hoodie, her body arching into me instinctively.

The press of her against every hard line of my body was pure torture, but it was a torture I craved. Would burn in hell to keep.

She was mine.

She just didn't know it yet.

But she would.

By the time I was done, there wouldn't be a single part of her that didn't know who she belonged to, and for once, I was ready to believe in something bigger than myself. Something that felt a hell of a lot like her.

I dragged my mouth from hers, only far enough to find the sensitive shell of her ear. "You're mine," I rasped, my voice a raw, guttural scrape against her skin. "You understand me, little raven? Every breath you take belongs to me now. Every shiver...every sound you make."

Her breath hitched, body trembling under my hands. God, she was so fucking responsive. So perfect.

She shook her head, her fingers flattening on my chest as she pushed me back. "It doesn't work like that. It's not that simple. This shouldn't have happened. You can't keep kissing me."

"So, you're saying you want me to kiss other girls? That I should touch them like I touch you? Let them put their hands on me?"

A flare of anger and jealousy streaked over her face. "Do whatever you want. We were never together, and we're not now."

"You're not running again," I whispered darkly, letting my teeth scrape gently down the line of her jaw. "You're staying. You're staying right here—with me." I kissed her again, stealing the tiny gasp that slipped from her lips, swallowing it like a drug I couldn't get enough of.

Nothing else existed. Not the cold bricks biting into her back.

Not the thin dusting of snow falling outside. Not the gnawing feeling that danger was still nearby.

Just her.

Just us.

The heavy thud of boots overhead jerked me out of the spell I seemed to fall under in her presence. Voices followed, a group laughing and talking as they came down the stairs above our heads.

Kaylor stiffened against me, quickly buttoning her jeans and adjusting her sweater, the dazed look in her eyes clearing.

Fuck.

My first instinct was to threaten whoever interrupted us, but I took her hand and led her out of the stairwell, knowing Evan waited for me in the parking lot. It was time we got the hell out of here.

13

KAYLOR

Evan pulled away from the curb, the black town car gliding smoothly into traffic as Kreed and I sank into the leather seats. The sky outside had turned a muted gray, the threat of a more serious snowstorm heavy in the clouds as perfectly shaped white flakes continued to dance from the sky.

With us tucked warm inside, Evan drove us toward the other side of town. Nothing was going to plan. The pompous ass just thought he could claim me, kiss me whenever he wanted, touch me. The worst part was that I let him. I liked it. Too damn much.

Only Kreed could bring me so much pleasure and rage within the same minute. One second, he made me feel treasured, and within the next, I was consumed with zapping jealousy at the thought of him with another girl.

Why did he put that image into my head?

Kreed's attention since I moved into his house had been solely on me. I hadn't seen him with other girls, and judging by my reaction, I didn't want to. It made me sick to think about him with anyone else, but how could I hate someone and still be so consumed? Possessive?

Affected? I didn't know what I felt anymore other than he made me feel.

I leaned my head back, exhaling. I just wanted one day without the world crumbling underneath me.

Tipping my head to the right, I glanced at the thorn in my side, studying his profile. His lips twitched slightly, knowing my gaze was on him. He had cuts on his knuckles and bruises that I hadn't noticed before. I grabbed his hand before I thought about it. "What happened?"

He shrugged it off, flipping his hand around to interlock our fingers. "Nothing. Just the repercussions of football."

Frowning, I pulled my hand away from his. "Why don't I believe you?"

A single dark brow shot up. "Are you worried about me, little raven?"

I snorted just as my phone buzzed in my pocket. Dropping his hand, I pulled out the device, Carson's face popping up on my screen. I caught Kreed's scowl as I answered and smiled faintly, pressing the phone to my ear. "Hey, Car—"

His voice came through in a frantic rush, tripping over itself, so fast I could barely make out the words. "Kay—oh my god—it's Kenny—I don't know what to do—I can't find her—no one's seen her—"

My stomach plunged. "Carson," I said, sitting up straighter. "Slow down. Take a breath. Tell me what happened."

Beside me, Kreed tensed, his focus snapping fully to me.

I hit the speaker button so he and Evan could hear too.

Carson took a shaky breath and tried again. "It's Kenny. She's missing."

My brain stuttered, refusing to process the words. "What do you mean, missing?" My fingers trembled around the phone, a sinking feeling forming in my gut.

"No one's seen her, Kay. Not since yesterday. She's not answering her phone. Her parents tried everything. They're filing a missing person's report right now." He was barely holding it together. "Have you heard from her? Anything?"

That desperate edge in his voice was raw and pleading, making my stomach churn. I almost wanted to lie to give him a fraction of hope, but instead, I stared blankly out the window, city lights smearing against the glass like watercolors, and whispered, "No. Nothing. I haven't talked to her since...the other day."

He swore under his breath. "This is bad. I have a horrible feeling. Shit. I don't know how it happened."

The color drained from my face. "When was the last time you spoke to her?"

"Yesterday morning. Before school. We had a fight." His voice dropped, thick with what I swore was guilt.

"A fight?" I echoed, meeting Kreed's troubled gaze for a moment. "About what?"

There was a pause. "It was stupid. We were arguing about you."

"Me?" My breath hitched. "What for?"

He didn't answer right away, and that told me enough. Whatever it was, it mattered, and it wasn't good.

Kreed shifted beside me, the leather creaking as he leaned forward slightly, eyes locked on mine.

Carson's voice pulled me back. "It doesn't matter. It was dumb. I should've let it go."

"You don't think she's really missing, do you?" he asked, rushing his words. "Maybe this is just one of her stunts. You know how she gets. She's impulsive. Dramatic. Maybe she just wanted attention or needed space or—"

"I'm sure it's something like that," I said quickly, too quickly. "Maybe she got stuck somewhere. Her phone died. Her car broke down or—"

"Her car's been at school since yesterday," Carson cut in. "She never drove home."

That froze me. "Since yesterday?" I repeated, my brows furrowing. "Why didn't you call me sooner?"

"I thought she'd show up! I really did. I kept checking my phone every hour, but then today, when she didn't come to school, I panicked. And when I got home—" He gulped. "The cops were already there."

My heart continued to drop as I shifted my grip on the phone. I was shocked I could still hold it. Nothing in my body seemed to want to function properly. "Did you track her phone?"

"Yeah. It's still pinging at the school. Like it never left. Can you try calling her? Maybe she'll pick up for you."

I nodded even though he couldn't see me. "I will. I'm coming over. You shouldn't be alone." I blinked hard against the pressure behind my eyes. "I'll talk to her parents. The police, if they're still there. We'll figure this out. Together."

There was a ragged breath on the other end. "We have to find her, Kay."

"We will," I vowed before ending the call. I stared out the window again, watching the world pass in a blur of gray and blue.

Kenny was missing.

Those words didn't fit in my mouth. They didn't feel real.

She was loud. Smart. Funny. Loyal. Literally the best friend anyone could ask for. She wasn't supposed to just disappear.

I fumbled with my phone in my hand like a lifeline. Kreed hadn't said anything, but his gaze was on me, waiting patiently. I didn't turn to meet it. I couldn't. Instead, I whispered to the dark interior of the car, "This can't be happening."

Not to Kenny.

Please, not to Kenny.

My call went straight to voicemail when I tried her number, and my texts went unread, but I had to try. The last fifteen minutes to my old neighborhood were fucking harrowing. I didn't know what to do with myself, my mind spiraling to the darkest possible scenarios. Kreed pulled my fidgeting hand into his, steady and strong, two things I desperately needed.

We pulled up to Kenny's house a few minutes later, the town car barely coming to a full stop before I was pushing the door open and stepping out into the cold. Evan called after me to wait, but Kreed was already there, rounding the car and falling into step beside me. "You're not going in alone," he stated.

I didn't argue.

There was no time.

As soon as I spotted the two cop cars, my chest seized; for a brutal, endless heartbeat, the afternoon bled away, and I was there again, standing in the cold, my parents' blood slick on the driveway, the wail of sirens clawing through the air louder than my own silent scream.

"Hey, it's going to be okay," Kreed said.

I nodded, drawing in a breath and lifting my chin. *I can do this.* For Kenny, I would do anything.

The porch lights spilled weakly across the dusting of snow, illuminating Carson's pale, stricken face as he yanked open the front door before we even reached it. "Kay," he said, pulling me into a desperate hug. His entire body shook. "God, I'm so glad you're here."

I hugged him back just as tightly, feeling the rim of his fear scrape raw against my skin. When we pulled apart, Carson finally noticed Kreed behind me, his eyes darting warily between us. I gave a small shake of my head and a pleading glance. The last thing I needed was the two of them to start shit. Carson seemed to understand, but he touched the side of his lip where the cut Kreed had left was still healing

Kreed kept his hand on the small of my back, a silent gesture of support I needed. "What the fuck is going on? Have they found her?" I rushed out. "Found anything?"

Carson had tears in his stormy, dark blue eyes. "She's gone. I don't think this is a prank. She's really missing."

My legs trembled, and I sank into Kreed, my back falling into his solid chest. I had to get a hold of myself. The only way we could find her was if we all kept our composure and a cool head. Falling apart wouldn't bring Kenny home.

The house smelled like coffee and something burnt, as if someone had forgotten a pot on the stove. Inside, the atmosphere was thick with despair. Kenny's mom sat on the couch, her face buried in her hands, shoulders heaving silently. Her dad stood stiffly by the fireplace, jaw clenched, talking to two uniformed officers with grim faces.

The severity of the situation hit me.

"Kaylor." One of the cops turned toward me, recognition flashing in his eyes. "We might need to ask you a few questions. Specifically, about the last time you spoke with Kennedy."

No one called her Kennedy. Not even her parents. "Kenny," I corrected. "She goes by Kenny, and whatever you need," I replied, my throat dry. "We last spoke a few days ago."

Kreed hovered a few feet behind me, his entire body humming with silent tension. He was a living weapon, poised to act if needed.

For once, I was glad he was here, not that he needed to know that.

The officer gave me a sympathetic smile and motioned toward the kitchen, away from Kenny's grieving mother. I followed, Carson and Kreed at my back like twin shadows.

As I walked, I couldn't shake the feeling coiling in my gut, the same sick twist of dread that had haunted me ever since Carson's call. Those girls who kept going missing over the last six months flashed through my memory.

There's no way she's *one* of those missing girls. I didn't even want to think about it.

Not Kenny.

Not my best friend.

Not the girl who spent almost as much time at my house as I did. Not the girl I'd spent hours on the phone with when we were supposed to be sleeping, talking about the future and boys and stupid dreams.

I tried to remind myself that she was smart. She knew all the dos and don'ts, all the shit girls had to think about when they were alone.

She couldn't have been kidnapped. There had to be a reasonable explanation for her disappearance.

The kitchen was dim, lit only by the fluorescent under-cabinet lights buzzing faintly. I perched on the edge of one of the chairs, my hands clasped in my lap to stop them from shaking.

Kreed stood behind me. Carson leaned against the counter, arms folded, his face pale but resolute.

The officer, Detective Harris his badge read, pulled out a small notebook and clicked his pen. "When was the last time you spoke to Kenny?" His voice was surprisingly gentle.

"T-two days," I stammered, voice scratchy. I cleared my throat and tried again. "I think. We texted that night. Just...normal stuff. Nothing serious." We'd been talking about Kreed and Carson and how much we hated guys. If I had known that would be the last time we talked... No, I refused to go there.

Harris scribbled a note. "No mention of plans? Meeting someone?"

I shook my head. "No. She said she had homework. She was going to stay in."

Another scribble. Another question. "Has she mentioned anyone new lately? Anyone she was seeing? Any new friends she was hanging out with?" He rapidly fired the questions.

"No." But even as the word left my mouth, a shadow of doubt fluttered in my mind. The truth was, I had so much going on in my life that perhaps I missed any signs of trouble or change in hers. We hadn't spoken as much since I transferred schools, but she'd been so fixed on Carson for so long, I never even considered there might be someone else.

The detective's pen paused. His eyes lifted to meet mine, shrewd and calculating. "Has Kenny ever talked about running away?"

"What?" I recoiled, anger flashing through my fear. "No. Never." The idea was preposterous. She loved her parents. She recognized how lucky she was and the privileges her parents allotted her. She'd never been a selfish person like most of the girls at the academy.

"That's absurd," Carson chimed in, mirroring my thoughts.

Kreed shifted behind me, the heat from his body seeping into my back, chasing the chill that had taken up permanent residency within me.

Detective Harris noticed, his lips pressing into a thin line. "We have to ask. Sometimes teens—"

"She didn't run away," Carson cut in. "Someone took her," he insisted. "It's the only thing that makes sense."

The detective's mouth pressed into a straight line. "We can't jump to conclusions, but we're exploring all possibilities."

What other explanation was there?

The cops had a few basic questions, but it seemed like they didn't have much to go on, which was beyond discouraging. With there not much else we could do, Kreed, Carson, and I left the Greys' household, promising Mrs. Grey that if we heard anything from Kenny we'd let her know immediately.

When we stepped outside, the ground was slick, covered in an inch of snow. My shoes crunched on the freshly blanketed white powder, leaving my imprint behind as we walked toward the car.

I glanced at the house I grew up in, the porch light casting a warm glow that once meant home. Now, it just felt foreign. Another family lived there. Another girl could be sleeping in my room, completely unaware of the memories soaked into those walls. My posters were probably gone, the scuff marks on the baseboards from my tap shoes painted over like I'd never existed. I couldn't wrap my head around the fact that I didn't live there anymore, that I'd never walk through that door again, never tan in the backyard with Kenny, or crash in the theater room for a movie night with bowls of popcorn and old blankets. It wasn't just a house... It was my life, and standing here now, watching someone else's light in my window, I felt the grief in a way I hadn't expected.

My phone buzzed. A single notification.

I frowned, pulling it from my pocket, seeing one message from an unknown number. The pit of my stomach twisted before my thumb even hovered over the screen. I halted as dread, pure, bone-deep dread, took hold of me.

The message lit up my phone with a quiet ping, unassuming. I shouldn't have opened it, but I did, and the second the image loaded, the world tilted. At first, my brain refused to process it. Then it hit me all at once, like a punch to the gut, and I gasped.

Oh, God, Kenny.

She looked so pale, deathly so, and every ounce of warmth had been leeched from her. Her wide, terrified eyes were ringed with smeared mascara, staring straight into the lens like she knew someone on the other end might still care. Might still come for her.

She was standing in front of a wall I didn't recognize, the backdrop nondescript and sterile. Hotel maybe. Warehouse. Wherever it was, it felt wrong. Cold.

She wore a skintight, glittery minidress that barely covered her thighs, an outfit she'd never wear by choice. Silver heels. Lips painted a harsh red though they trembled. Her hair, once so meticulously curled, now hung limp and stringy down her shoulders.

She looked like a doll someone had dressed up for a twisted game.

My stomach flipped.

My lungs forgot how to work.

A sob climbed up my throat, but I swallowed it, blinking hard as my vision blurred. I clutched the phone, wanting to reach through the screen, grab her hand, and pull her back.

Kreed, sensing the change in my form, immediately snatched the phone from my hand. A message had accompanied the photo.

She should be you. Will you give up your freedom for hers? If you don't, you'll never see her again.

Kreed swore violently under his breath, a pulse ticking at his temple as his grip on the phone tightened. "Who the fuck sent this?"

"What the fuck is it?" Carson barked. "What's wrong?"

Kreed didn't answer. He was staring at me instead. His jaw was locked, his whole body buzzing with violence he barely contained.

I turned away, pressing the heels of my hands into my eyes, trying to breathe, trying to think, but all I could see was Kenny dressed like...like she was for sale. Suddenly, I couldn't breathe. My chest hurt, each breath shallower than the last. The edges of my vision blurred, and my fingers went numb as panic climbed up my throat. I couldn't breathe. I couldn't think. The rush of blood buzzed in my ears.

Then Kreed was there, his hands gentle but firm on either side of my face. "Hey, hey—look at me, little raven," he said steadily. "You're safe. I've got you." I tried to shake my head, but he didn't let me pull away. "Breathe with me, okay? In...and out." His forehead rested lightly against mine as he mirrored slow breaths, over and over, until I started to match him, until the world stopped spinning, and my lungs worked again. "That's it," he whispered. "You're not alone. I'm right here."

It took a minute or two, but the edges of the panic attack slowly receded, and my breathing evened out.

Carson was watching us, his brows bunched together. He had my phone in his hand. "We need to show this to the police. They need to see this."

He was right. I had to march back inside and show this message to the cops. They would know what to do.

Kreed leaned in, grabbing my chin gently but firmly, forcing me to look at him. "Do you trust me, little raven?"

"What does that have to do with anything?" I retorted, my brain unable to predict where this was going.

"If you go in there and show the cops this text"—he held up my phone—"they'll kill her, and you'll still be in danger."

I couldn't let my mind entertain the idea of losing my best friend. "What do you want me to do then? I can't sit and do nothing."

"And we won't." Kreed snatched my phone from Carson to keep him from running off with it.

"This is bullshit," Carson hissed. "You're putting Kenny's life in *his* hands. The Kay I know would never be so reckless as to listen to this bullshit, not with her best friend."

I dragged my gaze from Carson to Kreed. "Are you suggesting I comply and give them what they want?" Which was me.

"No." His voice was lethal, a vow. "They're not getting you. Don't even think about it. I don't care who they are or how many of them there are. You are not going to them."

"But Kenny—" I started to argue.

"We'll get her back," he growled. "But we do it smart. We don't play by their rules. They want you scared, desperate. It makes you easier to control."

I didn't know what to do. I was so confused. How did I know which choice was better? Which road led to Kenny alive and home? "Do you know what you're asking of me?"

"I do."

Tears burned my throat, but I swallowed them down. There wasn't time for weakness. Not anymore.

Kreed's forehead rested against mine for half a second, grounding me. "Trust me," he whispered. "I'd burn them to the fucking ground before I let them hurt you."

I nodded shakily.

Because I had no choice.

Because deep down, even through the fear, I believed him.

"If you want my forgiveness, bring her home." It might not be fair to put such pressure and expectation on Kreed, but I was too distraught. This was my best friend, and I wasn't above playing dirty to save her.

I just hoped it wasn't a mistake.

14

KREED

Carson stormed off next door to his house. Good. He got in my way.

He made it very clear he didn't trust me, as he shouldn't, unless it had to do with Kaylor. This was one time I meant what I said. I didn't give a shit about him or what he thought. Hell, I didn't care about Kenny. I didn't even know her. The promises I made were for Kaylor. It was Kaylor I protected and would continue to do so. It was her. It had always been her.

She might not see it yet, but I did.

I had my theories about the sudden kidnapping of someone close to her, and I planned to explore them. Pulling out my phone, I sent the Crew a group message, telling them we needed to meet tonight. We had some shit to discuss. If we could uncover who the Viper traitor was, I was certain it would lead us to Kenny, and we had to move fast. If my suspicions were correct, it wasn't death waiting for Kenny. It was much worse.

I wasn't sure how Kaylor would handle the loss of someone else in her life. Especially to a sex ring. Finding her friend would keep Kaylor safe. Finding the traitor would keep Kaylor alive.

There had been whispers of the Vipers moving girls out of Elmwood, those no one would miss, for the last year, perhaps more, but people were talking about it more now that some of those missing girls were making headlines. Kenny wasn't their normal target. She didn't fit the mold of girls with broken or no homes, girls desperate to survive, or girls who wanted to get out of a shitty home life. The tricky bit would be safeguarding Kaylor while tracking her friend. We could afford no slipups. Evan alone wouldn't be enough. I needed my crew, and despite hating the idea, I would need my father's help and the Ravens. If anyone had details about the Vipers' activity, it was my father's crew. It had been too long since I paid a visit to the Rooftop.

Distancing myself from the Ravens would have to wait. I never thought anything could drag me back. This was why I loathed feelings. They made you do shit you promised you wouldn't ever do or, in my case, do again.

I snuck a glance at the girl who had changed my world to see how she was faring. Comforting girls in distress wasn't my specialty. I didn't know what to say or do. It summoned this protective feeling she instilled within me. I didn't fully understand why, of all the girls I'd been with, what made her different, a puzzle I wasn't sure I'd ever solve.

She couldn't sit still. Her knees bounced like she was trying to shake the nerves out of her. Fingers picked at the already ragged edge of her nail, and her gaze, vacant and unfocused, stared straight through the tinted glass window.

I didn't say anything. Just watched her, cataloging every subtle crack in her armor, but she sensed my gaze, turning toward me slowly, her legs folding in as her body curled slightly. "You think it's the Vipers. Don't you?"

Her eyes locked on to mine, wide, haunted, and too perceptive. She was tucked beside me in the back of the town car as Evan took a turn ahead.

She hadn't asked to live this life. She hadn't asked to be part of the game, but the heaviness in her gaze told me she was starting to understand, starting to see that trust was paper-thin. That crew life wasn't roses, it was rot, and some of us were already too far gone to crawl back out.

I blinked slowly, swallowing the burn in my throat.

She was figuring it out. That someone had betrayed her father. That monsters didn't always wear masks. There were dark corners of this world, and people would do all sorts of evil things when greed and money were involved. They might tell themselves their needs were more important than someone else's, but it was all excuses and bullshit.

I knew damn well the things I'd done, the pieces of my soul I'd lost, and I'd done so willingly. I was rarely the hero... Except with her, but I wouldn't classify what I was doing as heroic. It was selfish.

"I don't think it's a coincidence your best friend was taken," I said at last, voice flat with restrained fury.

Her brow furrowed, pain lacing every syllable. "Why not just kill me?" she whispered. "Why take her?"

I exhaled. "Because this isn't about quick revenge. They want leverage. Something they can use to keep you obedient. Killing you would create too much noise. With your parents' deaths already under suspicion, you drop next, and suddenly, the cops actually start asking questions. They can't risk that. This isn't personal. It's business. Cold. Calculated."

She looked down, her hand falling into her lap, clamped in a fist she didn't realize she'd made. "They're the ones who took those other girls... Aren't they?"

I didn't answer immediately.

Did I think it? Yeah. Deep down, I fucking did, but knowing and proving were different beasts. "It won't help to jump to conclusions," I replied. "Not until we're sure."

"I'm not asking for proof. I'm asking you. Your opinion. Just say it, Kreed. Say it's possible." Her lip trembled, but she forced it still. Her spine stayed straight even though she was on the verge of losing her composure.

I wanted to hide her from this side of the world. She'd already seen and witnessed traumatic shit, but if she stayed in my world, she would see more. I should be protecting her from myself. I was as much of the problem. Perhaps that was one of the reasons I wanted to be the solution, to correct a wrong. I had to start somewhere, and if I wanted her to trust me, I needed to be honest with her despite how dark the truth might be. She deserved the truth.

"Yeah. I think it's highly likely. All the more reason you shouldn't be involved. I'll take care of it. We'll find her," I promised, one I fully intended to keep while also keeping her safe. This needed to end, and I had a feeling before it was over, rules would be broken, lives would be altered, and there wouldn't be enough Vipers left of them to bury. I would kill for her. I would burn this whole fucking town to the ground if it meant keeping her safe. If the Vipers wanted a war...

They were about to get one.

Her throat bobbed, and for a brief moment, she looked...tired. Exhausted.

We pulled up to Brock's place, and even before Evan killed the engine, I sensed something was brewing inside... Something unpredictable and volatile.

I stepped out first, scanning the quiet street. Too calm.

Kaylor moved like a ghost beside me. She wasn't okay, and I didn't know how the hell to fix it. Not yet.

Brock swung open the front door before we reached the steps. His eyes locked on her, then slid to me. One look was all it took. He could tell something horrible had happened. Kenny's disappearance hadn't hit the news yet, so unless Kaylor had texted him, he didn't know what had occurred.

I handed him the phone without a word.

He took it, glanced at the screen, and everything about him changed. His face turned to stone. "Jesus Christ," he muttered, those cynical aqua eyes crystallizing.

Josie appeared behind him, peering over his shoulder as strands of pink hair fell into her face. "Shit," she whispered, her eyes flying up to Kaylor. She stepped past Brock to Kaylor, putting her arm around my girl. "Let's get you a drink."

I didn't know much about Brock's girlfriend, but I liked the way she handled situations because fuck if a stiff drink wasn't in order. Kaylor needed something to relax her.

Brock left the door open as he followed Josie and Kaylor down the hall. I assumed that was as much as I was going to get for an invitation inside. He still had Kaylor's phone, so I trailed behind, swinging the door shut behind me.

The rest of the crew filtered in from the living room like blood called to blood. Grayson. Micah. Fynn. Kenna. Mads. Ainsley. I'd spent years trying to keep my distance from this pack, but right now, I was fucking glad we were on the same side.

Brock passed Kaylor's phone around to the guys. The reactions were so similar, shock quickly giving way to fury. "They sent this picture ten minutes ago," I said, leaning against the wall. I was too turned up to sit. Josie had Kaylor at the table with the other girls. My gaze flicked to her before I continued. "It came from an unknown number with a threatening message demanding Kaylor trade herself for her best friend's life."

No one dared speak for a beat.

Micah broke the silence. "They want to swap her?" He laughed, but it was hollow and dangerous. "What the actual fuck is this?" He dropped Kaylor's phone in the center of the island, forking his fingers through his blond hair as Mads pulled out glasses from the cabinets behind him.

"No one's taking Kaylor anywhere," Brock stated. "We've got connections. We can try and trace the number, see if we can get a location."

"Doubt it," I muttered. "Burner phone. No metadata. These guys aren't amateurs."

Fynn was already moving, pulling out his laptop. "Still checking.

There might be something. A reflection. A shadow. Anything. They might not be amateurs, but even the pros fuck up, and I'm extraordinarily good at finding mistakes, even the tiniest misstep."

Grayson handed me a beer, and I gave him a quick nod of thanks. Beer wasn't my go-to drink, but I didn't want to get shitfaced. I needed to keep a clear head. I accepted the bottle as a gesture of goodwill, but I wouldn't be finishing it.

Everyone was moving. Planning. Throwing out ideas. Talking at once, and it made me realize I needed my crew. Without Raine, Maddox, Mason, and Nash, I wasn't doing anything. The Elite weren't the only ones with connections. I pulled out my phone, shooting Raine a message.

Me: **Need a meeting at the Rooftop. Can you send out the notice?**

Raine: **Names?**

Me: **Everyone.**

Raine: **Should I be concerned?**

Me: **I'll fill you in later tonight.**

Shoving my phone back into my pocket, I took a swig of my beer, my eyes searching out Kaylor. She was staring into her half-drunk glass of what I thought might have been bourbon Josie had poured her. I didn't want to leave her, but with a house full of people, she wouldn't be alone. Dropping my barely touched beer into the sink, I strode across the kitchen, bending down to murmur in her ear. "I'll be back."

She grasped my arm. "You're leaving?"

I nodded. "Just for a few hours. You'll be safe here."

"Where are you going?"

I brushed a kiss against her cheek, just below her eye, where the skin was still soft and a little flushed from the bourbon. "To earn your trust back, little raven."

THE NIGHT AIR bit through my hoodie as I pulled it closer around me, but it didn't touch the fire burning in my chest. Not tonight. Sliding into the town car's back seat, I met Evan's gaze in the rearview mirror. "The club," I said, giving him no other direction or information.

The Rooftop wasn't just a name. It was the top floor of my father's club with floor-to-ceiling windows and a private elevator coded with fingerprints and blood. A place where decisions were made, dealings were arranged, laws were broken, and lives were threatened.

Raine leaned against the bar when I stepped inside, flipping a butterfly knife between his fingers. The steel flashed under the overhead lights, but his eyes were dark and focused. "Are you going to tell me what this is about?" he asked without preamble.

I nodded once. "Everyone here?"

Raine smirked. "Even the old-timers showed. They're curious what could drag Kreed Corvo out of the dark."

The Rooftop was dim, lit only by the overhead pendant lights swinging slightly in the draft like a noose waiting for a neck. The air smelled of old cigar smoke and stronger liquor, and the floor-to-ceiling windows reflected back our silhouettes.

Every chair around the long, black glass table was filled. Crew from all corners of Elmwood, some still in their varsity jackets, some in weathered leathers, scarred hands folded or fidgeting, the smell of blood still faint on a few, sat shoulder to shoulder. Ex-cons, hustlers, and legacy members who'd grown up under Raven rule just like me. The Ravens didn't do temporary. You didn't walk away from the brotherhood unless you were in a box. Even then, they found a way to drag you back.

I hadn't stood in this room since the day I told my father I was done being his damn puppet. That was before he brought Kaylor into our house. Before she tore everything I thought I wanted to hell.

Now I was back because of her.

Mason slouched to my right, tapping a ring against the table.

Maddox leaned against the edge, arms folded. Raine was on his phone near the bar, only half paying attention but somehow listening to everything. Nash sat next to his father.

I didn't waste breath. "We've got a problem," I said, letting the room fall quiet. "What do we know about the missing girls?"

Heads turned. Conversations cut short. Chairs creaked. All eyes found me.

"Who's taking them?" I continued. "Where are they being held?"

Slate, one of the oldest at the table, gray at the temples, but still mean as hell, tilted his head. "Since when do we have an interest in human trafficking?"

"We don't," Huntley added. "It's never been our business or our style."

I pulled out my phone, slammed it face up on the table, and tapped the screen. The picture I'd forwarded to myself from Kaylor's cell glared back at us, Kenny pale and terrified, dressed like bait in a barely there minidress, eyes wide with silent screams.

Curses whispered around the table.

"She's the latest girl to have gone missing, and she just happens to be Kaylor Steele's best friend. Coincidence?" I arched a brow. "I don't think any of us would buy that."

"Shit," Briggs hissed under his breath. He leaned forward. "You think the Vipers?"

"I don't think," I snapped. "I know. This isn't a one-off. It's organized. Someone's running auctions in our city *and* making bank while they do it."

"Why do we care?" Cash asked. "You screwing the girl or something?"

Mason choked on a laugh. Maddox just lifted his chin, daring Cash to keep talking.

This was personal for me, but the crew didn't realize just how personal Kaylor and I were. I wanted to keep it that way. The less involvement she had, the safer she was, not just from the Vipers but from these guys sitting around the table. Once my father found out about this meeting held behind his back, I'd have to deal with the repercussions, but I was willing to pay them, regardless that it would put me deeper into Raven business, the very thing I'd been distancing myself from.

"No," I lied smoothly. "We care because it's a direct threat to our hold on the city. The Vipers are escalating. They're poaching from our streets, our clubs, our kids."

Raine finally slid his phone into his jacket. "We're losing face. That auction brings in high rollers. If we don't shut it down, they'll start thinking Elmwood belongs to them, and the Vipers will move into our territory."

"Which is the exact opposite of what we've been working toward," I said plainly, no bullshit. "This girl isn't their target." I picked my phone back up and held Kenny's picture up, forcing them to look at her. "She is a tactic to get Kaylor, which interferes with our plans." My father's plan that was, but everyone in this room knew the game, knew it wasn't just revenge my father sought. His grand scheme was to be the only crew in Elmwood, and taking out Kaylor's father was only a piece of the pie.

Hector cracked his knuckles. "You think someone inside is involved?"

"I think someone's talking. Or too scared to admit they know something. Either way, we're going to find out."

Raine stepped forward. "So we start rattling cages?"

"No." I held his gaze. "We start flipping them. I want ears on every block. You hear anything—anything—about missing girls, new players in town, side doors opening, whispers of movement at the docks, warehouses...I want names. I want locations. I want leverage. They're bold enough to try and force her hand by coercing her to walk into their trap on her own. We can't let that happen."

Raine placed his palms on the table as he leaned over it. "They're testing us. Seeing how far they can push. I'm done letting them play in our shadows."

"I think someone in the Vipers is running the operation," I said. "And someone in our backyard knows more than they're saying."

"The first step in getting the Vipers out of Elmwood is to take down this ring. No more underground auctions selling minors. It's bad for our business," I stated.

"Is this coming from you or your father?" someone from the back asked.

I didn't flinch. "I wouldn't be here if he didn't agree." A lie, but I'd worry about Daddy Dearest later.

Mason glanced sideways at me, lips twitching. He knew. They all did, but no one called me on it.

"This started personal," I continued. "But it's not just about Kaylor anymore. If this auction ring keeps expanding, drawing in buyers with sick fucking fetishes and deeper pockets, it cuts into every business we own. Strip clubs. Casinos. Trade routes. The next girl they take could be someone connected to this table."

That landed like a blow.

Some of them had daughters.

Most had sisters.

All had something to lose.

"Shit," Slade muttered.

I let that sink in. They had families, and what we all had in common was that we were here to provide for them, to keep them protected.

"Word is the next auction is in two weeks," Raine informed, straightening. "We need to shut it down before it happens."

I looked around the table. "They think they're untouchable. Let's prove them wrong."

Hector nodded. "I'll call in my guys."

Slate cracked his neck. "You'll have eyes on the docks by midnight."

Briggs muttered, "I'll check the southside clubs. There's a new face working security, too clean for the job."

A flicker of agreement passed through the room.

Mason's knuckles drummed against the table. "We're going to blow up their little kingdom."

"Start with the shadows," I said, already turning for the door. "That's where they hide their monsters." And one by one, they stood.

Old blood. New blood. United for one thing. Not because I asked but because they finally saw it, too.

The Vipers were coming for us.

And we were ready to bleed them dry.

15

KREED

When it was just the four of us left, me, Raine, Maddox, and Mason, I moved to the balcony, pushing through the heavy glass door and stepping into the night. Elmwood spread out below, streetlights flickering over cracked sidewalks, casting shadows that stretched like reaching hands. From up here, the city didn't look broken, but I knew better. It was rotting from the inside out.

I leaned on the steel railing, fingers curled forcefully enough to creak the metal. Behind me, footsteps thudded. Familiar weight. Familiar silence.

Maddox and Mason flanked my sides, Mason already flicking a lighter, the tip of a cigarette glowing red before he passed it to Maddox. Raine stood back, watching the skyline as if it held answers.

I drew in a deep gulp of the harsh air, letting the ice burn my lungs, exhaling in a puff of white fog. The cold didn't clear the anger out of me. Nothing could.

Maddox exhaled a cloud of smoke. "You should have called and filled us in before the meeting."

Taking the cigarette he offered, I drew in a drag. "There wasn't enough time. I had to move fast. The longer they have Kenny, the more danger Kaylor is in."

I passed the smoke to Mason, who took a long pull, filling his lungs. "You really think it's the Vipers?"

"Before Kaylor, I hadn't given the missing girls much thought, nor who was responsible," I said, my voice low. I'd been too preoccupied with my own rage to care. "But since Kaylor, I've been paying more attention. We know there's a traitor among them, and that person has a motive. They took Kenny to get to Kaylor. It's a warning shot."

Raine frowned, flicking his switchblade open and closed. "Her friend is a fucking message, and we'd be idiots not to read it."

"They could've killed her," Mason added, tapping the slim white stick, sending ash tumbling over the side of the railing. "But they didn't. That's not random."

"No," I said. "That's strategy."

Maddox held out two fingers toward his twin, signaling for the cigarette. "They're watching Kaylor," he said, bringing the smoke to his lips. The ember glowed orange against his face, casting harsh shadows over his angular features. "Maybe have been for weeks."

"Scouting her," Raine agreed. "Testing her reactions. And ours."

Mason let out a short, dry laugh. "And they were stupid enough to take her on school grounds."

"Bold," Maddox corrected, expelling a puff of smoke that disappeared into the night. "Or desperate."

"Do we have any guesses who?" Mason asked.

I finally peeled my eyes from the city and looked at them, at the ones who'd bled beside me, tortured with me, carried secrets so deep they didn't have names anymore. "Rusty. We start with him, her father's partner and friend."

Raine cursed under his breath. "It's always the friend."

"He probably had a secret hard-on for Kaylor's mom," Mason said with clinical detachment, "and now he wants the daughter."

"Don't even fucking joke about that."

Mason's lips twitched. "I like this new look on you."

A single brow shot up. "And what look would that be?"

"Jealous boyfriend," Mason replied. "It's a step up from the brooding asshole."

I grimaced. "First, I'm not her boyfriend. And second, I prefer being an asshole."

Raine glanced at me, shaking his head. "You would."

"They think we're fractured," I said, getting us back on track. "That I've gone soft. That she's a weak spot."

"She is," Mason said but not cruelly. "And you're not soft, not where she is concerned. Anyone with eyes can see that."

Maddox took another drag, his pale gaze fixed on something beyond the balcony. "Selling her off would be a good way to silence Kaylor without the heat of another dead body."

He wasn't wrong.

The image of Kaylor bound and forced into some underground trafficking ring clawed at my insides. Selling her off would silence her and punish me in the process. Clean. Cold. Strategic.

And it made my blood boil.

My fingers curled into fists at my sides, the burn of my nails digging into my palms the only thing keeping me from putting another hole in the wall.

"What's the move?" Raine asked, tone clipped.

"Let me see that picture again," Maddox said with the cigarette dangling between his lips as he held out his hand.

I reached into my pocket, fishing for my phone, and passed it off to him. I'd forwarded the photo from Kaylor's cell to mine earlier. He zoomed in, eyes narrowing as he scrutinized the details again. Maddox was always the more meticulous one out of the four of us. "She's not alone. Look," he said moments later. "Here—do you see?"

We all leaned in. He enlarged the far edge of the frame to a mirror in the corner of the room, slightly cut off. A sliver of someone else reflected in the glass. Big. Male. Tall. Bearded. His face wasn't visible, but I'd bet my life that it was Rusty. He was the one behind the camera.

"Fucking monsters. I'll kill him," Mason growled, always the first to lean toward violence.

He wasn't the only one. My vision turned red, painted with blood I was eager to spill.

"We need to put a tail on Rusty," Maddox said. "Follow him. See who he talks to. Where he goes."

"Not just Rusty," I said. "We need to know who he's working with. Who else helped move the girls. There's no way he did it alone."

"That's a long list," Mason said. "Too long for just us."

I hesitated. I hated what I was about to say. "You're not going to like this," I muttered. "But we need help. We need the Elite. Kaylor's already involving Brock. If we don't work with him, she'll do it behind our backs."

"I don't like it," Maddox said immediately. "We don't bring outsiders in."

"If it keeps her from running straight into the Vipers' Nest," I ground out, "I'll break every damn rule we have."

Maddox gave me a grin, eyes flashing. "Well, fuck. Didn't think I'd live to see the day."

Mason flicked the butt of the cigarette, grinding it under his boot. "We don't let anyone touch what's ours."

I turned back to the skyline, the city glowing soft and golden under a sky too calm for the war we were about to bring. "They're already dead," I whispered. "They just don't know it yet."

And when we were done, they'd never forget the name Kaylor Steele. They'd sure as hell never come near her again.

Or they'd beg for death long before we gave it to them.

THE COLD FOLLOWED me up the steps. I kept my hood low as I slipped around the side of Brock's house, boots silent on the gravel path. The porch light was off, no dogs barking in the neighborhood, just the whisper of branches scraping against the roof and the dull hum of tension in my chest.

I keyed in the security code like I'd done it a hundred times. Brock hadn't changed it. That said something. Maybe trust. Maybe stupidity. Hard to tell these days.

The lock gave a soft click, and I pushed the door open, softly shutting it behind me, and came face-to-face with a glint of steel. It was hardly the first time I had a weapon shoved into my face. Doubt it would be the last. I didn't move, didn't flinch, just stared down the gun barrel. The safety was off. Finger poised on the trigger, and Brock's eyes didn't blink.

But neither did mine.

Fuck.

So much for thinking I'd earned any trust.

Then again, I was sneaking into his house in the middle of the night, but he had to know I'd come back, that I wouldn't leave her alone. Clearly, she wasn't alone. He'd stayed. Did that mean his friends were also here?

A long second passed. Then he lowered the weapon with a grunt. "It's a good thing you've got a recognizable face. Two more seconds, and your blood would've painted my damn walls."

I arched a brow, slowly stepping farther inside. "You're saying that like I've never had a gun pointed at me before."

From the shadows, the rest of the Elite emerged. Micah near the stairs, Fynn from the hallway, and Grayson posted by the windows like a damn sentry. They hadn't come to talk but to interrogate me.

I crossed the kitchen and leaned against the counter, arms folding across my chest. "All right. Let's cut the bullshit. Say what's on your minds."

Micah went to the fridge and pulled out a beer. He twisted off the cap with a flick of his wrist, the metal clattering onto the counter. "We want the truth," he said, bringing the bottle to his lips.

"Everything you know. Start from the top," Grayson added.

I glanced at the gun still resting on the counter in front of Brock, its matte black surface catching the overhead light. "All you had to do was ask. The gun's a bit extra." No one smiled or laughed. Sighing, I gave them the rundown of the Vipers' possible involvement and the upcoming auction. I didn't dress it up. Didn't soften the edges, but I didn't give them everything either.

Not yet.

"And if I'm sharing, so are you," I finished, turning the tables. "I don't spill and tell for free. No more secrets."

No one jumped at the chance to agree to my terms. I wasn't exactly in a position to negotiate, outnumbered four to one with a loaded weapon within arm's reach of their leader, but that didn't stop me from trying.

Finally, Brock's head moved in a slight nod. The motion was reluctant, like it physically pained him to make the concession. "If it means we get Kenny back sooner, fine. A temporary truce seems manageable." He leaned forward slightly, those piercing aqua eyes fixing on mine with laser focus. In the dimly lit kitchen, they seemed to glow with an otherworldly intensity. The gun remained on the countertop between us, a silent reminder of the power dynamic at play. "You have a suspect?" he asked, his voice carrying traces of authority that made people confess to crimes they hadn't committed. "Someone you think is behind this?"

I hesitated.

It was one thing to talk strategy with my brothers and quite another to give away what might be my ace. But this was different. This was the Elite. Kaylor's family.

How much could I trust them? The question gnawed at me as I studied their faces. Any one of them could tip off our suspect, intentionally or otherwise. Information was currency in our world, and once I spent it, there was no getting it back.

My gaze drifted toward the hallway that led to the stairs, toward the room where Kaylor was sleeping. Safe. Protected because Brock had put everything on the line to make it so. When it came to her, he'd already proven he'd sacrifice whatever was necessary.

He wasn't the only one.

So would I.

"I've got a name," I said, eyes locking with Brock's. "But it's not confirmed."

"Let's hear it." Micah set his beer down with a soft clink.

I had nothing to lose and everything to gain. "Rusty." Not an ounce of shock rippled through the room, and it justified my suspicions. "You already suspected he might be more involved," I concluded.

Brock's jaw tightened almost imperceptibly. "We learned long ago that no one is who they portray themselves to be."

Fynn stepped forward, his movements fluid and predatory. He'd been the quietest of the group, but now his attention was laser focused, which in my experience made him someone I shouldn't underestimate. "What makes you think he's involved?"

I shrugged. "Call it a hunch."

Grayson scoffed. "You expect us to go on a hunch?"

I pushed off the counter, straightening to my full height. The marble was cold against my palms as I gripped the edge. "Believe what you want, but I don't trust him. Not with Kaylor. Someone betrayed her father, and my money is on the best friend. If I had to guess, her father discovered Rusty's side business, and he was using club resources to fund it."

"You have any proof?" Brock asked.

"Not yet, but I'm working on it. Why don't *you* trust him?" I threw the question back at them, curious if they had anything more substantial than intuition and doubt. The way they'd reacted, or hadn't reacted, to Rusty's name told me there was history there.

"Rusty and my uncle might have been friends, but I remember there being tension between them a few times at gatherings. Kaylor doesn't know this. I never told her, but at their crew parties, I saw Rusty make a move on her mom. He might have been drunk, but it was no excuse. She made it clear she wasn't interested, and let's say he got a little forceful until he saw me. I have no respect for someone who disrespects his friend by hitting on his wife, especially in the way Rusty did. It rubbed me wrong. To this day, I don't know if she ever told my uncle what Rusty did."

I agreed with Brock, and what he was telling me only backed up my suspicion of Rusty's character. He wasn't a nice guy and was just like someone my father would recruit. The pieces were slowly fitting into place. "We need to put a tail on him. Someone skilled enough that Rusty won't notice."

His aqua eyes glinted with what might have been anticipation as he exchanged a quick glance with Micah. "We know someone," he said, his voice carrying the quiet confidence of someone who'd already thought three steps ahead. "Consider it handled."

Brock's eyes narrowed to slits, the muscle in his cheek twitched once, twice, before he leaned forward across the counter. "Why didn't you tell us sooner?"

I ran a hand through my hair, buying myself a moment to choose my words carefully. "Because the second I point a finger without solid proof, the Vipers start sniffing around for answers. They'll want to know how I know, who told me, what evidence exists. And if I'm wrong about Rusty... Kaylor's the one who pays the price for my mistake."

No one argued with that.

"We don't have to trust each other, but if we want to take him down, we need to work together," Brock said.

Micah rolled his shoulders, working out tension that had been building since this conversation started. "Can we do that without killing each other?"

"You're the one with the gun," I reminded.

Grayson's expression twisted into a snarl. "As if you don't have one stashed in the house or a knife in your pocket."

My lips curved. "Touché."

Micah's laughter rumbled up from his chest, deep and genuine. He shook his head as if he couldn't quite believe the situation we'd found ourselves in. "Who the hell knows?" he said, dimples flashing as his grin transformed his entire face. "Maybe we'll end up friends when this nightmare is over."

"Don't count on it," Grayson muttered.

Fynn coughed and then cleared his throat.

"Well, regardless, this is going to be a hell of a team-up." Micah smirked as he pressed the beer bottle to his lips.

The cocky grin reminded me too much of Mason's. They had the same carefree, nothing-mattered playboy vibe. Having two of them on the same side seemed a reckless combination. "Is he always like this?"

"Yes," three in-unison confirmations echoed in the kitchen.

Brock's gaze didn't leave mine. "I had my doubts about you after the shit at the warehouse. I still do, but you showing up here, putting in the effort to protect from not just a potential killer but your father, means something and hasn't gone unnoticed by me. But...if you fuck up, fuck her over again, or hurt her, and I don't just mean physically, we'll end you."

Four very intimidating guys smiled at me. Not in a friendly manner but in a way that said they would take pleasure in causing me pain. I understood the threat all too well.

I wasn't sure how to feel about having Brock and the Elite watch me, but I was hardly surprised. "If I screw up again, I'll offer myself to you on a fucking gold platter."

Brock nodded, accepting my response.

It was time to add some ground rules of my own. "That being said, I want Kaylor involved as little as possible, and I don't want to tell her about Rusty until I have proof. I don't want to create any false hope or tip off the traitor by her being unable to control her emotions. She's been through enough. And if I'm going to keep her from doing something reckless, I need to know she's safe."

"We all have people we want to protect, but from personal experience, the girls in our lives don't like to be left out. We've learned the hard way about keeping them in the dark. You might want to rethink your strategy, mini boss," Grayson said, giving me unsolicited advice.

I didn't like the nickname or the advice.

The air had been cleared, and the Elite and Ravens knew exactly where they stood with each other. Now we'd just had to see how well we could work together. It should be interesting, to say the least.

Leaving the Elite in the kitchen, I headed upstairs, half expecting Brock to stop me or ask me where the hell I thought I was going. He didn't. Perhaps he could see that I needed her as much as she needed me, especially tonight. Those nightmares of hers wouldn't stay quiet for long. I knew from experience they always came crawling back when your guard was down, when the world went dark and silence made space for the shit you'd buried. Night didn't forgive. It reminded.

It wouldn't have made a difference if he tried to stop me. Lucifer himself couldn't have kept me from her room.

The door to her bedroom was cracked just enough for a sliver of hallway light to slash across the floorboards. Quietly, I reached out, fingers brushing the cool handle, and nudged the door open with a slow push. The hinges didn't creak. I slipped inside, the air faintly sweet with the scent of her, vanilla and something warmer underneath that made my lungs stutter if I breathed too deeply.

My eyes landed on her instantly. Kaylor was curled in on herself, limbs tangled in the blankets. Her face was half buried in the pillow, one hand clutching the edge, the barest crease between her brows. Even in sleep, she couldn't let go of whatever hell still haunted her.

It hit me square in the chest, an ache that never fucking let up.

She deserved better. Better than this room that wasn't hers. Better than watching shadows for movement. Better than having to count on a guy like me.

But she had me anyway.

No matter how many nights passed, how many plans we made to protect her, it wouldn't erase the fact that she'd never be safe enough until the threat was extinguished.

I crossed the room on silent steps, lowering into the chair beside her bed. My elbows dropped to my knees, fingers laced, eyes locked on the shape of her. I could have slipped into the bed beside her. Could have pulled her close and kept the nightmares at bay with the weight of my body, but I didn't want to risk waking her. If she could grab even a few hours of real sleep, I wasn't going to screw it up.

So I sat.

And I watched.

And I waited.

At some point, maybe an hour in, her body shifted as a soft sound escaped her lips, barely more than breath.

"Kreed..." My name. So faint it almost didn't feel real, but it was, and it wrecked me.

She said it like I was safety, like I was home.

Fuck.

My throat closed. I couldn't swallow past the ache, couldn't breathe past the effect she had on me. My fists curled against my thighs, nails biting into the calluses of my palms.

I didn't deserve that kind of faith. That kind of softness, but I was going to earn it anyway.

Starting tonight.

Starting with blood if it came to it.

I leaned back in the chair, bones aching from tension that never left. My gaze stayed locked on her, on the gentle rise and fall of her chest, on the shadows playing across her skin, on the loose strands of hair curling over her cheek.

She slept.

I stayed awake.

Just like it was supposed to be, and if anyone came for her tonight...I'd make damn sure they never walked away from here.

THE FIRST RAYS of morning light filtered through the curtains, painting soft gold across the walls. I hadn't slept. Couldn't. Not when every creak in the house had me ready to put my fist through someone's face. It would be dumb for someone to try to abduct her with a house full of notorious bad boys with reputations for revenge, but I refused to let my guard down. The second I did was the moment when they would strike.

It was what I would do.

Kaylor stirred, legs tangled in the sheets, mumbling something under her breath. Her brows twitched, lips parting, dry and sleep swollen. Slowly, like she was surfacing from somewhere deep, her lashes fluttered, and her eyes cracked open.

She blinked at me, eyes still hazy and unfocused. The light caught the silver strands of her hair, fanning across her cheek, catching on the slope of her collarbone like sunlight had chosen her and her alone to land on.

"Kreed?" she rasped.

I sat forward, elbows on my knees. "Morning, little raven."

Her gaze darted from me to the clothes I still wore, to the seat I hadn't moved from all night, and then back again. Her brows pinched together. "Why are you in the chair?"

I gave a half shrug. "Didn't want to wake you."

"How very un-Kreed-like of you," she mumbled, rubbing at her eyes. A soft flush crawled up her cheeks when she caught how close I still was.

I couldn't help it. A crooked grin tugged at my mouth. "What? You expected me to curl up next to you and spoon?"

She glared at me through sleep-heavy lids. "I expected you to take over the bed like you own the place."

"I do," I said, deadpan.

She snorted into her pillow. "And creepy. Sitting there all night. Watching me sleep."

Fucking adorable.

"Protective," I corrected. "Big difference." I leaned in, just enough to feel her breath against my skin. "Besides, you're the one who kept whispering my name all night. Figured I better stick around in case you needed me."

That got her.

Frowning, her lashes dipped low as she muttered, "You're lying. Unless I was cursing your name. That would make more sense."

I chuckled low, the sound rumbling from my chest. "You want me to tell you what else you said?"

She shot me a look. "Don't push your luck."

I grinned. "So you admit it."

Her eyes narrowed. "You're insufferable."

"Maybe," I said, resting my chin in my hand, elbow on my knee. "But you're stuck with me anyway."

Her mouth opened, but the snark she usually fired off so easily stalled. The silence that followed wasn't awkward. It was taut, crackling like lightning waiting to strike. Something raw lived in that moment. Something neither of us wanted to name, but reality shattered the calm like a brick through glass.

Her face changed. The softness drained out of her expression, replaced by a slow, soul-crushing dread. She blinked again, this time too fast, too hard. Her bottom lip trembled. "It...it wasn't a nightmare? Kenny?"

I didn't answer.

"She's really gone." Her voice broke. "Kenny's gone." Her fingers shook as she reached for the edge of the blanket, gripping it like it could hold her together. But it wouldn't. Nothing would right now.

I slid my hand across the mattress, found hers, and laced our fingers. Her skin was cold. Mine was burning. "I'm going to find her," I said quietly. "I swear it, Kaylor. I'm going to bring her home."

Her eyes lifted to mine, glassy with unshed tears. "And if you can't?"

I held her gaze, fierce and unflinching. "Then I make the bastards pay."

"Maybe it would be easier if I just gave them what they wanted. She's probably so scared. I could put an end to her nightmare, Kreed. I don't know if I can wait and hope we find her."

"You're not going to them," I said against her hair. The thought of her in the possession of someone so sick, someone who would sell one of their own to save their own skin... It made my chest burn with a protective instinct so fierce it nearly brought me to my knees.

"But she could die," she whispered, her voice fracturing like glass. "If I don't go—"

"We're going to find her," I cut her off, my voice harder than I intended.

"What if we're too late?" The question came out broken, raw terror bleeding through her words.

I pulled back just enough to look at her, to let her see the promise in my eyes, and kept our fingers tied together. "We won't be. She has the Ravens *and* the Elite looking for her. I'd say her odds of being found are pretty fucking good, little raven."

With big light-blue eyes, she looked at me, and I would have promised her anything in that moment, anything to banish that sorrowful expression on her features. "I'm scared."

Something cold and familiar stirred in my chest. Something that had been sleeping in the dark corners of my soul since the last time I'd made the mistake of caring too much. The thing that turned me into exactly what people feared when they whispered my name in the shadows.

For her, I'd become someone I didn't like very much, but what troubled me was whether, when this was over, she would look at me the same. Would she still want me? Would she see a monster?

KAYLOR

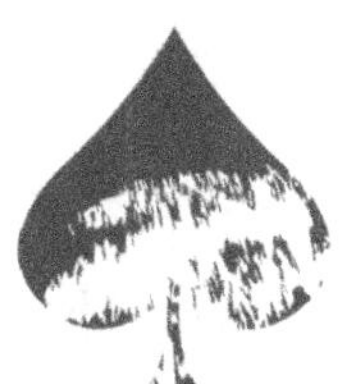

I stared down at our woven fingers, his hand enveloping mine, and it couldn't have felt more natural. His fingers were so much larger, stronger...marked. Each one inked with a suit from a deck of cards: spade, heart, club, diamond. Just a few of many tattoos inking his body, but it was the raven spread over his forearm that should have warned me he wasn't safe.

But he *felt* so damn secure, and that comfort I had from being with Kreed made my guilt magnify. I was in this lush bed with the most gorgeous guy I'd ever seen, willing to risk his life for me, and my best friend was in a locked glass cage. It wasn't fair.

My heart twisted painfully at the thought. As if my mind needed the reminder, flashes of that photo burned behind my eyes. It was my best friend, and yet it hadn't looked like her, and I was here...in a warm bed, wrapped in blankets, cushioned by comfort...and, worse, beside Kreed.

It would be so easy to follow his lead, to lean into him, to let him shoulder the burden of everything. But would that help Kenny? Would that get her back?

I hated how tempting it was to stay locked inside this room, for how my body ached for the comfort Kreed offered, even as my soul was riddled with guilt. What kind of friend was I? My best friend was trapped in hell, and here I was...being held like I was breakable and protected like I was sacred.

Maybe that was why it felt so wrong. What made me so special? Why hadn't Kenny had someone to protect her? Why hadn't *I* protected her?

It was making it damn hard to remember all the reasons I should be running away from Kreed. Why was it such a horrible idea to fall for him?

Drawing in a deep breath, I unwove our fingers and inched up into a sitting position on the bed. The soft hush of morning light spilled through gauzy curtains, the world too still, too quiet for how shattered I was inside. The air was cooler than I expected, or maybe it was guilt digging its nails in. "How long am I supposed to wait?" I asked, second-guessing my choice not to show the police the message I received.

If Kenny died because of me...

I'd never fucking forgive myself. Hell, I definitely wouldn't forgive Kreed. It would be the end of us for good. Did he have any idea of the enormous risk I took in trusting him?

He sat back in the chair, his eyes shadowed with tiredness but alert, always alert. "It hasn't even been a full day. Give us another forty-eight hours, and if we have nothing, we take that photo to the cops."

What if she didn't have forty-eight hours? I would go crazy. I couldn't imagine how horrible this was for Kenny. "What the hell am I supposed to do in the meantime? Twiddle my thumbs?" School was out of the question. No way could I focus on homework. At the rate things were going, I'd be lucky if I graduated this year.

"Go about your day. If they're watching you, watching us, don't let them think they've rattled you."

I wasn't sure I had it in me. I didn't have the acting and manipulation skills he had.

Climbing out of bed, I crossed the room, arms wrapped around my chest. I didn't want him to see me fall apart. Not again. He'd seen enough cracks already, and if I broke now, I wasn't sure I'd be able to gather the pieces back together. It created a vulnerability I didn't want to display. "I need to shower."

"Leave the door open, and I don't mean that in a creepy way. I just want to be able to hear you if something happens."

My brow lifted. "What exactly do you think will happen in the shower?"

"I don't discount anything, little raven. Even something as trivial as a shower."

"I'll be like twenty steps away. I think I'll be fine," I said, moving to the dresser and opening a drawer to look for clean clothes. "We're essentially in the same room. You don't need to hover."

His voice came from closer than I expected. I hadn't heard him cross the room, but I couldn't fault my distractedness. "And you're not going to do anything reckless?" He didn't want to leave me alone, but I needed the space. The tears I held back wouldn't be suppressed for much longer.

"When have I ever?" I forced a small smile over my shoulder, trying to prove I was good.

He gave me that dry look, the one that said he saw right through my bullshit. "Every single day since I've met you."

"Kreed, please. Fifteen minutes."

His eyes searched mine as if he were trying to see if I was lying. Maybe I was. Just a little. I wasn't planning to sneak out or do anything stupid... Not yet, but I did plan to fall apart. I did plan to let the scalding water drown out my sobs.

He sighed. "I'll give you ten."

I rolled my eyes even as I fought the tightness in my throat. "You're such a tyrant."

"And yet, I'm still here."

I didn't answer. Just turned and slipped into the bathroom, locking the door behind me. Screw keeping it open. I didn't honestly believe a lock would keep him out anyway. If I were in trouble, he'd find a way inside.

Only when I twisted the shower knob and the water roared to life did I let myself slide down to the tile floor, my knees drawn to my chest. My breath hitched, and then it was all crashing down—my guilt, my fear, and my rage at the world and myself.

I buried my face in my arms and let the sobs come, silent and shaking, as steam filled the room, and the sound of the running water drowned out the truth: This was my fault.

WITH PUFFY, red eyes I couldn't hide, I shuffled downstairs, my wet hair dampening the back of Kreed's hoodie. He left it on the bed for me when I got out of the shower, and I couldn't resist slipping it on. His woodsy sage and sea salt scent adhered to the soft material, enveloping me in a way that made it feel like his arms were around me.

Kreed wanted me to go on with my day as if my best friend wasn't fighting for her life. I wasn't sure I could. Doing so would require me to shut off my brain to keep from thinking about her, not a simple request for something that felt like it had its own will.

Somehow, by the light of day, everything seemed different. Definitely not clearer because I was just as uncertain last night as I was this morning about my decision. Maybe I should have gone to the police as Carson wanted. What was I doing thinking we could handle this alone? We were in fucking high school.

Not that I didn't believe my cousin and the Elite were capable because I'd seen the aftermath from people who'd crossed them. And Kreed...

He had an inside to a part of Elmwood I wasn't sure I wanted to be associated with, let alone know about. It might have been better if I'd been oblivious to the nefarious activity happening right under my nose, which my father had a hand in.

It wasn't too late. I could still go to the police. Or I could keep going down this path, trusting Kreed. *Or...*I could give myself up, trade my life for Kenny's.

Kreed and Brock would be beyond pissed. I didn't want to imagine what that would do to them, the rage it would set off, but if it was me being held, being threatened, they had a higher stake. They would have more determination to find me.

It wasn't that I didn't believe they would do their damnedest to rescue Kenny. They would for me, but if it were me instead... There was nothing they wouldn't do. Nothing. Frightening but also in a fucked-up way, comforting.

Of course, there was no way any of them would agree to such a stunt. They made their position in the matter very clear last night, but today was a new day. Perhaps we were all thinking clearer this morning. It was difficult to distinguish whether my emotions were making decisions or my head.

Whispers laced with sarcasm and muffled laughter floated down the hallway, their casual rhythm breaking the tense silence of the house. My socked feet padded against the hardwood, heart already prickling with suspicion. As I rounded the corner into the kitchen, I half expected to find my cousin and the Elite in a hushed strategy session with Kreed.

But instead, it was a memory I didn't expect to see again, one that belonged to another life entirely.

Raine was perched on the kitchen counter, casually spooning peanut butter straight from the jar. Maddox leaned against the fridge, pouring what suspiciously looked like rum into a coffee cup. Mason sat at the table, flipping a card between his fingers, the joker, if I had to guess, with a carefully stacked deck in front of him.

They were all here, sitting comfortably in my cousin's kitchen, Brock and the Elite nowhere to be seen.

I froze in the doorway. "What the hell are you guys doing here?"

Mason smirked, flinging the card in my direction so it sailed perfectly through the air, only for Kreed to catch it before it could smack me on the forehead. "Heard you missed us. Couldn't let that go unaddressed. Not in your time of need," the younger twin said.

I choked on nothing. "Your delusions are getting scarier."

Raine grinned as he pointed his peanut butter–covered spoon in Kreed's direction. A glob of the sticky spread clung to the metal, threatening to drop onto the pristine countertop. "If you can forgive this asshole," he said, nodding toward Kreed with theatrical emphasis, "surely you can find it in your heart to forgive us poor, misunderstood souls."

"I haven't forgiven anyone," I muttered.

Maddox tilted his head. "So you're not sleeping with Kreed?"

"Because I swear he was in your room last night," Raine added innocently, licking peanut butter off the spoon.

Hovering in the doorway, I glared at the four Corvos who were the bane of my existence. "You guys show up just to annoy me into a mental breakdown?"

"Pretty much," they chimed in unison, unbothered.

I rolled my eyes and crossed my arms. "Where's my cousin?"

"What, we're not enough?" Maddox asked, taking another sip of his drink. His Adam's apple bobbed as he swallowed, and when he lowered the mug, there was genuine hurt in his expression that I almost believed. "I thought we really bonded when you lived with us, shared trauma and all."

"If Kreed can't be reasonable," I snapped, "maybe you three can. You want to help? Then tell him"—My eyes locked on Kreed's—"that I should do the trade." The words left my mouth before I'd fully decided to say them, but I didn't take them back.

The air died.

Kreed turned so fast his spine should have cracked under the violent motion. "Do what?" he growled, absolutely furious.

I swallowed hard, my throat suddenly dry as desert sand, but I didn't back down. Not when Kenny's life hung in the balance. "They want me. That much is clear. We could use that. Set a trap. Trade me for Kenny—"

"No." The word exploded from his lips like a bullet, hitting me with the same devastating force. It ricocheted off the kitchen walls.

"Kreed—"

"Absolutely not," he snapped. "Don't even think about finishing that sentence. We talked about this."

I met his glare head-on, fire meeting fire. "They have her. What if it were me? What if I were the one missing?"

"I think you know what I would do. Besides, we have no guarantee they will keep their word. We could agree to the trade, and then what? They take you both and disappear before we even blink?"

"You won't let that happen." The certainty in my voice surprised even me.

"Now you suddenly have unwavering faith in me," he snorted, crossing the kitchen to Maddox and taking the bottle of rum, tipping it back.

Rum for breakfast. I couldn't fault him because I was contemplating having some myself.

Frustrated, I blinked back the tears stinging my eyes. To think I thought I'd purged myself in the shower.

"The cold truth is," Kreed continued, lowering the bottle and wiping his mouth with the back of his hand, "unlike Kenny, they won't keep you around to dangle as bait. You'll be sold immediately—probably within hours, and then my chances of finding you drop to practically zero." His silver eyes burned with a fury that made the air shimmer. "Assuming they bother putting you up for auction instead of just disposing of you outright. Is that what you want? To be sold to some sick freak for his personal entertainment?"

My stomach churned at the images his brutal honesty conjured. "You don't know what will happen. You can't be sure they won't let her go."

"I do. Because I know how people like this operate. You think they want you so they can hand over Kenny with a thank-you note? You'd be walking into a life you don't come back from."

Tears stung my eyes, hot and unwelcome. "She's my best friend."

Kreed's expression shifted in the hard mask. "I know what she is to you," he bit out. Then he was moving, crossing the space between us in two quick strides, his calloused hands coming up to cup my face with devastating gentleness. "But you—" His thumb brushed away a tear, the touch so tender it made my chest ache. "You're mine, little raven."

The breath left my lungs.

He wasn't asking. He was claiming.

"I already lost you once," he whispered. "I'm not doing it again. You don't get to offer yourself up like some kind of fucking sacrifice. I won't survive that."

Mason's chair scraped against the floor as he shifted, breaking the charged silence. "Okay, that was intense," he said, his usual smirk replaced by something more serious. The playing cards lay forgotten on the table. "Anyone else feel like they just witnessed a cosmic shift in the universe?"

"Shut up, Mason," Kreed growled.

"I'm not trying to be a martyr," I choked out, my words muffled against the small space between us. "I'm trying to do something."

"We are doing something," Maddox cut in, offering the bottle of rum to me as if booze would solve all my problems. "But using you as bait isn't part of the plan."

I nodded at Maddox, letting him know I definitely wanted a drink. "I'm not saying we go in blind," I said, turning toward all of them now, pleading. "But I'm what they want. That gives us leverage."

"Which is exactly why they don't get their hands on you," Mason said, less playful now. "They're not playing fair. We don't either."

"We'll find her," Raine promised. "But we all agree with Kreed. You're not the price."

I hated how much I wanted to believe him, but the truth was, part of me did feel like the price. Like I was a key someone else had decided to steal and use. I couldn't sit still while Kenny slipped further into hell.

I took the drink Maddox handed me and tossed it back, the rum warm as it coated my throat.

"You're unnegotiable." Kreed's refusal to even consider compromise, to bend even slightly, only made my secret decision crystallize into something harder than diamond.

I stilled... But not the way Kreed hoped. I'd give him two days. Forty-eight hours. And if by then Kenny wasn't home, safe in my arms, I would go to them. Even if it meant losing Kreed in the process, because if I didn't try... If I let her down...

I'd never be able to look at myself again.

THEY FLANKED ME LIKE SHADOWS.

Kreed on my right. Mason on my left. Maddox trailing a few paces behind. I didn't need to look to know they were there, hovering, protective, but present in a way that was both comforting and suffocating.

Corvo security detail, version overkill.

I hadn't wanted to leave the house, let alone show up to school. I didn't know how they convinced me otherwise, but here I was, pretending to give a shit about my education. Raine went to the club to check in, see if anyone had heard anything. I wanted to go with him. That was immediately vetoed, but the first chance I got, I was out of here. I'd find my own way to the club. Raine would be so pleased to see me, and I gave little fucks. If someone had the tiniest crumb of information, I wanted to know. I would leave no stone unturned.

Carson's one-word responses to my texts on the way to school nearly had me jumping out of the car. I got that he was upset and going out of his mind, but so was I. She was my friend too, despite my lack of presence lately, but he had to cut me some slack considering everything I'd been through. I was doing my best. I didn't want to lose them both in a span of twenty-four hours, but I couldn't help but feel as if Carson was pulling further away from me when we should be leaning on each other. He hated Kreed. I got it.

Hell, most days I loathed the man, but on the days I didn't, I somehow found my lips attached to his. As much as I wanted to hold on to my hate for Kreed and his brothers, I had to, at some point, accept that I didn't hate them.

Another problem for another day.

We stepped through the school doors, and the second I crossed the threshold, every pair of eyes swung in my direction. I hadn't even made it to first period, and I already felt like a freak show on display. Girl with the missing friend. Girl with the secrets. Girl with the Raven Crew. If only they knew the truth. I couldn't even imagine the rumors swirling around me and the crew. It wasn't enough that they'd singled me out, that I'd slept with Kreed, that I'd been living in their house. Now they were surrounding me like guard dogs with bared teeth, ready to attack.

There were parts of high school I despised, and the speed at which news traveled was high on that list.

I didn't care. At least, I told myself I didn't care. I tried to look on the bright side, which was very hard to do considering how gloomy shit was, but the upside of being at school was that I didn't have time to fall apart.

At lunch, I found Poppy at a table near the middle of the cafeteria. She perked up when she saw me and immediately slid her tray to the side, clearing space like I might bolt if she didn't. I was under strict orders by my Raven guards not to leave the school grounds. The fact that they were everywhere I turned hadn't given me the opportunity to skip out like I wanted.

I plopped onto the chair with a scowl, glancing over my shoulder to see which Raven would be joining me for lunch.

"Hey," Poppy said, drawing my gaze away from the crowded lunchroom. "I didn't expect to see you today."

"Wasn't really given a choice," I muttered, picking at my nails. I hadn't grabbed any food. Nothing sounded good. "Kreed basically threw me in the car."

Her golden eyes flicked behind me where, no doubt, at least one of the guys was lurking. "They're starting to scare me," she said carefully. "They've never acted like this before. Not with anyone and certainly not a girl. What kind of magical pussy do you have?"

If my lips had the ability to smile, I would have, but I couldn't muster the energy it took. It felt wrong to find humor or joy in anything. "You know I'm not sleeping with all of them." I toyed with a napkin left on the table from the previous period, twisting it into a spiral.

She plucked half of her sandwich off her tray, put it on a napkin, and slid it to me. "Just the one who commands the school."

I stared at the bread, knowing I should eat it, and how very Poppy-like to make sure I ate. She was a good friend. She and Kenny would love each other *if* they ever got the chance to meet. "I'm not sleeping with *him* either, actually."

She picked up her half of turkey and cheese between two slices of wheat bread. "But you're thawing. I can see it. Your will is wavering. He's working his way back into your heart."

Maybe he was, but my heart was awfully fragile currently, and he was making it difficult for me to hate him. "I don't have it in me right now to figure him out."

"If you need me to be the voice of reason on your shoulder, reminding you what an asshole Kreed Corvo is, I'm your girl." She took a bite of her sandwich.

"Thanks. I might take you up on it." Forcing myself to eat, I followed her and took a bite.

"I know it's probably the last thing you want to think about, but I have to ask..." Poppy reached over and gave my arm a gentle squeeze. "Any word yet?"

I shook my head. "Nothing."

A heavy silence fell between us, punctuated by the clatter of trays and the distant buzz of other conversations. I was about to change the subject and ask Poppy about Nash when a tray thumped down in front of me. I glanced up, watching Mason drop into the seat across from me. Half an apple dangled from his fingers, teeth marks sunk into its side, and that signature smirk, the one that looked like it came with a warning label, tugging at the corner of his mouth.

I stared at him, taking in the full effect of Mason and the damn dimples he threw around so carelessly. "What are you doing?" I asked flatly.

"Watching you," he said, casually biting into his apple.

"For fuck's sake," I muttered, pressing my fingers to my temple. "I can't even eat in peace."

"Wow." Mason turned the apple, the raven tattoo on the back of his hand flashing at me. It was identical to the one Kreed bore but on a smaller scale. All the Corvo boys had one. The crew's mark. "You and Kreed really have trust issues."

"You think?" I huffed, leaning back. "I don't need a bodyguard. Or a babysitter."

Mason's eyes danced. "Au contraire, you need both, my little kitten."

I groaned. "So we're back to that ridiculous nickname."

"It's adorable. You know it is."

"It's demeaning."

"That too," he said, unbothered. "But more importantly, it annoys Kreed. So it's a win-win."

I shot him a dull look.

Poppy blinked between us like she'd stepped into a completely different conversation, and maybe she had because beneath the banter, under the sarcasm, was this unspoken tension I didn't know how to navigate. And I didn't want to admit that having them here, even when it pissed me off, made me feel slightly less like the ground was falling out from under me.

Maddox loomed by the wall, pretending to scroll through his phone, but I caught his eyes flicking to me every other second.

"Do you guys take turns or something?" I asked, jerking my chin toward Maddox. "Is this part of some babysitting schedule I should be aware of?"

Mason's grin stretched wider. "We drew straws. I won."

"You didn't win." I rolled my eyes. "You volunteered."

"Semantics," he replied, winking. "If we're going full truth here, Maddox and Kreed would've fought me for the seat."

My chin rested on my head as I eyed him, my half sandwich forgotten. "I thought we were being truthful."

"You underestimate your appeal," Mason said, swallowing a bite of apple. "It isn't just Kreed who's fallen under your spell. We all have."

Poppy coughed, choking on her drink.

God, who would have thought I'd have multiple guys fighting over me? Brothers, nonetheless, and it wasn't even like they all wanted to sleep with me. At least I was pretty sure. "I don't know how. You literally hated me a few weeks ago."

He leaned in, resting his forearms on the table, his expression turning more sincere than I'd expected. "*I* never hated you, and I think that was the dilemma we all faced. We *wanted* to hate you, but you made it impossible."

I blinked, the power of his words sticking harder than I thought they would. "Why are you telling me this?"

Mason's hand moved across the table, his knuckles brushing against mine in the briefest of touches before pulling back. "Because I want you to know you're not alone. You matter to all of us, not just to Kreed. Turns out, we like living with a girl, and we've got your back. He isn't the only one who'd take a knife to keep you safe."

"Wow," Poppy whispered dreamily. "Where do I get one of you?"

Mason grinned without missing a beat. "I'd say I'm one of a kind, but my twin's literally glaring at us from across the room."

I followed his gaze to where Maddox stood, his eyes fixed on our little group with an intensity.

"This is literally history in the making," Poppy declared as she reached for her bag sitting on the floor. "Where's my phone? I need to document this moment."

"Have we ever hooked up?" Mason asked Poppy, tilting his head to the side as he checked my friend out with a glint of interest.

"Absolutely not," I cut in before Poppy could respond. "She's off-limits."

Mason's eyebrows shot up, and his grin turned wicked. "No one is off-limits. Well, except for you, of course." He winked.

I fixed him with my best don't-even-think-about-it glare. "She's hooking up with Nash, remember?"

Mason waved a dismissive hand. "Minor detail."

"You're unbelievable. I doubt he would feel the same."

"Nash isn't serious about anything, let alone anyone," he replied offhandedly.

I was too emotionally drained to deal with this. "Don't be a dick."

"It's true. He isn't saying anything that I don't know." Poppy caught Mason's gaze as she paused, worrying her bottom lip between her teeth. "I might be interested."

The conversation had somehow spiraled completely out of my control. "What is happening? No more sex talk. Where's Kreed?" I quickly shifted to what I hoped was a safer subject.

Mason shrugged, finishing the last bit of his apple. "Who knows. Doing Kreed shit probably."

My eyes narrowed. "What does that mean?" Just as I was about to launch the crust of my sandwich at Mason's smug, dimpled face, a shadow fell over the table. I glanced up, spotting a guy standing near the table, nervous, twitchy, maybe a freshman? He was rail-thin, his backpack slung low off one shoulder, and his eyes darted everywhere but my face. He held something out in his hand. A small, crumpled scrap of paper. Not a note from a teacher. Not a hall pass. Just a torn square like it'd been ripped from the edge of a notebook.

"Kaylor?" he asked, voice cracking as he zeroed in on me.

Mason straightened, dropping his apple core onto the table with a soft thud. His voice lost every ounce of humor. "Who wants to know?"

The kid flinched. His grip on the paper tightened before he quickly thrust it toward me instead. "This is for you, I think." His voice came out in a rush, and his eyes flicked nervously toward Mason as if he'd already decided this had been a huge mistake.

I didn't reach for it. Not right away. "Who gave it to you?" I asked.

The kid swallowed, shifting his weight from one foot to the other. "I-I don't know. Some guy in the parking lot. Said it was important."

My heart slammed once, every muscle in my body tensing.

Mason reached for the note at the same time I did, his fingers brushing mine before closing around the paper. "Let me," he insisted.

I didn't argue. Couldn't. A coldness was already coiling in my stomach.

He unfolded it slowly, brows furrowing as he read, and the playful tilt of his mouth vanished. His jaw flexed once. Then again.

"What?" I demanded. "What does it say?"

He frowned. Mason rarely frowned. That was Kreed's full-time job. "I'm not sure I should show you."

"No more secrets," I reminded him.

"Fuck," he hissed through his teeth, sparing his twin a glance as he slid the paper across the table.

I unfolded it, hands trembling. The handwriting was messy, scrawled as if it had been written in haste or fury, lacking any punctuation.

Ticktock, sweetheart, you're on a timer

One more day before the stakes rise, and so will the price

No cops No Corvo No games

We'll be in touch

My breath snagged in my throat, turning to glass. I stared at the ink like I could unwrite it. My fingers curled around the edges, creasing the paper. "They know I'm here," I whispered.

"Son of a bitch," Mason muttered, already grabbing his phone. His fingers flew across the screen as he stood. Across the room, Maddox's posture changed in a second. His back peeled off the wall, his light-green eyes hardening as he started toward our table.

Poppy glanced between us, brows drawn together. "What's going on? What is it?"

I pushed back from the table, the legs of my chair scraping loudly against the linoleum. I was standing before I even realized I'd moved. My knees wobbled beneath me, but I forced them to lock in place. "They sent me a message," I said, voice hollow. "They're watching me."

Poppy's eyes widened. Her mouth opened, but no sound came out.

Mason was already speaking low into the phone, voice clipped and hard. Probably calling Kreed. Or Evan. Or someone else on the Corvo payroll.

I stared at the note a second longer before balling it in my fist, my nails biting into the paper. This was their move. Their warning shot. They wanted me off balance. Shaken. Afraid. And it was working. Not for myself but for Kenny. They knew exactly where to stick the knife and twist it.

I couldn't give them the satisfaction.

I wanted to find out who this fucker was, and if he or they were part of my father's crew *and* had betrayed him, I wanted him to hurt as I had, to feel pain and fear. He needed to taste his own medicine.

As Mason filled Maddox in, I slid my phone from my back pocket, fingers flying over the screen, and hit send. For the first time since this whole nightmare started, I meant it more than anything I'd ever said.

I want this asshole to pay. I want revenge.

17

KAYLOR

My phone vibrated in the middle of digital art class, the sound rattling the table so loudly that the guy next to me spared me a glance. Aside from the clicking of keys and mice, the class was generally quiet, which made the buzz of my phone amplify. I quickly snatched it off the desk, desperately wanting the text to be news about Kenny.

Brock's name popped up on the screen. Using face recognition, I unlocked my phone, my eyes scanning over the message. For a second, I'd forgotten my earlier text at lunch and the damn note, hope of something positive clouding all other thoughts, but it all came crashing back as I read my cousin's response.

Brock: **Are we talking the Ravens or the kidnappers?**

Me: **Whoever was stupid enough to take my best friend.**

Brock: **And if you don't like what we find?**

Me: **It doesn't matter who. They dug their grave the moment they messed with my friends.**

Perhaps I was more like Brock than I realized.

I snuck a quick glance around the room to make sure no one

caught me on my phone. It went off again, and I assumed my cousin sent another text, but no, it was a message from Rusty. Word of Kenny's disappearance had probably gotten to him, and he was freaking out, as he probably should.

Rusty: **I'm sending someone to pick you up after school.**

Did any of the men in my life know how to ask instead of order? I sighed and checked the time. The last hour of school would be torture. I could only imagine Kreed's reaction when a Viper showed up on school grounds to pick me up. I hadn't seen him most of the day, and I wasn't even sure he was in the building. Did that mean Maddox and Mason would be waiting for me after the final bell?

They weren't.

Who waited for me was worse... And better. I couldn't decide.

The bell shrilled, slicing through the air like it couldn't wait to shove us all out into the chaos beyond the classroom walls. My fingers curled around the strap of my bag as I stood, my muscles aching from how tense I'd been all day. Every laugh in the hallway felt fake. Every face unfamiliar. Every shadow a potential threat.

I stepped out into the corridor, blinking against the harsh light spilling in through the windows. The late-afternoon sun was soft and hazy, a welcome change from the cold gloom that had settled over everything lately. Students pushed past me in waves, their voices a blur of weekend plans and complaints about homework, normal things that felt foreign now.

Kreed leaned against the far wall in a black hoodie, the raven tattoo peeking from beneath the shoved-up sleeves. His arms were folded, those silver eyes locked on me with a stillness that should've soothed me. It didn't. Not this time.

He shoved off the wall when I got close, his sneakers silent against the polished floor as he matched my pace. The familiar scent of his cologne mixed with adrenaline, maybe, or the lingering smoke from whatever underworld business had kept him away.

"You learn anything, little raven?" His voice was low, meant only for my ears, as we navigated through the thinning crowd.

"Yeah, how annoying you and your brothers are." I shifted my bag to my other shoulder, the weight of the laptop I hadn't opened feeling heavier with each step. "Where were you today?"

"Did you miss me?" The corners of his mouth lifted, but the smile didn't reach his eyes as he took my bag from me, slinging it over his shoulder with ease.

"Did you find my best friend?" I shot back, my throat narrowing around the words. Kenny's absence was a constant ache.

"Working on it." His hand brushed mine as we walked, a fleeting touch that sent warmth up my arm.

"Why the hell do I have to be here if you don't?" I halted, forcing him to turn and face me fully. The hallway stretched empty around us now, most students having fled to their cars or buses. I wanted to be out there helping, doing something, because my education was the furthest thing from my mind.

He ran a hand through his dark hair, the gesture betraying his own frustration. "Because normal is what keeps you safe. Normal is what keeps you alive."

I started walking again.

"Where are you going? Evan's parked over here." His voice carried a note of confusion as I headed toward the main entrance instead of the student lot.

"There's a car waiting for me. Rusty sent it." I braced for the reaction I knew was coming.

Kreed's jaw ticked, a muscle jumping beneath the stubble he'd let grow. His entire body went rigid. "You're not getting in that car."

I exhaled, my breath visible in the cool air as we stepped outside. "I have to."

"No, little raven, you don't." He stopped walking, his hand shooting out to catch my wrist. Not hard but firm enough to anchor me in place. "It's a bad idea."

The parking lot stretched before us, cars peeling out with

weekend freedom. "If I don't go, he'll think something's up. And if what you believe is true..." My voice trailed off, caught in that space between denial and dread.

He stepped in and tilted my head back to meet his eyes. His presence pressed against the storm inside me, steady and warm despite the chaos. "Then we can't have him suspecting you know anything," he finished for me, his voice rough. "Shit."

"It sucks when I'm right." I tried for levity, but it fell flat between us.

"Now is not the time to try to be funny." His free hand came up to cup my face, his thumb brushing across my cheekbone.

I sighed. "Trust me, there's absolutely nothing hilarious about the possibility that my father's friend betrayed him and then kidnapped my best friend. I don't want to believe he's involved. I've known him my whole life. I can't imagine him hurting me. Or Kenny."

Kreed's expression darkened, shadows gathering in his silver eyes. His grip on my wrist tightened fractionally before he forced himself to let go. "People lie. They hide who they are when they want something bad enough. And if Rusty's in this?" He shook his head, disgust twisting his features. "We need him to think you're still in the dark."

I nodded. "I need to look him in the face. If he's going to lie to me, I want him to do so while looking me in the eye."

"Every bone in my body wants to haul your pretty ass over my shoulder and put you into the trunk of Evan's car. Lock you up until this is over."

"It's a good thing you're not a neanderthal or a psycho." I managed a weak smile though my heart was hammering against my ribs.

"Right. Good thing." His sarcasm was heavy, loaded with all the things he wasn't saying. The way his hands closed into fists at his sides told me exactly how much restraint he was exercising.

"Besides, I'd just find a way to escape, so let's save us both the trouble."

He shook his head. "I'm coming with you."

"Is it safe for you to be at the shop?" I asked, hovering on the edge of the parking lot. "Maybe we should get Maddox and Mason. If the Vipers are involved—"

"I'll be fine," he said immediately, his hand moving to rest on my lower back, a brief touch that sent warmth spreading through my sweater. "I can take care of myself, but if you're going to do this, you need to make him believe you're letting the cops handle it, that you don't suspect a thing."

That wasn't the problem. The problem was, I wasn't sure I could take it if something happened to Kreed because of me. My chest seized at the thought, a physical ache that made it hard to breathe. I cared about the asshole even when I didn't want to. Too many people had been hurt. It had to stop.

"Kaylor?"

I turned at the sound of my name, my sneakers scraping against the asphalt. A familiar figure approached from across the parking lot, and recognition hit me. "Jesse?"

He looked exactly the same, tall and lean with dirty-blond hair that always seemed to need a cut. The greasy gray shop jumpsuit hung loose on his frame, the first few buttons undone, flashing the dirty white tee underneath. That same crooked grin spread across his face, the one that used to make the other mechanics shake their heads in exasperation.

"Hey, bubbles. Long time no see." He stopped a few feet away, shoving his hands into his pockets. "Rusty sent me."

The stupid nickname had me wanting to roll my eyes. Jesse was Rusty's son, but he never called him dad. Jesse had always been hanging around the shop until a few years ago when my dad offered him a job instead of just being a nuisance. Jesse was two years older than I, and he'd seen me at most stages of my life. When Rusty had first started bringing him around, I'd been in my bubble phase. I took a little bottle with me everywhere, hence the dumb nickname that had stuck.

Beside me, Kreed's entire body hardened, tension radiating off him. "Who's Jesse?" he grumbled, close to my ear, deliberately brushing his lips against the curve of my skin.

"He works for my dad. *Worked* for him," I corrected, the smile slipping from my lips as reality crashed back down. My throat constricted around the words, past tense still feeling foreign and wrong.

Jesse's expression softened, his hands coming out of his pockets as he took a half step forward. "I never got to tell you how sorry I was for what happened to him and your mom."

"Thanks, Jesse." I wrapped my arms around myself, suddenly cold despite the afternoon sun. "My dad always thought of you as the son he never had."

"He was a great guy." Jesse cleared his throat, looking down at his oil-stained boots. "The shop's not the same without him."

"As touching as this reunion is," Kreed interrupted, "we need to go."

Jesse nodded, stepping aside as he opened the passenger door. Kreed gave Jesse a not-so-friendly glare as we climbed into the truck, a beat-up Ford that had seen better decades. The bench seat forced us close together with me sandwiched between the two guys like some twisted version of a first date gone wrong.

This should be fun.

The testosterone radiating off them was thick enough to choke me, making the already cramped cab feel suffocating.

Kreed's thigh pressed against mine, solid muscle and barely contained energy. Leaning close, I whispered, "Are you jealous?"

His breath hitched slightly, and when he turned his head, our faces were inches apart. "Do I have a reason to be?"

The challenge in his silver eyes made my pulse quicken. Jesse was stable, cute, and funny, but he was a Viper. It would be trading one crew for the other. But most importantly, Jesse didn't make my teenage hormones go batshit crazy like Kreed did. "Maybe."

His mouth arched into a scowl I found too damn sexy. "Don't toy with me, little raven."

Jesse kept peering sideways at us during the ride to the shop, his eyes flicking between Kreed and me, and I couldn't help wondering what was going through his head. The engine rumbled beneath us, and I found myself gripping the worn fabric of the seat as Jesse took corners a little too fast. I couldn't help him figure out my relationship with the enemy. I still didn't understand what the hell was between Kreed and me. We shouldn't make sense on paper, and yet, when I was with him, it was the only thing that made sense in my life.

Kreed sat beside me, one knee bouncing in a restless rhythm against the floorboard. Not from nerves but from barely contained tension. This wasn't fucking awkward at all.

"We heard about your friend," Jesse said, his eyes on the road. The sympathy in his voice was genuine, which somehow made it worse. "You've had a rough go of it, bubbles."

The temperature in the cab plummeted. Kreed's knee stopped bouncing, and his entire body went predator still. "Call her that again, and this car will never make it to the shop."

The words came out quiet, conversational even, but there was death in them. Jesse's hands went rigid on the steering wheel, a low chuckle breezing through his lips. "Don't give me a reason to pull this truck over and show you what Vipers are really made of."

Fuck.

"Stop," I hissed through my teeth, my elbow jabbing into Kreed's ribs hard enough to make him grunt. I sent Jesse an are-you-kidding-me frown before pinning Kreed with a glare that promised retribution later. "Can we put the who's a better bad guy away for ten minutes? I just want to get to the shop in one piece. I don't know what's crawled up both your asses, but save it for when I'm not sandwiched between you."

Jesse's shoulders relaxed slightly, and he actually chuckled. "I'm pretty sure I can figure it out, and as much as I'd like to fault him for it, I can't. We're all protective of you."

Kreed made a growling sound in the back of his throat that definitely said Jesse was testing his patience and his restraint.

God, the last thing I need is a brawl in a moving car. I'd had enough of hospitals to last three lifetimes.

We somehow made it to the shop without anyone dying or spilling any blood on Jesse's truck. I stepped out onto the cracked asphalt and took a healthy gulp of fresh air, letting the cold fill my lungs. It felt good, cleansing, and I needed it before I went inside. My sneakers crunched over scattered gravel and oil stains that had seeped into the pavement over decades.

Everything about this place brought an odd mixture of grief, homesickness, and nostalgia; the faded blue paint on the building's exterior was peeling in familiar spots, and the neon sign still flickered erratically "Viper's Auto Pro" in letters that had lost their brightness years ago. I could clearly picture a younger version of me as a kid running through those glass doors or into the open garage after school, pigtails bouncing, knowing my dad was inside waiting with change in his pocket for the vending machines.

The moment we stepped inside the faded auto body office, the air immediately shifted to a familiar cocktail of old oil, cheap coffee, and secrets that seemed to cling to every surface. Dust motes danced in the afternoon light streaming through grimy windows, and the linoleum floor creaked under our feet. I didn't know if this was a complete waste of time or if it could be a trap. I also didn't know if Kenny had time for us to chase shadows, but I had to try.

"He's in the office," Jesse informed us.

My father's office.

A pang hit me in the chest at the thought of seeing someone besides my father behind his desk. Kreed trailed behind as I moved to the narrow hallway, leading to the garage, a bathroom, and the room my father had used as his workspace to run his shops.

My throat thickened, and as I curled my fingers into my palms, nails pressing crescents into my skin, I did my best to suppress the memories threatening to drown me. The phantom scent of my dad's aftershave seemed to linger in the air.

"You good, little raven?" Kreed asked when I stopped just outside the office door, my hand frozen on the brass knob that had lost most of its shine.

I didn't think I'd ever be whole again, the cracks in my heart still bleeding, but I tipped my chin and nodded anyway.

Kreed planted himself just outside the office door, his broad shoulder pressed against the frame, one hand braced against the wood. The position gave him a clear view of both the hallway and inside the office. "Leave it open," he said.

I rolled my eyes, but it was all for show because I was grateful he insisted. The door creaked on its hinges as it swung wide.

Rusty sat behind the desk, flipping through paperwork with weathered hands, his salt-and-pepper hair catching the light from the single overhead bulb. He looked older than the last time I'd seen him, deeper lines etched around his eyes, but his shoulders still carried the same solid strength I'd known since childhood. He was deep in a stack of bills, his reading glasses perched on the end of his nose.

When he sensed my arrival, his gaze flashed up from the papers, and his entire face transformed as his coal-dark eyes landed on me. The harsh lines of concentration melted away, replaced by something softer. "You came," he said, standing slowly, his chair groaning in protest. "Wasn't sure you would."

I forced a small smile, my lips feeling stiff and unnatural. "You said it was important."

"It is," he replied, and the grin he gave me was warm, the kind I'd grown up with until it sputtered and died the moment his eyes shifted to land on Kreed's imposing figure behind me. The temperature in the room dropped several degrees. "Didn't realize you'd be bringing a Raven."

Kreed grinned, hovering in the doorway, his silver eyes cataloging every detail of the room. "Miss me that much, huh?"

"Care to give me a minute with my girl?" Rusty's voice carried a note of challenge, his jaw setting in a way that reminded me uncomfortably of my father when he'd made up his mind about something.

Kreed's response was immediate and harsh. "She's not yours. Not anymore, and I'm not leaving her side."

Rusty didn't reply immediately, but strain zipped across the room like static electricity before a thunderstorm. He folded his arms across his chest, the motion making his work shirt strain across his shoulders, then settled himself on the corner of the desk with deliberate casualness. "Yeah, I figured." His smile was all teeth and no warmth. "Guys like you probably can't let her breathe without getting twitchy. Real protective or just real possessive, Kreed?"

"For fuck's sake," I muttered, stepping between them before Kreed could deliver whatever threatening response was brewing in that menacing expression of his. "Enough. Both of you. I'm not here for a pissing contest."

Rusty arched a graying brow, but his expression softened slightly as he focused on me again. "I heard about your missing friend. Kenny, right? It's why I wanted to see you."

I sank into the empty chair across from the desk, the same chair I'd sat in as a kid while Dad finished up paperwork, swinging my legs and waiting for him to take me for ice cream. The vinyl was cracked now, stuffing peeking through. "I need help. I need answers. I need to know if anyone's heard anything—anything at all," I pleaded. I was praying Rusty was the man I hoped he was and not a traitor, that the warmth in his eyes was real and not a mask. Surely, he would be willing to offer his services. But if Kreed was right...

The thought trailed off into darkness I wasn't ready to face.

Kreed wanted me to pretend I didn't suspect a thing, that I had no knowledge of a traitor among the Vipers. Asking Rusty for help was what I would have done, what the old me would have done without question. I would have run here at the first signs of trouble, seeking assurance from someone who was like family. So here I was, asking the man who'd bounced me on his knee as a child to help me find my best friend.

Rusty's gruff demeanor softened slightly as he leaned back in his chair, the harsh lines around his eyes smoothing out, and for a moment, I caught a glimpse of the man who used to sneak me candy when Dad wasn't looking. "I'm sorry, kiddo. I wish there was something I could do, but I don't know anything about those missing girls."

I nodded as the little amount of hope I'd been clinging to deflated like a punctured balloon. My chest felt hollow, scraped clean of optimism. Kreed wouldn't approve if I told Rusty about the ransom, about me being the prize they wanted, but I was tempted to spill my guts just to see his reaction. Would his face change? Would he get uncomfortable, shifting in his seat? Would he have no reaction at all, the kind of blank stare that came from already knowing the truth?

Rusty rubbed a weathered hand over his face, his callused fingers rasping against his beard. "I don't know what I can do. I haven't heard anything specific, but I'll ask around. See if any of the guys know something." He dropped his hand, meeting my eyes with what looked like genuine concern. "The streets don't stay quiet for long when bad shit's going down."

"Will you let me know if you hear anything? It doesn't matter when. I'm not sleeping much as it is."

His eyes held mine, and an emotion I couldn't quite name gleamed in them. "You know I'd never lie to you, and I won't fill you up with false promises, but I'll do what I can."

The words should have been comforting, but they sat wrong in my stomach, twisting like spoiled food. I nodded anyway, swallowing the bitter mix of hope and hopelessness sagging in my chest. Behind me, Kreed's hand settled lightly on the back of my chair, not possessive, not forceful, just there. "I appreciate it," I said, my voice barely above a whisper.

Rusty's gaze flicked to Kreed again, and this time, I caught the flash of darkness brewing behind his eyes, but he kept it leashed this time. His jaw worked silently before he spoke again. "You shouldn't be alone. Especially with *him*." The word dripped with venom, and Kreed's fingers twitched against the chair. "After everything we went through to get you out of that house, I still can't believe *he's* staying with you." Rusty leaned forward, his elbows braced on the desk, hands clasped like he was praying or planning. "Come to the nest. You'll have round-the-clock protection. No one will get through those doors without my knowledge."

The temperature in the small office seemed to drop several degrees, but I kept my gaze on Rusty, stirrings of wariness fluttering in my chest. Something about his words felt off. "How do you know that Kreed has been staying at the house?"

Rusty blinked, just once, but it was enough. His mask slipped for a fraction of a second before sliding back into place. "What kind of friend would I be if I didn't keep an eye on his daughter?"

"So you're spying on me?"

"I wouldn't call it spying, kiddo." His voice took on that patronizing tone I'd heard him use with Jesse and younger crew members, the one that meant he was about to lecture me like a child. He stood slowly, moving around the desk until he was leaning against its edge. "I know you've had a sheltered life because your father didn't want you to grow up as we did, but it's time to take the rose-colored glasses off. You're the daughter of a powerful crew don. He might not be with us anymore, but there are people out there who would use you to hurt us. You're still important to the Vipers."

Like you? I silently questioned, so confused.

"You're living with our biggest enemy." Rusty's voice hardened, losing any pretense of fatherly concern. "I know you think he might care about you, but I don't trust him. He's already hurt you once. He'll do so again."

The air behind me shifted, and Kreed's presence dominated the office. "You don't know shit about me, old man."

Rusty's lips carved into a humorless smile. "Your reputation speaks for itself." He tilted his head, studying Kreed. "Does she know about the things you've done? About your past? Or have you only let her see the good side of you?"

Kreed's laugh was hollow and empty. "You're assuming I have a good side."

The chair legs scraped against the worn linoleum as I stood

abruptly and put myself between the two of them. "It's probably best I leave. *And* I don't need your guys stalking me. I have enough eyes on me as it is. I wouldn't want one of them to get hurt."

Had that just come out of my mouth? I hadn't meant for it to sound like a threat, but when the words echoed back at me, it was precisely how they'd landed. My pulse quickened as I realized what I'd just done, issued a warning to a man who'd known me since I was in diapers.

Who the hell am I?

It was obvious that Kreed and the Ravens were rubbing off on me, their corruptness seeping into my bones like ink in water. I couldn't decide if I liked who I was becoming. The old Kaylor would have never spoken to Rusty that way, but this version of me, the one standing in my dead father's office, staring down a man who might have betrayed everything we'd built, she was different. Harder. They were changing me, and I wasn't sure if I was grateful or terrified.

"Watch yourself," Rusty said as I moved toward the door.

I paused at the threshold, my hand gripping the door frame. Without turning around, I shook my head. "I have all the protection I need."

I didn't glance at Jesse, who was still in the lobby as we passed by, despite feeling his eyes burning into my back. I hadn't thought about how the hell we would get home, but Kreed had taken care of it. Of course, he had. He seemed to anticipate my needs before I even knew I had them.

The familiar black town car idled in front of the shop, its engine purring softly. Evan stood as still as a statue beside the driver's door, his broad shoulders filling out his dark suit, sunglasses concealing his eyes despite the late-afternoon light.

The second the shop door shut behind us with a heavy thud, Kreed took my hand and ushered me toward the car with an urgency that made my skin prickle, as if he was preparing for someone to come chasing after us or strike me down from behind. His head turned constantly, his eyes scanning the street, the alleyways, and the windows of surrounding buildings.

"I really fucking hate that guy," Kreed grumbled, staring at the shop through the window as Evan pulled the car away.

"I think the feeling is mutual between the two of you."

"I don't trust him," he growled, his silver eyes narrowing. "I know you have your doubts, but I'm not wrong about him. My instincts are telling me he's the traitor."

The certainty in his voice made my chest clench. I shifted in the seat, turning my body toward him so I could read his expression. "And he might be, but it doesn't mean he's running a trafficking ring. You don't have to like him. What matters is getting Kenny home. The more people helping, the bigger our reach. Someone had to have seen something. Heard something."

Kreed's expression darkened. "If he is behind it, you need to know that I won't turn a blind eye. I will destroy him."

"If he is involved, you won't be destroying him alone. I'll be by your side." The vow came out steadier than I felt.

"Such violence. Dare I say it looks good on you, little raven." His gaze swept over me, lingering with fire burning in his eyes.

Heat crept up my neck. "Don't tell me you get hard at the prospect of me in black leather and brass knuckles." I tried to keep my tone light, but there was an edge to it.

"Brass knuckles, huh?" He leaned nearer. "Yeah, I could get behind that."

I shook my head but couldn't ignore the flutter in my chest. "There's something wrong with you."

"Yeah," he said, his hand reaching out to trace a finger along my jaw, the touch featherlight but burning. "You crashed into my life."

The truth in his words hit harder than I expected. Giving in to the pull I'd been fighting, I rested my head on his shoulder, feeling the solid warmth of him, the way his breathing hitched slightly at the contact. "Touché."

When we pulled up in front of Carson's house, Evan cut the

engine, but neither of us moved. The silence stretched between us, heavy with unspoken words. I stared at the familiar front door, the closed blinds, and the darkened porch light that Carson usually kept on. The house looked hollow, abandoned, like grief had already moved in and made itself at home.

Kreed's fingers found mine, intertwining without permission, his thumb tracing circles on my skin. The gesture was soft, intimate in a way that made my heart skip. "You sure you want to do this? He was pretty pissed last night. He might not be ready to talk."

I stared at the front door, imagining Carson behind it, probably pacing, probably not sleeping, probably drowning in the same helplessness threatening to consume me. My chest ached at the memory of his frantic voice on the phone, the desperation bleeding through every syllable when he'd called about Kenny. "I have to try," I said. "Since he isn't answering my calls or messages, he left me no other choice. I need to know if there've been any updates. I need to see how he's doing. Pissed off at me or not, he's still my friend."

Kreed tucked a stray strand of hair behind my ear, drawing out the movement longer than needed. His eyes searched mine. He gave a short nod, and I reached for the door handle, my heart pounding so hard I was sure he could hear it.

I barely got two knocks in before the door whipped open with enough force to rattle the frame. Carson stood there, and the sight of him made my breath catch. His usually perfect hair was a mess, dark circles shadowed his eyes like bruises, and his clothes looked as if he'd slept in them...*if* he'd slept at all since Kenny vanished.

His gaze landed on me first, and for just a heartbeat, relief flitted across his features before his eyes shifted to Kreed behind me, and his relief crystallized into something hard and cold. "Oh," he said flatly. "You brought him."

I didn't flinch, though his tone cut deeper than I wanted to admit. "Can we come in?"

He stepped aside without answering.

Kreed followed behind me, and the second the door shut with a decisive click, Carson rounded on me. "You think now's the time to play house with him?" His dark-blue eyes glared murderously at Kreed. "Our best friend is missing, probably locked up in some goddamn hell, and you're—what? Hooking up with him?"

The accusation hit like a slap, but I kept my voice steady. "Carson," I said softly, trying to reach the friend I knew was drowning beneath all that rage. "I'm doing everything I can to help Kenny. That includes working with Kreed—"

"Him?" Carson's voice pitched higher as he gestured wildly at Kreed, his hands shaking slightly. "What the hell does he know about helping anyone? His family has blood on their hands. Don't think for a second they don't have their own shady involvement in all of this."

Kreed didn't respond right away, but his silence hung dangerously.

Carson stepped close enough that I caught a whiff of liquor on his breath, invading my space. He didn't day drink, and I doubted he'd gone to school today, not that I blamed him.

Kreed, in a fluid half step forward, put him subtly between us. The movement was casual enough to seem natural, but there was nothing casual about the way his shoulders had set, the way his hands had gone loose at his sides.

Carson's eyes burned with a wild, desperate fury, making him look half mad. "You going to protect her from me?" The words dripped with bitter sarcasm as he snorted, chest heaving. "At least I didn't take advantage of her when she was vulnerable."

"That's enough," Kreed said quietly. "Cool off."

But Carson was beyond reason, beyond cooling off. His grief had twisted into something ugly. "I didn't have to trick her to fuck me." He hurled the words as he shoved Kreed, both hands slamming into his chest with all the force of his pent-up rage.

Bad move.

I gasped.

Faster than I could blink, faster than thought itself, Kreed had him spun around, and the thud of Carson's body hitting the wall went through the room. One of Carson's arms was pinned behind his back at an angle that had to hurt, the other braced across his upper chest, Kreed's forearm a steel bar forcing him still against the plaster.

Kreed leaned in so that his breath was hot against Carson's ear. "I don't want to hurt you," he warned. "But if you try to hurt her—if you so much as breathe wrong in her direction again—I won't stop at pain. I'll make you bleed."

The threat hung in the air, visceral and real. Kreed's muscles coiled beneath his shirt, the controlled power in every line of his body.

"Kreed!" I shouted.

He didn't move. Didn't even acknowledge me. His focus was on Carson, who was pressed against the wall like a butterfly pinned to a board.

Carson struggled, his face contorted in a mask of anger and shame, but he wasn't going anywhere. His feet scrabbled against the floor for purchase he'd never find. He had no training, no chance against someone like Kreed.

"Kreed," I repeated, firmer this time, placing my hand on his arm. "Let him go. Please."

His nostrils flared as he drew in a breath, the desire to make Carson pay for his words battling against whatever part of him still heard my voice. After what felt like an eternity but was probably only seconds, he slowly released Carson and stepped back, keeping himself positioned between us.

Carson turned around, immediately rubbing his wrist where Kreed had twisted it, his face flushed red with fury and humiliation. "You brought a damn attack dog into my house."

"No," I said coldly. "I brought someone who isn't afraid to get shit done. If you'd stop letting your emotions cloud your judgment for five seconds, maybe we'd actually get somewhere."

Carson stared at me, his mouth opening then closing as betrayal bloomed across his features, but underneath it all, buried beneath the anger and the wounded pride, there was hurt. So much hurt that it made my chest ache.

"I'm scared too, Carson. But fighting each other doesn't bring Kenny home."

Carson backed away from me, dragging both hands through his already disheveled hair as if trying to physically ground himself. I thought he might kick us out. Instead, he collapsed onto the arm of the couch. "I didn't sleep last night," he muttered. "I just kept waiting...for a message, a call, anything. I kept thinking maybe she'd just show up at the door, maybe it was all some massive misunderstanding, you know?" His laugh was hollow. "Like she'd just been at some guy's place and forgot to check her phone."

I nodded with understanding and stepped closer as Kreed stayed rooted just behind me.

Carson glanced up at me, and I saw the boy I'd grown up with, scared, lost, trying so hard to be strong. "But she didn't. And she won't. Not unless we do something."

"We are doing something. We're chasing every lead, talking to everyone who might know something. Rusty's putting feelers out on the street. The Corvos are watching every corner of this city."

The muscle in his jaw jumped beneath his skin. "I don't like you depending on *them*."

"I don't have to like it either." I met his gaze steadily. "But I'll use every tool I've got if it means getting her back. I'll make deals with devils if that's what it takes."

Carson looked past me to Kreed. "I don't trust you."

"I don't need you to," Kreed replied coolly. His hands remained loose at his sides, but there was steel underneath the casual posture. "I just need you not to get in our way."

Carson's weight shifted forward like he was preparing to launch himself off the couch, but he surprised me. Instead of exploding, he shook his head. "This is messed up."

"Tell me about it," I murmured.

I sat for a beat, watching Carson's face as he stared at his hands, at the red marks on his wrists, at anything but us. "Have her parents heard anything? Any new leads? Did the police find anything on her phone?" I asked.

Carson shook his head slowly. "Nothing. They're treating it like a possible runaway. Again. Just like the other girls."

"They're wasting time." I sighed. "We need to push harder. Find someone who knows something. And if the cops aren't going to move, then we will."

Carson finally looked, really looked at me, and I saw a glint of the old Carson, the one who'd always believed I could do anything. "You're not giving up, are you?"

"No," I whispered. "Never."

"You get one shot," he said, his gaze sliding past me to fix on Kreed. "One. If something happens to her because of you—"

"She's not your responsibility. She's mine," Kreed declared.

My breath caught, not surprise, exactly, but recognition. Like he'd just admitted out loud what had been hovering unspoken between us for weeks.

I didn't correct him. Didn't protest or deflect or make a joke to cut through the tension.

Not this time.

Because for the first time since this nightmare began, since Kenny had vanished and my world had tilted sideways, I didn't feel alone. And maybe that was the scariest part of all, how easily I'd let him become the thing I leaned on when everything else was falling apart.

18

KREED

Kaylor climbed into the car and immediately turned toward the window, her shoulders hunching inward like the weight of the world had settled there and was slowly crushing her from the inside out. Her spine was rigid, and her hands were folded in her lap, holding herself together, as if she let go even for a second she might shatter into pieces too small to put back together.

I hated it. Hated seeing her like this, hated that I'd been part of what drove her to this breaking point.

The engine hummed beneath us as I reached for her, then stopped short, my hand hovering in the space between us as if I'd hit an invisible wall. She looked so damn fragile sitting there, her reflection ghostlike in the window, and I didn't know if touching her would help or make her break faster. The uncertainty was killing me.

Then I heard a soft, choked breath she tried to smother behind her hand.

Fuck this.

I slid across the seat without hesitation, reaching for her gently as if she were made of spun glass and might dissolve at the wrong touch.

"Come here, little raven," I murmured, my voice rough with emotion I couldn't name.

Her head shook in automatic denial, but her resistance was weak. She glanced at me with eyes too bright, too glassy, and folded herself into my arms as if she'd been waiting for someone to say it was okay to fall apart.

My arms wrapped around her instinctively. She trembled with the force of her grief, silent sobs shaking through her. I held her tighter, one hand cradling the back of her head where her hair was silky soft against my palm, the other wrapped around her waist. She twisted the fabric of my hoodie hard enough that her knuckles pressed against my chest as I unbuckled her seat belt and pulled her onto my lap. "It's okay," I murmured against her hair, breathing in the scent of her shampoo mixed with salt and fear. "I've got you."

She buried her face into the curve of my neck, and with that surrender came the flood of emotions she'd been working so hard to keep wrapped up inside her. Her tears were silent, but they soaked through my shirt. Every shallow breath she took, every stiff shake of her shoulders, each one felt like a nail being driven into my goddamn ribs.

My hand stroked down her spine in long, slow movements, trying to soothe the tremors that kept rolling through her. I pressed my lips to her temple, feeling the flutter of her pulse beneath the delicate skin, then to beneath her eyes where tears tracked silver lines, then to the corner of her mouth, brief, barely there touches but enough that her breath hitched and caught.

She looked up at me with those light-blue eyes, now shiny and red-rimmed, full of sadness. Her cheeks were flushed pink from crying, her lips parted as she tried to catch her breath. My hand found the curve of her jaw, my thumb tracing the line of her cheekbone as I tilted her face to mine. Her palm settled over my chest, right where my heart was hammering hard enough that I was sure she could feel it.

The air between us grew charged. I wasn't sure who leaned in first, only that the space between us got smaller until it disappeared entirely. My breath mingled with hers, and I could feel the heat rolling off her skin, could taste the salt of her grief and the temptation buried beneath it, so sweet and dangerous and impossible to resist.

"I'm sorry," she whispered against my lips. "I hate crying. I hate being weak."

"You don't ever have to apologize to me. And you're not weak. You're the strongest person I know."

Her gaze dropped to my mouth, lingering there. "You can't say things like that to me. It makes hating you so freaking hard."

"Good—"

Her mouth closed over mine, and it was becoming my favorite thing when she stole my words with her lips. The kiss was tentative at first, her lips trembling against mine, but with us, a quiet kiss was hardly enough. She pressed closer, her mouth opening slightly as a soft sound escaped her throat that was part sob and part need. Her hands fisted in my shirt, pulling me down to her.

As if I could ever deny her anything.

I kissed her back because I'd been selfishly craving her taste for weeks, the sweetness of her lips, the way she fit against me like she was made for this, and the few moments I'd stolen were hardly enough to feed the craving. But even as my body responded, even as heat pooled low in my stomach and my fingers pressed into her waist, I wouldn't take advantage of her. Not ever again.

I'd give us both a few minutes of distracted heaven before forcing us back to the darkness waiting for us outside this car. Let myself taste her sadness, her fire, her need all mixed together on her tongue. Let her feel through the desperate press of my mouth how badly I wanted her.

Her tongue traced the seam of my lips, hesitant but hungry, and I opened for her with a low groan rumbling through my chest. When she shifted on my lap, pressing closer until there was no space left between us, the rapid beat of her heart fluttered against my chest.

My hand tangled in her hair, my fingers threading through the silky strands as I angled her head to deepen the kiss. She melted into me, all soft curves and warm skin, her body molding to mine. The sound she made when my teeth grazed her bottom lip was broken and needy, and it nearly undid every good intention I had. I wasn't used to denying myself things I wanted, and God, did I want her.

Neither one of us gave Evan a thought, so absorbed in each other.

Did I want to undress her and take her in the back of the car? With every fiber in my body, but I couldn't let this happen. Not like this. Not when she was using me as an escape from pain instead of choosing me for who I was.

I had to pull away even though it felt like tearing something vital out of my chest. Resting my forehead against hers, our breaths came ragged and hot as they mingled in the small space between us. Her eyes were still closed, her lips parted and swollen from our kiss, and she looked so beautiful it hurt.

"Little raven," I said softly. I brushed my thumb across her bottom lip, feeling the dampness there, lingering on the soft fullness before trailing down to trace the line of her jaw.

Her eyes fluttered open, confusion starting to shadow the desire that had been burning there moments before. Her brows drew together in a way that made me want to smooth the lines with my lips.

"I won't take advantage of you again," I murmured even as I wondered what the fuck was wrong with me. "You can use me all you want, but it has to be your choice."

"Use you—" She shoved at my chest, desire morphing into anger. The line was so easy to cross. I knew. "Is that what you think I'm doing?"

My brows lifted. "Aren't you? It took away the numbness, didn't it? Made you feel something that wasn't guilt and anguish. Don't get me wrong. I want you. Turns out, I always want you."

She sagged against me like all the fight had gone out of her, her body soft and pliant in my arms. "I never thought there would be a day when Kreed Corvo rejected me."

"This is the opposite of rejection, little raven." My arms tightened around her, one hand stroking down her spine in slow, soothing motions. "This is the most selfless decision I've ever made. If you were any other girl, I wouldn't be here having this conversation."

"Why me?" she whispered, the question so quiet I almost missed it.

"Why not you?" I countered, tilting her chin up so she met my eyes. "Why wouldn't it be you?"

Her lips parted like she wanted to argue, to list all the reasons why she wasn't worth consideration, but no words came out. Just a soft exhale ghosting across my skin that made my heart squeeze. "What have you done with Kreed?"

She had to stop saying my name all breathless and wondering. I was on the verge of throwing this good-guy act out the window and taking full possession of those lips, giving her exactly what she wanted and not giving a shit that we were in my car. "I don't fucking know," I admitted, "but this has to be your fault somehow."

Her chuckle was soft and short, like she didn't want to allow herself to feel anything but guilt and misery. It vanished from her lips as quickly as it had appeared, replaced by that haunted look that made me want to hunt down everyone who'd ever hurt her. I guess that would include me. Make that make sense.

Her head came to rest on my shoulder, the rhythmic in and out of her breaths caressing the side of my neck, a test of my rapidly fraying will.

I couldn't pinpoint exactly when shit had changed for me, when my concern had shifted from protecting myself to protecting her, from putting my family first to making her my priority. All I knew was that, somewhere along the way, she'd become the most important thing in my world, and I'd break every law before I let anyone hurt her again.

THE SECOND THE message came through Raine's burner, the buzz cutting through the quiet night air, I knew we didn't have time to waste. We were still parked outside Brock's house, the engine ticking as it cooled, while Kaylor was asleep upstairs in her room. The house stood dark except for the single lamp Mason had left burning in the front window, a signal that all was well.

Mason was inside with her, stretched out on the couch with explicit instructions to stay the fuck out of her room unless the damn house was on fire. I hated leaving her, but I'd made her a promise I intended to keep, which meant that despite every instinct screaming at me to go upstairs and crawl into bed with her, I had a lead to follow.

Raine leaned over from the driver's seat, his long legs pressed up against the worn leather, phone in his tattooed hand. The screen's blue glow cast harsh shadows across his angular face as his eyes scanned the message. "A girl matching Kenny's description was seen being transported through the South Rail district. Three nights ago. With two other girls. They were loaded into a black SUV outside the old cement factory."

Adrenaline flooded my system so fast it made my hands shake. Three nights ago. That would put the timeline right after Kenny disappeared.

"That's Raven territory," Maddox growled from the back seat, his voice rough with sleep but already alert. He turned to look at me through the partition, his eyes hard and calculating. "Why would the Vipers trespass? You think it's a trap?"

"Probably." I opened the door, the cold night air immediately biting through my hoodie and raising goose bumps along my arms. My boots hit the asphalt as I circled to the back of the SUV and popped the trunk with more force than necessary. "Doesn't matter. We're checking it out."

The trunk opened to reveal our arsenal, guns nestled in foam, magazines lined up like soldiers, blades gleaming under the streetlight. The sight of it all made something dark and hungry stir in my chest.

Maddox joined me at the trunk, his movements fluid and practiced as he began loading magazines into a Glock with an efficiency that spoke of experience. His fingers moved with mechanical precision, muscle memory taking over. "It doesn't make sense."

Raine stayed calm as always, but beneath the fall of his black hair, his eyes were focused. He was already dressed for this brand of work, black jeans molded to his lean frame, combat boots laced tight, and I caught the glint of a blade tucked into the back of the waistband of his dark jeans. "Kaylor?" he asked, glancing toward the house where a single upstairs window glowed softly. "You leaving her behind?"

My teeth ground together. I couldn't tell from his tone if he approved of the idea or thought it was a mistake, and that uncertainty scraped against my nerves. "Mason's inside with her," I said, checking the action on my own weapon. "He'll stay until I say otherwise. She doesn't leave the house. Not tonight."

And if my sneaky little fox somehow managed to slip past Mason, which, knowing her, she'd try, Evan and two of Brock's most trusted *friends* were stationed around the perimeter.

"She's gonna love that," Maddox muttered, checking the safety on his gun with a metallic click that sounded unnaturally loud in the quiet night.

"She doesn't have to love it," I replied as I slammed the trunk shut. "She just has to stay safe." Because if something happened to her while I was gone, if I came back to find her hurt or worse, I'd never forgive myself. The thought of her scared and alone, of coming home to an empty house and cold sheets, made my chest feel like it was caving in on itself.

Maddox snorted. "Are you sure this is the girl for you? She's a lot of fucking trouble, man." His eyes narrowed as he studied my face.

He was telling me. I scraped a hand through my hair, the cost of every wrong move, yet leading us here. "Regardless of my feelings, we owe her for what we did."

Maddox's frown deepened, carving harsh lines around his mouth. He kicked at a loose chunk of concrete, sending it skittering across the asphalt. "You think this lead's real?"

"Only one way to find out."

Raine grinned humorlessly. "I can't believe you're trusting her with Mason."

I shook my head. "I can't trust her with any of you. Mason just got lucky tonight."

"Let's hope he doesn't get lucky, or he'll be dead in the morning," Raine muttered.

"Just get in the fucking car and drive," I grumbled over my shoulder, heading back to the SUV, my thoughts spinning in circles that led nowhere good.

We drove, and the farther south we went, the more the city decayed around us like a wound that wouldn't heal. Boarded windows stared back at us like dead eyes. Graffiti-tagged concrete walls told stories of territory wars and forgotten dreams. Chain-link fences stretched between abandoned lots, their razor wire catching fragments of neon light from distant signs, leading to nowhere and protecting nothing.

The old building stood like a forgotten ruin against the bruised sky, its broken windows staring out like hollow sockets in a skull. Rust stains streaked down the concrete walls like dried blood, and weeds pushed through cracks in the loading dock where trucks used to bring hope in the form of honest work.

We pulled up down the block, headlights clicking off with a soft whisper. The engine ticked as it cooled. Raine was the first out, his hand hovering over the hilt of his knife, fingers flexing and releasing in a nervous tell he'd never quite managed to shake. "We're going through the side. Briggs said they were seen entering near the loading dock."

I nodded. "Maddox, you cover rear. Stay sharp and watch for runners." I turned to my right-hand man. "Raine, you're with me."

As we crept toward the building, our footsteps muffled by years of practice and necessity, adrenaline simmered beneath my skin. We'd been doing shit like this since we could walk. At least it felt that way. I'd never forget the first time the old man stuck a gun in my hand. It was a memory you never forgot. I told myself I was done with this shit, and I was. Once this was over, that was it. I was walking away from it all.

The air hung thick and stagnant, smelling like rust and mold, old concrete, and something else, something that made my nostrils flare and my gut clench, but we were getting closer. I could sense it.

19

KAYLOR

I woke up in darkness. The kind that pressed against your eyelids like velvet, making it impossible to tell if your eyes were open or closed, if the world still existed beyond the suffocating quiet. The bed beside me was empty, cold sheets stretched where warmth should have been. My hand instinctively reached out anyway, fingers searching blindly across the mattress for Kreed, expecting to find the familiar landscape of his body, the steady rise and fall of his chest. Nothing but cotton and disappointment.

My pulse jumped, a staccato rhythm too loud in the silence.

Pushing the covers off with more force than necessary, I sat up slowly, the cool air hitting my bare legs. I blinked hard into the dark, trying to force my vision to adjust as I swung my feet to the floor and strode toward the hallway. The hardwood was ice beneath my bare soles; each step a small shock to help clear the fog of sleep from my brain.

A faint flicker of light bled up from downstairs, painting ghostly rectangles on the hallway walls. Shadows danced and shifted, accompanied by the soft murmur of a television filtering up through the quiet house.

Kreed. It had to be him. Maybe he couldn't sleep either; maybe he was waiting for me to find him.

I padded down the stairs, each step careful and deliberate to avoid the creaks I'd memorized. His oversized hoodie from earlier hung loose around my frame, the sleeves swallowing my hands completely, the fabric still carrying traces of his cologne. The glow of the television drew me into the living room, but it wasn't Kreed sprawled across the leather couch.

Mason?

He sat there with casual confidence, one long leg draped over the other, remote balanced lazily in his palm. A smug little grin played at the corners of his mouth as he flipped through channels with a deliberate slowness suggesting he had nowhere else to be. The blue light from the screen cast angles across his face, highlighting the aristocratic line of his jaw and the mischief that seemed permanently etched in his features.

"What are you doing here? Where's Kreed?" I demanded, wondering what was going on. Nothing like going to sleep with one Corvo and waking up with another.

He turned toward me with that infuriating sparkle in his eye, the one suggesting he knew exactly how unsettled I was and found it endlessly entertaining. "Out. It's just you and me, my little kitten." His voice carried that trademark Mason drawl, honey smooth and designed to get under your skin.

I arched a brow, crossing my arms defensively across my chest. "Is that supposed to make me feel secure?"

"At least I'm not Maddox," he said with a shrug that somehow managed to be both dismissive and suggestive. He stretched like a cat in a sunbeam, all lazy grace and hidden claws. "Pretty sure he's got a hard-on for you."

My nose wrinkled at the mental image. "Let's save the dick talks for another night."

Mason raised an eyebrow. "Even Kreed's?"

Heat flashed up my neck, but I pushed through it with stubborn determination. "You want to talk about how impressive your brother's cock is? How fucking huge is it? How he knows exactly how to—"

"Okay, stop. You're right. Bad idea." He held up both hands in mock surrender, but his grin only widened, those dimples carving deep crescents in his cheeks. The expression lit up his whole face, transforming him from dangerous criminal to charming rogue in the space of a heartbeat. For a second, I almost felt sorry for the poor girls who didn't know better than to fall for Mason Corvo's particular brand of trouble.

"You didn't answer my question," I pointed out, steering him back to the topic. "Where is he?"

"Out with Raine and Mad."

My stomach twisted into a familiar knot of dread. "Did something happen? Did he—?"

"No, not yet." Mason's grin faded. He muted the television, plunging us into a quieter intimacy. "This is why he didn't say anything. He didn't want to get your hopes up."

That twinkle of anticipation that had bloomed inside me like a fragile flower fizzled and died. Of course. Hope was dangerous. Hope was sharp-edged and treacherous. I sank onto the opposite end of the couch, tucking my legs beneath me. "So what kind of 'not yet' are we talking about here? The kind where he comes home with good news, or the kind where he comes home bleeding?"

Mason studied me for a long moment, his expression uncharacteristically thoughtful. "You really want to know, or are you just asking because you *think* you should?"

The question caught me off guard. "I want to know. I *need* to know."

He leaned forward, elbows resting on his knees. "They got a tip about where they might be transporting. If it pans out, if they can get these girls out... It might give us leverage. Information. A way to trace this whole fucking network back to whoever's pulling the strings."

I didn't give a shit about the network. I cared about my friend. "And if it doesn't pan out?"

"Then they come home empty-handed, and we start over tomorrow. But Kreed..." He paused, running a hand through his dark hair. "He's not the type to let things go. He won't stop until he finds answers even if it kills him for your sake. Kreed doesn't give loyalty easily, but when he does, it's unbreakable."

The words hung between us, a bridge I wasn't sure I wanted to cross. "You think he's in danger tonight?"

"I think Kreed is always in danger." Mason's smile returned, but it was different now, guarded. "But he's got Raine and Maddox watching his back. They'll be fine."

"How did you get stuck here with me?"

"Someone had to make sure you didn't run off and get yourself kidnapped or killed."

My stomach suddenly growled so loudly and demandingly that even Mason raised a brow. "When was the last time you ate?" he inquired.

I pressed a hand to my abdomen, trying to remember when I'd last put food in my body that wasn't coffee or whatever passed for cafeteria sustenance at school. "Who knows." I shrugged. "I'm getting a snack. Do you want anything?" I offered as I pushed myself off the couch, needing the movement, the distraction of routine tasks.

"Anything but that hummus shit you're always eating," he called after me.

I rolled my eyes but didn't answer as I went to the kitchen. Only the faint night-light under the cabinet cast a warm amber glow, creating a small island of safety in the sea of black. I opened the fridge, the sudden burst of white light making me squint as cold air rushed out to embrace my skin. The shelves were better stocked than they had any right to be, Brock's doing, his quiet way of taking care of me when he wasn't here. I rummaged around halfheartedly, pushing aside containers of leftover takeout and bottles of water, not really seeing any of it.

That's when I heard it.

A faint buzzing, barely audible over the hum of the refrigerator.

I frowned, my hand freezing halfway to a container of strawberries. The sound came again, muted but persistent, like an insect trapped behind glass. I straightened slowly, letting the fridge door swing shut and plunge me back into amber twilight, my ears straining to locate the source.

I reached for my phone on the granite counter, fingers fumbling in the dim light, but the screen remained dark and silent. No new notifications. No missed calls. Nothing.

The buzzing hadn't come from my phone, so where? Had one of the guys left their device here? Was it Mason's? But he was still in the living room.

I turned slowly, every nerve ending suddenly alive and crackling with unease. The sound was definitely coming from behind me, somewhere near the kitchen table. My eyes landed on the chair where I'd carelessly dumped my bag earlier after stumbling through the front door, exhausted after seeing Rusty and Carter.

A chill ran down my spine, ice-cold fingers tracing each vertebra.

My feet felt heavy as concrete as I crossed the room. I unzipped the front pocket of my bag with trembling fingers, the metal teeth parting with a soft whisper. Digging inside, my hand brushed past the usual debris of student life, crumpled receipts, lip balm, and loose change until my fingers found something that didn't belong.

Something hard. Small. And definitely not mine.

A burner phone.

I pulled it out like it might bite me, the cheap plastic warm against my palm. I'd never seen it before. The screen glowed to life at my touch, no passcode, no security, nothing standing between me and whatever message had been burning a hole through my bag. A single text was displayed across the cracked screen, the words stark and brutal in their simplicity:

Tomorrow. Midnight. The old train yard off Route 19. Come alone. No Crew. No Corvo. No Cops. Or Kenny dies.

My breath caught in my throat. I reread the message, the words blurring slightly as my hands began to shake, hoping the letters would rearrange themselves into words less terrifying. My world tilted sideways, reality shifting beneath my feet.

The phone grew heavier in my hands, the message echoing in my skull like a warning siren that wouldn't stop screaming. *How the fuck did this phone get in my bag? When could someone have put it there? How long has it been in there?*

I tried to retrace my steps, but panic was creeping up my throat, making it hard to think clearly. I'd gone to school, sat through classes, eaten lunch, and pretended to care about assignments. The shop and then to Carson's after. That was it. I hadn't left my bag unattended except...

Except in the town car when Evan came to pick us up at the shop.

My mind began to spin as I thought back. I'd left it in the back seat while we went inside Carson's, trusting in the illusion of safety that Evan's presence provided.

That meant whoever was behind this had been close. Close enough to breathe the same air I breathed. Close enough to slip a phone into my bag without me noticing, to violate my space. Close enough to track me, watch me, maybe even follow me home to this sanctuary I'd foolishly believed was safe.

Could it have been Evan?

There was no way. Kreed trusted him explicitly, but did I? Evan had been employed by the Corvos for more than a decade, but he worked for Kreed's dad, *not* Kreed. Perhaps it was Donovan who ordered Evan to slip the burner into my bag. Nothing else made sense. I couldn't see how anyone could get past Evan unless he'd been distracted by something or someone. I made a mental note to ask Evan if anything unusual had happened while we'd been inside Carter's.

My stomach churned, a nauseating cocktail of fear and rage burning in my chest.

A low, static ringing filled my ears. If they could get this into my bag, slip past every defense and precaution, what else could they do? How long had they been watching?

The sound of footsteps broke through the fog of panic.

"Hey, you good?" Mason's voice came from around the corner before he stepped into the kitchen. His expression was open, relaxed even, but I watched it shift as his gaze landed on me, the way his pupils dilated slightly into confusion.

I froze like a deer in headlights, every muscle in my body locking up.

He looked from me to the untouched fridge, its door still hanging open and spilling light across the tile floor, then back to my face. The blood drained out of me so fast I felt dizzy, my vision swimming at the edges as I instinctively palmed the burner phone behind my back, the plastic warm and slick against my suddenly sweaty palm. I tried to keep my features neutral, to arrange my face into an expression resembling normal, but my heart was hammering so loudly I was sure he could hear it.

Too late.

"Are you okay?" he asked again. His brows drew together in a way that transformed his boyish features into someone older. "You look like you just saw a ghost."

My mouth opened, but nothing came out except a small, strangled sound barely qualifying as breathing. I licked my lips, tongue darting out nervously as I fumbled for something, anything, to say that wouldn't sound like the complete lie it was. "I...I couldn't decide what to grab," I muttered, turning toward the open fridge to hide the tremor that had started in my hands and was now spreading up my arms. I pretended to study the shelves with intense concentration, like the arrangement of leftover Chinese takeout and expired yogurt was the most important decision I'd ever made.

Mason didn't buy it. Not even close.

"Wanna tell me what's really going on?"

I clutched the phone behind my back. "It's nothing. I'm just tired. Haven't really been sleeping. Shocking, right?"

He didn't laugh. Didn't even crack a smile. "Kaylor."

I flinched, my shoulders jerking involuntarily. My name sounded different coming from him now, not teasing or fond but serious. Like he was giving me one last chance to tell him the truth before he stopped asking nicely.

He looked down, scanning me from head to toe with a systematic thoroughness that made me feel like he was cataloging evidence. My posture was too rigid; my shoulders were drawn up defensively. The strain in my voice was too high, and the words were coming too fast. The way my eyes wouldn't meet his, darting away every time he tried to catch my gaze. How my breathing had gone shallow and quick.

"What happened?" he demanded, sounding eerily like Kreed. He moved deeper into the kitchen, boxing me in against the counter and effectively cutting off any easy escape routes. "Don't make me call Kreed."

The phone burned in my hand, the threat in the message feeling more real, more immediate. *Come alone. No cops. No Elite. No Crew.*

If I told him... Kreed would find out within minutes. Wouldn't that be a good thing? Perhaps this was helpful, but something was holding me back. Something was telling me not to tell Mason about the burner phone.

But lying to them again? Keeping this from Kreed?

It made my gut twist into knots.

Mason stared at me, and I didn't know what to do. Every option felt like betrayal.

I forced a shaky breath, my lungs burning with the effort, and grabbed the first things I saw in the fridge, string cheese that had seen better days and a half-empty bag of grapes that looked lonely on the top shelf. My movements were jerky, uncoordinated, as if my body had forgotten how to function normally. Before turning around, I quickly stuffed the burner phone deep into the front pocket of

Kreed's hoodie, the fabric soft and oversized enough to hide the tell-tale bulge.

Mason hadn't moved.

He was still watching, suspicion darkening his usually playful light-green eyes until they looked almost gray in the amber kitchen light. "You sure nothing happened?"

I nodded too quickly. "Yeah. Sorry. I'm just...overwhelmed, I guess." The words were clumsy on my tongue. "It caught up to me for a second. I'm okay now."

He didn't look convinced. Not even a little bit. His eyes never left mine, and I could see the promise there: this conversation wasn't over. "All right. But grapes are a sucky snack. You got any popcorn in this place? Some candy, preferably chocolate."

"I'm sure there's a box of microwave popcorn in the cabinets," I retorted.

He nodded. "I'll find the popcorn, and *you* can take your grapes, but don't un-pause the movie until I get back."

I rolled my eyes. "I wouldn't dream of it." Leaving Mason in the kitchen, I took my pathetic snack that I really didn't want and rushed back into the family room. A few minutes later, Mason plopped back down onto the leather couch with a giant bowl of popcorn, filling the room with the aroma of butter and salt. The grapes couldn't compete.

I sat at the opposite end, and if I had any chance of getting my hand in that bowl, I had to move closer. Mason played the movie, and my stomach made a hollow ache. I glanced at the grapes and then at the popcorn. The choice was obvious.

Unfolding my legs, I inched to the center cushion. Without saying a word, he put the bowl between us. We munched through the first five minutes of the movie before he picked up his drink and offered it to me.

I took a big swig, thirstier than I realized before the presence of booze registered. "Is there rum in this?"

He shot me a cheeky grin. "Is there any other way to have a Coke?"

"Should you be drinking on the job?"

He shrugged. "The way I see it, I'm the one who lucked out tonight. I'd rather be here with you than out there hunting monsters."

I took another sip before passing it back to him, and the message on the burner phone sat heavy on my chest. My thoughts were too loud. Too fast. Racing like a hamster on a wheel that wouldn't stop spinning.

Alone. No cops. No Elite. No Crew. The words kept going off in my head. Each repetition made them feel more real, more urgent, more impossible to ignore.

They'd said to come alone, and I believed them. Believed that deviation from their script would mean blood on my hands, consequences I couldn't live with. I didn't trust that Kenny would survive if I didn't follow their rules to the letter. So, I'd go. I had to. The decision sat in my chest, heavy and cold and absolutely final.

It was a decision I'd been teetering with all day, and getting the text just seemed to solidify what I had to do, but that was the easy part. The hard part was going to be getting past Mason, Maddox, Raine, Brock, and eventually, inevitably, Kreed.

I slid a glance toward Mason, who had stretched his long legs out on the coffee table and was now chewing popcorn like it was his job, completely relaxed despite the undercurrent of suspicion radiating from him. There was no way I could sneak out with all of them on watch, not unless I leveled the playing field somehow. Not unless I made them sleep through it.

The idea came like a whisper in the dark, but it stuck to my brain like a burr, impossible to shake once it had taken root.

Sleeping pills.

Aunt Char suffered from insomnia, and I was positive I'd seen a bottle of sleeping pills in her bathroom when I'd gone hunting for a toothbrush. I didn't want to kill anyone, just knock them out long enough for me to escape. Nothing Google couldn't help me calculate: the dosage, timing, and delivery method. I could crush the pills into powder. Mix them into drinks. Hot chocolate, perhaps, or booze.

So, while Mason watched his movie, I silently planned my own death sentence. If he only knew what was going on inside my head. The betrayal they would all feel. I'd wanted revenge, just not like this.

The thought made my stomach stab with self-loathing. I hated the idea of tricking them, especially Kreed, but what other choice did I have? They wouldn't let me go. Not willingly. Not when they found out what I was planning. Kreed would lock me in a room before he'd let me walk into what was obviously a trap, and part of me, the smart part, the part that wanted to live, knew he'd be right to do it.

But Kenny's life was still hanging in the balance, and I was the only one who could tip the scales.

"Hey," Mason said, tossing a kernel of popcorn into the air and catching it in his mouth. "You're thinking too hard over there. I can practically hear the gears grinding." He flashed me that trademark grin, but his eyes remained assessing. "Want me to change the movie to something more romantic? Or a comedy? Something that doesn't require actual brain power?"

I startled, my body jerking as if I'd been caught doing something criminal. Which, technically, I was about to be doing. "No, this is fine. Just..." I forced what I hoped was a believable smile, but it felt like stretching plastic wrap across my face. "When will Kreed be back?"

"Late. Could be hours yet, depending on what they find." Mason's expression softened slightly, genuine concern creeping in around the edges of his suspicion. "Maybe you should try and get some sleep. Come here." He opened his arm, his fingers indicating for me to move.

I chewed on the corner of my mouth, my lips tasting like buttery salt.

"Just sleep." He gave me a lopsided grin. "I promise not to cop a feel...unless you want me to."

I rolled my eyes, contemplating if resting in his arms was a very bad idea, but I always slept better in Kreed's. Mason wasn't Kreed, but he was as close as I would get. "You swear to keep your sneaky hands off me."

He lifted both hands in the air. "You have my word."

I double-checked to make sure he hadn't crossed any of his fingers, because that was just the shit Mason would pull. Grabbing the throw blanket, I scooted into his arms, my head resting on the space below his shoulder, and curled into him. His arms came to rest around me, and he felt warm and safe. Different from Kreed, but it did the trick. I closed my eyes, trying to clear my head of thoughts, but a dose of guilt hit me, and it had nothing to do with using Mason as a human pillow.

Tomorrow's deadline loomed like a thundercloud on the horizon. I had a mission. A terrible, dangerous, probably suicidal mission that would either save my best friend's life or end mine.

And for better or worse, I was going alone.

SUNLIGHT FILTERED SOFTLY through the curtains, warm and golden as it washed across my skin. I blinked slowly, muscles still heavy with sleep, my eyelids fluttering against the brightness. The familiar ache in my lower back told me I'd been lying in one position too long, but as awareness crept in, I realized I wasn't where I'd fallen asleep in Mason's arms.

I was in my bed, but I wasn't alone.

How did I get here was my first thought. My second...

Fuck.

I didn't... I wouldn't have...

No way I slept with Mason. Like I hadn't been that tired. Had I?

Lifting my gaze, a rush of air expelled from my lungs at the sight of Kreed's gorgeous face. His arm was slung across my waist like he was still protecting me even in sleep. His face was half buried in the crook of my neck, stubble scratching against my collarbone with each slow, deep breath. Heat radiated from his body, seeping through the thin fabric of my shirt until the steady thrum of his pulse beat against my shoulder blade.

Oh, thank God.

But unfortunately, the relief at knowing I hadn't gone to bed with his brother didn't last long as the message from last night slammed into the forefront of my mind.

Today was the last time I'd wake up beside Kreed like this.

Tonight, I was leaving him behind.

Tonight, I'd be gone.

Tonight, I'd betray his trust.

And he didn't have a clue.

Oh, how the fucking tables have turned.

I stayed perfectly still for a moment, afraid that even the slightest movement would shatter this fragile bubble of peace. My ribs rose and fell in careful rhythm, matching his breathing as I memorized the weight of his arm and the scratch of his stubble against my skin. The way he seemed to instinctively pull me closer even as he slept, his fingers twitching slightly against my hip bone. One lock of dark hair had fallen across his forehead, and I fought the urge to brush it back.

I shouldn't wake him, not with what awaited him, but I couldn't stop myself from turning my head just enough to study his face.

He looked...peaceful. And younger somehow. The harsh lines around his eyes had softened in sleep, his jaw unclenched for once. As if the constant tension he wore during the day, the rigid set of his shoulders, the way his hands always seemed ready to reach for a weapon, had finally loosened its grip. There were no edges on him right now, just soft, steady breaths and a quiet that made my heart ache.

This morning, I wanted something selfish. Something simple. Just a moment with him that didn't involve fear, or loss, or the world pressing down on both of us until we could barely breathe.

I shifted slightly to face him, the mattress dipping under my weight as I propped myself on one elbow. My fingers hovered above his cheek, trembling slightly, and without even thinking, I traced the line of his jaw with my fingertip. The contact was featherlight, but he leaned into it unconsciously. I brushed against the faint shadow of a bruise near his temple, purple and green at the edges, a reminder of yesterday's violence.

That warmth in my chest bloomed, unfurling like sun-drenched ivy, curling through my ribs and spreading outward until my whole body hummed with it. I wanted to memorize every version of Kreed. The good and the bad. All of him.

God, he's beautiful.

And he didn't deserve any of this.

Screw it. Why didn't we deserve one day of happiness before I blew up both our lives?

I missed that feeling. The butterflies taking flight in my stomach. The electricity that made my skin feel alive. The part of me that still believed in moments that made all the scars worth it, that whispered maybe, just maybe, some things were worth fighting for.

I leaned in slowly, heart thudding against my ribs so hard I was sure he'd feel it. My lips hovered just above his for a moment so I could taste his exhale. I could feel the pull between us, magnetic and heady, every nerve ending in my body suddenly awake and aware of the space between us, the narrowing distance, and the anticipation making my hands shake. The ache had been building for weeks.

I closed the distance. My lips brushed his softly, a question pressing against his mouth. It was barely a kiss, more like a whisper of contact, but he tensed beneath me, and the answer came immediately.

Kreed stirred, a soft sound rumbling in his chest as his lips parted slightly. His breath caught as I kissed him again, deeper this time. His hand came up slowly, fingers finding their way into my hair, threading through the tangled strands. He pulled me closer with gentle insistence, lips pressing more firmly against mine, and I melted into him.

Heat flooded my veins, pooling low in my stomach as his other hand found the small of my back, his fingers splaying wide against my spine. I could taste the salt of sleep on his lips and feel the way his pulse jumped beneath my palm when I pressed it to his throat.

"Good morning," he murmured against my mouth, voice rough with sleep, making me want to kiss him again. His eyes were still closed, but a smile tugged at the corners of his lips.

"Morning," I whispered as I kissed the corner of his mouth, then his jaw, then that spot just below his ear that made him shiver.

His arm tightened around my waist, pulling me flush against him until there was no space left between us. Just skin and warmth and the steady rhythm of two hearts beating in sync. For a moment, I let myself pretend this was real. That tomorrow wouldn't come and I'd still be here, but even as I kissed him deeper, even as his hands mapped the curve of my spine with reverent fingers, I couldn't shake the cloud hanging between us.

By sunset, this would all be a memory.

By sunset, I'd be the villain in his story.

The thought should have made me pull away, should have made me stop this before it went any further. Instead, I kissed him harder, poured every apology I'd never be able to say into the space between his lips and mine, and tried to memorize the taste of his trust before I shattered it completely.

That familiar rush surged through me, sparks blooming in my belly, spiraling outward, the sensation creeping up my spine, vertebra by vertebra, until every nerve ending hummed with electric aware- ness. He kissed me like he needed to feel something real, something that could cut through whatever darkness had been chasing him. Like he didn't know this was goodbye.

And God, it hurt.

My fingers gripped the fabric of his shirt, the soft cotton bunching between my knuckles as I pressed closer, desperate to steal just a little more of him. The heat of his chest seeped through the thin material, his heartbeat accelerating against my palm.

His mouth moved over mine with a quiet hunger, restrained but deep, each kiss deliberate and consuming. His teeth grazed my bottom lip, and a soft moan escaped him when I responded by sliding my tongue against his. My free hand found the nape of his neck, my fingers threading through the short hair there, and he shivered against me.

I melted into him, pouring everything I couldn't say into the way I kissed him, every apology, every confession, every desperate wish that things could be different.

He shifted above me, one hand bracing against the mattress while the other cradled my face, his thumb stroking along my cheekbone with devastating gentleness. My hands slid under his shirt, feeling the solid muscle beneath my palms, the way his breathing hitched when I traced the ripple of his abs.

He broke the kiss for just a moment, forehead pressed to mine, both of us breathing hard in the small space between us. His eyes fluttered open, heavy-lidded and dark, causing my stomach to flip and dive. His pupils were dilated, lips slightly swollen from our kisses, and his fingers were still tangled in my hair as if he didn't want to let go. "What was that for?" he asked, voice rough and thick with sleep and need.

I swallowed hard, trying to keep my face neutral, my heart locked behind a glass wall that was already showing hairline cracks. "I wanted to," I said simply.

His brow arched slowly, those silver eyes studying my face with an exposed intensity. The corner of his mouth twitched. "Why does this feel like a trap?"

The question hit closer to home than I wanted to admit. I forced a smile, just a little one, trying to keep it light. "Will you make me breakfast?"

Kreed rolled onto his back with a groan, one arm flung dramatically across his eyes as he dragged his other hand down his face. The movement pulled his shirt up slightly, revealing a strip of tanned skin that made my mouth go dry. "Not until you tell me what you've done with Kaylor?"

"Maybe I just realized life's too short to hold grudges," I said, rolling onto my side to face him. The mattress shifted under my weight, and I propped my head on my hand.

"Hmm." He gazed up at me. "I don't think I trust anything that comes out of that gorgeous mouth of yours."

I laughed softly, but there was a quiver in it I couldn't quite suppress. "Then why'd you kiss me back?"

"Because I'm a sucker for girls who taste like trouble."

My chest squeezed like someone had wrapped a fist around my heart.

Yeah. Trouble. That's exactly what I was.

And if things went sideways tonight... He might never kiss me again. I was the one betraying him, but staring at the hottest guy I'd ever seen, I wanted one last day to pretend, to commit every line of his face to memory, every piece of this version of us that would die with the setting sun.

I was so falling in love with him. It was about time I admitted it. At least to myself. I didn't know if I had the gumption to tell him, but it didn't seem fair to profess such a thing and then run away. Kreed was the type of guy who would hate that.

Hell, he might hate me come tomorrow morning when he realizes what I'd done.

20

KREED

I didn't cook often, but when I did, I liked the ritual of it; something about cracking eggs and flipping pancakes made me feel halfway normal. The sizzle of bacon filled the air, the skillet spitting tiny drops of grease. I shifted the strips with a fork, watching the edges curl and crisp, the meat releasing its fat in a satisfying crackle. Behind me, the kitchen island gave a subtle creak as Kaylor settled herself on top of it, legs crossed, followed by the soft rustle of fabric as she adjusted her position.

"You know," she said slowly, "I'm honestly a little surprised you know what you're doing."

I didn't turn around, just let a smirk tug at the corner of my mouth as I focused on the pan. The bacon was almost perfect, crispy but not burnt. "Surprised, huh?"

Her sudden shift in attitude toward me made me leery, setting off every alarm bell I'd learned to trust over the years. She had kissed me this morning, initiated contact with a hunger that still made my skin burn when I thought about it. I wanted to believe it was a step in her forgiving me, but it couldn't be that simple. Not with Kaylor. Nothing was ever simple with her. Something was going on beneath that carefully neutral expression, and I planned to figure it out, but in the meantime, I could go along with the masquerade or truce, whatever this was.

"Yeah. You don't exactly give off gourmet chef vibes." Her legs swung over the edge.

I flicked her a glance over my shoulder, taking in the picture she made perched on the counter. Her hair was a complete mess, silver strands wavy from sleep and tousled by my fingers running through it earlier. Her shirt—my shirt, I realized with a jolt—hung off one shoulder, revealing the elegant line of her collarbone and a small freckle I'd never noticed before. Her lips were still slightly swollen from our kisses, fuller than usual and still a tempting shade of pink that made me want to abandon breakfast entirely.

She was smirking, but the faint shadows in her eyes betrayed her. She was trying to act normal, but why? What changed?

I played along, turning back to the stove and reaching for the carton of eggs. "There's a lot you don't know about me," I said, cracking the first egg against the edge of the pan. The whites spread and sizzled, edges beginning to set almost immediately.

"I'll believe it when you make me something edible," she shot back.

"Then prepare to be impressed, little raven." I cracked the second egg, then the third, watching as they cooked alongside the bacon.

She laughed softly, genuinely amused this time, and damn, if a warmth that had nothing to do with the heat from the stove spread inside my chest. "What happened last night? I woke up and you were gone. Mason said you were following a lead."

The fork in my hand stilled, bacon grease popping in the sudden silence. I stiffened for half a second before forcing myself to stay casual, sliding the perfectly cooked eggs onto a plate. The yolks were still runny, just the way I liked them. I turned off the burner and set the pan aside, the metal scraping sound against the stovetop.

When I turned to face her, she was watching me wide, expressive eyes that seemed to see straight through every wall I'd ever built. Hopeful and wary at the same time, clinging to optimism.

"We found a location," I said slowly, choosing my words carefully as I leaned back against the counter. The plate was warm in my hands, ceramic heated by the food. "But by the time we got there, they were gone. The place was stripped clean. No girls, no guards, just...empty rooms and the smell of bleach."

Her shoulders slumped, and the hope in her eyes sputtered, threatening to go out entirely.

"But..." I added, placing the plate in front of her on the counter, my knuckles brushing against her knee in the process. The contact was electric. "That's not the end of it. If anything, it's proof we're on the right track. Moving them means they know we're getting close, that the pressure we're putting on them is working."

She picked at the corner of the toast without really looking at it, her mouth pressed into a firm line.

"Hey," I said quietly. "We're not giving up. None of us are."

She nodded, but it was slow. "I just want her home."

"I know." I understood that desperate, clawing need to protect someone you loved, to bring them back safe, no matter what it cost you. "And we'll get her. I swear to you, we'll bring her home. I don't break promises."

"What if she's already gone?" she whispered, the question so quiet I felt it more than heard it. "What if we're too late?"

My hand came up to cup her face, my thumb stroking along her cheekbone in a gesture that was becoming as natural as breathing. "Then we'll deal with that if it happens. But right now, today, we keep fighting. We keep looking. We don't give up."

She closed her eyes, leaning into my touch. Maybe we were both just clinging to each other in the middle of a storm, pretending we could weather it together.

For now, that was enough.

"Now eat," I ordered, making her roll her eyes, but she picked up her fork anyway.

We were halfway through breakfast when she flicked a piece of egg at me. The small chunk hit my shoulder with a soft splat and dropped onto my plate, leaving a greasy spot on my shirt.

I glanced up slowly, one brow lifting in mock disbelief. My fork paused halfway to my mouth as I stared at her.

Kaylor grinned as if she hadn't just committed an act of war, her eyes sparkling with mischief. She popped another bite into her mouth and chewed like the innocent little liar she was.

"Oh, that's how it's gonna be?" I set my fork down. "I'd expect something like that from Mason but not you."

She swallowed her bite and tilted her head, still playing innocent. "I don't know what you're talking about."

The lie was so blatant, so perfectly delivered with a sweet smile, I almost laughed. Instead, I pushed back my chair and stood, my movements predatory.

Her smile froze, eyes widening as she realized she might have miscalculated. "Kreed…"

Too late.

I rounded the kitchen island, and she bolted to the other side. Her laughter rang out, bright and genuine, as she scrambled away from me. I wasn't even trying hard, just enjoying the chase, giving her enough head start to make it interesting.

Her socked feet nearly slid out from under her on the smooth floor as she darted around the corner, arms windmilling slightly to keep her balance. The sight of her trying to run in those ridiculous fuzzy socks was almost too endearing for words.

"You're going to regret that," I warned, making her squeal with laughter.

"Not if you can't catch me," she shot over her shoulder, breathless from running and laughing at the same time.

That was when I decided to end the game.

I lunged forward, closing the distance between us in two quick strides. She shrieked, the sound dissolving into helpless laughter as I hooked my arm around her waist and pulled her back against me.

Her spine hit my chest with a soft thump, her body fitting perfectly against mine as I spun her around. The momentum carried us both until her back pressed against the kitchen cabinets, the cool wood a stark contrast to the heat radiating between us.

Her breath came fast from the chase, and her heart beat against my forearm where it crossed her ribs, quick and fluttering. She stilled, the laughter fading into something more dangerous. Her hands came up to rest against my chest, her fingers spreading wide over my shirt to steady herself.

Our eyes locked, and everything else seemed to fade away. My hand stayed planted at her waist, my thumb stroking along her hip bone through the thin material, while my other hand came up to push a strand of hair from her face. The silky strands slipped through my fingers like water.

Kaylor looked at me like I was the only thing in the room, like the rest of the world had simply ceased to exist. Her lips parted slightly, just enough to make my breath catch, and my own desire reflected in the centers of her eyes.

That same gravity was pulling us together again, that invisible force existing only between us, dragging me into the storm of her. I leaned in, giving her every chance to stop me, to pull away, to remember all the reasons this was complicated.

But she didn't. She tilted her face up toward mine, and that was all the invitation I needed.

I kissed her.

Not quick or soft like this morning but deep and lingering. I needed her taste to stay with me long after it ended. I wanted to memorize the exact shape of her lips, the way she sighed softly against my mouth. Her arms wrapped around my neck, her fingers threading through the hair at my nape, and I lifted her easily, setting her on the countertop. Her legs slid around my waist, her ankles locking behind my back, pulling me. I pressed my hard-on against her, the thin material of her silky underwear an annoying barrier to the heat I wanted to surround me.

The kiss deepened, becoming desperate, and I tasted the sweetness of orange juice on her lips and felt the way she trembled slightly when I traced the curve of her lower lip with my tongue. My hands found her thighs, my fingers spanning the width of them as my thumbs stroked along the sensitive skin just above her knees.

Her fingers tangled in my hair, tugging hard enough to make me groan against her mouth, and I sank into her, starving for this moment. Maybe I was afraid she would remember she hated me, but I'd take every fucking kiss she was willing to give and then some.

My mouth moved from her lips to trace the line of her jaw, then down to the sensitive spot below her ear that made her breath hitch. She tilted her head back, giving me better access, and her pulse raced beneath my lips.

Fuck. Not another girl wrecked me like she did.

"You're mine, little raven," I murmured down the column of her neck, pushing the neckline of her shirt out of my way so I could press my lips there. The loose material fell off her shoulder, sliding down her arm and exposing the top of her breast, an invitation I couldn't resist. "Tell me who you belong to. Say the words." I dragged my mouth lower.

"I belong to myself."

I shook my head, pushing the fabric out of my way and taking her nipple in my mouth as I swirled my tongue around the pointed bud. "Wrong answer. Try again."

"Kreed," she growled, but it ended on a moan when my teeth grazed her nipple. Her nails dug into my scalp, but I enjoyed the sting, enjoyed knowing it was my mouth that got her hot and bothered. I very much loved the fucking combination.

My lips curved as I trailed my fingers up the inside of her thigh, moving higher and higher. She shivered, but it wasn't enough. I wanted her aching and whimpering my name. I dipped down between her legs, pressing my mouth to the inside of her thigh where my fingers had been seconds ago. My tongue darted over the softest flesh I'd ever had against my lips, her skin a mixture of sweet and salty I craved.

Her head fell back as one hand went to brace herself on the counter, and the other stayed buried in my hair. I hooked a finger into the corner of her black panties, and—

The front door opened with a soft click, and a familiar voice called, "You two better not be screwing where you eat."

Every muscle in my body went rigid as reality came crashing back in. Kaylor's hands stilled in my hair, her breathing ragged against my ear, her heart hammering against my chest, matching the frantic rhythm of my own.

I'm going to kill him.

Kaylor pulled back slightly, eyes wide and lips swollen from our kisses, her cheeks flushed pink with embarrassment and lingering desire. She looked thoroughly debauched, hair mussed and shirt askew, and it took every ounce of self-control I had not to tell my brother to get the hell out.

I straightened, turning my head with a growl. "Maddox, this better be fucking good."

He stood in the doorway, his eyebrows raised in that particular expression of wanting to kick my ass. "People eat here," he grumbled, his gaze shifting to Kaylor and lingering. I knew he kind of had a thing for her, but I was starting to wonder just how deep this thing was rooted inside him.

My brothers and I never fought over a girl. There had never been a girl worth our time to fight over.

Until now.

Kaylor tugged on the stretched neckline of her shirt that had fallen so low down her shoulder that I could see the plump mound of her breast. If I could see it, so could Maddox.

My gaze narrowed. "How did you get in?" I demanded, automatically stepping between him and Kaylor, blocking his view even though the damage was already done.

"The door was unlocked," he said with a casual shrug, his lips twitching.

That stopped me cold. "It shouldn't have been." I never left doors unlocked, never. It was a basic security measure that had been drilled into me since I was old enough to understand the dangers lurking right outside my doorstep. Hell, sometimes the danger was within the walls of the home meant to keep you safe. "I distinctly remember locking it."

"That's a *you* problem, not a me problem," he replied with infuriating logic.

"Mad..." I sighed, dragging a hand down my face in frustration. Behind me, Kaylor slid off from the counter, her feet hitting the floor with a soft thud.

"Fine," he said, waving a dismissive hand toward the hallway like he was doing us some great favor. "I'll check the perimeter since you were obviously too distracted to do it yourself, but you can take your lips and hands off her for two minutes and check the rest of the house." He turned and disappeared down the hall before I could say anything else.

I faced Kaylor, my eyes devouring her, all tousled, flushed, and embarrassed. She never looked hotter except when she came. That was by far my favorite look. "Well, that was a mood killer," I muttered.

She let out a soft, breathless laugh, and my dick hardened. "Little bit. Probably for the best." But even as she said it, her hands came up to rest on my chest again, and I saw in her eyes that she didn't really mean it. That she was as reluctant as I was to let this moment end.

"I disagree." I didn't miss the way her eyes clung to me, drinking in every detail of my face as if she knew something I didn't. Her gaze lingered on my mouth, then traveled up to meet my eyes with an intensity that made me ache.

I was seconds from grabbing her, shoving her against the counter, when the door opened again with a soft swoosh of displaced air. "I swear to fucking—"

Mason strolled in first, his crooked grin already plastered on his face like he'd been waiting outside just long enough to make an entrance. He gave an exaggerated once-over of the kitchen, taking in the forgotten breakfast plates and the general state of dishevelment we'd left in our wake.

Raine followed behind, his movements more measured as his dark eyes scanned the evident situation, and the idiot grinned. "Are we interrupting something?"

Kaylor leaned her hip against the granite counter with fluid grace. Her arms folded across her chest, the movement drawing my attention to the way my shirt hung on her frame, still wrinkled from sleep and our other...activities. Her head tilted slightly. "All four Corvo boys under one roof with me," she mused, half to herself. "Not sure if that's a treat or a punishment."

Mason's smirk widened, eyes glinting with mischief as he leaned against the door frame, a joker card flipping between his fingers. "Depends on the night."

Maddox circled back into the kitchen. Without asking permission, he reached over and grabbed a half-eaten strip of bacon off Kaylor's abandoned plate, biting into it with a satisfying crunch. "It's a punishment," he said around the food. "For us."

Kaylor snorted. "Fair."

I turned to face Raine fully, squaring my shoulders. "Does Dad know what we're up to?"

He didn't blink, but I caught the slight twitching around his eyes. "He knows."

"Knows what, exactly?" I pressed, the kitchen suddenly smaller with all of us in it.

Raine ran a hand through his perfectly styled hair, the gesture leaving it slightly mussed, a rare crack in his usually immaculate facade. His sigh was heavy, laced with exhaustion that came from carrying family secrets. "That we've been using Crew resources to chase this down. The safehouses. The contacts. The intel channels. All of it."

My jaw clenched. "And he hasn't put an end to it?"

"We're on borrowed time," he said flatly. "He's letting it play out, for now, but that leash is getting shorter every day."

Kaylor's head swiveled between us, her frown deepening with each exchange as the wheels turned in her mind, trying to piece together the politics she'd never fully understood. "Why wouldn't he want to help? He has the power. The reach. You guys clearly have access to things no one else does."

"Because helping you," Maddox cut in as he leaned back against the counter, "doesn't benefit him. Not unless he can twist it into something that gives him leverage."

"Like using Kenny's rescue to pull you back under his thumb," Mason added, his tone losing all traces of humor. When Mason got serious, it meant the situation was worse than anyone wanted to admit.

I nodded grimly, dread settling in my stomach. "That's the more likely play. He lets us find her, makes himself look like the hero who allowed his sons to save the day. Suddenly, you owe him everything. He's got you again, and this time, he won't let go so easily."

Kaylor's face paled except for two spots of color high on her cheekbones. "I'm not going back," she snapped. "I don't care what he does. I'd rather burn before I let him use me again."

"You might not get a choice," Raine retorted. "Not unless we move faster than he can."

We were walking a tightrope with no net. One wrong move could send everything we'd worked for crashing down.

I looked at each of them in turn—my brothers, all brilliant in their own broken way, all carrying scars from the same man who'd shaped us into weapons. We weren't always on the same page, but right now, we were all aimed at the same target. "This means no more distractions. We keep our eyes on the objective. No second-guessing. No slipups. If Dad's circling like a vulture, we're not just racing the kidnapper, we're racing him too."

Mason gave a lazy shrug. "Good thing we're smarter."

"Debatable," Maddox muttered under his breath, earning himself a frown from his twin.

Kaylor padded against the cold kitchen tiles as she pushed away from the counter, restless energy having her pace. "What happens if he tries to interfere? If he pulls you back in, pulls *me* back in?"

"Then we don't give him the chance." I shifted my weight, planting my feet wider. "We finish this before he makes his move."

"And if he does make a move..." Raine rolled his shoulders back. "We'll be ready."

Kaylor's pacing stuttered to a halt mid-step. She turned toward me. No words, no accusations, just those light-blue eyes boring into mine, searching for lies I might be hiding.

Trust lived there in the depths of her gaze, fragile and new as morning glass. But raw and familiar fear lived there too, fear that came from knowing the one person you hated most in this world had the power to steal back everything you'd bled and clawed your way free from.

The distance between us stretched like miles and inches all at once.

I took a step forward, then another. When I reached her, I lifted my hand slowly, giving her time to pull away, to tell me to back off, to remember all the reasons we were supposed to be enemies.

She didn't move.

My knuckles brushed down the length of her arm, from shoulder to elbow, skin warm against skin. The contact sent electricity racing up my fingers, but I kept my touch light as air. "He's not getting you back. I don't care what it costs."

The room went still around us. For the first time in weeks, we weren't snapping at each other, and somewhere beneath the fragile peace, beneath the warmth of her skin under my fingers, I knew with bone-deep certainty that the storm wasn't done with us yet. Not by a long shot.

The fact that I was touching her, and Kaylor hadn't jerked away or told me to go to hell, didn't go unnoticed. Especially not by the peanut gallery currently crowding the kitchen doorway.

"Well, well." Mason's voice cut through the moment. He propped one shoulder against the doorframe. "Did you two finally kiss and make up?"

"I don't know about making up," Maddox grumbled. "But they were definitely making out when I walked in."

Kaylor's cheeks flushed, but her chin lifted in defiance. "We weren't—" She stopped, shook her head, and shot my brothers a steeling glare before flipping Maddox the bird. "Don't you guys have somewhere else to be? Like literally anywhere else?"

The four of us just grinned.

SOMETHING WAS OFF.

I'd been watching Kaylor for three hours straight, and every instinct I'd honed over the years was screaming at me to pay attention. She was being...*nice*. Every word that rolled off her tongue came with sugar on top instead of her usual sarcasm. She smiled too often, but it couldn't quite erase the sadness she tried to bury in her eyes. If I didn't know better, I'd say she was trying to distract us. Trying to distract me.

And the fact that it was working, that I kept catching myself staring at the curve of her lips when she laughed, only made me more unsure about what I was feeling.

She was up to something.

Hours later, when the afternoon light had shifted to deep gold and the house had settled into that pre-dinner lull, I cornered the three of them near the den. "Keep an eye on her," I said, pitched low enough that my voice wouldn't carry beyond our circle. "All of you."

Maddox arched a dark brow. "You think she's gonna make a run for it?"

"I think she's lying or hiding something." A liar recognized a liar, and I was skilled at lying.

Raine nodded. No protest, no questions.

Mason smirked. "Only you would be suspicious because a girl can't keep her hands off you. Maybe she's just tired of resisting Kreed Corvo's irresistible charm."

Raine and Maddox snorted.

I ignored him. Had to, or I'd end up doing something stupid.

I left to go check in on her while we waited for the call on Raine's phone to come in and made my way down the hall. I was halfway past the library when slender fingers wrapped tightly around my wrist, pulling me sideways before I could react.

Kaylor.

She stood framed by the soft evening light filtering in through the slatted blinds. Golden rays cut across her face in horizontal stripes, turning her skin luminous. Her hair was wild, silver strands catching the light, but it was her eyes that held me, locked on mine with wicked intensity.

My head angled to the side. "What are you doing?" I asked, trying to sound firm, trying to inject some authority into my voice, but the words came out rougher than I'd intended, betraying the effect she was having on me.

She stepped forward, slow and intentional, her feet silent on the Persian rug, closing the distance between us by inches, until there was barely a breath of space left. Her gaze dropped to my mouth, lingering, before dragging back up to meet my eyes.

My hands itched to reach for her, to tangle in that wild hair and pull her against me, but I forced myself to stay still, to wait and see what game she was playing.

Because this was definitely a game, and I was starting to think I was already losing.

"Kaylor—"

Her name barely made it past my lips before she cut me off, her hands pressing onto my chest as she pushed me deeper against the wall. "You've been watching me all day." I could see the flecks of light in her blue eyes, could count the freckles scattered across her nose.

"Because you're up to something, little raven."

The admission hung between us, raw and honest. Her pupils dilated slightly, and her tongue darted out to wet her bottom lip. "And if I told you"—she stepped into me, eliminating the last precious inches between us until her chest brushed against mine—"that you're right? That I am up to something?"

The contact sent fire racing through my veins. The soft cotton of her shirt rubbed against my chest, and I swallowed the growl rising in my throat, the sound vibrating deep in my chest. My hands twitched at my sides, fingers curling into fists as I fought the urge to either push her away from me or pin her against the wall. "Then I'd tell you to start talking. Now."

She tilted her head, studying me with those knowing eyes. A slow smile crept across her lips. "What if I'm not ready to talk?"

"Then I'd ask what the hell this is," I snapped, gesturing between us with a jerky motion that betrayed how rattled I was.

"This," she whispered, rising on her toes so her lips were barely an inch from mine, "is just a girl locking herself in a room with a boy whom she no longer wants to pretend she doesn't want." Her fingers found the front of my shirt, fisting the fabric as she watched the array of emotions move into my features.

On one hand, I was desperate to believe her, but another part of me warned that this could be a trap. I'd waited for this moment, waited for her to admit she felt something for me, so long that I couldn't trust it...trust her...trust myself.

Fuck yeah, I had trust issues, but with Kaylor, I wanted to try. I wanted this to be so real it fucking hurt.

The air between us crackled with a dangerous tension that made smart people do stupid things. I leaned down, my breath stirring the wild strands of her hair. The scent of her shampoo filled my nostrils, making my head spin. "Whatever you're planning, little raven. I will find out. And when I do—"

There was no mistaking the way her breath hitched. "You'll what?" Her eyes darkened, but there was a challenge there too. "Punish me?"

Jesus. She is trying to kill me.

My hands moved without conscious thought, wrapping around her wrists. I peeled her fingers away from my shirt, holding her hands captive between us. Her pulse hammered against my thumbs where they pressed against her skin.

Her expression wavered between excitement and disappointment, but the look was there and gone so quickly I might have imagined it, but I caught it regardless.

I held her gaze, refusing to let her look away. "I don't want to hurt you. *But* don't test how far I'll go if you're putting yourself in danger."

For a moment, vulnerability flashed in her eyes. Then her lips curved in a smile again, promising trouble delivered in spades. "It just so happens I'm really good at tests," she said, her voice carrying that same husky quality that made my knees weak. "Don't question everything," she whispered. "For an hour, I just want to pretend like my life isn't in shambles. I'm not asking you to be my boyfriend." Her fingers traced the edge of my collar, the light touch sending sparks across my skin. "You want me. I want you. Can't it be that simple?"

I shook my head. "Nothing about you and me can be simple."

"Kreed," she said breathily.

My name, so soft and desperate and full of need, made something primal unfurl in my chest. I closed my eyes for a heartbeat, fighting for control I was rapidly losing. "That's unfair, little raven, and you know it."

Her lips curved in a smile. "Looks like I picked up a few things from living with the Raven Crew after all."

"Not funny."

"Kreed," she said again, her fingers tangling into my hair. "Stop stalling and fucking kiss me before someone comes looking for us."

My fingers settled on her hips. "You sure about this?" I asked, studying her face for any sign of doubt, any speck of uncertainty.

"Because once I cross this line, there will be no going back. Not for either of us."

She nodded. "Yes." Her free hand came up to rest against my chest, right over my heart, and I wondered if she could feel how it was racing. "I don't want to think about what you've done. Or what I've lost. Or what's waiting for me tomorrow. I want this. I want *you*."

Something in my chest cracked open.

I didn't rush. I didn't throw her against the bookshelves even if every nerve in my body screamed for her. I leaned in slowly, brushing my knuckles along her jaw as I tipped her chin up. Her breath caught as I kissed her.

Soft at first, her lips molded to mine with a tremble, fucking unraveling me. I pulled her in, one hand tangled in her hair, the other gripping her waist like she might vanish if I let go. She pressed into me, sighing into the kiss like it was the first time she'd exhaled all day. She pulled me in again. This time, the kiss was heavier. Fiercer. Full of need that left no room for lies.

I spent a lot of time thinking about kissing her, about what I would do when I got the chance to touch her again, to be with her. I stopped trying to figure out what it was I liked about kissing Kaylor more than any other girl. I gave up trying to figure out what made her special. She just was.

My hands skimmed down her curves with deliberate leisure because I wanted to draw this out for as long as possible, savor every lick, touch, kiss, tremor, and moan. But I was still a guy, and it didn't take long for my craving to overcome reasoning. I longed to feel every inch of her nakedness pressing into me.

"I think I noticed something on your shirt," she murmured against my mouth, her fingers drifting to the hem of my tee.

"Oh yeah?"

Her head angled to the side as she took my bottom lip between her teeth. "It's got to go."

"You're the boss."

"Careful. I might like having control over you." She tugged at my shirt, and I helped her lift it over my head. Her gaze captured mine, and with a twist of her lips, she lifted her arms in the air. "My turn."

"With pleasure." I rid her of her shirt, tossing it to the side.

She melted into me as my lips reclaimed hers, and I lifted her easily, her legs wrapping around my waist. I carried her to the reading chaise, half shrouded in shadows, the moonlight filtering through the tall windows painted silver across her skin, and I swore I'd never seen anything so heartbreakingly beautiful.

Pushing up, my fingers made quick work of the button and zipper on her jeans, shimmying them over her hips and down her legs. Her silky, white panties were next to go, leaving her bare for my feasting. And I was fucking starved for her.

There was no resistance when my fingers stroked her clit, warmth and wetness making it effortless to slip inside her. One finger. Then two.

Her back bowed off the oversized chaise, lifting her perky breasts closer to my face, and fuck, if I would die a happy man in this moment.

"Jesus, you're hotter than I remember," I rasped, the words slipping out like a confession I couldn't take back.

She cocked an eyebrow, strands of her silver hair framing her gorgeous face. "Is that so?" That smirk told me she knew I was so damn lost in her. Giving her pleasure only amplified mine...so perhaps we were lost in each other.

I bent lower, teeth grazing her nipple before my mouth closed over it, my tongue circling slowly. Her nails dug into my shoulder. "I can't seem to get enough of you," I murmured against her skin.

"Good," she said, dragging her nails down the length of my chest, leaving faint trails of heat in their wake. "I want you addicted."

My gaze locked on hers, heat and passion tangled in the same breath. "Careful what you wish for, little raven." I pressed my mouth to the scar on her shoulder, the one that still made my heart tighten every time I saw it. A bullet had pierced her there, so close to ending everything. If she'd moved a step the wrong way, or if the shooter's aim had been off by a fraction, she wouldn't be here at all. My life without her was a hollow, colorless thing I didn't even want to picture.

She reached between our bodies, wrapping her fingers around my dick. "I want you inside me. Now."

I didn't think I could get harder. She proved me wrong as the pad of her thumb grazed the slick tip of my cock. A deep groan vibrated in my throat. "God forbid, I deny you anything."

She guided that throbbing part of my manhood to the opening of her core, and I gave her what she asked for, my hips thrusting once. It was all it took for me to be buried deep within her. The sound that left her, low, throaty, was enough to make my control snap, her body tightening around me, and I set a rhythm that was part claim, part punishment. Kaylor clung to me, nails in my back, urging me to move harder. My forehead dropped to hers, my breath ragged as I ground out, "You have no idea what you do to me."

Her lips brushed mine, a ghost of a kiss, her smirk still there even in the chaos. "Then show me."

And I did, driving into her with every ounce of want, tenderness, and devotion I had left in me until there was nothing else in the room, nothing else in the world, but her. No games. No lies. No past. The rest of the world fell away.

21

KAYLOR

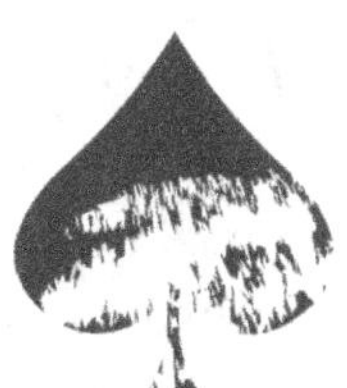

The fire in the hearth had burned low, amber flames dancing lazily over charred logs, casting shifting shadows across the walls. I was curled into Kreed's side, my head resting against the solid warmth of his chest, skin still flushed from what we'd shared. His arm wrapped around me, muscles relaxed but still protective, the steady rhythm of his breathing almost enough to calm the turmoil inside me.

Almost.

My fingers trailed the black ink sprawled across his skin, following the intricate lines and shapes etched into him like a map. The tattoos were warm under my touch, raised slightly where the needle had gone deepest.

I soaked up everything: his scent, cedar with hints of sea; his warmth, the way it seeped into my bones and chased away the cold that had lived there for so long; and the low hum of contentment vibrating in his throat when I moved closer. I was trying to stamp it all into memory, to burn these moments into my soul so deep they'd never fade.

These were my last minutes with him, and I wanted to press

them into my bones like flowers between book pages, but the tighter I held on, the more everything inside me threatened to slip loose.

I blinked hard, trying to keep it all down. The tears burning behind my eyes. The ache squeezing my chest. The desperate, clawing grief of what I had to do tonight, but my chest trembled anyway, a shudder rolling through me before I could stop it, betraying every emotion I was trying to hide.

Kreed felt it. Of course, he did.

His body tensed beneath me, instantly alert. He tipped my chin up with gentle fingers, thumb brushing beneath my jaw in a tender way that made my heart stutter. The touch coaxed my gaze to his, and I found myself drowning in silver eyes that saw too much. His brows furrowed, concern etching lines across his forehead. "Don't tell me you're already regretting what happened."

I shook my head fiercely, hair whipping across my shoulders. "No. No regrets."

His features softened. "What is it then?" His thumb traced my cheekbone, wiping away a tear I hadn't realized had fallen. "Kenny?"

I swallowed hard, the movement painful in my throat. I nodded because it was easier than unpacking all of it, but it wasn't just Kenny.

Not really.

It was everything. It was the rising panic in my chest, whispering that I was running out of time. It was knowing I'd just given the last unbroken piece of myself to someone who'd already ruined me in a hundred different ways and still managed to put me back together again, piece by shattered piece.

I never imagined in a million years I would feel such heartache having to say goodbye to him. Not after what happened at the warehouse and not after all the blood and betrayal. Not after all the venom we'd spit and swallowed and all the ways our crews tried to destroy each other.

And yet, here I was.

Falling harder with every breath.

That was the cruelest twist of all.

"I didn't mean to get emotional," I whispered, blinking fast as the tears slipped free anyway, hot trails down my cheeks. "I'm sorry. It just...it hit me."

Kreed's arm tightened around me, tugging me flush against him until there was no space left between us. His lips brushed my temple, warm and reassuring, the kiss soft as a whisper. "Don't apologize for feeling something."

"I wasn't supposed to," I murmured against his skin, breathing in that scent I'd grown addicted to. "That wasn't in the cards for us."

The fire cracked and popped, sparks dancing up the chimney. "Don't give up hope. Not yet. I'm waiting on a call."

I lifted my head slightly, hope and fear warring in my chest. "Another lead?"

He nodded once, jaw set with determination. "A new location. We're not done, not even close."

I hesitated. "The Crew?"

Kreed's mouth curved in a faint but tired smile, lines of exhaustion bracketing his eyes. "No. The Elite this time. I forwarded your cousin the data I got the other day. Figured it couldn't hurt to have more eyes on it."

I let out a slow breath, hope blooming in my chest. "And?"

He shrugged. "It was useful."

"Good." What Kreed didn't know was that I was banking on that information being what saved me. I might be freeing Kenny, but I needed Kreed to find me. The irony wasn't lost on me, trusting the one who had a part in destroying my life to become my salvation.

He looked down, brows drawing together as if he saw something through the tears, as if he could read my mind. His eyes searched my face, and I wondered what he found there.

I hadn't anticipated this panicky desperation gripping me, everything inside begging me to stay by Kreed's side. It was basic survival instincts, but Kenny wouldn't be in this mess if it weren't for me. I owed her everything.

I owed her my life.

I LAY LONGER than I should have, cocooned in Kreed's embrace, my skin still tingling from his touch as I absorbed his warmth like a dying star soaking in the last of its light before burning out. His arm was heavy across my waist, his fingers splayed possessively over my hip, and for a moment, I let myself pretend this was real. That we had time. That tomorrow wasn't coming for us both.

But the hands on the clock continued to tick past, and eventually, I peeled myself off the couch, the separation like tearing skin from bone. Kreed released a groan of complaint, his arms reaching for me instinctively, his fingers grasping at empty air. His eyes were still closed, dark lashes fanned against his cheeks, but a frown pulled at his mouth. "Don't go," he muttered.

I wish I didn't have to. I really do. "I need to pee," I whispered, wrapping my arms around myself to ward off the sudden chill. He wouldn't protest further when my bladder was in question, giving me the excuse I needed.

"Hurry," he mumbled, still mostly asleep.

I'd never seen a more tempting sight in my life than Kreed naked and aglow by firelight. The flames painted his skin in gold and shadow, highlighting every ridge of muscle, every line of ink that decorated his chest and arms. He could have been an ancient god of war, beautiful and dangerous and utterly mine... At least for a few hours he had been.

I bit my lip hard enough to taste copper. *Move, Kaylor. If you don't go now, you won't be able to leave.*

My brain somehow got the message, forcing my feet to move one in front of the other. Each step felt like walking through quicksand, my body fighting my mind. The ache in my chest grew heavier, spreading outward through my veins.

It was time.

Time to do the one thing I told myself I wouldn't. To lie. To manipulate. To betray those who had betrayed me first, but this wasn't about revenge. The Corvo boys somehow managed to do the impossible; they'd redeemed themselves, proved they were more than the monsters I'd thought them to be. But it wasn't enough.

I had no choice. Not really.

This was about Kenny.

And if I didn't do this... If I didn't make the trade, if I didn't show up at that meeting spot alone, she'd pay the price. I couldn't let that happen. Not when her blood would be on my hands, not when I was the reason she'd been dragged into this nightmare in the first place.

Even if it meant becoming the villain in their story.

Kreed would be fuming when he figured it out, but I was counting on his anger to make him come after me. If anyone could find me, it was him. I had to believe that, or this whole plan would fall apart.

Phase one of sacrificing my life: slip sleeping pills into their drinks. Pretty messed up, but they'd done way worse to me. That thought didn't make the guilt any lighter.

I tiptoed upstairs, the hardwood cold beneath my bare soles. The house was quiet except for the distant murmur of voices from the living room and the soft crackle of the dying fire. I crept down the hall to Aunt Char's bathroom, my heart hammering so loudly I was sure someone would hear it.

She and my uncle were still overseas and would be for a few more weeks. Hopefully by then, this would all be over and I could get back to living my life like a damn normal senior on the verge of graduating. Hell, I prayed I could still graduate. I prayed I'd still be *alive* to graduate.

Aunt Char's bathroom hadn't changed in years. The same sleek tub in the corner and the same French tiles around the bathtub. It still smelled faintly of eucalyptus and old lipstick, scents that reminded me of childhood visits and simpler times. I opened the cabinet behind the mirror, the hinges squeaking softly in protest.

I rummaged past ancient cold medicine and dusty hairpins, bottles of expired vitamins, and tubes of face cream. Finally, I found what I was looking for...the sleeping pills. I didn't know how strong they were, but I had to take my chances.

I tipped a handful, smooth white tablets that looked so innocent, so harmless, into my palm. This was the part that crossed a line. The point of no return. Once I crushed these, once they were in the drinks...that was it.

I just needed enough to knock out four Corvos who never let their guards down. Four Corvos who would try to stop me if they knew what I was planning. And of course, I couldn't forget Evan and his friend outside.

My stomach rolled as I cradled the pills in my hand. "I'm sorry," I whispered to the mirror, as if speaking it could somehow make it better, but the apology was ash on my tongue, bitter and worthless. My reflection stared back at me with hollow eyes, and she didn't forgive me.

As I trotted downstairs, I passed the boys in the living room. The TV was on low; none of them were really watching. They were busy on their phones, scrolling through social media or checking messages.

Maddox was sprawled in the big armchair, one leg thrown over the side, completely relaxed in a way I'd rarely seen him. Mason had claimed the other end of the couch, his feet propped up on the coffee table. Raine sat cross-legged on the floor, his back against the couch, looking younger than his years in the flickering light.

They trusted me. That was the worst part. They'd finally let their walls down, and I was about to exploit that trust in the cruelest way possible.

I swallowed hard and kept walking, the pills burning in my closed fist as I made my way into the kitchen. My hands shook as I pulled ingredients from the cabinets, the simple act of making cocoa feeling like preparing for execution. Whipped cream swirled in thick clouds. Shaved chocolate curled from the block like delicate flowers. Anything to make the taste stronger, richer, more decadent. Anything to hide the bitterness of the crushed pills burning a hole in my pocket.

One by one, I doctored each mug. Kreed's first. Then Maddox's, Raine's, and Mason's. I made two more for the guards outside, pouring them into black thermoses.

The pills dissolved quickly when I stirred them in, leaving behind nothing. I made one for myself as well. The only one untouched. No pills. Just warm milk and cocoa, because I knew someone would notice if I didn't have a drink too.

The mugs steamed on the tray, cheerful and innocent, but I knew better. They weren't comfort. They were betrayal in disguise, wrapped in whipped cream and good intentions.

My heart raced so loudly I was sure they could hear it from the other room, the sound thundering in my ears. I wasn't doing this because I didn't care. I was doing this because I did, and if it cost me everything, Kreed, the Crew, the trust we were slowly rebuilding, I'd carry that burden, because if this worked, if I made the trade and brought Kenny home, the cost would be worth it.

I just had to survive it first.

I lined the mugs up on a tray, but the moment I picked them up, the enormity of what I was doing nearly buckled my knees. My hands trembled so violently I almost dropped the whole damn thing, cocoa sloshing dangerously close to the rims.

"Fuck," I hissed, unable to believe I was doing this.

The night air bit at my skin as I stepped out onto the porch, two black thermoses warming my hands. The guards stood in their usual spots, shadows against the pale moonlight. Evan was by the stairs, and the other guard leaned against the railing, his eyes scanning the tree line. They tensed when the door squeaked open, hands moving instinctively toward their weapons, but relaxed when they saw me. Just the harmless girl they were protecting.

If only they knew.

"Sorry. I didn't mean to startle you." I offered a tentative smile. "Thought you guys might want something to warm you up."

They exchanged a glance, some silent communication I couldn't read, before Evan gave the expressionless approval. "Appreciate it."

"Hot cocoa." I handed over the thermoses, wondering if they could feel my hands shaking or smell my nervousness. "Don't worry, I didn't spike it."

What the fuck? Why did that come out of my mouth?

Evan cracked the lid and sniffed it, steam rising into the cold air. "Thanks. You should probably head back inside. It's cold tonight."

One of the coldest nights of the year. Of course, it was. I'd checked the weather earlier, some desperate part of me hoping for a storm to delay what I had to do. I lingered long enough to see them take the first sips.

One step down.

Now the hard part.

Inside, Raine and Maddox were in the living room arguing. Mason was half asleep on the couch, his head leaned back against the cushions, scrolling on his phone. Kreed stood by the window, his back to me, phone pressed to his ear. His shoulders were tense, one hand braced against the window frame as he stared out into the darkness.

"She said the guy had a tattoo behind his ear?" Kreed asked. A pause, and I could practically hear him processing information. "No, that sounds like the same runner from the old warehouse. You're sure it was him?" Another pause, longer this time. "Brock, I swear, if this is another dead end—"

I froze, breath catching in my throat.

Of course, it was my cousin on the other end of that call, and whatever he was telling Kreed, it sounded serious. Hopefully, it wouldn't mess with my plan. I was running out of time, and I couldn't afford any surprises. The tray in my hands grew heavier with each step, four steaming mugs balanced precariously as I approached the living room.

Maddox glanced up first. "Is that what I think it is?"

"If you think it's hot cocoa, then yes," I replied, setting the tray on the coffee table and somehow not managing to spill a drop. "It's like the only thing I can make. My mom taught me."

Mason swung his legs over the side of the couch, sitting up with a grin, reaching for a mug before anyone else could. He groaned in delight as he took a sip. "Holy hell. Marry me."

I rolled my eyes. "You're too high maintenance for me."

"And Kreed might kill you," Raine added, directed to Mason as he gave me a curious glance. I didn't meet his gaze. I couldn't. "Besides, if Kreed fucks this up, I'm swooping in."

I choked on my first sip of hot cocoa, and not because it was too hot. "I'm not marrying any of you. There's no way my last name will ever be Corvo."

Kreed's leg shot out, his boot connecting with Raine's shin in a kick that made his brother grunt. He was still on the phone, pacing near the window with his free hand gesturing as he spoke in low, clipped tones, but obviously, he was also tuned partially into the conversation with me and his brothers. Multitasking had always been one of his more annoying talents.

"I'd let you keep your last name," Maddox offered, and I was afraid he might be serious.

What the hell was happening? Why were we talking about *me* marrying any of *them*?

Kreed ended his call and turned, brow furrowing in concentration. "Thanks," he muttered, reaching for the last cup without thinking, sipping absently before he sat down beside Maddox.

I took mine and curled into the armchair opposite them, tucking my legs beneath me like it was any other night. "Who was that?" I asked, pretending my ears hadn't been straining to catch every word Kreed said.

"Brock," he replied, rubbing his temple. "He thinks he might have a photo of one of the smugglers. It's not the best, a still from CCTV footage."

I sucked up a half-melted dollop of whipped cream. "Where did Brock get the footage?"

Kreed lifted a brow at me over the rim of his mug. "Do you really want to know, little raven?"

"It might be information we should share with the police," I suggested.

"They have it." His response was clipped.

"How would...oh." The picture started to come into focus. "Brock obtained it from the police, I take it."

"I'm not saying anything," he replied.

I lifted my mug back to my lips to give myself time to think, to process this new information. The ceramic felt cold against my palms now despite the warm liquid inside. *Let it go,* I told myself, the words repeating in my head like a mantra. Let them chase their leads. Let them run in circles for one more night because if everything went according to plan...

By tomorrow morning, Kenny would be free. And I would be gone.

I couldn't even think that far. All that mattered was getting through this night. One step at a time. It was all I could handle, or I'd lose the thin thread of bravado I clung to.

I watched them sip. Watched as the rich brown cocoa disappeared from their mugs. My fingers gripped my cup, but I barely touched the drink inside. My stomach was a mess of guilt, nerves, and anticipation, churning so violently I doubted I could have swallowed even if I wanted to.

Raine was the first to show signs. He yawned and rubbed at the back of his neck, rolling his shoulders.

"Long day?" I asked casually.

He nodded. "I haven't slept much lately. Think it's finally catching up to me."

Maddox stretched out over the arm of the couch. "Shit, is it just me, or is it really hot in here? Did someone crank up the heat?"

"It's the cocoa," Mason muttered. "Sugar crash. That stuff is deadly."

Kreed didn't say anything. He was still watching me from across the room, mug half finished in his hand, a slight furrow between his brows as if he was close to working something out but was missing one piece of the puzzle.

I kept my eyes trained on the fire crackling in the hearth. *Don't look at him. Don't look guilty. Just breathe.* My brain was convinced that if Kreed stared into my eyes, he'd be able to read every one of my fucking thoughts. He had an annoying, uncanny ability to know shit. I couldn't take the chance, regardless of how ridiculous or superstitious it might be.

Mason's head dropped back against the couch. "I'm tapping out. I'll crash on the floor if I have to."

"No one's sleeping on the floor," Kreed said, pushing off the wall, but the movement wasn't as smooth as usual. His balance wobbled slightly before he caught himself.

My nerves skyrocketed. He was going to find out. He was going to know it was me. "Are you okay?" I asked, genuine concern in my tone. What if I'd given them too high a dose?

Shit, what if I kill them?

I nearly spilled my guts, confessed my sins.

"Yeah." Kreed blinked a few times, then looked down at his mug. "Just tired. Didn't realize how fucking tired."

"Maybe we should all get some sleep," I offered carefully.

Maddox didn't even answer. He was already slumped sideways, legs stretched out, head tilted at a weird angle on the armrest. Raine wasn't far behind, shifting to lie across the opposite couch with a low groan.

Mason tried to stand, then changed his mind, and sank back into the cushions, his eyes fluttering closed.

I held my breath as Kreed stepped toward me, his gaze locked on mine. His hand touched the back of the chair I sat in, then slid off as he swayed slightly. "Kaylor," he murmured.

I got up, abandoning my drink to slip my arm around Kreed's waist. "Let's go upstairs." *Before you fall on your face.*

He didn't fight me as I helped him down the hall to the staircase. "You... You've been different today."

Shit.

We climbed the stairs, Kreed holding on to the railing, moving at a snail's pace. "Different how?" I asked too quickly.

He blinked hard, trying to focus. "Like you've forgiven me," he muttered, gripping my bedroom door frame. Kreed might be seconds from passing into a deep slumber, but the man still had moves. With a fluid motion defying his drowsy state, he trapped me between the frame and his body, one hand over his head supporting him, while his other hand captured my chin. His thumb traced along my jawline, the calloused pad of his finger sending shivers down my spine. "Have you forgiven me?" His breath was like a feather-soft kiss against my lips.

I gasped softly. How the hell could he do that? Churn me up and tug on my fucking heartstrings? Somehow, a nearly sleepwalking Kreed was still as hot as he was fully awake.

My eyes connected with his half-lidded silver ones. *Shit.* How had it happened? How the hell had I fallen in love with him? I hadn't wanted to admit it. Still didn't want to, but it was there inside me. The warm glow haloing around my heart. It was easy at first to believe what I felt was nothing but lust and hormones, but I couldn't continue to lie to myself. I'd lied enough tonight.

Lifting my chin a fraction higher, my hands slid up the flat of his stomach to rest on his upper chest where his heart beat steadily under my fingers. "You always knew I was going to forgive you."

His mouth brushed against mine. "Is that a yes?"

"Yes," I murmured.

His lips captured mine, the taste of chocolate lingering as his tongue slipped into my mouth, mingling with mine. This could be our last kiss for days. Weeks. Months. Years. Hell, it could very well be our last kiss ever.

We both deserved for it to be fucking memorable, not that Kreed would remember much, but I'd never forget this moment.

I guided him to the bed, my hands on his waist as he swayed slightly on his feet. He lowered himself onto the mattress with the careful movements of someone fighting against heavy limbs, but he didn't go alone. His hands attached to my waist before I could pull away, his fingers digging into the soft material of my shirt, and I ended up landing half on top of him in a tangle of limbs.

"This is better," he whispered, his nose buried into my hair, his arm slung protectively over me.

Fuck. Better for who?

I had to untangle myself from him or risk rousing him when it was time for me to leave. I couldn't give him the chance to stop me, but it was so damn tempting to curl against him and close my eyes. I stared at him, a silent tear streaking down my cheek.

Please don't hate me. I don't have a choice.

Within minutes, the only sounds in the room were his soft breathing and the howling of wind beating against the windows. Lifting his arm to the side, I pulled the blanket up over him and held my breath, waiting to see if he would remain asleep. *I think I'm in love with you,* I mouthed, needing to say the words at least once even if he never heard them.

This was it.

The house was quiet. The boys were down. The clock had started ticking.

As gently as I could, I climbed out of bed, sparing one last glimpse at Kreed. *You better find me, or I'll never forgive you. For real this time. I'll be waiting for you.*

I crouched at the side of the bed, fishing out the burner I stashed there. The phone's screen glared in the darkness, the single message still stamped across the screen. I reread it one more time, not because I didn't know the words but because I needed to look at something other than the trembling of my hands.

If things went sideways… If they found it while I was gone, they'd follow but not in time to stop me. I needed a head start. Just enough to get in and get Kenny out.

This had to be my choice.

My risk.

I had twenty-five minutes. Just enough time to slip out of the house unnoticed and do the one thing I swore I would: get my best friend back. Even if it meant I never saw them again. Even if it meant never seeing Kreed again.

Carefully placing the burner on the pillow where my head had lain minutes ago, I moved quietly to the stairwell, each creak of the wood a thunderous boom in my ears, but no one stirred. The house had fallen into a deep hush. I stood at the top of the stairs, watching the darkened hallway stretch before me. Down below, the soft hush of firelight still danced in the living room, casting golden shadows into the hall.

They were still out. Asleep.

I waited another beat.

Still nothing.

Clutching the hoodie around me, I passed through the kitchen, the warmth from earlier already faded. I avoided the family room entirely. There was no way I was risking stepping too close even if they were all out like lights. I already had one miracle.

Two would be pushing it.

I slipped through the back door, letting it close behind me with the softest click.

22

KAYLOR

The night air hit me like a slap, cold and biting, but it snapped my nerves into place. I ran across the lawn, my heart in my throat, wind nipping through the sleeves of my hoodie. Through the yard, around the gate, and straight into the trees where Carson's BMW was already idling near the road, headlights off, taillights glowing faint red in the dark.

I climbed into the passenger seat and shut the door quietly behind me, rubbing my hands together to chase the cold that went deeper than the icy temps created by fear and adrenaline.

Carson didn't say anything at first. He gave me a sidelong look, dark-blue eyes narrowing, like he wanted to ask questions he knew he wouldn't like the answers to. But, to his credit, he kept his mouth shut, but his eyes said a thousand words. He was still pissed at me, yet he showed up for me when I asked.

"Thanks for coming," I murmured.

Carson's sandy hair hung longer than usual and didn't have a stitch of product in it, two things he tended to be meticulous about. His eyes were red from a combination of lack of sleep, stress, tears, and worry. "You said it was about Kenny. *And* you didn't give me much of a choice."

"That's because I didn't want you to talk me out of it."

He rubbed at the back of his neck before glancing at me. "Talk you out of what exactly, Kay?"

I buckled myself in, the leather warm and buttery against my frozen fingers. "You don't need to know anything else. It's better that way. Just drive me to the old train yard off Route 19."

His expression looked as if he wanted to push me into telling him what we were doing in the middle of the night, but in the end, he only nodded and threw his car into gear. "I'm surprised you're alone. No security? No backup? No reinforcements? You sure about this?"

I stared out the window at the empty road stretching into the dark. "I've never been more sure about anything."

As we drove, Carson kept stealing glances at me, and his energy seemed as restless as mine. Each mile we passed only tightened the knot in my chest. The train yard wasn't far now. My hands clenched in my lap, nails digging crescents into my palms.

Carson's fingers wrung the steering wheel as we paused at a stoplight. There were no other cars at the intersection. "I don't see how this will help Kenny."

One of my laces on my boots had come undone. I bent to quickly tie it. "Just stay in the car. Wait for me. I'll only be a few minutes."

"Maybe I should come with you—"

"You can't," I interrupted, my head whirling in his direction, squashing the idea before he let it take root. "I need to do this. This is something *I* need to do. This is my fault, Carson, and I need to fix it. Let me fix this."

"Is that why you asked me instead of *him*?" he asked, disgruntledly. "Because you knew he would never let you get out of the car?"

I assumed he meant Kreed. It was no secret Carson wasn't a fan of any Corvo, but especially Kreed. "I asked you because you're my best friend, and I needed you." It might not be fair to play with Carson's emotions, but it was the truth. Regardless of what he felt for me, I cared about Carson, and I knew he'd never let me down, despite how much I disappointed him or hurt him, even if I never intended to.

He sighed, staring out the front windshield into the night. "I don't like you going alone. I'm not about to lose both of you."

His fears were far too valid. "Don't worry about me. I'll be fine." I had not one but two crews and the Elite who would potentially move heaven and earth to find me.

"You should've told Kreed," he argued, words I never thought Carson would utter.

"I thought you despised him."

"Trust me, I do. I'll never understand what you see in him, but he has the means to do whatever it takes to keep you alive." Regret lived in his tone, and most of those means he alluded to might be illegal.

"No," I said quietly. "I couldn't. He'd try to stop me, and if this goes to hell, I can't have anyone else getting hurt."

He clearly didn't like my very stupid plan.

"Feel free to fill him in once I'm gone," I joked, trying to ease the tension. My body was wound so damn tight I wasn't sure I could move out of the car.

Carson frowned. "That's not funny." We reached the turnoff onto the gravel road leading to the abandoned yard, and he killed the headlights. The world dimmed around us into nothing but darkness.

"This is good," I told Carson. "You can drop me off here." I had to show up alone, which meant this was as far as I'd let Carson come, but I wanted him close enough that when Kenny was set free, he'd be the one to find her.

"You've got ten minutes," he muttered, nothing in his expression happy. "Then I'm calling Kreed if you're not back." He made it sound like a threat, which would have made me smile except my mouth muscles lost the ability to curl.

Ten minutes should hopefully be more than enough. How long did it really take to kidnap one person and release another? I nodded, hand already on the door. "Thank you, Carson. Seriously. I mean it."

I took one long glance at my best friend, swallowing back the lump of emotion in my throat. I'd see him again. I refused to believe otherwise.

Taking a deep breath, I gathered my last tendrils of courage and started to open the door. My hand was on the handle, my fingers trembling.

"Don't," Carson said, his voice cracking as it broke the silence. "Kaylor, don't go."

I turned to him slowly, blinking under the streetlight. "I don't have a choice."

"Yes, you do. You always do." Unsnapping his seat belt, he shifted in his seat toward me. "This is my fault."

"Don't be ridiculous. I'm responsible for Kenny being kidnapped. It's my fault, Car."

He shook his head. "You're not the only one to blame."

I stilled. "What do you mean?"

Carson ran both hands through his hair, his features stressed. "I was pissed. Seeing you with him...*living* with him. With *them*. Hooking up with...him. It was like watching a car crash I couldn't stop. You were spiraling."

I blinked, confused. "Carson—"

"You didn't seem to care, Kaylor! The guy kidnapped you, and you...God, you were still looking at him like he hung the damn moon."

My stomach dropped, a sick wave of realization starting to take shape.

"I was trying to protect you," he continued. "I *am* protecting you. Or at least...I thought I was. Rusty promised he'd get you away from the Corvos for good. Said he could help and keep you safe from them."

The words struck like bullets. Cold. Unforgiving. I shook my head, denial rising like bile. "Holy fuck." My voice cracked. "This isn't happening."

He reached for my arm. "Kay—"

"You didn't." I yanked my arm back as if his touch burned. "Carson, tell me you fucking didn't help *him*." Suddenly, that doubt I had about who Rusty was as a person became less muddled.

His silence said everything.

I laughed. Bitter. Disbelieving. "Are you kidding me right now? You're supposed to be my best friend. You're supposed to trust me."

"I didn't know what he was planning, not exactly. I thought he just wanted to get you out. Away from them. Away from *him*." Even now, after what he did, he had venom in his tone when he spoke about Kreed.

"You mean Kreed," I snapped. "Say his damn name. You can't even do that, can you?"

Carson's jaw clenched, his eyes rimmed with guilt and a darker emotion. "Everyone knows what kind of guy he is. He's an asshole. He's dangerous. He was taking advantage of you, and I couldn't just watch it happen. I've loved you forever. I was waiting for you to realize it too, but then everything went to hell."

I stared at him, numb and hollowed out. "So you thought Rusty was the solution? Who are you to interfere? How is what you did any different than what Kreed and his brothers did? Why, because you love me?"

"I was trying to save you," he murmured weakly, his eyes begging me to understand.

"No," I whispered, fury threading through the tears stinging my eyes. "You weren't saving me. You were trying to control me. Just like everyone else."

The engine ticked in the silence that followed. I looked back at the train yard. Chains, shadows, and fate waited for me on the other side of the fence, but what gutted me more was that the boy who used to ride bikes with me down Shady Court...just handed me over to the wolves.

I'd been so worried and focused on Kreed that I never for a second thought that Carson would be the one who hurt me the most. Kreed's betrayal pierced my heart, but Carson's...it cut deeper.

"Fuck," I muttered. "I can't deal with this right now. Because of what you did, I have to save our friend. You have no idea what you've done."

"Don't go," he begged. "I'll go instead. This is my fuck-up. I'll fix it."

"How? They don't want you, Carson. It's me. And you just handed me to them on a silver platter with a big fat bow."

His head hit the back of the seat seconds before his hands slapped against the steering wheel, making me jump. "I fucked up."

"Yeah, you did." I glanced at the clock, seeing I only had a few minutes. "I need to go."

"Kay, I—"

"Don't, Carson. Just don't. Save it for when I get it out of this mess, and you better hope I do." I stepped out into the cold and slammed the door behind me, the crunch of gravel under my boots sounding like gunshots in the quiet.

The old train yard loomed ahead like a graveyard in the night, rusted tracks gleaming in the moonlight. My breath fogged in the air as I moved forward, one step at a time. Steel skeletons of old boxcars lined the tracks, reminding me of forgotten tombstones, their paint flaked and faded, their wheels locked in place by years of rust. The silence here was unnatural. So still it rang in my ears. No wind. No animals. Not even the creak of metal. Just me and the sound of my own heartbeat thudding in my chest.

This was it.

No turning back now.

I was going to be sick, but my roiling stomach wouldn't stop me. Nothing would.

The moon barely made it through the thick blanket of clouds above, casting only the faintest silver sheen over the decaying landscape. Every shadow seemed to move when I wasn't looking, making me jumpy as hell.

I kept going, one foot in front of the other, the soles of my shoes scuffing over gravel, toward the meeting point, an old switching tower in the center of the yard. A perfect place for an ambush. I knew it. They knew I knew it. But here I was

Halfway to the tower, I saw the light. It blinked once, soft and brief. A signal.

My pulse leapt in my throat. I stopped walking, eyes narrowing as I scanned the tower's windows. A single silhouette passed behind the broken glass.

This is it.

I took a slow, deep breath, forcing my shoulders to relax. Panic would get me killed. I had to be calm. Be smart. I had to think like a Raven, like Kreed. *God, he is going to kill me once he finds out what I've done.*

My fingers clutched my phone in my hoodie pocket as I kept walking. I'd left it on but silenced the ringer, knowing it would ping my last location, knowing Kreed or Brock could easily track me. I was counting on it... Counting on them.

By the time I reached the base of the tower, a figure stepped out from behind one of the boxcars. He was dressed head to toe in black, his face shadowed beneath a hood, but his posture was unmistakable.

"You're alone," the man said, voice distorted by a mask.

"You said to come alone," I pointed out, surprised how level I sounded when internally I was freaking the fuck out. "Where's Kenny?" I asked, getting straight to business. I wanted this over with, and I wanted to see my best friend, to be assured they hadn't played me.

The figure tilted his head. "You'll see her soon enough."

My fingers twitched at my sides. "You got what you wanted. I'm here."

"Almost," the man replied. "Toss me your phone."

Shit. Of course, they were smart enough to ask for it, but I didn't have to give it to them.

"Don't make me search you," he added at my obvious hesitancy.

The threat sounded like something I definitely didn't want to experience, his hands groping my body. Here was hoping they wouldn't destroy it or turn it off. All hope wasn't gone. I pulled it from my pocket and chucked it onto the gravel.

Another figure appeared then, behind the first. He was taller and watched me with a creepiness that made my skin prickle.

He went to where my phone had landed, lifted his foot, and smashed it down on the screen. I watched in horror as the device shattered. Bending down, he fished through the debris, picking up the chip before crushing it under his boot as well.

"Walk," the first man said, motioning toward the tower.

My chest deflated, pressure clamping on my lungs. Now was not the time to have a panic attack. I had to stay strong. "I-I'm not going anywhere until I see my friend. Where's Kenny?"

The two men at the base of the switching tower didn't flinch. They were silent shadows standing between me and what I'd come for. There was just enough distance between us that I could run. Maybe even make it back to Carson's car if I didn't trip. If they didn't shoot. If they didn't catch me.

A lot of maybes.

The first one, the one who'd spoken, tilted his head as if amused. "You want proof we're not bluffing?"

"I want her. Now," I snapped. "Or this deal is over."

He held my stare for a long beat. Then he gave a small nod to his partner. "Get the girl."

The second man disappeared between the rusting boxcars, his boots crunching against the gravel. *Stay calm. Keep breathing.* Easier said than fucking done. One wrong move and this whole thing fell apart.

A minute later, he returned. And he wasn't alone.

Kenny.

My knees nearly gave out.

She was bound and blindfolded, her steps stumbling as she was led into the clearing, the little black dress she wore leaving her defenseless against the cold night. My eyes did a quick scan of her body, searching for any evidence that she'd been abused. I couldn't find any outward marks, no cuts or bruises, but that didn't mean she hadn't suffered. I knew all too well that trauma couldn't always be seen with the eye. At least, she was alive.

"Let her go," I said, heart in my throat. "Take the restraints off. I said I'd come willingly. No hassle, but not until she's free." I wasn't a complete moron.

The leader glanced at me again, weighing the situation. I nearly told him to just get Rusty if he was having a difficult time making decisions because, after hearing Carson's confession, I was fully convinced now that he was the traitor. Then the leader nodded once more, and the second guy grumbled but moved to untie her hands.

The moment the blindfold came off, Kenny's tear-streaked face found me. Her eyes, puffy and wild, locked on mine. "Kaylor?" Her voice was thick with disbelief and fear. "What—what are you—"

Before she could finish, the guy gave her a rough shove in my direction. She stumbled forward, her bare feet digging into gravel, and I moved on instinct, catching her before she hit the ground.

"Oh my god," she breathed, shaking in my arms. "You shouldn't be here. You don't know what they're planning—"

"I know," I whispered in her ear as I leaned in, tears blurring my vision. "But you need to listen to me. Carson's waiting in the car down the road. Go. Run. Don't stop. He'll take you to Kreed."

She pulled back just enough to look into my face, eyes wide. "What? No—no, I'm not leaving you—"

"You have to," I said, my voice firm now. "It's the only way we both make it out of this. You have to tell Kreed everything you know. He'll find me."

Her chin trembled. "Kaylor—"

"Go," I said again, urgent now, my hands shaking her shoulders as if I could snap her into reality. "Before they change their minds."

The man behind us gave a bark through his mask. "Time's up, dolls."

I turned and pushed Kenny gently in the direction of the road. "Run," I whispered.

She hesitated. Just a breath. Just a heartbeat. Then she turned and did what I asked. Ran.

"Go after her," the masked leader roared.

"No!" I screamed, but the other was already moving. Before I thought about what I was doing, I took off, launching myself onto his back, my arms wrapping around his neck. I squeezed with everything I had, praying it would slow him down as I did my best to make a nuisance of myself.

It didn't work for long. He was bigger and stronger, and with minimal effort, he had me flipped off him. The asshole tossed me to the ground, hard, and I landed with a jarring thump on my back, a jolt of pain lancing through me, but I rolled, lifting my head to see Kenny disappear into the night. Only when I couldn't see her anymore did I push myself to my feet, glaring at the masked douchebags. "You got what you wanted," I said, raising my chin a fraction. "Let's finish this."

The leader motioned toward the tower. "Pull a stunt like that again, and you won't be as lucky as your friend." His furious eyes shifted to his partner. "Go after her." He grabbed me under my arm. "You. Inside. And move your ass."

I hesitated for a breath, and then I commanded my feet to go. As I climbed, splinters caught my palms where the railing had long since rotted. My legs felt like lead, like I was dragging fear up each step with me. I walked slowly.

When I reached the top, the door to the tower groaned open, and as I crossed the threshold, the air changed. He followed behind. Inside was empty... Except for a chair bolted to the floor and a camera set up on a tripod facing it.

A horrible thought sowed terror into my mind, and before I could run, before I could scream, the prick came, a piercing sting in the side of my neck. My hand flew up, but it was too late. The world tilted, and my legs buckled.

As I crumpled to the ground, my captor's voice echoed distantly, as if it were already behind glass. "You've given me quite the run for my money, kiddo."

It was no fucking surprise that I recognized Rusty's voice, and the last thing I saw before darkness consumed me was the lens of the camera blinking red.

Recording.

Then nothing.

Just dark.

WHEN I CAME TO, it was like surfacing through tar. My head throbbed with every heartbeat, my limbs were heavy, and my thoughts were slower than they should have been. The smell hit me first, lilies and fresh linens. So out of place I was sure it was a trick.

I sat up with effort, blinking against the warm amber lighting overhead, and realized I wasn't in a cell. I was in a room. No, a suite. My head fucking spun, and my hand immediately flew to my temple, the other stabilizing myself on the bed. Whatever drugs they gave me, they were potent, the side effects lingering in a nasty, unpleasant way, much like a hangover. The irony wasn't lost on me. I'd drugged the Raven Crew to get here, only to be drugged myself.

Talk about karma being a motherfucker.

The dull throbbing beating against the sides of my head didn't subside, but eventually my vision cleared, and I got a clearer look at my surroundings.

What. The. Actual. Fuck?

Ornate crown molding trimmed the blush and gold walls. The bed I lay in was massive, layered in silk sheets with thick, fluffy pillows that smelled like a luxury hotel. Plush rugs muffled the sound of my bare feet when I swung my legs over the side and stood.

It was beautiful.

And terrifying.

Nothing about this place screamed prison, but I felt the bars all the same.

The windows were tall and curtained but sealed. No way to open them. No sound came from beyond them, no movement, no air. When I reached for the glass doorknob, I wasn't surprised to find it locked from the outside.

Of course, it was.

A gilded cage was still a cage.

I turned slowly, taking it all in. The vanity lined with untouched perfume bottles. The corner chaise stacked with plush blankets. A walk-in closet full of expensive dresses, most with tags still on them, designer brands, hand-beaded gowns, and lingerie that made my stomach pitch. It didn't look like the same space that Kenny had been held, but I couldn't be sure. Not really.

Not that it mattered. It was a mask. A fantasy. A beautiful lie to convince me I wasn't in hell, but I knew better.

A silk noose still tightened.

When I spotted the camera mounted discreetly in the corner of the ceiling, I knew this wasn't comfort. It was control.

I strolled through the space carefully, my fingers shaking as I opened the vanity drawers. Lipsticks. Hairbrushes. But no hidden weapons unless I planned to kill my kidnapper with a mascara wand. The closet had shoes in every size. I pulled open one of the drawers, hoping maybe, just maybe, they had been careless.

Inside were stockings. A drawer of jewelry. Diamonds and pearls and gold, probably real, probably worth enough to buy my freedom if that was how this world worked.

But it didn't.

This wasn't about value.

It was about ownership.

And that scared me the most.

Not the chains I didn't see but the fantasy they expected me to accept. And they were watching my every move. The door to my room finally opened, and I saw him.

Fucking Rusty.

He stepped inside, and his presence immediately sucked the oxygen out of the room. He looked so out of place in his oil-stained boots on the shiny tile, echoing far louder than it should have, and yet, he was a king entering his castle.

The bottom of my stomach dropped.

I didn't know why I expected him to look different. More sinister, maybe. More bloodstained. But he looked the same. Maybe a little grayer at the temples. Maybe his face had softened with the price of living well while the rest of us grieved and survived.

But it was him.

The man who called me kiddo and ruffled my hair. The man who showed up to family barbecues, who slipped me twenty bucks when my mom wasn't looking, and taught me how to patch a tire when I was thirteen. Who had unveiled Donovan's deception but carefully kept his own hidden. The man who used to call my dad his brother. How could he be him and also be someone who heartlessly stole people and sold them as if they were meaningless dolls?

His gaze swept over the room, indifferent. Not even stopping on me. "Nice to see you awake," he said lightly, like we'd bumped into each other in a grocery store aisle and not in a fucking nightmare of his own making.

My throat burned. "How could you?"

His eyes flicked toward me, quick and impersonal. "It's not so bad, right?" He gestured vaguely toward the silk sheets, the opulent walls, and the mirrored vanity. "They'll take care of you here, and soon you'll be living a life of luxury just like you're used to."

I almost laughed. Almost. The sound got stuck somewhere between fury and disbelief. "How fucking cliché," I spat. "My father's best friend killed him. The one person he trusted the most. Or maybe he didn't trust you. Maybe he figured you out too late, uncovered what you were doing behind his back, and instead of owning your shit, you decided to silence him. You betrayed him. The crew. You sold out the people who would've bled for you. For what? A fatter paycheck? A bigger cut of the fucking pie?"

His mouth twitched. Not quite a smile. Not quite a wince. "You wouldn't understand."

"Try me," I snapped, taking a step forward, my nails digging into my palms. Not that I would believe a word out of the bastard's mouth.

He sighed and looked up, toward the corner of the ceiling at the camera. Watching. Always watching. Then he looked back down at me like I was a child having a tantrum. "This goes beyond me. It's much bigger than your dad ever realized. Bigger than any of us small-town players." He spread his hands wide, palms up in a gesture of false helplessness. "I didn't build this machine, kiddo. But I'm not stupid enough to stand on the wrong side of it when it comes rolling through."

"You're on the wrong side," I shot back. "You're selling girls like livestock. You're going to sell *me*." I didn't know that for an absolute fact, but every instinct I possessed screamed that it was true.

He didn't deny it, confirmation in the absence of words. "You don't belong in Elmwood anymore," he said finally. "It's not safe for you. Not anymore."

"Don't you dare pretend this has anything to do with my safety." The rage building inside me was volcanic, molten, and ready to erupt. "This is about you and your cowardly ass. About protecting your own worthless skin. It always has been. You don't give a single shit about me, and you sure as hell didn't care about my dad when you sold him out."

His mask slipped for just a fraction, something ugly surfacing behind his eyes before the practiced neutrality slammed back into place. "I can assure you I took no pleasure in making the tough decisions your father couldn't."

The casual dismissal of my father's character and his death, spoken like it was some unfortunate business transaction, shattered what little control I had left.

"Fuck you!" I hissed and lunged.

My body moved before my brain could catch up, pure instinct and fury driving me forward. My nails found his face before he could even think to react, digging deep furrows from his temple to his jaw. Skin tore like paper under my fingertips. He shouted in shock and pain, stumbling backward as red bloomed beneath his eye, the blood dripping steadily into the starched collar of his white shirt.

"You little bitch!" he growled, one hand flying to his face while the other shot out to steady himself against the wall. His fingers came away slick with crimson. "You're lucky they still want you pretty, or I'd—"

But I wasn't done. Not even close. The taste of his blood in the air only fed the fire burning in my veins. "You're going to pay for what you did to Kenny," I seethed. "For what you did to my parents. I'll fucking kill you myself." The vow vibrated in my chest like a struck tuning fork, resonating with every beat of my heart.

His hand dove into his jacket pocket, his fingers closing around something that made him straighten with renewed confidence. I couldn't see what it was, but the motion was enough to freeze me in place. Even through the red haze of rage, some primitive survival instinct reminded me I wasn't invincible.

He straightened slowly. Blood continued to smear across his cheek in abstract patterns. "Calm down," he snapped, his voice regaining its earlier authority. "Or I'll have them pump you full of sedatives again. And I'd really hate for you to miss the show."

The blood in my veins went ice cold. "What show?"

His eyes darted to the camera again, just a blink, barely perceptible, but I caught it.

And I knew.

"Who's watching me?" I demanded, my voice climbing toward hysteria. "Who the fuck is watching me right now?" Lightning struck somewhere behind my ribs, sending electric panic racing through my nervous system. My breath came fast, instantly evoking terror.

His smile was the answer before he even opened his mouth. "Just a few potential buyers. Turns out you're worth significantly more to me alive and undamaged than as a corpse."

"No," I said, backing up until my spine hit the wall. I shook my head frantically, like I could physically dislodge the horrifying thought taking root in my brain. "No, he'll kill you for this. When he finds out—"

Rusty's smile widened. The expression didn't reach his eyes. "Who? Your boyfriend? That Corvo psychopath?" He laughed humorlessly. "Kiddo, you'll be gone before he even knows where to start looking."

It was my turn to smile. The expression felt foreign on my face, dangerous in a way that surprised even me. "Then I really can't wait to see the look on your face," I said, my voice dropping, "right before you fucking die."

His expression slipped, a shadow of doubt gleaming in his features. "You're worse than I thought. He's really done a number on you." The door slammed shut between us with the finality of a coffin lid closing. Then came the locks, clunking into place one after another in a mechanical symphony of captivity.

One. Two. Three.

I stared at the hairline seam in the door frame, the blood still hot in my veins, rage and terror mixing into something combustible.

Three locks.

Rusty thought that would be enough to keep me contained.

He had no idea who Kreed Corvo was.

And he had absolutely no fucking clue what I was willing to do, what lines I was prepared to cross, to get back to the people I loved.

The camera blinked at me from its corner perch, recording every moment of my captivity for its unseen audience. But let them watch. Let them see exactly what they thought they were buying.

They were about to learn that some cages couldn't hold what lived inside them.

And just how fucking sharp a raven's claws could be.

23

KREED

I woke up cold.

Not just physically, but the type of cold that sinks into your marrow and tells you something's wrong before your brain has even caught up. The taste in my mouth was wrong, bitter and chemical, like I'd been sucking on pennies. My arm stretched across the sheets, my fingers searching through the rumpled fabric for her.

Empty.

No Kaylor.

The realization hit me like a physical blow. I sat up fast, the sudden movement making my head whirl as my chest already began compressing with a familiar panic. The bedroom was still dark, pale moonlight trying to bleed through the heavy curtains, casting everything in shades of gray and shadow, but all I saw was the twisted bedding where she should have been and the gaping absence of her presence, no indent in the pillow, no lingering warmth, nothing.

Where was she? And how the hell did I get upstairs? My thoughts moved through thick fog, memories fragmented and unclear. I vaguely remembered Kaylor helping me as I stumbled

around in the middle of the night, legs heavy as lead, and falling into bed with her.

It was unusual that Kaylor woke before me, mostly because I hardly seemed to sleep these days. My internal clock had been shot to hell for weeks, hypervigilance keeping me on edge even when exhaustion threatened to drag me under.

A part of me longed to roll back over and continue sleeping, to sink back into the merciful oblivion that had claimed me. God knew I freaking needed it, every muscle in my body aching with a bone-deep fatigue that came from running on fumes and adrenaline, but there was this whisper in my ear, insistent and urgent, urging me to find her. I was never one to ignore those little nudges of intuition; they'd saved my life too many times to count.

Something felt off, and I wouldn't be able to fall back asleep until I knew she was safe.

I shoved off the covers with more force than necessary, the fabric tangling around my ankles as I swung my legs over the side of the bed. I yanked on a hoodie from the chair nestled in the corner, the soft cotton still carrying the faint traces of her perfume. I glanced at the bathroom, but the door was wide-open, darkness yawning beyond the threshold. No water running. No shower steam. No little raven.

"Kaylor?" I called out, my voice bouncing off the empty walls as I moved into the hall. The sound came back to me hollow and unanswered, making the house feel even more cavernous than usual.

I wandered from room to room, poking my head into each doorway before trotting downstairs. The grandfather clock in the hallway ticked with metronomic precision, each second stretching like an eternity. Nothing. Kitchen—empty, coffee maker cold and unused. Library—empty, books sitting undisturbed on their shelves. The air itself felt different, charged with an absence that made my skin crawl.

Family room.

Not empty, but no freaking Kaylor.

My gut twisted like someone had reached in and grabbed my

intestines with both hands. Two of my brothers were sprawled across the couches in various states of unconsciousness. Something was very, very wrong.

I kicked the couch Maddox was sprawled on, my foot connecting with the leather hard enough to make the whole thing shake and squeak. "Get the fuck up," I growled, my voice rough with sleep and growing unease.

Maddox groaned, the sound coming from somewhere deep in his chest. His dark hair was plastered to one side of his head, and there were pillow lines pressed into his cheek. He blinked slowly, pupils dilated and unfocused. "The hell, man?" he mumbled, squinting up at me through barely open eyes.

"She's gone." My voice sliced through the drowsy atmosphere. "Kaylor's gone."

That got them moving... Or trying to.

Raine was already up, his legs swinging over the side of the other couch with the fluid motion of someone whose body was used to snapping to attention, but even he moved slower than usual. He ran his fingers through his disheveled onyx hair, the strands sticking up at odd angles, as Mason stumbled into the room. His eyes were puffy and red-rimmed, and he kept blinking like he was trying to clear his vision, one hand braced against the door frame for support.

"What is all the fucking ruckus?" Mason mumbled, rubbing sleep from his face with the back of his hand. "It's the damn middle of the night."

He wasn't half wrong. A quick glance at the TV showed the time in glowing blue digits—4:47 AM. We were teetering between really late or really fucking early, depending on your outlook. But the wrongness in my chest told me this wasn't about inconvenient timing.

"What do you mean, gone?" Maddox asked, pushing himself up to a sitting position. His movements were sluggish, and he gripped the couch arm for leverage.

"I can't fucking find her. That's what I mean. She isn't anywhere in the house." The first tendrils of real fear began to wrap around my heart.

"Did you check with Evan?" Raine asked, already reaching for his phone. His fingers fumbled with the screen, taking two tries to unlock it.

"Not yet, but my guess, they haven't seen her." I watched as he scrolled through his contacts, fighting against the sluggishness that seemed to have claimed all of us.

"I'll check the security footage," Raine stated, steadier now, falling into the familiar rhythm of problem-solving mode.

"You don't think they were ballsy enough to come here and take her, do you?" Maddox asked, and the question hung in the air like smoke, heavy with implications none of us wanted to consider.

Raine shook his head, his pale eyes moving from the mugs on the coffee table to mine. The empty ceramic vessels sat there like evidence, chocolate residue still clinging to the bottom of each one. Four mugs. Four of us. But only three had been drained. "No."

We were thinking the same thing.

The realization hit us simultaneously, settling over the room like a shroud. The way we'd all fallen into such deep sleep. The chemical taste still coating my tongue.

She wouldn't have. Would she?

But even as the thought formed, I knew the answer. The cold certainty of it settled in my chest, heavy and undeniable. She would. She had. To save her friend.

And we'd let her.

"We were drugged," I whispered, the truth tasting bitter on my tongue, matching the chemical aftertaste that still lingered in my mouth. "She spiked the drinks. Look around. Do you feel rested? That wasn't fucking just hot cocoa." I gestured wildly at the room, at their sluggish movements, at the way we were all still blinking like we were trying to clear fog from our vision.

"No way." Mason shook his head. "Kaylor is too...naive for that shit. Besides, where would she get the stuff to knock us out?" Disbelief warring with the mounting evidence.

"I believe it," Maddox said, sitting forward now, elbows on his knees, staring at the empty mugs on the coffee table like they held all the answers. His jaw worked silently, grinding his teeth as the pieces fell into place.

The four of us stared at each other, sharing a holy-shit look that spoke volumes.

"That little minx," Raine murmured.

"I'm going to kill her," I muttered. Right after I kill whoever had her.

I turned and stormed back into her room, my bare feet slapping against the hardwood with each furious step. I was retracing every inch, every clue, my eyes scanning the pristine surfaces like a crime scene investigator.

That's when I saw it.

The burner phone.

Sitting right in the middle of the bed like a final goodbye, its black screen reflecting the pale morning light filtering through the curtains. The sight of it confirmed every terrible suspicion that had been building in my chest.

I snatched it up, my fingers flying across the screen. There was only one message.

Tomorrow. Midnight. The old train yard off Route 19. Come alone. No Crew. No Corvo. No Cops. Or Kenny dies.

"Fuck." The word exploded from my throat as I punched the headboard hard enough to feel it crack beneath my fist. Pain shot up my arm, but it was nothing compared to the agony tearing through my chest. Wood splintered, and a sliver embedded itself in my knuckle.

"She went alone," Raine muttered behind me. I hadn't heard him enter the room, not over the roaring screaming in my head, but suddenly he was there, his light-green eyes scanning the same message over my shoulder.

"She was never supposed to go at all," I ground out, pacing now like a caged animal. My feet wore a path in the hardwood, back and forth, back and forth. "I promised I'd keep her safe. I vowed I would get her friend back, but she didn't trust me. And now she's fucking gone."

Every step sent another jolt of adrenaline through my system, but there was nowhere to channel it, no target for the rage building inside me like a nuclear reactor about to melt down.

My phone vibrated in my back pocket, the sensation cutting through my spiral of self-recrimination. I whipped it out, studying the number with narrowed eyes. It was local but not from anyone I knew. The digits stared back at me, anonymous and somehow ominous.

"Are you going to answer that?" Raine prompted.

I swiped to accept the call and put it on speaker with mechanical movements. "Who is this? And you better have a damn good reason for calling me."

"Kreed?" The voice was frantic.

It took me a heartbeat to connect the voice, to place it among the chaos of my thoughts. "Carson?"

"I—I have Kenny," he rushed out, the words tumbling over each other in his haste to get them out. "She's here. She's safe."

I didn't give a shit about Kenny. It was Kaylor I was out-of-my-ever-loving-mind concerned about. I froze, my pacing coming to an abrupt halt as I already knew where this call was going. "Where the fuck is Kaylor?" I prompted.

"She didn't come back. I begged her not to go. She told Kenny to run. Said something about this being the only way to save them both... She didn't come back. I tried to wait. I didn't know what to do."

His sentences jumbled, not altogether making sense, but I got the gist of what happened, and my throat muscles constricted until I could barely breathe. I squeezed my eyes shut and turned away from Raine. "She made a trade," I said softly. "She traded herself."

For her best friend.

And I let her.

Because I'd been too fucking comfortable, too trusting, too distracted to see what was right in front of me. I'd known damn well she was acting out of the ordinary yesterday. Was that why we'd slept together? Had that been some kind of goodbye?

Fuck that.

We weren't saying goodbye. I refused to let her go. She was mine, and I had every intention of getting her back.

I fought the urge to hurl the burner in my other hand against the wall just to hear something break that wasn't my heart. "Where the fuck are you, Carson?"

"I just left the old train yard off Route 19."

In the background, I heard soft whimpers. Sniffling.

Kenny.

I had nothing against her. Not really. But knowing she was safe, cradled in Carson's arms, breathing, alive, while my girl was gone, suffering, locked in some goddamn nightmare that only got darker by the hour? I snapped.

My fist went clean through the drywall beside me, a crack of violence louder than Carson's voice. Dust showered down my forearm as white fragments scattered across the floor.

"You better fucking hope I find her. And soon." I threatened. "Because if I don't, I won't just kill you, Carson. I'll make you feel every second of what she felt."

A pregnant pause. "I wouldn't stop you."

Not what I expected. Not even close.

Something pinched in my chest, not sympathy but a question I didn't have time to ask. What the hell did he mean by that? What exactly had he done? Was it guilt over letting Kaylor go? Or was it something more?

I hung up without another word. Let him stew in his own self-loathing until I was ready to deal with him. Right now, Kaylor was all that mattered.

Mason, Maddox, and Raine stood nearby, all silent. Watching me. Reading the war in my expression. None of them asked what was wrong. They already knew. It was clearly written in every line of my face.

I was unraveling, rage boiling in my gut, scraping up my throat, clawing for release. Every breath I took burned. Every second that passed without her was a scream I couldn't voice. I was on the verge of crashing out, losing my shit, but I couldn't afford to give in to the emotions, not when Kaylor needed me.

Not yet. Not when she still needed me to stay sharp.

Before I could speak, the burner phone on the table buzzed.

Once.

Twice.

Mason was closest. He snatched it up. "Shit." The curse breezed through his lips as he handed it over, eyes unreadable. "You're going to want to see this."

New Message.

One video.

No number. No ID. Just a timestamp—ten minutes ago. I clicked on it with shaking fingers. And there she was.

Kaylor.

Her face filled the screen, shadowed and pale. Her silvery hair was down, a little tangled. She looked...calm. Too calm. Like she was pretending. Like she was barely holding herself together under whatever monster had forced her in front of that camera.

"Kreed..." Her voice was quiet, steady, her light-blue eyes wide. "If you're watching this... Don't come looking for me. That's what they want me to say, but fuck their speech."

My pulse stopped.

"I don't have much time," she continued. "I'm sorry. I'm so sorry. You were right. I should have trusted you sooner, but I need you to make good on your promise. Do what you're exceptionally good at."

She rushed the words, trying to get everything in as those emotionally filled eyes of hers silently pleaded with me. A door flung open off camera, and from the shift in her gaze and their set determination in her features, I knew she was almost out of time. "I forgive you. And I lo—"

The screen went black. Silence stretched in the room like a noose. No one moved. No one breathed. "No," I muttered. "No, no, no." My chest heaved. My brain scrambled.

What promise?

I hated promises. I didn't hand them out. Not unless I meant them. They were too damn heavy to fake. But then it hit me, hard enough to stagger. *I'll always find you, little raven. That's a promise.*

My eyes burned. My jaw locked.

This wasn't a goodbye. It was a dare. A challenge in a whisper. She knew I didn't back down. Kaylor knew me better than anyone, knew that I never listened when people told me no, and I sure as fuck wasn't about to start now. She wanted me to hear between the lines. She wasn't telling me to let her go. She was counting on me to do the opposite. She was still fighting.

And so was I.

I was about to become the Vipers' worst nightmare. I was about to show Rusty the true monster he thought I was, and anyone who stepped into my path would be nothing but collateral damage.

My hand snapped back, hurling the burner across the room, but it didn't hit the wall with a satisfying crash. The device landed straight into Raine's hand as he caught it like the wide receiver he was known to be in high school. "As much as I sympathize with your need to smash shit, this might come in handy in finding her. Assuming you want her back."

I looked up, breathing hard, a storm in my eyes. My brothers knew me well. "I'm gonna tear them apart," I said. "Rusty. The Vipers. Anyone who had a hand in this."

"They just declared war," Maddox said under his breath.

I nodded once. "Good. Because I'm going to fucking destroy them."

"Kreed?" Raine's voice was steady but urgent. "What's the move?"

They stole what's mine. And I didn't take kindly to thieves. "We're getting our girl back."

My girl.

TO BE CONTINUED...

Thank you for reading!
Kaylor and the Crew's story will conclude in
ENDGAME

xoxo,
Jennifer

JOIN MY DISCORD - It's new! I'm excited to dive into Discord and connect in a more personal way with readers. It's a great safe space to meet bookish friends! https://discord.gg/6eQcmjh64j

JOIN DARK DIVAS READER GROUP - My reader group is the best place to talk books and get up-to-date information. https://www.facebook.com/groups/1217984804898988

SIGN UP FOR JL WEIL NEWSLETTER - Get free books just for signing up. https://www.jlweil.com/vip-readers

FOLLOW ME ON FACEBOOK - Click the follow button on my Facebook page for notifications on what's happening. https://www.facebook.com/jenniferlweil

CHECK OUT MY SHOP - Get signed books and merch at my online shop! https://www.jlweil.com/shop

AMAZON - Click the follow button on my Amazon page and you'll get an email for each new release from me. https://www.amazon.com/stores/J.L.-Weil/author/Boo8A1AQGO

INSTAGRAM - I post pretty pics of my books and teasers. https://www.instagram.com/jlweil/

Check out my Amazon Author page for a collection of all my books available!

ABOUT THE AUTHOR

J.L. Weil is a USA TODAY Bestselling author of teen & new adult paranormal romance, fantasy, and urban fantasy books about spunky, smart mouth girls who always wind up in dire situations. For every sassy girl, there is an equally mouthwatering, overprotective guy.

You can visit her online at: www.jlweil.com or come hang out with her at JL Weil's Dark Divas on FB.

Stalk Me Online
www.jlweil.com
jenniferlweil@gmail.com